GROUND ZERO

RAIN STICKLAND

Paperback ISBN-13: 978-0994950031
Paperback ISBN-10: 0994950039
Kindle ISBN-13: 978-0-9949500-4-8

DEDICATION

To all those who have dedicated their lives to rescuing animals.
Luckily I count some of you among my friends. There is no finer
human being than one who protects a creature more vulnerable
than him or herself.

CONTENTS

ACKNOWLEDGMENTS

Thank you once again to Amanda K. Woods for putting up with my irritating nitpicking with respect to my cover. Graphic design falls well outside my milieu, and in fact gives me a splitting headache from which none of us will recover should I ever stop whining.

And thanks go again to Steve Kovacs, who was nagged into giving me information regarding personal security, martial art instruction, and insight into the vagaries of the world of criminal justice. I'm pretty sure I owe him my soul at this point.

My friends deserve a round of applause for putting up with my disappearing acts, as well. Particularly Sarah Lyons Fleming, who guided me through life as a new author, and Typhanei Celeste, who treats me like I always know what I'm doing. Much love to Marlin Woosley, as always (I *really* hope you attain the dream you've been working toward so hard). I'm a terrible human being, I realize, so thank you for not telling me to take repeated long walks off of very short piers. They all know I'm crazy, and appear to like me anyway.

Last, but definitely not least, to my readers, who have now made it possible for me to do what I love as obsessively as I want to, I give my deepest thanks and appreciation! Your kind e-mails mean more to me than you'll ever know.

1 ~ WHAT YOU DON'T KNOW

"I killed your father," Mackenzie blurted at her daughter. Cameron's mouth dropped open in shock, but then another expression crossed her face. Betrayal.

"You *lied* to me? *You?*"

"No, I didn't. I told you he was killed trying to rob some people. I just didn't tell you that we were the people he was stealing from. Or that it was me holding the knife."

"But *why*? Why wouldn't you tell me that? And why are you suddenly telling me this now, after hiding it for over twenty years? For that matter, what else have you been keeping from me?"

"First of all, not everything about me is any of your business, though in this case it actually is. There may be a lot of things I haven't told you, but other than this there isn't anything else I feel has anything to do with you. Granted, I can't think of much I haven't told you anyway.

"As for why I haven't told you, mostly it has to do with time passing and me no longer thinking about it. You were a baby at the time, so I couldn't tell you then. I wasn't about to tell you while you were still in school and might feel like you had to keep secrets from your friends. It wasn't technically a secret, since the cops were called and the whole thing was written off as self-defense. Small children wouldn't understand that, though, and if the other kids had known about it, you would probably have been tormented by them for it.

"As you got older it became one of those memories that lose their importance and potency as time passes. I've had a lot of things happen to me throughout the years, and that was just one of them. Granted, it sort of stood out for me since I've never killed anyone else, but I dealt with the guilt as best I could. There were quite literally more important things to be getting on with, however," Mac finished.

"More important than killing my father?" Cam's tone was incredulous.

"Well, I figured our survival was the biggest priority, so ... yeah. That about sums it up. I'm guessing you want an explanation," Mackenzie said.

"What do you think?"

"Ah, sarcasm. Guess I deserve that. I haven't exactly explained this very well. It just wasn't very easy to start the conversation, so I figured being blunt and getting the words out would jump-start things. Well, here goes nothing.

"I was working on the budget when he broke in. I had just over a thousand bucks sitting on the kitchen table, and I was trying to figure out how we were going to pay six hundred in rent, another two hundred in hydro, a hundred for the gas bill, and still be able to afford diapers, baby food, and groceries.

"Your father looked at the money like it was some sort of windfall, and grabbed it off the table. My brain was going a hundred miles an hour, trying to figure out what I would do without that money, because I sure as hell wasn't going to fight him for it. He turned to me with a knife in his hand. One of those folding ones, but the blade was about five inches long. He was telling me he was going to kill me for being such a whore, because he apparently thought I was turning tricks to get that kind of money. He accused me of screwing all his friends, too, which was laughable since he didn't actually have any.

"I should have kept my mouth shut, but I was starting to panic, thinking that if I died you would end up starving to death. *He* sure as hell wasn't going to remember that he had a kid in the bedroom down the hall. Never mind caring enough to take you to someone who would care *for* you. I begged him not to leave you without a mother. I regretted saying it as soon as the words left my mouth, because he got this horrible look on his face.

"By this point he was being pretty casual about the whole thing, and the knife was just sort of dangling from his fingertips. I didn't even think about what I was doing. I snatched it away from him and was holding it with the point toward him. He sort of lost his mind and ran at me, and to this day I couldn't tell you if I purposely allowed him to impale himself, or if I just didn't have time to react." Mackenzie fell silent and waited for Cameron to speak.

"Holy fucking shit!"

Mackenzie waited again, but nothing else seemed to be forthcoming.

"Would you say something else please! The suspense is killing me," Mac said, her tone anxious. She couldn't help thinking she had waited too long to tell Cam about this, but there hadn't been a pressing need until now. Cameron was showing every sign of suffering from PTSD and guilt over killing Gerry in August, though, and Mac could no longer stand idly by. Cam needed to know someone close to her truly understood what it felt like to kill someone.

"I don't know what to say, Mom. Give me thirty seconds to absorb, would ya?"

Mackenzie couldn't sit still. She had cornered her daughter in the kitchen as soon as Cam had come back from the ferret building, because she wanted to get the confrontation over with, so she took advantage of their location and got up to root around in the fridge for something to snack on. She grabbed some of the cookies she'd made the day before, and pulled out the jug of goat's milk to go with them.

"Here. Have some cookies. Maybe that'll help you absorb better," she told her daughter, and slid the container toward her. Cameron automatically grabbed one of the cheesecake cookies Mac had figured out how to make from the goat cheese that was so plentiful on their farm now. She'd taken a lot more satisfaction

4

from homesteading-type activities than she had expected, and busied herself coming up with new things, but she knew she'd go back to take-out in a heartbeat if it were at all possible.

"So I take it all this happened before you started working as an accountant for that big garage then," Cam finally said.

"A few months before, yeah. We were dead broke back then. You wouldn't remember it, but it was not a happy time for me. I had just turned eighteen, and summer was starting to kick in something fierce. Air conditioning was a luxury we couldn't afford in my wildest dreams in those days, and I remember sitting at that table, wanting to cry because there was no way I could even afford to buy some cheap ice cream at the grocery store.

"Thankfully the guy at the garage took a chance on me, *and* on my two years of high school accounting, and gave me a job. From there things got a whole lot better for us. It meant putting you in daycare, but at least my boss was understanding the few times I got called out of work for emergency situations with you. My work could be done on a fairly flexible schedule, since I didn't need to be there answering phones or anything, but a lot of employers aren't that nice.

"I really learned that lesson later, working for that corporation in Toronto. I wasn't very good at taking orders from people anyway, and I decided that was enough for me. I was sick of working for idiots who knew less than I did about their own jobs, and then having to take crap from them. It was a really good thing I left, though. The money was a hell of a lot better for consulting work. I only did that part-time, of course, but even that was more than enough to live on. I just needed variety," Mac said. Cameron nodded her head in response.

"No kidding. How long did it take you to get bored with accounting? And then later on it was investment stuff. Of course, most people would have been bored with those types of jobs right from the start, but you were really into them at first."

"I'm so bad for that. That's why I've always got my head stuck in a book, learning something new. Between my curiosity and my need to keep my brain engaged, there aren't a lot of subjects I haven't learned at least something about. And I took classes, too. A lot."

"Well, I'm glad you knew how to raise chickens and grow vegetables, because otherwise we'd have been screwed. I certainly wouldn't have survived when the shit hit the fan."

"That wasn't any of my doing. I was raised on a farm, and, believe me, I hated it. I despised having to weed the garden, especially, and we had a big one. Then there were the animals. I'd no sooner make friends with one of them than we were eating them for dinner."

"Seriously? Ugh. That's just mean. I'm so glad I never met your parents," Cam stated emphatically.

"I wasn't going to let them within a mile of you, and it had nothing to do with the chickens and rabbits. Flopsy and Mopsy aside, there was a lot of other cruelty and sickness in that house. I might have gotten pregnant young, and with the naïve hope that my even-less-mature husband would rescue me from that life, but I wasn't completely without a sense of self-preservation," Mac explained.

"While I don't blame you, considering what you've told me about other things your family has done, it was still hard to explain to people why I never saw my grandparents when they weren't actually dead. People just don't get it when you say you don't speak to your family. It's like they think all families have to love each other."

"Believe me, I know. I've lost track of the number of times I've had people say, 'How can you *not* talk to your own mother? She's your *mother*!' Like that's some sort of guarantee she's good, kind, and loving, and there's no chance at all she could be anything else. Actually, my mother wasn't all that bad, but my father was a nightmare. But so long as my mother stuck with him, and willingly sacrificed her kids' welfare just to stay with him, there was no way I could have a relationship with her. She obviously didn't care that much about her children."

"What happened with your brother, then?"

"Don't know, really. None of the people I was friends with around here would have told me anything that was going on with him, because they knew I wanted nothing to do with him. He was even worse than my father in some ways. I'll put it this way. He used to get really excited when our father would let him slaughter the animals. That should tell you something of his personality. Most farmers look at it as a necessary chore. He thought it was fun, and couldn't wait to get at them. Our father encouraged him."

"Nice," Cameron said with a sneer.

"The whole bunch are like that on my father's side. They beat their dogs and leave them outside in the middle of winter – and that was before winters started getting so mild up here. Forty below wasn't uncommon back then. I couldn't wait to get away from this area when I was in high school. Every girl I knew wanted to get knocked up just to go on welfare or get married. Maybe my situation didn't seem all that different, but I actually wanted you. Not as a means to an end, but because I wanted to have a kid. I was really young, but I really wanted to have a baby. I really wanted to have a husband, too.

"I had this fantasy where I would finally matter to someone, and because of that fantasy I made some big mistakes with men. Brad was one of them. So was Allan, though we never got married. At the same time I can't really consider him a mistake, because he was good with you. He loved you like you were his own, and not many men can do that. You were three when we started up, and you should have seen how happy he was the first time you called him 'Dad.' He was so thrilled."

"I know, mom. You've told me that story a zillion times. Always nice to hear, though. I sometimes forget how lucky I was to have someone like him. Or you for that matter. I mean, you went through your childhood with parents that not only didn't give a shit about you, but treated you like shit, too. I had two parents who really loved me. I can't imagine having a kid at seventeen, and being able to care for him or her. I can't even imagine being a parent now!"

"Good. Hold that thought, because this really isn't the time for you to be making me a grandmother. I can only be grateful you're not at all like me in that respect. Hell, I don't even want anyone else getting knocked up. Chuck and Kayla are content with the kids they have, and Gilles and Felicia both feel they're too old for that now, though her daughter, Melanie, might want kids with John one day soon. Whatever they decide, I'm still glad they're here on the farm with us. And it's not like we have to worry about Kelly and Annette having kids," Mac concluded with a smile.

"Or Carol and Samantha," Cam added.

"Not together at least. Anyway, you've had time to ponder the situation. Are you okay with it all?"

"Well, gee. Do I really have a choice? It's not like you can go back and change things, any more than I can. We both killed someone, and that isn't exactly a temporary thing," Cam said with more of her own brand of sarcasm.

"No, it's really not. It's the one thing that's hard to explain to someone who's never killed anything before, or who has no respect for life. Even hunters. It's why I can't kill the animals we have, and why I chose animals that would give us eggs and milk. I can't consciously choose to kill something. It's not in me. Not if it isn't directly related to defending myself or someone else.

"I can tell you I'd much rather have been the one to kill Gerry, than have that load on your shoulders. I've borne it once before, and I'd have done it again, but that's not something I can do for you. I'd have protected Neil in a heartbeat, and probably wouldn't feel anywhere near the guilt you're feeling now, though it's hard to think of ending the life of someone who was as young as my daughter. It's just that you had never even spoken to him, so you have no idea how bad he really was, other than what I told you. He really was a waste of life.

"I know you feel guilty. Not just for killing Gerry, but also for feeling guilty. Am I right?"

"Yeah, but how did you know?"

"It was how I felt. Brad would have hurt you somehow. Possibly killed you. So I felt guilty for my own guilt, knowing I should have been glad as a parent that he was dead and couldn't hurt you. I figured you would feel similar emotions when it came to Neil, and probably myself."

"Please tell me Neil doesn't know I feel that way," Cam responded miserably.

"He knows, and he understands. You don't have to worry about that. He's not a child who doesn't understand complicated human emotions. That's the thing about people. Our feelings are never simply one thing or another. And the older we get, the more nuanced those emotions are.

"Neil's probably one of the most emotionally intelligent people I've ever met. He knew when we first got together how easily our so-called whirlwind romance could freak out someone like me, and despite wanting to move in immediately, he was willing to back right off and let me do things at my own pace.

"It was because of that that I was able to jump into marriage with him so easily. Well, and the whole apocalypse thing, too. I mean, we both knew it wouldn't be long before we wouldn't be able to get married at all, so I took a big chance and jumped into it with both feet. Thankfully it's worked out okay, because you would have had good cause to shoot me if it hadn't. I put all of us at risk," Mac said ruefully.

"Sort of, but not entirely. You already knew his property backed onto ours, so we weren't likely going to be able to avoid him. There was every chance we'd have run into him anyway. And he was a prepper. At least you knew he wasn't going to come over here out of desperation, to try and take everything we had. If he'd been a psycho of some sort, we'd have been screwed either way. Well, except for the fact that we're armed and all that.

"Speaking of security measures, though … I really don't feel good about the motion sensors being on such a low sensitivity setting. Maybe if we had more cameras," Cam said worriedly. Mac knew Cameron had been getting a little paranoid about their security, and assumed it was a consequence of the situation with Gerry.

Cam did a lot of walking now, too, and Mac had a sneaking suspicion she was patrolling the perimeter of their property. She was certainly gone long enough every day, and she wasn't spending the time with Kirk and Leigh at Neil's old cabin. She'd hated having to ask them about it, since she felt like she was checking up on Cam, but Kirk and Leigh were both worried about her, too.

"Neil and I will be doing some scavenging once the roads are clear. Maybe we can stop in at an electronics store. We've already used up the cameras I bought before the world went to shit. Since Neil hadn't bothered with that kind of stuff, I ended up using our spare cameras over there to make sure Kirk and Leigh would be okay. Now there are some gaps, so you're right. We can find some cameras, I'm sure. I just have to make sure they're compatible with the software we're already using, because it's not like I can download drivers from a website now."

"When did you and Neil decide to go scavenging?" Cam asked with a surly bite to her voice.

"Huh?"

"Nuh-uh. You know exactly what I'm talking about, so you're not allowed to play dumb. I wouldn't believe it anyway. We bought this property together, remember? I'm twenty-three, not some child who has no say in the matter. You should have discussed this with me, but now I'm suddenly hearing about what you and Neil have decided to do. You obviously weren't intending to ask me to come along. Or Billy for that matter. He's nineteen now, so I'm sure he would want to know what you and his dad are up to, don't you think?"

Mackenzie let out a sigh. Cameron was right. She was so used to just making any decisions she felt needed to be made, without consulting anyone. Not even Neil. Now she was being called on it.

"Okay, you're right. I'll explain why Neil and I decided to do things the way we did, but it doesn't change the fact that we should have talked about all this together." Her statement was enough to mollify Cam for the time being, but Mac didn't think it was going to be that easy. Cam was going to want to come with them, so she would have to convince her to stay behind somehow.

"There needs to be two of us to lift and move things, because we're going to a summer home Neil knows about where they have some PV panels. With all the extra people we have on the farm now, we're just barely scraping by on power at the moment – especially with so few daylight hours – so we need more panels. More panels are useless without the deep cycle batteries to store the power, so we plan to stop at one of the marinas, too. At least one person has to be knowledgeable enough to deal with the panels and batteries, which means me, Neil, or Billy.

"We don't want any more than two people, because we're planning to fill the truck and trailer with everything we can find. Things like mattresses, because we've currently got kids sleeping with their parents, and couples sleeping on single beds. It's not healthy for the kids to be in bed with their parents at this age. Katherine is a teenager, for one thing, and Chuck and Kayla need their privacy. We can build them extra rooms, no problem, but that doesn't help without beds to put in them. And Katherine should *not* be sleeping in the same bed with her brother.

"Aside from that, I want to get a few boxes of books from the library. Some of the topics are very specific, and the person going to get them has to know what they're looking for. There isn't likely to be anything in-depth about sustainable energy, or even permaculture, in a small-town library, but I'd like some stuff on diesel engines for a project I have in mind. Plus I need books on boating, the Great Lakes, and local geography. Mariner-type maps if they have them.

"In other words, I *have* to go, and Neil is really the best choice to come with me when it comes to muscle and knowledgeable assistance. We should have made it a group discussion. I'm just not used to working that way. Hell, you know what I was like with my business. You tried working for me for a while, instead of having to do factory work, but that didn't work out so well for either of us."

"Okay, I'm really irritated with you at the moment, so I'm not going to talk about it right now. Maybe you're right about who should go, but the way you went about it makes me want to disagree with you just on principle. We'll talk about it later," Cameron said shortly.

Fuck, thought Mac.

"Alright, so how about we get back to the original point of this discussion. I told you about what happened with your father so you would know I understood what you were going through. He was the same sort of person Gerry was, too. I know there has to be a part of you that's wondering if he might have straightened himself out if he'd had the chance, and I'm here to tell you that he would only have gotten worse.

"At least Brad had the excuse of being spoiled. He was used to getting whatever he wanted, so when he got older he continued to take things, whether people wanted to give them to him or not. That was another reason I didn't tell you the whole story about your father's death. I wanted to be sure you were old enough to understand that you didn't inherit anything bad from him. He was just spoiled. He wasn't really born evil. I completely blame his parents.

"I don't think that was the case with Gerry, though. Apparently his family was really nice, but they didn't spoil their kid," Mac continued.

"Then there was me. If you knew I had been the one to kill your father, it was possible you would wonder if both your parents were psychos, and you were destined for the same. You had to be able to understand the whole self-defense thing, and that I wasn't the type to go around killing people without a damn good reason. It's not like I make a habit of it."

"Well, I'm sure Neil is relieved to know that," Cameron said with a laugh. "Assuming he knows, of course."

"Yeah, he knows. I probably should have told you first, but I wanted his advice. If I hadn't, I probably wouldn't have said anything to him. After all, it can't be very comfortable for him to know that his wife has killed one of her previous husbands. At least the second one survived marriage to me," Mac joked, but then sobered quickly.

There was every chance that Mitch was dead, since he hadn't

made it out of Hamilton when things went south. She had tried to help him a couple of times, but he'd screwed up his chances and she'd finally given up on him. She didn't feel good about the likelihood of his death, but there was only so much she could do.

"You don't know he's dead, mom," Cameron said abruptly.

"He probably is. Still, he made his own choice. I'm not happy about it, but I'm not going to kill myself trying to help someone who won't even help themselves."

"What about Ian?"

"Ian's different. He tried to help himself, but his insulin will only last for so long before it turns toxic. I figured out a way to help him with that, so I'm going to help him. He'll be okay for now, at least until I can figure out how to pilot one of those boats down at the marina. Then I just have to get down to Cleveland."

"Ian could have done what you did, and found someone to make the insulin. He could have set himself up the way we did, too. You have a rescue complex. That's what it is. You run around saving people all the damn time. We have, what, over twenty people living here now?"

"Yeah, yeah. Whatever. We won't be so stretched for food and power next year so it won't matter. It also means you don't have chores to do every damn day either, so be grateful they're all here, Cam."

"I am, actually. I'm just saying you're compulsive about saving people. I just hope you don't take it too far and get yourself killed. Not only do I not want to lose my mother because of someone who can't take care of themselves, but I also don't think anyone else wants you out of the picture either. Not one of us has done what you managed to do, and things could fall apart here without you," Cam said soberly.

"Don't worry. I'm not planning to be stupid about it. My big risk was trusting Neil, and that's completely out of character for me. You know that. Besides, everyone is expendable to some extent. You and Billy have the knowledge between the two of you to run this farm if you have to. In fact, Neil and I will be counting on you to do just that when we head to Cleveland in the spring."

"I'm thrilled," Cam said sardonically.

"It doesn't have to mean a bunch more work for you. Everyone is already sharing the load. The planting will be done before we go, and we're only planning to be gone a couple of weeks. I have an idea about using something with an engine, but I've got to work it out first. Neil and I don't know how to sail from a practical standpoint, and I'm not real comfortable with what I've learned from reading about it thus far. Most of those boats run on diesel engines, so it's possible we can use one of those. It would sure as hell make things a lot easier if we can pull it off."

"Yeah, but where are you going to get the diesel from?"

"We're looking at a completely different alternative, actually. I'll explain it to you later if we can make it work. Diesel's still an option, though I'd have to calculate how much fuel we'd need in order to get there and back. Or we'd end up going into various towns to scavenge more on the way. A bit more of a risk that way, though."

"No shit it's more risk that way. You did say that you would have to pass between Detroit and Windsor, right? Isn't Detroit a really rough city? Or will that matter now?"

"I honestly don't know. I'd think Detroit would be pretty much wiped out. Maybe not entirely, but people were already desperately poor there. I mean, the city went bankrupt six or seven years ago, I think, and they never really came back from that. Some people would have had gardens, but then a lot of people had guns, too. The ones with the guns will probably have killed anyone with food in order to take it from them. The question is, would they have known how to continue growing it? I doubt it, but it's possible people are still alive there.

"To be on the safe side, we'll try to avoid any of the big cities. There are plenty of small towns along the way, and we'll stay pretty close to the shoreline so navigation isn't so risky. I'm not sure if the GPS will still be working. It depends on whether or not the US Army is still functioning and maintaining ground communication with the satellites. And then there are storms and stuff, where we'll want to be able to get to shore if things get dicey."

"Well, that's just great, mom. You've really boosted my confidence now."

"You and me both."

2 ~ CONFRONTING DEMONS

Cam sat in her bedroom, completely pissed. She didn't really understand why, since she'd agreed that it was for the best that her mother go with Neil for the scavenging foray. In fact, she'd agreed a couple of weeks ago. But for some reason she didn't understand, she was really angry that she hadn't been able to go with them. Adding to her anger was the fact that her dad was disappearing for days at a time, going on supposed camping trips. Like they weren't already living rough enough.

She stomped around her bedroom, grabbing the things she would need for her usual hike around the property, and decided that this time she would definitely be doing the whole circuit. Just circumnavigating the property she'd bought with her mother a few years ago would take her at least an hour, and that was at a pretty fast clip. Adding Neil's to that would mean she'd be gone all day. *Perfect*, she thought. It was just what she needed to blow off steam.

When she grabbed her pack from the walk-in closet she glanced at her bow. It was hanging on its rack, untouched since they had finally managed to get the main house put up. In fact, she hadn't even moved it into her room. She was pretty sure her mother had done that. Cam had cringed even at the thought of touching it. Thankfully the fatal arrow was no longer in her possession. It had still been lodged in Gerry's body when it had been removed from the scene.

Thinking about her bow made her even angrier. She'd allowed that little pissant to take away something from her that she really enjoyed. The more she thought about it, the more irritated she got.

It felt good, she suddenly realized. Like she could breathe fire. And right then she wanted to be a tornado of aggression. Not to destroy, but to cleanse the cobwebs from her veins. Her mind felt awake for the first time since August. That was months ago, and now she was furious with herself for the time she'd wasted. She knew the rage wouldn't last, but she was going to put it to good use in the meantime.

Cam pulled on her arm guard, and with a violent gesture she grabbed the bow from the rack. The compound bow had a mounted quiver, so the only other thing she needed was her glove caliper release. She had to rifle through her pack to find it before she could put it on.

It was habit now to carry her Glock 22 with her on her treks, so she made the usual checks to be sure a round was chambered and then slid it into the holster at the back of her jeans. Her knife went in another holster beside it. She tucked in the tail of her shirt, but threw her coat on over it. At the moment she really wished she had a shoulder holster, because there was no way she would get to her gun in time if there was a need for it, but she'd have her bow this time. She'd have to remove the coat anyway, if she was going to get in any archery practice.

She was just about to head downstairs when her laptop beeped. An outer perimeter sensor had gone off. The dual-technology, microwave and passive infrared sensors rarely gave off false positives, and were currently set to a fairly high body weight, so rabbits and squirrels wouldn't set them off. A jolt of adrenaline lit up her already overactive nervous system. Without thinking twice about it, she checked the location of the breach and left the room. This was just what she needed.

Tromping through the brush in the most direct path possible, Cam was wishing she had some training in bush tactics. She knew she sounded like a bull in a china shop. Her mother could move like a cat when she wanted, but then she'd grown up in the boonies. Cam's only experience with moving quietly had been walking around their Hamilton apartment in her sock feet. Not exactly aboriginal tracker material.

She could have brought the sling for her bow, but knowing there was a possibility of an intruder made her glad she was keeping it in her hand, ready to draw on whoever it might be. Granted, it really wasn't likely to be anything more than a deer, and there were no cameras to cover this area. The only way to find out was to physically check. That was fine with her. Cam was much too agitated these days to just sit at her laptop and watch things on the screen.

As Cam approached the area of the offending sensor, it dawned on her that she might have made a really big mistake. She hadn't told anyone about the potential breach, much less where it was, and if Gilles or Chuck weren't keeping a steady eye on their own computers, Cam knew she could find herself in a bad situation very quickly. Her adrenaline spiked again, and fear began inching its way through her body.

Stupid! You giant, fucking idiot, she cursed herself silently. It was too late for that, though. If something was going to happen, she would need to deal with the situation as it was, and not worry about her regrets. Those could come later, assuming things didn't go terribly wrong in the meantime.

When Cameron picked up the sound of a branch snapping, she automatically drew back on her bow.

"Drop the bow," the voice said behind her, and in her semi-panicked state she interpreted it as a warning. Since it had been drilled into her to do exactly the opposite, Cam didn't follow that order. Instead she spun around and slipped sideways so she had cover behind a tree. She aimed automatically at what she considered a threat, and drew back on her bow until the pulleys took over the work.

"Who are you, and what the *fuck* are you doing on our property?" Her demand for answers was met with empty, raised hands, and elevated brows. She was relieved to note that the older man standing in front of her did not appear to be armed. Telling her to drop the bow had probably just been his way of saying she had nothing to worry about, but she wasn't stupid enough to assume he wasn't dangerous.

"I'm not here to hurt anyone, or steal anything," he responded softly.

"Answer the questions," she ordered. Cam realized she was in a bit of a predicament here, since she wasn't going to walk this guy back to the house. She had no intention of letting him see the farm. How the hell she was going to get him to leave, and have any kind of guarantee he was gone, however, was the real issue. She needed some sort of backup here, and since no one knew where she was, she wasn't going to get it unless she did some fast thinking.

"My name is Brian Newman. Maybe you knew my son, Gerry." Cameron's heart started racing. Gerry's father. The very last person she wanted to meet up with.

"What makes you say that?"

"You look like you're about the same age, so I thought maybe you went to school with him, though I don't recognize you. I thought I knew everyone from around these parts. There's only a couple hundred people around here. Or there were anyway," he finished dryly.

"Okay, you told me your name, but that doesn't tell me what you're doing around here. I know who belongs in this area and who doesn't, and you sure as hell don't belong on our property."

"I was just cutting through to get to Neil McKinnon's place, though you might know him as Mac. That's what everyone out here usually calls him. He runs the knife store in Rosseau. It's been closed down now since the summer, for obvious reasons, so I haven't been able to go talk to him there."

"What do you want with Neil?"

"I'm guessing you know him then. I've got some questions I wanted to ask him," he said. Cam had a pretty good idea what those questions would be regarding, and she didn't think it was a very good idea for him to get those answers right about now, so she continued to draw things out as she tried to come up with a solution to her current problem.

"About what?"

"I don't see that it's really any of your business, but I'll tell you anyway. You might be able to answer some of those questions, considering the fact that you're aiming a bow and arrow at me. My son was killed last summer, and I think Mac – Neil as you call him – might know something. The police didn't tell me much about it, and I'd like to know the truth. I don't think that's too much to ask."

"You won't get any answers from me, so you'll have to talk to him yourself. What you can't do is trespass on our property in order to do so. The world may have gone to hell, but we have a right to protect ourselves. I don't want to hurt you, but I will if I have to. Turn around," Cameron added. It had taken her a while, but she'd finally figured out a solution.

"You going to shoot me in the back?"

"Not if you do what you're told. Just do it," she snarled. When he'd finally complied, she eased off on the bow string and reached up under her jacket to pull her Glock from its holster.

"Alright. If it'll ease your mind you can turn back around. I just didn't want you trying anything. I need to fire a few shots in the air to bring some people here. You need to leave the property, and I have to be sure that you do. I can't do that without help." With that, Cam fired three shots into the air. She knew someone would come when they heard them.

"It won't be long, so just relax for a bit," she said, much more calm now that it seemed as though the situation was under control. Brian tried to talk to her while they were waiting, but she cut him off.

"Like I said, you're not going to get any answers from me, so don't bother. I didn't grow up in the area, or go to school with your son, and we didn't know each other." It was nothing less than the truth. She'd never even spoken to him. The only time she'd heard his voice was when he'd called her mother a bitch on the video her mother had recorded while she'd streamed it live. Cam didn't think hearing a single word qualified as knowing someone.

At the time her mom had been trying to avoid having to kill Gerry, despite the fact that he was bent on raping her. Streaming the video meant he wouldn't get away with it if he did, and since he didn't actually move on her physically, he could walk away without consequences. The only problem was, he'd refused to give up. Every additional encounter had resulted in him being on the losing end of things, until he'd shown up at Neil's and fired his rifle at him for interfering.

Brian attempted some small talk, but Cam wasn't taking any chances. She didn't want him knowing anything about her, or her mother. She would leave it up to her mother and Neil to decide what he would be told, if anything. Obviously the police had notified him of his son's death, but beyond that she didn't know what he knew. Not much, apparently. She was going to have to talk to Gilles about it, since he'd been the cop doing the notification.

Think of the devil, and the devil appears, she thought, nearly laughing at the absurd notion, when Gilles popped silently out of the brush in her direct line of sight. Cameron was grateful when he asked her what was going on, without addressing her by name. He might have been a rural cop, but he wasn't a bumbling fool apparently, and didn't give the game away. Maybe there was a reason her mother had so much respect for him.

"This is Brian Newman, or so he calls himself. He was looking for Neil McKinnon to ask him some questions about his son's death, and decided to take a shortcut through our property. I told him he would have to find another way to his friend's place, and wanted to be sure he went that way."

"Sure, I know Brian," Gilles responded. "I'm the one who told him about his son, in fact."

"You didn't tell me much," Brian said with a snort of derision.

"There was a reason for that, Brian. But since you seem like you need to hear more, I'll tell you what I was trying to avoid saying the first time. Your son shot Neil, and he was killed while trying to fire another round at him. I thought I was doing you a kindness by letting you think it was an accident. You've had more than enough people tell you bad things about your kid, and I didn't want to add to that when there was no need," Gilles responded calmly. Brian abruptly sat down on the deadfall behind him, his legs apparently unable to support him.

"I see," he said softly.

"I'm sorry, Brian. In hindsight it might have been better to be completely honest with you, but I'm still not so sure about that. Maybe you needed time to adjust first before you heard this. I don't know. I'm not a shrink. And that was the only notification I'd ever done. I'm sorry if I made things worse for you."

Cameron watched Brian take a few deep breaths, obviously trying to steady himself. Part of her desperately wanted to confess to him. She wanted to atone and ask for forgiveness, but she didn't dare. Maybe under different circumstances she might have done so, but with the precarious state of the world at the moment, rocking the boat seemed like a really bad idea. He looked up at her suddenly, and she just as quickly looked away.

"Can you tell me who it was that killed him, Gilles?"

"That's not something I'm willing to do," Gilles responded, his tone polite but firm.

"I'm pretty sure I already know the answer anyway," Brian said harshly. "Under the circumstances, I'm guessing the person felt they had no other choice, and I'm not going to do anything about it anyway. I just wanted to know."

Cam had a very hard time breathing. This was bad. She should never have come out here with her bow. Brian suspected she was the one who had killed his son, even if no one was confirming his theory. She needed to talk to her mom about this. Of course, her mother wasn't going to be too happy with her when she found out about her traipsing off by herself to check out a potential trespasser, and without telling anyone where she was going.

Yeah, she was in serious shit. It didn't matter that she wasn't a kid anymore. She had just acted like one, or at least partially, and she was going to hear about it. Thankfully her mother was going to be a lot more concerned about their safety. Cam had learned her lesson about going off half-cocked, at least, even if nothing too bad had come of it for the moment. She had no idea how things would pan out later on. This whole thing could turn out to be a huge mistake on her part. One she wouldn't be making again.

"Go back and tell Chuck to bring the truck to the end of the road here," Gilles was saying to her. Cam nodded, relieved that Brian wasn't going to be trusted to just leave the property. They would take him home and make sure of it. He would have to walk back again if he chose to do anything, which would give them some time to figure out what to do.

As Cameron walked away, she was also grateful that she wasn't going to have to continue to sit there with Brian. She could no longer look him in the eye, and felt like shit for having killed his son. She couldn't even say she was sorry, without admitting her guilt.

When she finally broke into the clearing, Cam was extremely irritated to find Billy standing there, waiting to see what was going on. For the moment, however, she ignored him. She had more important things to worry about. Since Chuck was standing there with him, she didn't have to go looking, and was able to give him Gilles' message right away. Chuck didn't say anything. He just turned and headed for the main house to grab the keys.

"You okay, Cam?"

"I'm fine, Billy. It's being handled," she said, resenting the fact that she felt like she had to answer to him. For the sake of peace and harmony, in the house that she and her mother shared with him and his dad, she had to be nice, but that sort of obligation always made her cranky. He'd obviously been paying attention while she explained things to Chuck, however, because he couldn't seem to resist talking about it, even though her tone should have been enough to warn him to leave it alone.

"Do you think he knows it was you? Is he going to be a problem for us, do you think?"

"He gave every indication that he assumed it was me, yes, but as for whether or not he's going to be a problem, how the fuck should I know? He said he wasn't planning to do anything about it, but he could easily be lying. Or he could change his mind later. Neither of us confirmed his suspicions, but the fact that neither of us tried to lie and say he was wrong means he's going to assume he's right. That whole 'silence is taken as assent' kind of deal, or whatever the hell the saying is."

29

"Okay, so maybe we should assume he's going to come after you then," Billy continued worriedly.

"I'm already assuming that, Billy. I'm not stupid," she snapped, but when he gave her a look that made it clear her actions would indicate otherwise, she rolled her eyes.

"Okay, fine. I was stupid to go out there on my own, and I'm sure my mother isn't going to be happy about it. I won't be doing it again, but I really don't feel like talking about this right now," she said, her tone daring him to keep it up.

"Just try and remember next time that we're all at risk when you do stuff like that. And we care what happens to you, too." So saying, Billy turned and walked away.

"Aargh!" Her snarl was for her own benefit, as she stormed back to the house. Cam was already pissed at herself. Not just for making a mistake, but for taking things out on Billy. He really hadn't done anything wrong. Except maybe the comment about caring what happened to her. She did *not* need to hear that kind of shit from him. His hero-worship after she'd killed Gerry and kept his dad from getting killed was bad enough. That was just embarrassing. Him crushing on her was pissing her off.

She didn't share Billy's interest in any way. If she had she'd have made the usual goo-goo eyes at him that people did when they were flirting. She'd be trying to spend time with him, instead of trying to avoid him. To be fair, he wasn't overbearing about it, and he was perfectly willing to be friendly toward her even if Cameron wasn't attracted to him. He didn't even try to pull that stupid 'friend zone' bullshit with her, where a woman's only worth was in whether or not she was willing to sleep with a guy.

Then again, Billy was having to fend off Katherine and her overt attempts to catch his eye. In his case, however, the girl was far too young. Five years' difference when the girl was fourteen was way too much. She was still a kid, even if she didn't think so herself. Never mind the fact that Chuck would probably string him up by his testicles for going near her.

If Cam had felt any chemistry toward Billy, at all, she might have gone for it. Even before the world had gone to shit, her sex life had been sporadic at best, and now it was completely non-existent. She didn't think there was much hope of that improving, but if Gerry's dad was still alive, maybe other people were, too.

Cam certainly didn't want to sleep with Billy just to get laid. He wanted more than that, and she'd only end up hurting him. She wasn't the kind of person who could easily live with herself after using someone for sex. A trait she'd obviously inherited from her mother. She had no hang-ups about the act itself, but one-night stands weren't something either of the Thane women went after. There had to be more to it than that.

She hung her bow on its rack, and stripped off the glove. Her jacket and the arm protector came off next. She would have removed the jacket to practice her archery, hence the need for the arm protector, but there hadn't been a chance to get in any practice. Cam let out another sigh of frustration. At least the numbness wasn't seeping back as quickly as she'd feared. The anger that had

31

propelled her out the door was mostly gone, replaced by simple irritation.

Since the purpose of her treks around the property were to check for trespassers the sensors might miss, the day hadn't exactly been wasted. The odds were against there being someone else stepping onto their land in the same day. Being in the middle of nowhere had its advantages, after all. She decided against going back out for her planned perimeter walk.

The cold sweat from the earlier adrenaline spike was making her shiver, and she felt kind of gross, so Cam decided another shower was in order. Then she could go over and see Kirk and Leigh, and tell them about the events of the afternoon. She could use the radio, but she was in the mood to hang out and maybe play some video games for the first time in ages.

Her mother would want to talk to her when she got back, but that probably wouldn't be for hours yet, and she was in no mood to wait around. Even the thought of doing so had her feeling resentful. No, that conversation would have to wait.

Cam showered and changed, then headed out through the greenhouse area at the back of the house once again. She wanted to avoid running into anyone who might want to talk to her about what had happened. A few minutes later she was stomping across the bridge they had built just before winter, which allowed them to cross directly back and forth between the two properties, without using the roads. It was wide and strong enough to support driving a truck over, in case they needed to move large items in addition to people.

Even now, during a time that should have been the coldest part of winter, there was very little snow, and the ice on the river was merely a thin crust. Cam thought of the stories her mother used to tell her about the neck-deep snow she'd played in as a child. Cameron had never experienced snow that deep. She'd grown up in the city, in an area that was below most of the Canadian border. They'd had high heat and humidity every summer, and very little winter to speak of. It wasn't unusual to have no snow for Christmas, and things had only grown warmer as she'd gotten older.

Now, even further north, at most Cameron had seen about six inches of snow. And it hadn't lasted very long either. A few days earlier she'd heard her mother say something about the winter wheat coming up soon. They'd planted it in the fall after their vegetables had finished for the season, so they would have something to use for flour by spring. Once they harvested that, they would be putting in vegetable gardens again, and growing more fodder for the animals.

Cam kicked at a two-inch crusty blob of snow that marred the otherwise bare path leading away from the bridge. The only reason it hadn't melted was because of the shelter of the evergreens above her head. Things stayed pretty dark and cold under the gigantic pines. The sudden shade had her shivering a bit, so she picked up the pace. Another ten minutes would see her at the cabin, and she was really looking forward to relaxing with her friends. She had almost lost them seven months earlier. The experience had reminded her to value them, and she hadn't been spending enough time with them.

Kirk and Leigh had nearly been trapped in the city when the grid began to collapse. They were living in Oakville at the time. Unbeknownst to her and her mother, their car was in the garage when Cam messaged them to get up to the farm, waiting to have its timing chain replaced. When Cam told her mother that they wouldn't be able to make it, her mother suggested they rent a car instead. She would have paid for the rental, even, but that hadn't been necessary. It turned out their car was a lease anyway, so they just left it there for the leasing company to reclaim.

Just as she reached the porch steps, Cam got a nasty surprise. Apparently Billy had headed directly here after he'd spoken to her. She could hear him talking to Kirk on the other side of the house where they'd set up a target to practice their archery. Kirk and Leigh had taken lessons with her and her mother, and they had their own equipment. It sounded like Billy was learning to use it. Well, that was just great. Here she'd been hoping to get away from everyone, and now she was going to have to put up with Billy instead of being able to chill.

Maybe her day could have gone a whole lot worse, considering the whole thing with Gerry's father, but at the moment it felt like a disaster. She already felt bitchy and miserable, looking for a way to decompress, and Billy's presence meant she was going to have to clamp a lid back down on her emotions. Granted, it was really the first time since August that she'd even had normal emotions, so she should probably be grateful. A few weeks earlier she'd been completely numb, but her mother's big revelation had jarred something loose inside her.

Cam took a deep breath. She needed to think before she came face to face with Billy. And she needed to calm her temper. She could really use a punching bag right about now, and as much as she might wish Billy could stand in lieu of one, it wasn't something she could do. So she let her mind wander, and thought about whether or not she could make one of her own. She started to think about its construction, and having to use dirt rather than sand. Their shopping spree at the sewing shop before all the stores had closed meant they had whatever materials she might need, but she wasn't sure if the thread they had was strong enough. She was in the middle of wondering if she could use paracord instead, when Billy walked around the corner, startling her from her thoughts.

"Hey Cam!"

"Jesus Billy. You scared the crap out of me!"

"I didn't mean to. You must have been in the middle of some pretty deep thoughts if you didn't see me coming," he said with a tentative smile.

"Nothing important, or philosophically deep. Just pondering how I might be able to make a punching bag," she responded.

"Uh, okay." His tone was leery, as if it had occurred to him that she might have considered him for the role, which made Cam chuckle.

"Hey, if I'm making one, you don't have to worry that you'll end up with any bruises. I'll take out my frustrations on inanimate objects. Anyway, was Kirk teaching you to use his bow?"

"Yeah. I've been coming here for a while now. I guess you didn't notice."

"I haven't been noticing anything anyone does, Billy. Don't take it personally. I have a lot on my mind. Speaking of which, I just came over here to spend some time with my friends so I can zone out for a bit. Don't take that personally either. I just really need some time and space right now to relax."

"I was heading back to the house to get Gowan anyway. I can't bring him here when I'm firing arrows at a target. He might get hurt, or he might bump me so that someone else gets hurt, you know?"

Cameron just nodded at him. The Doberman her mother had rescued, along with a bunch of ferrets, had attached himself to Billy. They were fast friends now, but like a lot of dogs he was a little too enthusiastic sometimes.

Billy left her to her thoughts finally, and Cam walked cautiously around the end of the house, rather than going up on the porch to the door. She took a quick look to see if Kirk was firing at the target, but when she saw him yanking arrows out of it to replace in his quiver, she relaxed and walked toward him, smiling as she spoke.

"Dude, have I got some crazy shit to tell you!"

3 ~ FINDERS KEEPERS

"There are a hell of a lot more people alive than I've been expecting," Mac said, worried that it might impact their safety at the farm. Some of the people had come running outside when they'd heard a vehicle driving past, while at other homes curtains were wrenched aside so they could look out to see what was going on.

"You make it sound like it's a bad thing," Neil replied.

"It might be. If they're desperate, and there are enough of them, it could be a very bad thing."

"If they survived the winter, they have their own food stores, and they're probably going to be putting in gardens again very soon. You don't really want people to die out completely, do you?"

"They have just as much right to survive as we do, but they may not have what they need to put in new gardens. A lot of people bought new seeds and seedlings every year, in order to start up their gardens. Most don't know how to save their seeds, and most seeds were engineered so people couldn't get seeds from fruits and veggies anyway. Not to mention the fact that if any of these people know who you are, and where your cabin is, there's a good chance they'll try to get to your place to help themselves to a working vehicle. In addition to our food," she said.

"Leaving the farm was a risk. We both knew that. I can't guarantee those people we passed don't know who I am, but none of them seemed familiar to me, and we're already pretty far away from the cabin. It's a very long walk. All we can do is wait and see. In the meantime, could you try to concentrate on the job at hand, honey? I'd like to get these panels off the roof before one of us falls twenty feet," he said rather curtly.

"Sorry," she muttered, irritated by his tone even if he did have a point.

"It's a damn good thing we brought two ladders, cowboy, because these panels are heavy. It's definitely going to take the both of us to get them down," she finished, her breath coming out in a woofing sound when she momentarily took the weight so Neil could get positioned properly on his ladder. Once he had, he took the weight so she could do the same. Between them they guided the PV panel to the ground, a step at a time.

"We should have brought some rope. Are we taking all of these?" Neil asked.

"We probably should, though I'm not feeling really enthusiastic about it right this second," she replied, as she stood on the ground and stared up at the eavestrough far above their heads.

"Well, let's get the next one, and we'll take it as it comes," Neil decided.

It took them two hours, with a number of breaks just to be on the safe side. By the time they were done, Mackenzie's arms and legs were trembling. Each panel had taken them fifteen minutes, but now they had eight of them on the ground, ready to be put in the truck.

"Maybe we should have gone for the mattresses first. That would have been better cushioning than the blankets we brought with us," Mac said with some concern.

"Not much we can do about it now," Neil said, shrugging. "Whoever's driving will just have to be careful, and we'll head straight from here to the furniture store by the Pentecostal church. We can take a look for marine batteries on our way to the library instead. Probably a bunch where the boats are docked by the town bridge. I'm not sure what you hope to find in the library, though. You're talking about some fairly obscure technology. Most people didn't know about it before the grid collapsed, so I can't see the library in Huntsville having any books on it. Hell, you'll be lucky if they have a book explaining solar energy."

"Oh, I know. I don't really expect to find anything, but even having books on diesel engines will be a big help to me," Mac replied. "I only really understand gasoline engines. When someone starts talking about glow plugs, I'm lost. The only reason I know it's possible to convert to using vegetable oil, is because of some stuff they had on the news about it years ago. Besides, I still need the books on boating and sailing. I was thinking they might have a section with marine maps, too, seeing as there are so many lakes and waterways around here."

She tilted her head to the left, stretching out her neck, and then to the right. She was already tired and sore, and wasn't looking forward to hauling boxes of books out of the library, but it had occurred to her that she'd like to conserve some of those books. Anything to do with medicine, food preservation, agriculture, science, or technology could turn out to be a big help to them, and she loved books just for their own sake. She hated to think of them being left to rot.

They arrived at the furniture store without incident. First they stacked four queen-size mattresses inside Neil's large horse trailer, and stowed the photovoltaic panels between. They added a couple of twin mattresses on top, and it wasn't until they had finished standing up the remaining four twin-size mattresses in the trailer, that trouble came calling.

The shuffling gait had the unwelcome thought of zombies popping into her brain, but she shook her head to clear it. This was nothing more than severe malnutrition. At his first, nearly incoherent words, however, she felt the first flicker of fear and disgust. Neil stilled for a second, but then began to circle around to the driver's side of the truck.

"Eat you," the disheveled stranger said, his voice a harsh, gasping sound. Apparently he hadn't been talking a lot lately, or someone had tried to strangle him at some point.

"Dude," Mac began, while backing up. "You're not gonna eat me. You might be starving, but I can give you some food. Real food, not human. We carry emergency packs with us."

"No. Eat you."

The light of madness in his eyes made her think further conversation was probably pointless, but she needed to try. She really didn't want to have to hurt the guy, though killing him might be a mercy. He'd obviously taken in more than he could handle, and it sounded as though part of what he'd taken in was human flesh. She understood survival, but he seemed to prefer eating humans to regular food sources now.

"You're *not* going to eat me, or anyone else. I can give you real food, but I'm not letting you gnaw on me no matter how hungry you are. If you try, I'm going to have to hurt you. You don't want that, do you?"

Her hand was on the grip of her gun when he lunged jerkily toward her, his halting steps slowing to a stop when he saw her brandishing the weapon. He was apparently sane enough not to directly challenge a bullet. At least not by himself. It wasn't until she began sidling toward the passenger door of the truck that she saw the others.

"Neil," she said softly.

"I see them," he responded just as quietly. "We need to go. Now." So saying, he pulled open his door. Mackenzie continued to brandish the Glock 22, giving Neil time to get the truck started and in gear.

"Mac! Get in the fucking truck!"

She wasn't arguing. Her pulse racing, she leapt in. He was

pulling away from the warehouse-like store before she'd even closed her door. When the door-latch clunked into place, she yanked at her seatbelt, causing it to jam on her first attempt.

"For fuck's sake," she snarled, forcing herself to pull the belt slowly the second time. Patience wasn't one of her virtues at the best of times, and with panic added to the mix she wanted to scream at the belt mechanism.

"Okay. So *that* just happened," Mac said breathlessly, as she settled back against her seat with her heart still fluttering. Neil let out a chuckle at her choice of words.

"Yup. It sure did. You still want to head to the electronics store in the mall?" Neil glanced at her as he waited for her response. Mackenzie took a moment to consider the issue.

"Cameron's right. We need those cameras. Our security has gaps. And, after seeing those freaks, I like being vulnerable to outsiders even less than I did before," Mackenzie replied. She shuddered and wondered how long it would be before she felt like eating again. She considered herself a pragmatic sort, and knew she was just as likely to resort to cannibalism as anyone, if her survival were at stake. But she was pretty sure she'd never start *preferring* that to other food sources.

"Well, at least they weren't moaning about brains," Neil quipped. Mackenzie snorted. It probably wasn't the least bit funny, but she'd always been the sort to think of strange things as an adventure rather than a frustration.

"Probably the closest thing humanity will ever come to actual zombies, I suppose. I've never been a big believer in zombie apocalypses. Then again, there were those bath salt drugs that had people trying to eat other people while they were high on them. We've done some pretty nasty stuff to ourselves as a species."

"Well, zombies aside, how do you want to do the mall thing? I'd prefer to go in together, and stay in visual contact, rather than one of us outside waiting with the truck. Especially after seeing that bunch. I'm not too keen on either of us running into a group like that while we're alone. What do you think?"

"I think you're right," Mac said. "It's a different set-up from the library, with outside doors everywhere, despite most being the employees-only kind. Just too many ways in and out for a person outside to know what's going on. So, we go in together. I think with the library we can both go in to make sure it's empty, and then you can stay with the truck since I know what I'm looking for. Good thing we brought the headlamps, though. Both those places are going to be pitch black inside. What do you want to bet the glass doors at the mall will already be broken?"

"Nothin' doin'. I'm keeping my money. There's no way that place wasn't raided for food, what with the grocery store being attached. It has its own set of doors if I remember correctly, but there would've been other items worth looting in the main part of the mall. Thankfully security cameras wouldn't have been high on anyone's looting wish-list, but that's assuming the local stores even carried them for sale. I'm betting most of the people were dead within the first month in town, with the exception of those who considered other people a food source."

Mac didn't respond. She hated to think of all the people that had once lived in Huntsville. It had been a beautiful town. Too damn crowded in the summer with all the tourists, or terrorists as she and her friends had called them, but beautiful all the same. Well, at least there were no crowds now, and tourism was a thing of the past. Aesthetically-speaking, Huntsville could still be considered beautiful. Just really empty, with a lot of long, brown grass no one had been able to cut at the end of the previous summer, which had withered during the winter months.

The sadness crept up on her. It wasn't until that moment that she'd realized how much of the beauty of the town had come from the people living there, peacefully enjoying small-town life. Since she'd spent such a large portion of her life avoiding people as much as possible, the sentiment caught her completely off guard.

"Why is it that it's only now, when people are either dead or crazy, that I'm starting to think they weren't so bad after all? I guess I'm like everyone in that respect, not appreciating something until it's too late. It's not just that, though. There's a rhythm that's missing in the world now. Kind of like someone blowing air across the top of an empty bottle, rather than a whole band playing. I think we were *supposed* to be a part of this world, but we went too far with it, and now we're not playing the part we should have played," she finished softly.

"Honey, that's just what humans do. We overreach. And it's not just with bad things, either. Even when we're doing something for a good cause we overreach, like with activism. People would go too far with it, alienating others who might have been a help to their cause. Humans just aren't that reasonable or rational, and we sure as hell don't think ahead very much about the consequences of our actions. Or inactions," he added ruefully.

"Ain't that the truth. At any rate, you were right not to bet against me. Looks like both big sets of doors are broken. It's a good thing, too. I want to make as little noise as possible. Hopefully the sound of the truck hasn't caught anyone's attention. Thankfully that furniture store is such a long way from the mall."

Neil pulled up to the doors and turned off the motor, while Mac looked up at the big signs over what used to be Zellers, before the large department-store chain had gone belly-up. Walmart moving into Canada had certainly had an impact on their bottom line.

"I always wondered what they put in here after Zellers crapped out. It's not easy finding big-name stores to take over those giant leases. Target took over some of the stores in the cities, I know, but then they pulled out of Canada. I'm surprised to see Winners and SportChek here, though. There aren't even a lot of Winners stores down in the bigger cities." Winners was a clothing store that sold new, but discounted, name-brand stuff. She'd seen cashmere for a fraction of the cost in some of them, but their stock wasn't consistent. Neil just shrugged.

"I was just thinking it was too bad they'd only have summer stock," he said. "Not that it's getting all that cold these days. We sure as hell don't need down parkas anymore."

"Well, we've got everything we need for clothing anyway, and that's not what we're here for. I mean, if you see something in the electronics store that you think will be useful, by all means grab it, but I don't want to be spending time looking into the other stores."

"What about the new arrivals?"

"What? The 'Spring Collection' you mean?"

"No," Neil said, and snorted out a laugh. "I meant the new arrivals at the farm, doofus. Fashion wasn't a concern of mine even when it might have mattered to someone, much less now when there's no one to impress. I was thinking that the kids in particular might be outgrowing some of their clothes sometime soon. Never mind shoes. We could grab a few boxes of cross-trainers from SportChek. They might have some sporting goods that would be useful, too."

"Hmm. Maybe. If we're quiet, and constantly checking to make sure we haven't attracted any visitors, we should be able to grab some boys' and girls' clothes. Pyjamas and underwear, too. Katherine's got the whole puberty thing going on, so I'll get some bras for her in different sizes. Seeing as it'll take a few trips to get stuff, that gives us the opportunity to keep watching for unwanted company. We just have to make sure we do everything together."

"Alright," Neil said, giving a nod.

"Let's get the cameras first then, just in case. We can keep going back in for other stuff, but we get only the truly necessary stuff first. And, of course, I'm pretty sure there's a book store in here, too."

"Alright, fine. Let's go before all my hair falls out from old age."

"You're right. We should go. I'm pretty sure it's already thinning," Mac said with a smirk, laughing outright when he growled at her. She slipped out of the truck with a smile on her face, reaching behind her seat for the metal pry-bar. She closed the door as softly as she could, and once Neil had done the same she stood there listening for a few moments.

"Sounds clear," she said softly. Putting her free hand on the grip of her Glock, she headed toward the second set of broken doors, Neil walking softly beside her. Once they had stepped through the metal framework of the doors, they both paused to listen again. There was nothing. Not even wild animals had come foraging in the mall, apparently, which meant the humans had cleaned out every scrap of food, including anything in the garbage bins that was fit to eat.

She glanced questioningly at Neil, who nodded back at her, and without speaking they headed straight for the electronics store. It had originally been a Radio Shack, but they'd been bought out long ago by a big chain conglomerate. The roll-down security bars had been bent, but surprisingly they hadn't been forced open. Mac figured it was likely people were more concerned with food than diodes, headphones, or circuit boards by that point. Without power to run any of the items, they were nothing more than paperweights to people who were starving.

The pry-bar made short work of the lock that latched into the floor, though it made a terrible screeching sound that Mac was sure would bring people running. She motioned for Neil to turn off his headlamp, and turned her own off to wait for any response to the noise she'd made. When no one appeared, they cautiously pushed up the roll-down bars and then spent a few minutes listening again, hardly daring to breathe. The silence stretched endlessly, with no echoing footsteps or shuffling feet to intrude upon it.

When nothing changed, even in the air currents, to indicate that anyone else might be present, Mac stepped past the threshold of the store and turned her headlamp back on. Neil followed suit. The storage room in the back was unlocked, and though there was very little inventory in there, they found plenty of empty boxes they could use to pack things in for carrying. They had a couple in the truck, but they needed those for their trip to the library later.

"We should grab some circuit boards and electronic components, too," Neil said.

"Yeah, it would be good to have extras to repair things. I'm no great shakes at electronics, but I'm sure someone else will find the time to mess around with stuff like that. I've got some books already for anyone who wants to learn, too."

"Those kids' starter kits would be a good thing. We don't have much stuff for Chuck and Kayla's kids with regard to education. They've gone the last few months without any sort of classroom learning."

"You're right. Now I feel like a hypocrite. I've always gone on about how important it is to keep learning throughout life, and now there are kids I'm responsible for who aren't getting an education," Mac said, disgusted with herself.

"Jesus, honey. It wasn't a judgment against you in any way. You're trying to help a bunch of people survive that you weren't counting on. It's not your responsibility to make sure anyone gets an education, or even that they have food to eat. It's up to Chuck and Kayla to deal with their kids. I just thought they'd like to have the stuff, that's all."

"Alright, alright. Now that you mention it, though, it's one more reason to make sure we go to the library. Those kids need books to read. I don't have anything appropriate for Katherine even, much less Chris or Amelia. Now I'm wishing I had a lot more boxes … and a lot more room in the truck and trailer."

"Well, we've still got the back seat and the cargo bed to fill, and there's space for a row of boxes on top of the mattresses in the trailer, so I think we're covered. And we'll take extra boxes from the mall here. We don't want to be at this for the rest of the night anyway. So, let's get it done, and get what we can."

"Yeah, yeah. Time to shut up and get to work, I know." Mackenzie snagged a box and headed back out to the display part of the store. She took a minute to listen again for human presence, but there was nothing.

As she stacked cameras, small boxes of diodes and triodes, and various computer components, she couldn't help feeling like she was stealing. It didn't matter that the company no longer existed, or that most likely no one associated with the company was still alive. It just felt weird. It had been the same at the house where they had scavenged the photovoltaic panels.

"Why does this feel like theft to me?"

"I know," Neil said in agreement. "We both know it's stupid, but it's so ingrained in us to think of stealing as wrong. Yet, when I think about corporate greed, and the theft from their own employees and all that, I don't feel quite so bad about it. In fact, I kind of feel like taking every damn thing in here, except that there might be someone else who needs it."

"You're right," Mac said with a laugh. "Now I feel a whole lot better."

Fifteen minutes later they were taking a pair of large boxes out to the truck, walking cautiously through the main aisle of the mall. They paused at the broken entry doors, but found nothing to alarm them, so they put their boxes in the back seat and went back for the other two from the electronics store. They didn't bother with boxes for the clothing they looted from Winners. They just took stuff from the children's section right off the racks, ensuring a good sizing selection. If stuff didn't fit now, it might later, or if someone added children to the mix.

An hour later Mac called a halt.

"That's enough for the time being. We've only got three kids on the farm. We already grabbed stuff for them to do from the electronics store, including some toys and instruments, so I think they're set. And I'm exhausted."

"Okay, let's head to the docks for batteries, and then hit the library, so we can get our asses back to the farm to play mother and father bountiful. You're not the only one who's tired."

"Are you okay?" Mac's tone was worried. She knew it, but couldn't help it. Neil getting shot had been a terrifying ordeal, and she was concerned that his one lung might have been permanently affected.

"I'm fine," Neil said, his exasperation obvious from his curt tone. "We've had at least three hours' aerobic exercise thus far, and that would tire anyone out. You have to stop worrying about me."

"Maybe," she said, as she climbed into the driver's seat. She waited for him to buckle up in the passenger seat before continuing.

"It's just that there have been other signs to indicate that you might not be quite up to par just yet," she said cautiously, waiting with bated breath for his response.

"And those signs would be?" He gave her a direct look, with one brow raised, as though daring her to say it. She started the truck and started pulling out of the mall parking lot to give herself a moment to figure out how to phrase it. Then she decided blunt honesty was her best bet, even if it wasn't as diplomatic or tactful as she might have liked.

"Sex. We're not having sex anywhere near as often as before. Of course, I didn't expect us to continue banging each other six times a day or anything. I figured that was because we were just starting out together. And then we couldn't while you were recovering. But now, if you're recovered, why are we only having sex once a week? I'm gonna run out of batteries," she joked.

"Well, you probably should have picked up more at the electronics store anyway, but aside from that there's a very good reason we haven't been making love. You keep running away from me."

"What? What the fuck are you talking about? The last thing I'd do is run away from you if you were wanting to have a bit of fun."

"It might be the last thing you want to do, but that's exactly what you're doing. You've been pulling away from me, and I'm pretty sure it's subconscious. I know it's not a chemistry thing, because I can see you react to me every time I touch you. I think it's more that you're worried and don't want to risk it. Every time we *have* managed to have sex, you've pretty much taken over the whole business so I'm not doing any of the work. I think part of you is terrified that it'll be too much for me."

"Fuck." Mackenzie thought about it as she pulled across the town bridge, parking on Main Street.

"It needs to change, Mac. You have to stop looking at me like I'm the infirm, because I gotta say, when it comes to you I'm about as firm as it gets."

"Very punny. Jerk."

"Come on, honey. There are a few boats down there, so let's do what we came to do. We can take care of that other business later." Mackenzie's breath left her in a rush at his words. Nope, there was definitely no problem with the chemistry between them. Just the thought of him taking care of business, as he put it, was enough to get her all riled up. She shook her head to clear it, making him laugh knowingly.

"Yeah, yeah. Yuk it up. Now stop distracting me. We can't afford that right now," she chastised. He sobered instantly.

"You're right. Sorry. Let's go."

The batteries only took a few minutes, and then they were heading over to Minerva for the books. She parked facing the wrong way, with the truck parallel to the wheelchair ramp. The library was locked up tight, so Mac used her knife's glass-break point to punch out a small portion of the thick safety glass in one of the doors to reach in for the lock. She had taped over the section so it would make as little noise as possible, but they still waited for a few minutes to be sure no one came running. It didn't take long to discover that the library was empty. They hadn't really expected anyone to be in it anyway. It wasn't as though there was a shortage of available shelter, and the doors had still been secure.

Mac went back to the truck with Neil to grab a couple of the boxes they'd snagged from the mall, and headed back into the library to fill them. She found plenty of books on boats and sailing, in addition to books on diesel mechanics, and was carting out a filled box within minutes.

"No sign of anyone yet?"

"Nope. I sure hope those assholes who wanted to eat us aren't the only people still alive in this town, though. That would really suck," he said. Mackenzie was in wholehearted agreement.

"Well, there's always the likelihood they'll end up eating each other, which will solve that particular problem. There will only be one left at the end, and eventually that one will die of starvation after a while."

"There can be only one," he quipped in a Scottish burr.

"This isn't The Highlander. Though I guess it amounts to the same thing since it involves killing off other people. Alright. I've got the other box packed, so I'd better go get it. Then I need to go into the children's section and pack up at least one more box there. The trick will be finding something that doesn't glorify mental illness and unhealthy relationships, that will still be interesting reading for a teenager."

"So Twilight is out then, I guess?" His question made her laugh.

"It's so nice to be married to an intelligent man."

"Remember that the next time you're losing an argument with me."

With a smile she went back into the library to get the rest of the books. As she was carting out the last box, however, she stopped smiling. She was hearing an unfamiliar voice through the partially-broken door glass.

4 ~ Misery and Company

Mac waited by the door, attempting to listen to what was being said. From what she could make out, the person speaking was a woman, though her voice was rough and hard to make out. It sounded as though she was begging for food. Mac put down the box, freeing up her hands just in case, and headed cautiously through the door.

Neil didn't acknowledge her as she came up behind the woman, who was facing away from Mackenzie. She was leaning to the side, holding a child against her hip who couldn't have been more than a year old.

"It's alright. We've got some food we can give you. We brought some with us in case we ran into anyone who needed some right away. We'll have to dig it out first, so why don't you talk to my wife while I get it?" He nodded toward Mac when he made the suggestion.

The woman gasped and turned around, fear turning her body rigid. The baby in her arms didn't cry, even though he looked scared and upset. Mac frowned, unintentionally frightening the woman even more.

"Sorry, I didn't mean to scare you," she said softly. "My face tends to do its own thing. It's even worse when I'm not thinking about anything. I think they call it resting bitch face." She tried out a smile to put the young woman at ease, but it didn't seem to work.

"I didn't hear you come up behind me. Normally I hear everything!" Mac was starting to get the picture.

"I take it you have reason to be paranoid, then. I wondered when your baby didn't cry. It's okay. We're not part of the roving band of cannibals, if that's what's worrying you. We don't want anything from you. We've got plenty of our own, non-human-flesh food. How have you been surviving on your own here in town, if you don't mind me asking?"

"I moved back here to live with my mom when Jake was born. She had a vegetable garden, and did a lot of canning. I don't know the first thing about gardening. Or canning for that matter. We haven't been eating people, though, if that's what you're wondering."

"I wouldn't necessarily blame you if you'd had to resort to that. It's just that we ran into a group that seemed to prefer human flesh to other sources of food, so I had to ask. What happened to your mom?"

"She died within a week of the power failing. She was on dialysis," the young woman said, her expression bleak. Mackenzie's heart dropped like a stone inside her chest. If they'd known, they could have saved her mother's life by providing power for a dialysis machine.

"I'm really sorry. I would imagine anyone who had kidney problems fared about the same as your mother. Most diabetics, too. My name's Mackenzie Thane, by the way, and my husband there is Neil McKinnon, if he hasn't already introduced himself." She held out her hand to the woman, who probably wasn't any more than twenty years old.

"I'm Lisa Johnstone, and like I said, this is Jake. His last name is Johnstone, too. His father never bothered to claim him, so I never bothered to give him his last name."

"I wouldn't have either. In fact, I didn't. My daughter has my last name. Depending on what we decide here, you might be meeting her. I take it you're not set up very well for survival at this point, if you're looking for food."

"Not at all. I'm still breastfeeding Jake, so he's okay so long as I get enough food to produce milk, but I haven't got any left. I've been going through houses, trying to find something, but they all ran out of food and starved long ago. It's been something of a horror-show for me, because damn near all the houses have bodies in them. I'm just glad Jake is too young to understand what they are, because I couldn't leave him on his own."

"He's awfully quiet for a baby," Mackenzie noted.

"He never really cried a lot, but after this happened I had to use a technique from a romance novel I read one time. Every time he cried I'd blow into his face to stop him. It was a book set in the 1800s, with Native Americans and all that, and they trained their babies not to cry so their enemies couldn't find them. I figured I'd better give it a try and see if it worked. Thankfully it did, but I have to watch to make sure he eats when he needs to, and that I change him regularly enough."

"Huh. Wish I'd known about that when my daughter was a baby. But then, she was colicky, so it might not have worked as well."

"Here's a granola bar, Lisa," Neil said, as he handed her the bar. Lisa looked at it like it was manna from heaven.

"Oh thank you!"

"We've got more food with us in the truck. You just need to take it a bit slow if you haven't eaten in a little while," he cautioned her. She tore open the foiled-paper wrapping with her teeth, and when she bit into the bar she moaned. Mac had to laugh.

"We've got a pretty good set-up where we are, if you're looking for a better situation," Mac offered. Tears filled Lisa's eyes.

"You're kidding me!" Her mouth was still somewhat full, so it came out muffled, but Mac got the gist of what she was saying.

"Your mother didn't happen to be Michelle Johnstone, did she?" Mackenzie wasn't looking forward to the answer, but she had to know.

"Yeah, she was," Lisa said, when she'd finally swallowed the last of the granola bar. "Did you know her?"

"I went to school with her. Man, I'm really sorry. She was a very decent person. I don't think I saw her after high school, but we were sort of friends during our public school years. I veered off with a rougher crowd, so we parted ways, but it wasn't because I didn't like her." Mac was depressed. Neil came up and put his arm around her shoulders. She could tell that he wanted to do the same for Lisa, but since he didn't know her he wasn't comfortable offering her the gesture.

"I guess I'd better grab that last box of books. Neil, we should empty out part of that back seat so there's room for a car seat at least. Lisa can sit on the bench with us. I'm assuming you live nearby, Lisa. Centre Street?"

"Just past the dental clinic, yeah."

"Okay, if you want to come back to the farm with us, take Jake back to your place to pack up a few things. We'll finish up here, and then pull the truck over. Make sure you grab anything vital, because it's going to be a long time before we come back here. I sure hope you're using washable diapers, because we don't have any disposables at the farm. The youngest kid there right now is seven years old."

"You've got kids there, too?" Lisa's eyes were alight with curiosity.

"Just three that could be classified as children. The oldest is fourteen, and all three are the kids of an old friend of mine. Chuck Forrest used to be a cop here in Huntsville, actually. You might recognize him when you see him. He's kind of hard to miss, since he's really tall. Anyway, let's get going. We've been away a lot longer than we planned, so my daughter and Neil's son might start getting worried soon. This is the first time any of us have really left the farm since shortly after the power went down."

"How far is it?"

"We're near Rosseau, but out in the boonies," Mackenzie said. Lisa tilted her head to the side, apparently considering her situation.

"It's not like I've got any better options right now, though I don't like leaving my mother's house empty like that."

"When you do come back to it, I'm sure everything will be exactly as you left it. The only people we've seen in town were the ones in that small group, and they're only interested in one thing. By the time you get back, hopefully they'll all be dead and gone." Mac turned back to grab the box from the library's entrance. She heard Lisa turn away with her son to head back up Minerva toward Centre Street. By the time she brought the last box to the back of the trailer, Neil had already cleared a section of the back seat. Everything had been stuffed on top of the mattresses in the trailer.

"I wonder if she's got a crib mattress and stuff," Mac said, when she looked inside the trailer to see that there was still a bit of space on top.

"If she's got her own mattress, we can probably fit that, too. We can grab that for her while she watches Jake. She doesn't know us," Neil continued. "She's not going to want to leave him with either of us just yet."

"Yeah, but let's not leave the keys in the ignition, just in case."

"You're such a trusting soul, honey."

"I was a complete fool with *you*, wasn't I? Cameron should

have smacked me silly for that, though it looks like everything worked out okay there," she said with a smile.

"You're human, and I have powers beyond the ken of mortal man. Or woman." Neil grinned at her as he spoke.

"So far beyond that no one has ever seen them," she retorted. "Come on. Let's go get our new guests." She shook her head at herself.

"Stop it," Neil said.

"Stop what?"

"Stop calling yourself a fool for bringing someone else back to the farm. We both knew we wouldn't be leaving anyone here if they needed a place to go. Or food. And no one at the farm has room to complain about it, since they're alive because we did the same for them."

It meant another thirty minutes to pack everything they could fit into the trailer, but then they were finally on their way back. It wasn't until they climbed into the truck for the last time that Mac began to relax. She hadn't even realized how tense she'd been until that moment, but she sighed in deep contentment when she plunked her ass down in the middle of the front bench.

Once they were on Aspdin Road and up to speed, Neil put his arm around her as he drove with his left hand. It reminded her a bit of her youth, and being snuggled up against whatever boyfriend she had at the time. Not that there had been many. Once she'd gotten married and then pregnant at sixteen, those sorts of boyfriends hadn't been a priority. The dating scene changed dramatically for her once she'd had Cameron, too.

Neil stopped the truck when they reached the concealed entrance to the farm, and got out to press his thumb to the biometric scanner plate that was hidden in a hollow at the back of a tree. Lisa gasped beside Mac when the gate swung open.

"Holy crap! It's like being in a spy movie," she said wonderingly.

"A little bit, yeah. My daughter and I made sure this place was hidden. We were expecting things to go south."

"What do you mean? Why didn't you warn people?" Lisa sounded shocked to the core, as only a young person can.

"I did, actually. I warned people constantly. It's just human nature to ignore things that require action. I was told by a guy I used to work for, who was a former Ontario Hydro executive, that the power outages would get worse, and that eventually the grid would come down. My friends called me paranoid for wanting to set up a place that was off the grid, but I didn't care. I knew it needed to be done if my daughter and I were going to survive. When the shit hit the fan, a few people needed a place to go, so they sort of straggled in after-the-fact. And then there were the animals."

"Animals? What animals?"

"She means the fifty ferrets, dozens of goats, and even more dozens of chickens," Neil said with a bit of a laugh. "And a Doberman, along with some cats and other dogs that she rescued while I was recovering from being shot." At the last bit he glared at

Mac. That had been a bit of a sore point between them for a while.

"You don't need to bombard her with everything just yet, thank you very much," Mac said crisply.

"Ferrets? You have ferrets here? Wait a minute. Did he just say fifty ferrets? He was kidding, right?" Lisa sounded like she was choking.

"Fifty-two if you count the two I already had, though they don't mix with the ones from the shelters." Mackenzie waited to see if Lisa would call them rodents, but she just seemed really excited.

"I always wanted a ferret, but they didn't have any around here. When I went to Nipissing University up in North Bay I couldn't have pets, and then I got pregnant with Jake. My life was a bit too complicated at the time to have pets. I already had my BA, but I was still trying to get my teaching certificate. I was taking some of the courses through their distance learning program, and was just about to start my practical when the world sort of went to hell. Oh wow," she finished, when she saw the open area before her.

Gilles stepped up to the truck when Neil rolled to a stop at the house. Mac's heart started pounding.

"Oh, God. Something's wrong. Let me out!"

It couldn't have been more than five seconds before Mac was standing in front of Gilles, but it felt like a millennium.

"What is it? What's wrong?"

"Nobody's dead or hurt, Mac. Relax. But we've got a situation to deal with," Gilles said. He shoved his hands in his pockets, as though unsure how much to tell her.

"Gilles, spit it out. What the fuck is going on?"

"Well, you're probably going to want to have a chat with your kid, because she could have gotten herself into some serious trouble. She's fine, but she went off on her own to check it out when a sensor lit up. She played it pretty smart after she ran into the person who tripped the sensor, but she also got lucky. The worst part of it is, she ran into Brian Newman. Gerry's father." Gilles left it at that, giving her a few minutes to sift through the situation in her mind. As it was, Mackenzie was reeling.

"Honey, we need to get Lisa and Jake settled a bit, so let's go into the house to finish this conversation. For that matter, we can all get something to eat while Gilles fills us in on the details."

Mackenzie nodded abruptly. Instinctively she wanted all the answers right that second, but she knew Neil was right. If Cameron was okay, she didn't need to go crazy. At least not yet.

"Maybe we should ask Cameron to join us in the kitchen," Mac said, as they walked into the house.

"You'll have to radio over to the cabin then. Billy came back from his archery practice saying she was there. Guess she wanted to hang out with her friends," Gilles said, raising one shoulder in a half-shrug.

"Is she upset then?"

"Not that I could tell, but I don't really know her that well. She hasn't been particularly social with any of us since we got here, and she was a baby when we knew her before."

"She's had a lot to deal with in the last few months. You know that," Mac said, her tone defensive.

"Oh, I know. I wasn't complaining. Just seems weird to me when I think of what you were like at that age. How we all were for that matter. We talked about anything and everything. I remember losing my cousin, getting shit-faced, and bawling on your shoulder one night. Then you did the same with me when you found out one of your old boyfriends died."

"Yeah, but you're not her tribe of friends, either. She's got Kirk and Leigh, and if she's gone over there she could very well be there to unload. I think you're right that she's been holding a lot in over the last few months, but killing someone isn't something her close friends are really going to understand. She didn't know I would understand better than anyone." When she stopped speaking, Gilles gave her a strange look.

"What do you mean?"

"I never told you, I know. It wasn't until I told Cam that I realized how long I'd been holding it in, and how many people I loved that didn't know that one big thing about me. I was the one who killed her father. The police knew. It was self-defense. I think," she finished lamely.

Mackenzie realized then that they'd arrived in the kitchen, and Lisa was staring at her, wide-eyed. She grimaced.

"Relax. I don't make a habit of it. He's the only person I've ever killed, and it wasn't done with conscious intent," she said acerbically.

"Uh, Mac, what do you mean you 'think' it was self-defense?"

Gilles was giving her the same look Lisa was.

"I mean, he was threatening me with the knife, but I managed to grab it from him. He lunged at me, and the knife was already pointing toward him. I'm just not sure if I had time to move the knife away, and *if* I did, whether or not I *would* have. He was there, threatening to kill me over a lousy thousand bucks, and when I begged him not to leave my daughter without a mother, he got this look on his face like he was going to head off to her bedroom first. That's when he stopped paying attention to the knife he was holding, and I grabbed it to keep him from doing whatever it was he was thinking of doing to Cam."

"I would have done the same," Lisa said, touching her arm gently. "Jake's birth father wasn't violent like that, but even thinking about someone being a threat to him fills me with fear. I've basically felt like that ever since my mother died. Occasionally I would hear people outside on the street, and the first thing I would do was grab the big knife out of the block on the kitchen counter."

Gilles' expression was one of understanding, as well, now that she'd explained things a little bit better. Mac could see he was curious about their new arrival, too.

"Oh, shit. I'm sorry, Gilles. This is Lisa, and the little one is Jake, though I guess you've surmised that already. We found them in town. I went to school with her mother, Michelle. But there's something a little more urgent we need to discuss regarding survivors."

While Mac was explaining what had happened in town, Neil pulled out the makings for soup and sandwiches. It might not be a full supper, but they were both too tired to do anything major for dinner. Added to that, Lisa wasn't used to eating full meals anymore, so simple would be better.

"Is Jake eating any solid foods yet? You said you were still breastfeeding him, but I thought maybe you might have been giving him some of your mother's preserves," Neil explained.

"Not very much, though it hasn't been easy. I know he needs more sustenance than he can get from my milk, but there was so little food I was trying to spread it out for both of us. I'd like to start him on solids, but I don't know what I can give him now."

By the time Mac had finished telling Gilles about the cannibals, and he'd gotten over his disgust a little bit, Neil had already boiled up some peas and carrots and was just dumping them into the blender.

"Why don't I feed him the vegetables while you eat? You're still really hungry, I'm sure," Neil said.

"I don't know if he'll take food from a stranger. Then again, he hasn't really seen any strangers until now, so maybe he'll be fine."

When Neil smiled at Jake, and held out his hands to see if he would reach for him, Mac felt her heart constrict. The kid looked nothing like Neil, but Mac couldn't help wishing in that moment, that it was possible for her to have more children. Neil would have been the father she'd always wanted for her kids.

"Mac!" The sharp quality of Gilles' voice indicated that she had missed something he'd said.

"Sorry. What?"

"I asked if Huntsville was the only place you saw people like that."

"Oh, right. Yeah, they were the only ones that we know of, but then they're also the only people we interacted with, aside from Lisa. Everyone else just stared as we drove by, so we have no way of knowing how they've been surviving. Of course, they were in remote areas, so they could easily have their own gardens and such. Most people did out here, even when there were grocery stores."

"True," Gilles responded thoughtfully.

"Gilles, would you mind helping me move the exercise equipment out of that room over there once I'm done feeding Jake here?" Neil nodded his head to indicate which room he meant, and Gilles said he would.

They hadn't really discussed where they would be putting Lisa and Jake, but for now it was the only thing that made sense. There was a toilet and shower directly off the room, though none of it was really finished yet. Just the floor was down because she'd gone with radiant, in-floor heating when she'd been planning the building.

The other closed-off rooms in the house were already occupied, and there were no spare cabin-like buildings they could move into, though Mac made a mental note to start planning one. She had no problem with sharing land and supplies with people. Not even strangers. But when it came to her privacy she was very leery of sharing her own house for long stretches of time.

It was a good thing it was already the end of February. The lack of snow was also a blessing. They could get started on another building right away. Of course, they had to get the new panels set up, too, so their power reserves weren't hitting close to empty by the time the sun came up every day. They already had six cabins built for the people who had come along after the power went down, so those eight panels would be a big help. She had originally bought more than enough to supply power to the main building, and the building that was being used to house the ferrets, but circumstances had changed with all the extra people.

"How did you get this place started?" Lisa was looking at Mac, waiting for her answer and spooning up more soup in the meantime. Mac had just taken her first bite of the sandwich Neil had shoved in front of her right before he started feeding Jake, so she tried to swallow it in a hurry. Instead it stuck in her throat.

"Hang on," she choked out, and ran around the counter to get herself some goat's milk. Once she'd managed to finish swallowing, she offered some to Lisa who looked like she wasn't so sure about drinking it. When she did finally try it, the surprise on her face made Mac laugh.

"I know. I was expecting it to be really weird-tasting myself the first time I had it, but in a way I was looking forward to it. It's lower in lactose than cow's milk, and I'm lactose-intolerant. I love milk, though, and everything it goes into, so having the goats has been great.

"To answer your question, I've been planning this place for about twenty years. My daughter and I bought the land a couple of years ago, finally, and it wasn't long after that we bought the steel buildings. I waited until they had something appropriate in their clearance section on the website, and then bought what we needed at a huge discount. I had a rough idea of the dimensions I wanted, and what framing style I needed. So, someone ordered this building first, and for one reason or another cancelled the order. I probably only paid about fifty or sixty percent of what it would have cost to order my own building."

"Yeah, but where did you get the money for it? This couldn't have been cheap," Lisa said skeptically.

"It was around a hundred and fifty grand, even with all the solar panels and whatnot, which is way less than most people pay for a house and land. When you don't have to pay for labour, you can do a hell of a lot more with your money. And I was lucky enough to be making a very good living. I did start-up consulting, among other things, and we lived in a really crappy area of Hamilton while we waited to do this. That allowed us to pay cash for everything, instead of making mortgage payments. Though I suppose now that it would have been fine to take on a mortgage. It's not like the banks exist anymore to demand payment.

"We had just managed to put in our first garden when I saw things were getting really bad. We weren't exactly ready, and we had to scramble around to get the goats and chickens we needed.

We've been breeding the chickens as fast as possible, too, so we can switch the ferrets over from kibble to eggs. I had a lot of kibble already, since I'd always planned to go get the ferrets from the various shelters, but I know it'll only last so long.

"We have to keep everything balanced, too, and calculate what we really need to feed everyone who lives here, and still supply the livestock. No point in having too many eggs, and then having to feed a bunch of unnecessary chickens. I chose chicken eggs and goat's milk for our protein, because I can't bear to slaughter animals. I grew up on a farm, so I should probably be more practical about it, but I still can't do it," Mac said ruefully.

"Everyone here feels the same way?"

"Not really, but since there's been no need so far to make that decision, we've all just left things as they are. Gilles knows how to hunt, as do I when it comes to a theoretical standpoint, but we haven't done so. Neil used to hunt with his mother when he was a kid. I'm sure others are capable, too, but I haven't asked."

Mac polished off her sandwich while talking to Lisa about the room she'd be staying in temporarily with her son.

"We don't have anywhere else to put you until we get another building put up, but you'll have a bit of privacy still anyway. I'm not real good about having people live with me, since I tend to be pretty solitary, so we'll have you in your own place pretty quick. There won't be a lot of furniture in it, until I get a chance to build some for you, but at least you'll have your beds and a home of your own."

"You tend to be solitary? I wouldn't have guessed that from the number of people I saw when we drove up, or the size of this place."

"I'm lucky enough to have friends who understand me. Anyway, Gilles and Neil are getting your room ready for you, so you can at least get yourself settled for the night. There's plenty of food in the fridge and cupboards, so feel free to take whatever you need or want. If you throw your dishes in the dishwasher, we'll get along fine. There are a lot of ways to entertain yourself here, too. Someone will have to show you how to access the server for the movies and TV shows we have stored, but I don't have time right now. I hate to just leave you on your own like this, but I have a serious situation I need to deal with."

5 ~ The Truth Will Out

"Okay, Gilles, tell me everything," Mac demanded.

"It's probably not as bad as you think, though I'm sure you're going to want to say something to Cam about her going by herself to check out a sensor without telling anyone she was going." Gilles went on to explain everything he knew about the situation.

"So you were already on your way to check it out when you heard the shots then? And you didn't tell him Cam was the one who killed Gerry?"

"No, but you could tell he knew it was her. He's not the kind of guy to go after her, Mac. He just wanted some answers is all. I hated having to tell him his son tried to kill Neil. It broke his heart, but I don't think it was unexpected. He knew what his son was, even though he tried to raise that kid right."

"I still need to meet him and see for myself. I won't take chances with my daughter like that," she said.

"I know. I'd be doing the same thing if it were my kid, and it wouldn't matter to me what anyone said," Gilles responded, patting her shoulder.

"Fuck. This is the last thing we need right now. I need to be getting ready to head down to Cleveland. Ian's insulin will be turning toxic soon. Sarjit has managed to make some the old-fashioned way, but it doesn't do any good to have it here, when Ian needs it down there."

"Brian doesn't have a working vehicle, and they live a good twenty klicks from here, so he's not coming back tonight anyway. You've got time to get over there to talk to him. He's got to work things out in his own head in the meantime. I think he's more concerned about getting his son's body back so he can be properly buried."

"Oh," Mac said with a cringe.

"Yeah. It's still at the hospital. The power went down before any autopsy could be done," Gilles said, his face contorted into a grimace. The thought wasn't a pretty one. Without freezing or embalming, there wouldn't be much of a body left. Mac didn't know much about human decomposition, but she knew it wouldn't be something any loving parent would handle well.

"He can't go there and see that," she said.

"No, you're right. If he doesn't have something to bury, though, he just might at that. Not that I really want to see it myself, and I'm sure Chuck won't either, but we're probably the two with the most responsibility to do something about it. We chose to be cops, and we knew it wouldn't always be speeding tickets and community relations. The question is fuel. Do we really want to spare it for something like this?"

"That's something I wanted to talk to you about anyway. What do you know about vegetable oil conversions?"

"Huh?"

"Okay, well that answers that question. I'm guessing not much."

"Vegetable oil conversions of what?"

"Diesel engines. Do you remember on the news a few years back, there was a surge of people converting their diesel engines to run on used deep-fryer oil? They were getting it free from the restaurants," Mac said, trying to prod his memory.

"Now that I know what the hell you're talking about, yeah. I actually know quite a bit about it. I was considering doing that with a car, but unless you could get the oil for free it wasn't really worth it. I think restaurants started charging for it in some cases, and buying the vegetable oil new cost at least as much as paying for diesel, if not more. So I never bothered. And burning diesel wasn't any harder on the environment."

"Not burning it, no. But it was the fact that it was a fossil fuel, rather than something more sustainable like sunflower oil that made the conversion better for the environment. Anyway, I made sure I had seeds I could grow so I'd have cooking oil in the future, and I bought a press for the same reason, so technically we can provide our own fuel if we can find a way to convert the diesels. We've got three trucks that run on it. It would have been better to have cars, since they don't burn as much fuel, but maybe we can find something that's been abandoned later.

"The real reason I'm asking is for getting down to Cleveland, since we already have pretty much everything we need right here on the farm. A lot of boat motors run on diesel, and I'm pretty sure the waterway goes from here all the way down to Lake Erie. I just have to double-check a book I grabbed from the library to see if there are any locks or canals that might be a problem on the way." Mac chewed her lip worriedly as she thought about it.

"Weren't you planning to use a sailboat?"

"I'm not real confident of my ability to operate one without killing myself, and Neil isn't any more knowledgeable than I am. Sails are a complication I'd rather not deal with if I don't have to. An engine is something I can understand. I'd like to find something that's got both, just in case, but if I have to pick one or the other I'd rather go with a motorboat if we can get the fuel together for it. Thankfully diesel doesn't go bad as easily as gasoline, but whether or not people used it up is another story."

"Let me think about it, and see what I can come up with. I do remember that the oil has to be pre-heated in order for it to work, so maybe I can jury-rig something," Gilles said. "How are you planning to get the oil for now, though? It's gonna be a while before you can harvest enough seeds for that."

"Looks like I'm going to be breaking into a bunch of fast-food joints. I have to wonder if it'll matter whether or not the oil is rancid, though. I mean, that oil has been sitting there for a number of months now. Will it break down and become unusable, do you think?"

"No idea," Gilles said with a shrug. "Guess we'll just have to find out. If I can put something together to make this work, we should have a test engine to mess around with, not one of the truck engines or a boat engine you're planning to use. No point fixing something that ain't broke, until we're sure we're not going to be breaking it."

"Good point. Alright, let me know what you come up with. In the meantime, by all means take Chuck to get Gerry's body. Wait until I've had a chance to talk to his father, though. I'll let him know what you're doing and maybe that will ease things between us all. This is a tense situation, and it could get bad if we're not careful."

ം ◆ െ

"What the ever-loving *fuck*, Cameron?" Mackenzie snapped furiously, the instant Cam walked through the kitchen door. The recipient of Mackenzie's temper hunched her shoulders.

"Uh, I take it you talked to Gilles," Cameron said hesitantly. Obviously she didn't want to get specific, just in case Mac was pissed about something else.

"Did you suddenly become a commando when I wasn't looking?"

"Uh, no." The hunch in Cam's shoulder's only became more pronounced, and it pissed Mac off even more.

"So, what exactly made you think you should confront a

potential intruder all by yourself then? Have we got a hidden supply of testosterone that I'm unaware of?" The sarcastic remark instantly offended the other occupant in the room.

"Bad decision-making isn't solely the province of masculinity, thank you very much," Neil cut in.

"Maybe not, but the majority of it is."

"Okay, well you have me there, but I don't think that's the issue this time, so let's stick with the problem at hand, shall we?"

Mac shrugged a shoulder and turned back to her daughter to await her defense. It was a while before anything came out of her mouth, and what did come out was hardly satisfactory.

"I was pissed off and wasn't thinking straight."

"Great. Let me guess. You were still sulking about not being able to go on our little scavenging trip, weren't you?"

"Something like that," Cam responded with a half-shrug of her own. "Besides, it's not like I'm the only person around here who's made a bad decision."

Mac almost choked on her ire. And the worst of it was that her daughter was right about her risky choices, which was a very bitter pill to swallow. Not that she felt it excused her. After all, her decision hadn't led to any disastrous consequences.

"Is that how we're going to start living? Every time someone makes a mistake or a choice the others don't agree with, everyone else gets to make one, too, just so we're all even? Is that what you think we should be doing? Or do we play a game of one-upmanship, where we try to outdo one another? Never mind the fact that you made your decision based on a childish need to get back at me for something."

Rather than shouting at Cam, Mackenzie's voice went really quiet. Cold, rigid logic poured from her mouth, rather than temperamental fury. The longer she spoke, the less sarcasm she used, until there was nothing left beyond the hard words.

"Did you realize at any point that you were making a mistake?" she finally asked. Cam took her time responding, and Mac knew it was because she was trying to swallow her own temper.

"Yeah, but it was too late by then. Brian was already behind me, telling me to put down my bow."

"I want the details. All of them. What did you do then?"

"I ducked behind a tree as I was turning around to aim at him."

"Alright. That was the smart thing to do. What then?"

Cam gave her the whole story, and as Mac listened to her daughter the tension eased from her shoulders. Cam might have made a poor decision, but from that point forward Mac couldn't find fault with any of the other choices she'd made. She wasn't even sure if she would have thought to fire a few rounds in the air to bring help herself, and so she nodded her approval.

"Okay. All we can do now is see what this guy has to say for himself. Gilles, Chuck, and even Neil here, think Brian isn't going to cause problems, but I want to see for myself what he's like." Mac glanced apologetically at her husband.

"I'm sorry. I trust you. I do. But this is my daughter, and I don't even want to trust my own judgment where she's concerned. I've got to do whatever I can to make sure he's not a threat," Mac said, appealing to Neil for his forgiveness.

"Honey, I'm not hurt or offended. Your first priority is Cam right now, not my feelings, so do whatever you have to do."

Mac heard sincerity in Neil's words, but by the same token she figured he'd prefer it if she was willing to take him at his word. Whatever his preferences, however, she was still going to do what she felt needed to be done. If it caused problems between them, then they'd have to deal with those later. Neil must have seen the doubt on her face, because he went on.

"I don't know Brian all that well. I've given you my impression of him, but I could be wrong, so I'm really not bothered that you want to form your own opinion. We were never close friends. Just enough that I felt comfortable talking to him about his son when he first started stalking you. We didn't really socialize or anything."

"Since the world kinda fell apart right after we met, I have no idea what you did to socialize around here. You didn't talk about having any really close friends, except maybe Carol and Samantha," Mac said.

"At the time even they were mostly friendly with me simply because I was Sam's boss. The odd coffee or dinner maybe. I wasn't anyone's idea of a party animal," Neil said with a self-deprecating smirk.

"You sound like my twin. All I did was work and plot and plan. Sort of like a criminal mastermind, but without the criminal element," she joked. Then she turned back to Cam.

"Since you realized you were making a mistake before anyone had to tell you, can I assume you won't be doing something like this again? No matter how pissed off you are?"

"I might make mistakes, mom, but I'm not stupid. If there's another alert, I won't go out to check it without letting someone know, or taking someone with me. I was thinking I need to learn something about bush tactics, though. Even if I go out with someone else, I don't want anyone getting the drop on me," Cam said, her tone hesitant. Mac almost smiled at the lingo her daughter had almost certainly picked up through movies or first-person shooter games.

"I'd rather you didn't go out to check sensors at all, but it's not an ideal world. Gilles would probably be the best person to teach you that, or maybe even Neil. What do you think, cowboy? How extensive is your hunting experience?"

"I think Gilles is probably far more capable in that respect. I haven't gone hunting since I was a little kid. He used to go every season, didn't he?"

"Yeah, alright. I'll talk to him. Besides, we won't be here for a couple weeks. It's best that she learn what she can, as soon as she can. She and Billy are going to be running this place when we're not here, so who knows what they'll have to deal with? When we get back with Ian, though, I'm going to ask him to teach her jiu-jitsu." Mac watched her daughter's face light up.

"Seriously?"

"Absolutely. There's no one I'd rather have teaching you. He was the acknowledged expert and master in his style, so you might as well learn from the best. It'll keep him out of trouble while he's here, what with learning how to make his own insulin at the same time," Mac said with a shrug.

"While he's here? I kinda figured he would just stay with us like everyone else does," Cam said.

"He's still got family outside Cleveland, so he's not going to want to stay. Aside from the insulin, and very limited electricity, he's got a pretty good situation there. His relatives have a small farm where they have some laying hens. Not sure about veggies and stuff, but we can send him back with plenty of seeds if they don't already have a garden of their own. He's got his pond with tons of fish in it, too. He had it stocked years ago, and then never fished in it, so they multiplied like crazy. Must be a pretty deep pond, because Cleveland winters used to be pretty cold. A shallow pond would have completely frozen. Then again, I have no idea whether or not fish survive being frozen. I wouldn't think so, but what do I know?"

"You're rambling, mom."

"It's your fault. You've got me all freaked out," Mac replied in a snarky tone.

"Hang on," Cam said, and trotted off toward the hall that led to the main door. Mac looked after her in bemusement, and then glanced at Neil who merely shrugged in response.

"Where did Billy disappear to? I would've thought he'd want to be here for when Cam got chewed out. I'm sure he must have something to say about it," Mac said.

"Maybe he already said something, since we were gone a pretty long time, and Gilles said this happened almost immediately after we left. I'm not sure where he is now, though. I checked earlier to see if he was in his room, but he wasn't there. Probably hiding from Katherine somewhere. That girl is *tenacious*."

"I know, eh? Granted, she's fourteen, so that's to be expected. Thankfully you raised Billy to be a decent guy who won't take advantage of her. There are plenty of guys who would, jailbait or not. Of course, that was back when there were actually plenty of guys. Now? Not so much," she concluded sadly.

"Hey! I'm right here, you know? From my perspective it's not as though you need a bunch of guys. You've already got me." Mac was saved the need to answer by Cam's timely arrival, ferrets in hand.

"Here. Have a ferret," she said, thrusting Pickle at her mother while she nuzzled Squeaker. Mac would have liked to have made some sort of retort, but her daughter knew her well. It was a given that her attention would be drawn immediately to the furry bundle in her arms. It was well known that she was as bad as a dog with a squirrel, when it came to the distraction provided by ferrets. Seeing them reminded her of something, though.

"I take it you got Lisa and Jake settled okay?"

"They're fine, though I wouldn't doubt Lisa's taking a well-deserved siesta," Neil replied.

"Who are Lisa and Jake?" Cam's bewilderment made Mac

laugh.

"A lot happened while we were gone, and it wasn't just here on the farm." So saying, Mac filled her in on the rest of the details.

"So, basically you just encountered the real-life version of the *zompoc*," Cam said when her mother was finished.

"The what? Oh, wait. You mean the zombie apocalypse?"

"Yeah, that."

"Near as I can figure, however, they're nothing more than crazy cannibals at this point. The only way they're the walking dead, is the fact that they're most likely going to be dead in a short while. Kind of like that death row thing. You know? Dead man walking," Mac prompted when Cameron looked blank at the reference.

"Is *that* what that means?"

"Well, yeah. How can you not have known that? You saw Green Mile more than once, did you not?" Mac was incredulous.

"A few times, sure. I guess I just never made the connection. Weird," Cam said with a shrug. And it hardly mattered anymore. It wasn't as though there was still any such thing as popular culture. There would have to be enough people in the world for something to actually be considered popular. The few that were left were probably so scattered throughout the world, that what was known in one culture was just as likely to be unknown in another. Movies might be the exception, but properly translating a turn of phrase was a complicated thing.

"Anyhoo, let's just worry about the world we're actually living in, shall we? We have more than enough on our collective plates without worrying about a system that no longer exists," Mac said.

"Okay, so I take it these people will stay on the farm with us? Lisa and Jake, I mean. Not the cannibals," Cam clarified with a smile.

"Definitely not the cannibals, no. I'm assuming Lisa will want to stay, and we've already discussed building another small cabin. The Bowflex and treadmill have been put in here for now to keep Jake safe, though it means not letting Pickle and Squeaker run around. I don't fancy them having a chew-fest on the rubber part of the treadmill.

"Now, take the boys back to the bedroom for me," Mac said to Cam, once she'd taken a turn snuggling Squeaker. "Neil and I need to discuss strategy for tomorrow's little meet-and-greet." Mac waited tensely, until she was sure Cameron wasn't going to argue the decision.

ဆ ◆ os

Mac woke up mid-morning, which was unusual for her, but she'd had an anxious sleep waiting for the events of the day to unfold. A quick breakfast of mushroom and goat-cheese omelet was enough to set them up for a few hours, and they were on their way less than half an hour after climbing from their bed.

When they knocked on the Newmans' door twenty minutes later, her stomach was tied in knots, and her Glock was tucked in its holster, situated very visibly in the front of her jeans. She really hoped Brian was the kind of person everyone was saying he was, but she knew that kind of hope was dangerous. It might lead her to miss things if she wanted so much for it to be true. She stepped to the side after knocking, in case there was a shotgun behind the door, though Neil remained where he was. She glared at him for it.

When the door opened fully, with no weapon in evidence, it was a little anti-climactic for her. Her hand stopped hovering over the Glock after she'd given him a good scan. His son had looked like him, she noticed, though the father was a lot cleaner. It made her wonder what they were doing for water.

"You look like her," he said, staring straight at her. The similarity of his words to her thoughts was almost enough to make her laugh. Almost.

"Hey, Brian. Mac here wanted to know a little something about you, seeing as it was her property you trespassed on yesterday, on your way to come see me."

"Mac, eh?" His lips twitched, reminding Mackenzie that everyone in the area still thought of Neil as Mac, because his last name was McKinnon. He didn't say anything about it. Just told them to come on in.

"That's okay, Mr. Newman. If it's all the same to you, I'd like to be able to see your face while we're talking. Your porch here probably has a bit more light."

"The deck out back is even brighter. You might as well come through the house and see what I've got that you might consider a threat. Geraldine's inside, and it would probably do her good to meet you. This is a difficult situation, especially for her, and I'd like to see it resolved as best it can be."

"Alright," she said reluctantly, giving him a nod. "I guess we can do that."

The house wasn't particularly dark, so Mackenzie relaxed a little bit more. Brian's matter-of-fact attitude went a long way toward reassuring her, so she could see why everyone had such a good impression of him. Geraldine was a surprise. Somehow she'd been expecting a flowered housedress. Instead she was wearing a good-quality pair of jeans and a long fisherman sweater. Her hair appeared to be freshly cut in a sassy swing, too, though the streaks were natural.

"You're the woman my son was bothering?" Her blunt question was another surprise.

"Yes, ma'am. I'm Mac."

"You might as well call me Geraldine. Why don't I make us some coffee, and we can talk about all this?"

Mackenzie headed through the kitchen door behind Brian, with Neil following her. The deck out back was stunning. She hadn't known there would be a lake view from the front. There were a lot of trees on either side, but the land in the back had been cleared long ago, creating a gentle slope down to the water. The late-morning sun reflected almost blindingly from the surface.

"This is really nice," she commented. Brian nodded agreeably.

"We spend most days out back here. Geraldine has her garden there, and I fish off the dock for our dinner. Breakfast and lunch too now. It's quiet, and we need that right now."

"I don't blame you," she said softly. "I doubt very much I'd ever want to see another person if I lost my daughter."

"Sit down and we'll get to all that in a bit. You're not going to need your Glock." He was making sure she understood that he knew a thing or two about weapons, apparently, and she was wondering why. He'd gone to a lot of trouble to assure her he wasn't planning to pick up one of his own. Unless his wife had one under her sweater, she didn't think either of them were armed. He was wearing a white undershirt with a button-down lumberjack shirt flapping loosely over it, and Mac could see he wasn't concealing a piece with it.

"Just the same, I've gotten used to carrying it," she said in warning. "You seem to be doing alright over here. That woodstove I noticed inside helps a lot I'm sure. What do you do for water, aside from the lake I mean."

"Had to jury-rig a rainwater collection system when the well pump and pressure tank stopped working. Actually set up a system to have a hot water shower in the basement, using a gravity feed and a tank we can set up on top of the woodstove. I can show it to you later if you like. Even used an old bicycle to pedal-power a sort of washing machine and spinner. We've got some friends we can trade with, too, though we haven't really bothered with that. Not much we need so long as we're clean and fed. I wasn't gonna have us trying to wash in cold water in the winter, though. How about you folks?"

"We were prepared for it, mostly. Solar power to start, and we got lucky with a flowing artesian well that didn't really need a pump or pressure tank, but we have those, too. We started working on wind turbines over the winter, which provided a bit of extra power even though they weren't very efficient, but now that the roads are clear we got some more PV panels and marine batteries. We ended up with more people than we originally planned for, so our power ran down close to nothing every day, but at least we had it."

It was another mild warning, letting him know about the extra people, but she just didn't feel a threat coming from him. It was sort of making her feel like an idiot, but she was a mother. Even before she'd become a mother, she'd been ridiculously overprotective of her friends.

"You sound like you're from the city, but not quite. You mind me asking where you came from?"

"Not at all. I was raised in Muskoka, but moved to the city when I married at sixteen so my first husband and I both had a shot at having decent careers. When it came time to buy land, though, I wanted to be back here."

"That explains it," he said, nodding at her. "What family?"

"Thane," she said curtly. "And if you know who they are, then I'm sure you won't be too surprised when I say I didn't remain close to them."

"Funny how that works, isn't it?" He was nodding again, thoughtfully, and with more than a little sadness. "We're generally considered good people, and we tried to raise Gerry to follow that lead. As you saw for yourself, it didn't work out very well for us. Or for him. You came from a family like the Thanes, who are *not* generally considered good people, and yet you and your daughter both seem to have turned into fine human beings. All the arguments about nature versus nurture don't answer questions like that. Sometimes people are just good. Sometimes they're not. And there's no genetic or environmental reason for it."

Mackenzie had nothing to add. She knew it was true. Everyone had to be taken for the person they were as an individual, not based on the circumstances of their birth or how they'd been raised. Sure, in many cases nature and nurture had a large impact, but the exceptions still baffled everyone and caught them by surprise.

There were a few minutes of bustle and awkwardness when Geraldine brought out the coffee. Then she sat down and pushed away all of that confusion with a single, bold statement.

"From what my husband says, your daughter most likely did the job that I was afraid to do, I'm sorry to say." The blunt words from Gerry's mother made Mac grateful she hadn't tried to swallow any coffee just yet.

"Our son was an evil little shit from the time he was born. I'm sorry, Brian, for saying that, but you know as well as I do that it was true. In fact, it's far more true than most people in this area realize. You know all those childhood symptoms they talk about on the true-crime shows? The ones for serial killers?" When Mac nodded, she went on.

"He had them all, except for the bed-wetting thing. He started out with animals. So we sold off our livestock and took him to therapy in North Bay. He started watching extremely violent and graphic sexual content online, so we got rid of the internet and got him to another therapist. When the situation developed with you, we actually hoped that they would catch him and arrest him before he managed to kill someone. The only reason we gave him a place to live here, was because we were trying to keep an eye on him. Otherwise we'd have told him to leave as soon as he turned eighteen.

"We couldn't have pets, and he figured out a way to turn on the porn on our satellite service. One day, a couple of months before he started going after you, he came after me in a way I never thought I'd see my own son do. I had to stand there with a knife in my hand to get him to leave me alone, but even that wasn't enough until I cut his hand when he tried to grab me. I knew Brian would kill him if he found out, so I didn't tell him until a few weeks ago when he told me he was going to go looking for answers. As much as I wanted Gerry gone from my sight, I felt it was my responsibility to watch him."

"You didn't have to tell me all this," Mackenzie began. "So why *are* you?"

"Because I want your daughter to know, assuming she's the one who managed to kill him, that she may have saved my life, too, and maybe countless other women. He would have started with rape, if he hadn't already. He certainly tried it with me. Then it would have progressed. Most likely to torture and murder. His last two therapists agreed with me, but unless he actually did something to a human being, there was little that could be done. He was an adult by that point, and we could no longer have him institutionalized without going through the court system."

Mackenzie needed a few minutes to absorb what she was hearing, so she took her time and drank some of the coffee. She almost moaned at the taste.

"How do you people make coffee this good? I don't get it. I've got a really nice machine. I've read the directions on the coffeemaker, and on the coffee containers themselves, countless times. I *still* cannot make a decent cup of coffee." Her words relieved a bit of the tension.

"That's my wife for ya," Neil stated laconically. "Always focusing on the real issues."

"Hey, coffee is going to be a luxury in this part of the world very, very soon. It's definitely an issue. Especially when I keep ruining it."

"Salt," Geraldine responded with a smile. "I always put in a bit of salt. Though I do try to brew it right, too. It makes a difference."

"When did you guys get married, Mac? Sorry, I mean Neil," Brian said with a short laugh, when both of them hesitated after opening their mouths to respond at the same time.

"About eight months ago. It was right after I talked to you that last time, and just before the power died in this area. It was already down in most of the cities by then. We got the licence from the town hall in Parry Sound on the Monday morning, and then we were hitched that afternoon. A friend of ours was able to do the ceremony, because she was a JP."

"I didn't realize when you were talking to me about her that you two were involved, but it makes sense now. Truth be told, I wasn't worried much about *why* you were telling me. I was too busy thinking about wanting to kick Gerry's ass. He might have been named after my wife, but he sure as hell didn't take any other part of himself from her." With that they were back on topic.

"I want you to know something," Mac began haltingly, knowing there was no going back now that she was about to confirm their suspicions. "My daughter has been miserable since that day. Until she went out to check on the sensor alert yesterday, she hadn't picked up her bow. We had to move it for her when we put up the main building, because she wouldn't even look at it. This hasn't been easy for her to live with."

"Taking a life shouldn't be an easy thing, no matter whose life it is," Brian responded. "I volunteered for the CAF when Bush Sr. started that brouhaha in Kuwait, and Canada joined in the fight. I didn't know it at the time, but it was already winding down by the time I got through boot camp. I was only over there for a month, but it took me a few years to get past what I had to do in that time, and the things I'd seen. No matter who you kill, it damages you.

"Neither of us knew that Geraldine was pregnant when I shipped out. We were very lucky that I was back home in time to be there for her through most of it, but I often wondered if maybe

93

I'd brought home some of that evil and passed it on to my child. Since nobody knows how that works, I suppose it's as good an explanation as we'll ever get. I had recovered enough that we were talking about maybe having another baby, when we started noticing that Gerry was a little different.

"At first we put off having more children so we could concentrate on figuring out what was wrong with him. When we knew what it was, we decided not to have more. It's a shame, really, because Geraldine was a damn good mother to that kid, but we couldn't risk it. Not just the possibility that we'd have another like him, but also that he might harm a younger sibling."

"It makes us sound so terrible," Geraldine quietly stated.

"I don't think it does," Mac responded. "I think it's heartbreaking that you felt you had to make that choice. Very few people are capable of looking at their children realistically, and you did everything humanly possible to get help for him and try to turn him away from that path. I can't think of a single other thing you could have done. When he became an adult, he made choices that went against everything you tried to instill in him, and they were his choices, not yours."

Geraldine had started crying, so Brian reached for her hand. He held it up to his mouth and rubbed her forearm with his other hand. Neil laced his fingers with Mackenzie's. She looked down at their joined hands and then covered them with her other one.

"You gave him real love," Mac began again. "You might not think you did, because of the way he made you feel, but you gave him the kind of love that a majority of parents can't even imagine. You did the hard work to give him his best chance, even when your own feelings were working against you. I don't think a lot of people have that kind of love in them. Most of us take the easier road. Denial."

"Thank you for that," Brian said gruffly. "Geraldine was right about your daughter probably saving a lot more lives than she realizes, and I hope you'll tell her that we said so."

"I will. I've been trying to find a way to help her deal with it. She didn't just feel guilt for killing your son, either. She also felt guilty because she seemed to think it meant she felt bad for Neil not being killed, and probably myself, but we both knew that wasn't really how she felt about it. She just hated having blood on her hands.

"Cam's always been pretty tough and cynical. When we took archery lessons, then later went to the gun ranges to learn to shoot, I guess she figured she'd be perfectly fine with using those weapons. She wasn't expecting to feel bad afterward, despite the fact that I tried to tell her it's never quite what you imagine it will be when you have to kill someone." Mac realized she would have to explain, when both Geraldine and Brian looked at her in confusion.

"Her father broke in to our apartment when Cam was just a baby. He had a knife that I managed to get away from him when he was distracted. I was standing there holding it when he ran at me. I faced up to it and called the police and all that, even though I was scared shitless. It was written off as self-defense, though they could have called it an accident, too, I suppose.

"To this day I don't know if I actually had time to turn the knife away from him. I had to deal with the aftermath, and I wasn't expecting the guilt any more than Cam was. She didn't know about it until I told her a couple of weeks ago. She only knew he'd been killed while trying to rob someone. She didn't know it was me. I've never lied to her about it, but I didn't want her growing up with the knowledge that her father had been killed by her mother. Her father had grown up spoiled by his family, and he seemed to think he was entitled to whatever he wanted."

"Sort of like our Gerry," Brian said. "Except for the part about being spoiled. If anything, he was a bit deprived because we had to permanently remove most of his privileges. That sense of entitlement, though, seems to be a commonality."

"I don't know what it was with some of the kids the baby boomers and our generation raised," added Neil. "I'm thankful Billy was never like that, and Cameron isn't either, but some of those overly-entitled shits still sprang from good people. Hopefully we'll find some answers to those questions before we start repopulating the earth."

6 ~ BENEDICTION, PERHAPS

Cam watched Gilles and Chuck slice off a long piece of plastic sheeting from the roll just inside the door of the ferret building. She was in there helping Kelly and Annette mix up raw eggs with kibble when they came in. The reason for the plastic was well-known to her, and she shuddered at the thought. Chuck and Gilles didn't look any more cheerful about the prospect than she felt, but Cam was grateful it wasn't going to be her at the hospital, attempting to transport the body of the man she'd killed.

When her mother had come home the other day from seeing the Newmans, she seemed to have relaxed a great deal about the situation, though she intended to remain on her guard to some extent. Cam was shocked when her mother suggested that she meet with Geraldine, and though she dreaded it, some guilty, self-destructive part of herself agreed to the meeting.

One of her reasons for being in the ferret building was to get a much-needed dose of ferret-therapy, or *ferrapy* as her mother called it. The furry little monsters soothed her nerves enough that she finally felt okay with leaving that afternoon, even though another, saner part of her thought she was being a bit stupid in meeting the mother of her victim.

At least she was getting it over with before they would be seeing what was left of their son. Cam wouldn't be staying there long, and it had been arranged that Gilles and Chuck would make the morbid delivery an hour or so later. When her mother ducked her head inside the building and nodded at her that it was time, Cam suddenly felt really nauseous. She wasn't ready for this.

She had to wonder how many people had ever carried on a face-to-face conversation with the parents of someone they'd killed. She sincerely doubted that it had been very common even when the world was fully populated, but then not many people were left, so maybe things would end up being done a lot differently in the future. If that was the case, she could only hope she was never in this position again.

Cam hopped into the passenger seat of her mother's truck. It was supposed to be a twenty-minute drive, but Cameron didn't notice a single second of it. She was too immersed in her personal terror.

"We're here, Cam," her mother said gently. "I'm going in with you, so there's no need to panic. I'm also armed." Her mother bared her teeth in a semblance of a grin, which looked more feral than anything else. Cam couldn't even open her mouth for fear the contents of her stomach would take the opportunity to escape.

"Look, Cam. They've both said he deserved what he got. I told you that. I just think it'll mean a lot more to you if it's coming directly from them. Okay?"

Cam nodded jerkily in response, still not opening her mouth. Then she opened the door and got out, so she could get it over with and go home. Brian, and a woman she assumed was Gerry's mother, came out onto the front porch. Her own mother led the way up the steps, and indicated the woman with a sweeping motion of her hand.

"Cam, this is Geraldine. Gerry's mother." Cam turned rigid. She really, really wanted to back away when Geraldine took a step toward her. In fact, she wanted to bolt right back to the truck and drive away. Instead she stood her ground.

Suddenly she was enveloped in the woman's arms, and she didn't know what to do with herself. She was *not* a hugger, and this was just frightening.

"It's okay," Geraldine whispered to her. "We'll talk about it a little more later, but I just wanted you to know that it's okay." Much to her horror, Cam felt the sobs coming out of her before she could do a single thing to stop them.

"It's okay," Geraldine whispered again, and just rocked her until she was done crying. When she finally pulled back, Geraldine held her at arm's length. Cam could barely see through her swollen eyelids, but she could still see the apparent warmth on the other woman's face.

"I'm sorry," she started to say, but Geraldine interrupted her.

"There's no need for that. Brian was right when he told you that you did what you had to do. There's more that you don't know about our son, but for now let me just say you've probably saved a lot more lives than you realize. It's not easy to lose a child, but I think it might have been harder for me to live with him being responsible for someone else losing their child. Your mother brought you here so we could talk to you a bit. From what your mother told us, you've been carrying around a lot of pain, and I wanted to ease some of that if I could."

"I don't know what to say," Cam said in a croak through her tight throat.

"There's nothing you have to say. I'm just sorry you're suffering because you did what you had to do to protect your family. My husband knows a little something about the guilt from all that, but then so does your mother. They might be able to help you if you let them. All I can do is tell you that nobody blames you for it. It's not much."

"It's kind of everything, actually," Cam corrected. "I didn't want to hurt anyone, much less kill someone. You should be blaming me for it."

"You prevented others from being hurt or killed, and we'll explain shortly the other reasons we're not blaming you for it. We recognized our son for what he was, and what he was becoming. We tried to stop it, but that didn't work out so well. If you want to come inside for a bit, we can tell you the rest."

"Okay. Thank you," Cameron responded quietly. Geraldine just smiled and then headed over to her husband's side. Cam looked at her mother in confusion. She didn't know what to make of these people. Especially Geraldine. From all appearances she seemed to be very understanding and forgiving, and it didn't sit right with Cam for some reason.

Maybe it was guilt. Or maybe she just couldn't understand a parent whose first loyalty wasn't to their own child, whatever the circumstances. She knew her own mother might kick her ass for doing stupid things, but she'd never abandon her or take sides against her when push came to shove. Then again, she wasn't a wannabe rapist or outright murderer. Maybe that changed things.

Cam followed them into the house, and by the time Geraldine was finished explaining things about her son, she felt a little bit better about the unprecedented level of understanding from Gerry's parents. She was still wary of too much kindness coming from anyone, but at least she could sort of see why they felt the way they did. Or the way they said they felt anyway.

"Man, that had to be so hard for you." It was all Cam could think to say at first. "I mean, mom has a fascination with pretty much everything, and is always reading books about a lot of stuff, and she went through this phase where she studied serial killers. I was in high school at the time, and borrowed some of her books for a class project. I know about the signs and all that.

"I don't know what I would do if I saw my kid doing those things. I guess exactly what you did. Then again, there doesn't seem to be a cure for it, since they don't know why it happens. It's kind of like a disease or a mutation maybe. These things just happen. Some kids are born with Autism. Some have eyes that are two different colours. Some are sociopaths or even psychopaths. And it's not like there's a way to stop it, so obviously it's not the parents' fault, whatever the difference is.

"I understand now why you say he might have hurt other women. He tried to hurt you, and then he tried to hurt my mother. It wasn't a one-time thing with him. I still can't feel great about it, but it doesn't feel as selfish as it did before. Does that make any sense?"

"It makes perfect sense," Geraldine replied, as she patted Cam's hand. "You believed you were protecting people you know, and to find out it wasn't just for your own benefit means it wasn't all about you or your loved ones. I keep going over things, trying to pick apart every little decision I made when he was growing up. If I had done this, would he be any different? Or, if I had done that, maybe."

"I've been doing the same thing for about seven months now. I kept wondering if I had taken away any chance he had to get beyond what he was doing. From what you've told me, it doesn't sound like it, but I'll never know for sure."

"I'm really glad we had this chance to talk, Cam. If you ever feel up to coming to visit us, you'll be welcome at this house."

Cam could only nod, because her throat was a little tight again. She had such a hard time with kindness, understanding, or sympathy. They seemed to trigger her emotions when she was feeling vulnerable, instead of soothing her. Geraldine squeezed her shoulder.

It seemed like the right time to say goodbye, so Cam thanked them and headed back to the truck. Her mother stayed behind for a moment, presumably to explain that Gerry's body was on its way. It was not a conversation Cam wanted to be a part of, so she was relieved her mother waited until she was at a discreet distance before saying anything.

On the ride back to the farm, silence filled the cab of the truck until they were rolling to a stop in front of the tree that housed the hidden fingerprint scanner for the concealed gate. She was suddenly very grateful for the extra layers of concealment and security her mother had implemented. Not to mention the new cameras they had already installed to fill in the gaps. Cameron was also having major second thoughts about her mother and Neil sailing away to Cleveland in the next few weeks. This really didn't seem like the time for it.

Her dad wasn't exactly reliable companionship or security these days either. She'd tried to talk to him about it, but he would only say he wanted to live out in the bush for a bit. Cam couldn't argue that it seemed to do him some good, because he usually came back pretty content, but she needed him right now, just like she needed her mother.

"Mom, is there any way you could postpone your trip? It's dangerous. You have no idea what's out there on the water or in the cities or towns along the way. You have no idea what you're doing when it comes to sailing, and it could take a lot more than the few weeks you were planning on. Do you even know which way the current flows, or how to sail against it? What if you can only go one way?"

"We've been over this, Cam," her mother said, more than a little exasperated. "If Kirk was going to die without insulin, would you say we shouldn't do everything we can to get him some? I've been planning for the need to make insulin since long before this all happened. You know that. I made sure I had the instructions printed out from how it was made by the guy who discovered it, just so I could be sure I'd be able to help Ian. He's my best friend. I'm not letting him die when I can do something to prevent it."

Cam didn't want to worry her mother, since she understood she felt she had no choice, so Cameron kept quiet about all the things that were picking at her peace of mind. Besides, it was just a feeling, which was nowhere near enough to convince anyone, not even herself, that there was any kind of problem. She would just have to take steps while they were gone to ensure her own safety, along with everyone else's. No more making impulsive decisions, either.

"We're going to try to convert the motors on one of the boats to operate on vegetable oil, Cam, like we're planning with at least one truck. Gilles is looking into it, and if anyone can make it work, he can. If he can, that means a much easier trip, and potentially a faster one. Particularly if we have to go against current or wind."

"If he can. Is that the brainstorm you were referring to before?"

"Yeah, but I didn't know if it was possible. It wouldn't be if Gilles hadn't already looked into it years ago for his own vehicle.

He at least knows the principles behind making it work, which is a lot more than I know. He's a much more able mechanic than I am, and I know dick about diesels," her mother finished.

"That's a first! Don't you know something about everything?"

"Not quite, though it would be nice if it were true. I really wish humanity had made it to the point of having the ability to upload knowledge and information directly into the brain. I'd have gotten my doctorate in everything."

"Then you'd have nothing left to learn. What on earth would you do with yourself?"

"Very funny. What I'd do is use the knowledge, of course. Like they say though, 'If wishes were horses, beggars would ride.' Not every dream can come true, and I'm grateful enough to be alive for the moment, and have everyone I care about still alive, too. That's more than a lot of people can say now," her mother said, and Cam could hear the sadness in her voice.

"I figure, if those people were stupid enough to believe nothing bad was happening, and that they didn't need to prepare, the world is probably better off without them in the gene pool. Granted, without you as my mother, I probably wouldn't be here either."

"The problem is, it wasn't just smart people preparing for this, even if it was the smart thing to do. There were paranoid and violent people, too, training in survivalist camps. Most of those were probably a joke, unless they had someone with actual military experience doing the teaching. Thankfully we haven't run into any of those types. Just some ordinary, run-of-the-mill cannibals," her mother said, with a twist to her mouth.

"Well, I certainly feel better about you leaving now. Thanks for reminding me."

"You really think they're going to walk in exactly this direction for about thirty or forty kilometres? Please. Besides, you've got the extra cameras now, and plenty of firepower. We already had enough of that before Gilles showed up, but he added tremendously to our stockpile, as did Chuck. We've got at least five handguns between us, in addition to all the long guns.

"Seriously, Cam, we're not going to be gone that long, and we're sure as hell not telling anyone outside the farm that we're going. We'll be back before you know it. Once you start getting some training from Gilles in hunting and bush tactics, you'll probably feel a lot better. Once Ian's here, we can work on our little handicap when it comes to close-quarters combat. Ian would be the first to tell you that a gun is a lot more helpful in most cases, but everything you have in your arsenal is a worthwhile tool."

Now that her mother had reminded her of that one advantage of having Ian on the farm for a while, Cam stopped feeling so whiny about the whole thing. She'd wanted to take martial arts lessons for as long as she could remember, and if she could take them from someone who was an actual master of his style, so much the better.

They walked into the back door of the house to find Billy and Neil sitting with Lisa at the serving counter. Billy was holding Jake while Lisa spoon-fed him an unidentifiable mush. He seemed to like it, though. He was smacking his lips and giggling after every bite.

Cam had to smile. Jake was still at a stage where she found him cute. In a couple of years, though, she'd probably find herself prying him off her leg. For some inexplicable reason, kids loved her. She couldn't understand it, because for the most part she really didn't like being around them. She didn't have the heart to be mean to them, or shout and chase them away, but she avoided them if possible.

In the short time Lisa and Jake had been staying in the house, however, Billy seemed to have become really attached to Jake. Apparently he loved kids, which made Cam very grateful he'd eased off on the hero-worship and puppy-love looks he'd given her for most of the time she'd known him. She wasn't sure if she would ever love someone enough to want to raise even one kid with them, let alone multiples, and Billy just didn't do it for her that way. She could handle thinking of him as a step-brother or something, but that was it.

It really was depressing to think that she would probably never find anyone at all now. If decent partners hadn't been thick on the ground before the world went to shit, they were truly verging on extinction now. Watching Billy with Jake and Lisa was also giving her the sneaking suspicion that at some point even Billy was going to be out of the running. So much for any sort of back-up plan. And although she considered the thought crass and selfish, and felt guilty for it, it was nothing less than the truth. It had been some comfort to think there was at least that possibility, whether he was someone she really wanted or not.

Cam shook her head at her aggravating thoughts. The fact remained that she really had no interest in him beyond a potential fuck-buddy should things get desperate, and so she didn't deserve to have that comfort from him. He was too decent of a human being for her to treat him that way.

She went past everyone and headed into the kitchen. It had been a really emotional day, especially for someone like her. Cameron wasn't interested in having emotional days. She liked hers to be as drama-free as possible. If things kept going the way they were, however, she might seriously consider doing some container-gardening in her room, so she could live off those vegetables and never run into another human being as long as she lived. If it weren't for the lure of eggs, cheese, and mushrooms, it sounded pretty reasonable to her.

Grabbing a container of the latest batch of cheesecake cookies her mother had made, and some milk, Cam decided she was taking her hoard up to her room where she could play non-stop computer games. It was a good thing they had hundreds of them stored on the server, because she was finally getting weary of her self-appointed guard duty. *Let someone else hold down the fort for a while*, she thought.

As she passed by everyone again on the way to the wide, straight staircase, Billy asked where she was going.

"Nunya," she answered, smirking visibly.

"What the hell is 'nunya' supposed to mean?" His frown echoed the confusion in his voice. Neil and her mother were both laughing, though.

"It means, 'Nunya' business," she retorted snappily, and headed on her way.

"Finally," she heard her mother say, relief in her voice.

"Finally what?" Billy was really confused now.

"Finally she's getting back to her old self."

7 ~ EMBARKATION

"Did Brian and Geraldine seem shifty to you?" Mac's question was asked to the truck cabin at large. "Maybe we shouldn't go right now. And what about this year's crops? We just got those in the ground."

"For the hundredth time, Mac," Gilles replied in exasperation, "Brian and Geraldine don't even know you're not going to be there. Seeing as we've managed to find a motorsailer, *and* convert the two engines to run on vegetable oil, you're probably only going to be gone for a couple of weeks. If you do ten or twelve hours a day, it should take less than a week to get down there. It's not bloody likely we'll get any frost, since we barely had any during what was supposed to be winter, and it's now past the beginning of April. That's why we planted early, remember? It's not like it was when we were growing up, and our parents had to wait until May long weekend to plant. We've got a really long growing season now.

"You've got plenty of oil, already filtered, both in the main boat and the dinghy. Just remember to switch back to the diesel tank for a few minutes if you're planning to shut down the engine for more than a few minutes. The oil needs to be run through completely. Then wait a few minutes before switching back to oil when you start up again.

"You've got a radio so you'll know exactly what's going on here, too, which means you can still nag us to death. Every single house on the farm has weapons of some sort, in addition to the usual assortment of firearms, and you've also got your own. The dinghy is loaded with everything you need in case your boat sinks, including some diving gear we grabbed from another boat. The gauges show that the tanks are full, so if there's anything you need to check underwater, you'll be fine. Does that sum it all up for you, or are you determined to rant and fret and worry until you drive us all nuts?"

"Damn it, Gilles!"

"Damn it, Mac," he returned.

"Mom, I'm going to be fine, the farm is going to be fine, and the ferrets are going to be fine. It's two weeks, if that. You can probably get there in five days. You said so yourself. By the time anyone even knows you're gone, if anyone knows, you'll already be back with Ian."

"The ferrets," Mac whimpered. "They've never been without me for so long."

"Yeah, and for the first few days they won't even notice that you're not there. It's you that's going to miss them, not the other way around." Cam was getting just as irritated with her as everyone else.

"So what? If they could swim for hours on end, or at least had life vests of some kind, I'd probably bring them with us. I'm just worried, and I don't want to leave the farm. There are too many things that could go wrong, with no support services there to back you up."

"Honey," Neil began, showing his own annoyance now. "In case you're forgetting, Gilles and Chuck were both *part* of the support services. Then there's Annette. She certainly did a great job with me, and that was a gunshot wound. I doubt they're going to encounter anything as dangerous as that."

"Yeah, mom. You're the ones who aren't going to have any backup, not us. It's not like there's a Coast Guard, or whatever the hell it used to be on the Great Lakes. If something happens while you're on the boat, you'll be on your own."

"If y'all don't stop this endless whining, I'm gonna turn this truck right around … " Gilles left the joke unfinished, but Mac knew the so-called punch line.

Billy was the only one who wasn't speaking. Mac could see that he was worried, and Cam's comment hadn't helped.

"We're going to be fine on the water. We know the risks, and the lack of support, which was why we made sure to load the dinghy with everything in advance." They had made it to the dock by then, so there was nothing left for them to do, other than say good-bye and get going. Gilles had only come along to drive Billy and Cam back to the farm, just in case they were too upset to drive.

Mac didn't want them off the farm by themselves anyway. There hadn't been enough time to assess the situation in the surrounding areas. They only knew that there were quite a few people still alive, because they had already been living on farmland. When they got back, Mac was going to see about getting in touch with more people for trading foods and services.

Neil had originally suggested they bring more people onto the farm, but Mac had been very resistant to the idea. At least he'd agreed that it was best to wait and see how things shook out in the aftermath. There had never been such a major test of humanity's character before, and Mac wasn't taking any chances.

People could pull together in the worst of times, but they could also turn on one another. It mostly depended on whether or not there were people who felt entitled to more than was fair. That also happened in the best of times, however. Like when there had been a group of *one-percenters* claiming the vast majority of the wealth and privilege. That selfishness was part of what had led mankind to the brink of extinction. And it still might. They were no longer polluting their atmosphere, but there was a lot of damage locked in and waiting to happen.

Mac looked at her daughter, hoping she would have a chance to raise a kid of her own, or at least grow old without struggling to breathe. Cam rolled her eyes when she caught her mother's look.

"I'll be *fine*, mother!"

"No," Mac responded with a smile. "It wasn't that. Believe it or not I was thinking about something else entirely." She grabbed the pack with their clothes, while Neil grabbed the electric cooler with Ian's insulin. They had just picked it up from Sarjit, the pharmacist they traded with. There was enough for a few weeks, just in case they ran into any issues along the way. They still didn't know how long this stuff would keep, so Sarjit only made it up a month at a time, and his daughter was the only person they knew of that was taking it. Apparently the dosages had taken some fiddling, too. With all the test strips expiring, things were very complicated that way.

That made her wonder if insulin pumps would help. They had to continuously test the blood, so maybe that was a better long-term solution. She would have to find out how they worked if they managed to find one. That could wait until she got back and could talk to Sarjit, or "Sergeant" as most people called him, about it. She'd have to take Ian to see him anyway, so he could be shown how to make his own.

Mac didn't think he was going to like having to do it himself, but like most people he would do what was necessary to survive. Mackenzie didn't even like to *think* about what was done to the animals to get insulin from them, and she paid as little attention to that part of things as she could. Growing up on a farm meant she wasn't naïve in the least. She just didn't want to be a party to animal torture or killing. Hence the fact that they all lived on milk and egg products instead of actual meat.

It was time to get started, so Mac grabbed Gilles, then Billy, giving them each quick hugs. Then she turned to Cam.

"Try to put on some weight while we're gone, would ya? I don't mean this aesthetically, either. Ordinarily I don't say anything about weight, since it has a lot less to do with health than people used to think it did. It's more that there's a very real possibility of people getting sick and not having medical attention, and having a little extra weight on us can mean the difference between life and death. After all, we don't have to worry about zombies chasing us, and it's highly unlikely those cannibals will be an issue for us. Be healthy, but pack on some pounds if you can. The fact that you needed all new clothes out of what we brought back worries me."

"I think I've already started to gain some of the weight back. I'm not walking miles every day and forgetting to eat anymore."

Mac pulled her into a tight hug, more relieved than she wanted her daughter to know. In fact, Cam's emotional state had probably been even worse than she'd suspected, so Brian's intrusion a couple of weeks ago had turned out to be good for her. It couldn't have come at a better time.

"Okay, as much as I'd like to just stand here and fret all day, we've got a city to discover and a man in potential distress to rescue. Though I'm sure he'd hate being compared to a damsel in any way," she said with a smirk. Mac got a kick out of teasing Ian with that one. He was so stereotypically masculine in that respect, she couldn't resist giving him a good poke now and again.

"Good luck, mom. Go save Macho Man. We'll be fine here, but you be careful." Cam gave her a quick squeeze before stepping back.

"Don't worry about us. We've taken steps to ensure the survival of this expedition," Mac said with a wink. "Now, to boldly go where millions have gone before."

"You ready, honey?"

"Yeah, let's get this showboat on the road. Water, whatever."

Mac untied the mooring lines while Neil started up the engines. They hadn't actually tested them yet, because they hadn't wanted to attract attention at the marina, so Mac was relieved when she heard them fire right up. The truck drew enough curiosity as it was, but people didn't know what they were doing when they were driving around. Firing up the boat before they were ready to leave would have advertised the fact that there was a working boat that might have some supplies on board. The supplies could be replaced, but they didn't want to have to convert more boat motors to vegetable oil. And motorsailers weren't exactly thick on the docks, either.

She gave her daughter one more quick hug, and then climbed the ladder onto the deck of the boat. She ducked her head into the cabin.

"Get me outta here before I start bawling my head off, okay?" Her cranky order had Neil smiling at her in sympathy.

"Don't worry. I might just make a fool of myself by joining you. I haven't spent much time away from Billy since he moved back in with me."

Since the boat had been left with the bow facing out, Neil didn't have to try to maneuver backwards. When planning their trip and reading about everything they would have to do, they had both agreed that they wouldn't try anything too complicated. Neither of them was very skilled or knowledgeable with any kind of motorboat, much less a sailboat, so they wanted to keep things simple and avoid potential mishaps.

One of the things Mackenzie had learned about the learning process throughout her life, was that trying to be really good at anything right from the beginning was a good way to set herself up for failure. She liked to be perfect, and to just know everything, but in practical terms, as opposed to theoretical, everything took time and practice. When she'd first taken up electronics, she'd been so frustrated when it had taken her weeks to learn how to solder. Her first time sweating a plumbing joint had been an unmitigated disaster, and she still didn't like to think about it. She figured learning to operate a boat was going to run along similar lines, and they could not afford to screw it up, so they would do nothing more than the basics that were necessary to get them from point A to point B.

As the boat slipped away from the dock, Mackenzie shielded her eyes from the sun glaring off the water. It was bad enough that she already had tears burning in them, but the glare was making it worse. She moved to the rear of the boat to keep Cam in sight for as long as possible. Saying goodbye to the ferrets that morning had been just as difficult. She knew Cam was right, and that they wouldn't start to miss her for a while, so at least they were okay.

She reassured herself that it would only take a couple of weeks, assuming everything went according to plan. Then again, she rarely assumed anything would go according to plan. *Shit happens, crap occurs*, she thought with a mental shrug. They would get through whatever they needed to get through. When she could no longer see the marina, Mackenzie headed back to the cabin.

"I take it you talked to Ian about meeting us at that yacht club," Neil said when she joined him.

"Yeah, Edgewater Park at any rate. He knows the way there. It'll be a bit of a hike for him, so I made sure he still had plenty of insulin for when the extra exercise played around with his blood sugar levels. He's used to working out every day, but not hiking for a full seven or eight hours. That's a completely different type of workout."

"He'll be fine. You really like to worry, don't you?"

"No, I really don't. I just don't have much choice in the matter. It helps me think of all the little details that everyone else seems to miss, though. Like storing our emergency supplies in the dinghy," she reminded him with a jab in the ribs.

"Alright, ya got me there. Along with the non-perishable food, and the fishing stuff in case we need more food, though we'll have to remember to grab the insulin cooler. Good thing we've installed a cigarette-lighter plug for it in the dinghy. Cam's right about us being on our own out here, though. As beautiful and peaceful as it is, it's a bit disconcerting. I'm glad we're staying pretty close to the shoreline. We can always head for land if a big storm hits."

"See?" Her sense of humour was back in full swing. "And who

thought about that when they were busy worrying?"

"You know, maybe it's not that you like worrying so much as you like being right about everything. Not to mention being bossy. Ouch!" His yelp indicated that her jab found its mark once again.

"And apparently you don't much like your flaws being pointed out, either. Jesus woman. Trim your nails, would ya?"

For good measure she poked him again, grinned like a Cheshire cat, and then leapt nimbly out of reach when he made a grab for her.

"Keep that up and I'm going to tie off the helm so I can have a go at you."

"Which would mean I'd have to have you walk the plank for mutiny and dereliction of duty. Stay at your post, sailor," she ordered. Neil just snorted in response.

They had smooth sailing for the day, Mac taking her turn at the helm after Neil had been standing there for a few hours. She'd had a quick meal before taking her shift, despite a mildly queasy stomach, and Neil went to grab some food for himself once he was relieved.

"O captain, my captain," Neil called out to her when he returned a while later. Mackenzie just laughed.

"Unless we're putting a north and south dividing line on this boat and changing into grey and blue clothing, I'm not sure that line is appropriate."

"Huh?"

"You're quoting civil war poetry, cowboy. It's got nothing to do with sailing as far as I know. It was written about Abe Lincoln. Don't ask me anything else about it, though. Poetry isn't my strong suit. It was one thing I never had any interest in. Aside from a little Poe, and that dying of the light piece from Dylan Thomas, none of them really spoke to me. And you can probably blame Rodney Dangerfield for my love of the Dylan Thomas one."

"Rodney Dangerfield made you love a poem? That's just weird," he said in wonder.

"Oh, shut up. It was that movie, *Back to School*, where he's a rich guy who falls for an English professor. He performs the poem for an oral exam. Did a good enough job that I just really responded to it. Every now and then I'll go back and read it, because it reminds me to fight for my survival. Pretty inspirational for a prepper, actually."

"Yup, still weird."

"Oh, for cryin' out loud," she complained. "Can't I just like a poem?"

"It's the Dangerfield connection that weirds me out, not the fact that you like the poem. It's actually a great one. I like it myself. Isn't that the movie where he jokes that he's going to donate his body to science fiction?"

"That would be the one. One of my first RDJ movies, too."

"RDJ?"

"Yeah," Mac said, much aggrieved by his lack of understanding. "Robert Downey, Jr. The guy is practically Hollywood royalty. Not that I was ever real keen on the whole celebrity thing, but he's a hell of an actor. Weird, but funny. I liked seeing him get past a lot of his issues. Did you ever see the video for that Elton John song, *I Want Love*, with RDJ in it? Made me want to cry."

When Neil gave her a look of skepticism, she got cranky.

"Okay, so what if I did cry? It's not a crime, is it? I'm allowed to cry at things that move me."

"I'm not saying there's anything wrong with it. In fact, I didn't say anything at all. But no, I didn't believe you when you said it only made you *want* to cry. I know you too well, honey."

"Huh. Anyway, what did you want?"

"When?"

"When you started quoting civil war poetry and we got off on this tangent about more of my numerous flaws," she said grumpily.

"Oh, nothing really. Just seemed like something I should say in greeting. Guess I'll know better next time."

"You should have known better this time. Besides, you were just trying to illustrate how bossy I am by calling me captain. It's not like you actually think of me as your captain."

"Well, you do have a bit of an impact on the direction of my life, so it's really not that far off, but you're not my boss, no."

"I beg to differ," she said pertly.

"You can beg all you like. In fact, you could get started now, and then we'll be ready for tonight when we're at anchor."

"You're quite the comedian. You might even give Rodney Dangerfield a run for his money. Now that he's dead," Mac said with a sidelong look.

"I'll be the one laughing tonight."

"That's probably for the best, since certain parts of the male anatomy don't respond well to laughter."

"Honey, I guarantee you will *not* be in any mood to laugh," he spoke into her ear, sending a spear of heat through her body.

"You know, we could stop right here," Mac began, slightly breathless.

"It's your call, Captain." Neil's voice in her ear again was all it took to convince her.

⁎ ⬤ ⁐

In the grand scheme of things, losing half an hour for sex wasn't that big a deal. She was feeling guilty, she realized, or she wouldn't be trying to justify anything. Sex was just sex, Mac mentally lectured. It was a natural, and necessary, function of life. Then again, with Neil it felt more vital. Like breathing. Thankfully things were back on track there, now that she was making a conscious effort not to push him away out of fear for his health.

The additional jostling of her body, however, had left her feeling even more nauseous. Mac had made sure to bring Gravol with them, just in case one or both of them failed to adapt to being on the water. The only problem was, taking them usually made her fall asleep.

"Grab the wheel, would ya?"

Neil sort of stumbled over and did what she asked. She took a long look at him, and noticed he was looking pretty pale.

"Oh, shit. Not you, too. Well, this should be fun," she said, and went out to the dinghy to pull the small bottle out of the medicine kit she'd packed. She used her teeth to pierce the seal at the top after she'd removed the safety cap, and shook an orange tablet into her palm. Mac replaced the cap, put away the bottle, and pulled her KA-BAR from its sheath. Once she'd split the tiny pill in half, she gave one piece to Neil and stuck the other under her tongue. They each downed their portion of the pill with a swallow of water from the bottles they carried clipped to their belts, and then Mac took over again at the helm.

"Go lie down, cowboy. You look like you feel a lot worse than I do," she said gently, and rubbed his arm. When his shoulders lurched a bit at her touch, she hastily removed her hand and left him to his own devices.

She ignored the nausea as best she could, taking comfort from the fact that it would probably be gone shortly, and concentrated on heading west to Tobermory. They were on Georgian Bay at the moment. Once they rounded Tobermory, they'd be heading almost straight south to Sarnia. They would take St. Clair River through to Lake St. Clair, and then use Detroit River to cut between Detroit and Windsor to Lake Erie. Once they hit Erie there was nothing complicated about getting to Cleveland.

Mackenzie chuckled a bit when she remembered Ian's initial reaction to her plan to take a boat down to meet him. When she'd first told him that it was possible to get from the marina near her farm all the way to Cleveland, he'd thought she was kidding. He didn't realize how interconnected the waterways were in the Land of Lakes. Of course, people who didn't live in the area were often astonished by the sheer volume of water there.

It was actually kind of odd that Mac didn't have any real boating experience. She didn't count the canoeing she'd done at camp when she was a kid. Her parents had been more than happy to get rid of her for a couple of weeks every summer, so some of her best memories were of that time. It had only bothered her that the camp had been a Christian one. She'd hated organized religion even then.

She considered herself a spiritual person, but she didn't believe all the crap written in the so-called holy bible. She had more of a connection with nature than she did incense and crackers, and she would never understand why people, who supposedly believed that their great and wonderful god had created their beautiful planet, would treat an amazing gift like that with disdain. It was like the boss level of hypocrisy and contempt to her way of thinking. And it was a terrible way of saying thanks for the life that they had been given.

When darkness started falling and it was time to drop anchor for the night, they were just past Tobermory. As was the norm for her, a 'road trip' was taking longer than planned, but then she was very reluctant to travel at maximum speed just yet. There wasn't really a rush to be there, and it was better if they took their time and avoided any accidents. Sinking the boat would add more hardship to their journey than she liked to think about, though they were prepared for the possibility. They just wouldn't be very comfortable if it happened. Especially if they had a third person to bring back in a small dinghy.

Much to her relief, the lights on the boat were solar-powered, so she didn't have to trip over her own feet in the dark to get the boat ready for the night. Or at least, get it as ready as she knew how to. She had a list of things she was supposed to do, and she followed it, but she wasn't at all confident that she was getting everything right. Ian would actually be a big help there. He'd had a motorboat at one time. He didn't know how to pilot a sailboat, specifically, or in this case a motorsailer, but he had some experience otherwise.

Just to be on the safe side, Mac used the radio to contact him. It gave her a chance to let him know where they were, as well as get some pointers for dealing with the myriad tasks associated with safe boat operation. She was just finishing up when Neil poked his head in the door, looking only slightly better than he had earlier.

"Okay, Ian. I'll let you know when we're about eight hours out from Edgewater Park. I don't want you to have to wait there for too long, but by the same token, I don't want to be sitting there with an obviously working boat that's drawing unwanted attention. You think Bella's gonna be okay to walk that far? Over."

"That dog would walk to China if she could. Over."

"Just make sure you bring something for her feet, then. Ointments, bandages, and first aid stuff if you've got it. You don't want to end up carrying an eighty-pound dog. Over."

"Yes, ma'am. Just pretend I'm saluting you like a good soldier. Over." Mackenzie was not going near the good soldier remark.

"I'll talk to you later then, Ian. Over and out."

"I didn't know you were planning to get in touch with him again," Neil said in what sounded like a slightly irritated tone, though she figured it was probably caused by the same thing that was turning his face green.

"I wasn't. I just wasn't that confident about my boat-handling skills. I didn't want us to wake up and find ourselves in the middle of some sort of disaster."

"Probably for the best. Why don't you radio the old homestead, and let them know we're okay. We told them what time to expect to hear from us, and it's getting on that time now. Cam may be tough and cynical, but she's still going to be worried about you. I know Billy isn't happy about this trip."

"Yeah, I noticed he was pretty quiet. Is he mad at me for putting you at risk like this?"

"No, of course not," Neil snapped. "You're not putting me at risk. I am. I'm a grown man who does the things he chooses to do, honey, and you don't make those decisions for me. So it's me he's a little pissed at. He doesn't blame you for wanting to help a friend. Actually he thinks you're pretty remarkable. He also understands why I had to come with you. For the most part anyway. I think maybe part of him feels I'm choosing you over him, because if something happened to me, then I chose to die rather than stay home with my son. By the same token, you're my wife, and if you left me behind I'd be in the position Billy is in right now."

"Cam, too, when you put it like that. But then Cam knows what it means to risk your life to help someone. Not in an extreme way, but in the little things she used to do in her everyday life. When homeless people came up to her to ask her for money, she gave it to them if she had it. It's considered a risky thing to do, because you have to get close to a stranger who might not have the best intentions. Sometimes it's a ruse. I made sure she knew the risks in what she was doing, but I never asked her not to do it. She didn't do it when she was young, of course. It was only as she got older and was working full time that she even had money to give away.

"We take risks in everything we do, and I'm sure Billy knows that. We're being as careful as we can be, and we're going to make it back in one piece. But you're right. They need to hear from us."

8 ~ SENSORY INUNDATION

"I'm warning you now. We all swear like a bunch of sailors, especially when we're playing, so you might not want Jake to hear us," Cam said to Lisa, who merely shrugged in response.

"Not really my biggest concern with him right now," she replied sardonically.

"Yeah, good point. Though you're going to be okay, you know? My mother has a habit of taking care of people, even though she hates the very thought of being a caregiver in the normal sense. Like she doesn't do the nursing or sick thing with people usually, or make giant meals and stuff. Okay maybe she does. She just does it on her own schedule when she feels like it, or when it's absolutely necessary. So, sure, she's kind of a failure at not doing the caregiver thing. She's just weird about it."

Lisa burst out laughing.

"You have the strangest relationship with your mother, I have to say."

"You don't know a tenth of it. We've been acting a lot more like normal people in the last few months. Not at all the way we usually do. Man, I can't even remember the last time I called her a bitch to make her smile. I'll need to catch up," Cam said with a grin.

Kirk and Leigh were planning to come over for a gaming night, and the real treat was that Leigh had been developing a new game. Before the world's freefall, it had been a hobby of hers, and now she had all the time in the world to indulge it. This was the first one she felt was ready for them to play, and they were all excited about just having something new. None of them really cared if it was great or anything, so long as it was different. It sort of felt like a miracle in a way. As if the world hadn't really ended.

The game console at the cabin had originally belonged to Billy, and it had a mod chip in it so he could play burned games on it, which meant Leigh could burn the games she created and they would actually work. The intent hadn't been to pirate games in Billy's case. It was just that his dad had been a prepper, like Cam and her mom, and he'd made backup discs of the games they bought. Without a mod chip the backups wouldn't have worked if the originals had been damaged in some way.

Cam got the entire stock of cheesecake cookies from the cabinet, grabbed a single big bag of potato chips, and five candy bars – one for each of the adults, since Lisa was joining them. Jake was too young to eat that kind of thing, or at least an entire one by himself, and he wouldn't know he was missing out on anything. It felt like a massive indulgence for Cam, though, breaking into the junk-food stash, but it had been months since she'd even looked at the chocolate bars. She was just now getting her appetite back.

Despite the festive atmosphere of a game-and-junk-food night, Cam took her responsibilities seriously. Her laptop would be open beside her the whole time. Gilles and Chuck were technically both keeping watch, but Cam and Billy had been left in charge. She could tell that didn't sit well with Gilles, though Chuck seemed content with it. He was more of a follower-type, while Gilles was a more assertive kind of guy, and he probably didn't think he should be taking orders from someone fifteen years younger than he was. Not that Cam cared what he thought about it. He was her mother's friend, but she barely knew him, even after several months of living at the farm together. They just hadn't interacted that much. He had his family, and she had been stuck inside her own head after killing Gerry.

Leigh and Kirk arrived and got the console set up in the living room. They had only played for half an hour when a sensor alert sounded on Cam's laptop. It was a completely different area from where Brian had triggered the sensor, so it concerned her even more. She picked up one of the two-way radios that had been part of the haul from the electronics store, and spoke into it.

"Yo, guys, did anyone get that alert?"

"Hey Cam," Chuck responded. "Yeah, I've got it covered, and Jim is with me. We'll look into it. Go back to whatever you were doing."

Cameron stared at the two-way, more than a little insulted. It was the verbal equivalent of a pat on the head, and she'd had enough of being treated like a little kid.

"Look, just let me know what it is when you find out. Nothing is showing on the camera feed, and I don't like being kept in the dark," she snapped.

"Okay. Calm down. I'll keep you posted."

God, she hated it when people told her to calm down, but it would be stupid to keep the conversation going when he needed to go and check out why the sensor had gone off. Sometimes you just had to swallow whatever it was that you wanted to say, in the interest of getting results. It was one part of being an adult that she didn't like very much. She'd been taught to speak up for herself, but there was a time and place for that she supposed. She was going to have to make it clear to everyone, however, that patronizing her wasn't something she was going to put up with anymore.

With the game temporarily suspended until they found out what was happening with the sensor alert, they decided to make something more substantial to eat. Billy offered to do the cooking.

"I can make some stir-fry. Dad taught me to cook, but I don't get much chance since he usually does it for everyone."

"That sounds really good. With lots of mushrooms, okay?" She got up and went with him to the kitchen to help.

"I don't think that'll be a problem," he said with a grin. "We've got plenty of the damn things. We should probably start making cream of mushroom soup and handing it out to people once our parents get back. It's kind of hard to use everything up before it goes bad, and those are things we've got a lot of. We can freeze it, too. It's a good thing we all seem to like those foods, but it doesn't leave us with much variety, except when we tap into the ARKs or canned goods."

"Yeah, mom doesn't really like to use anything from those, because the food supplies in those buckets will last twenty years, unlike the milk and fresh stuff. Even when we can or freeze things to preserve them, they only last six months to a year, if we're trying to play it safe. Still, we need variety. We'll get more of that when we put in the bigger garden this year, but right now it's a pain."

They were in the kitchen, pulling out what Billy needed for the stir-fry, when Cameron was struck by the container of sunflower oil she was holding.

"This is what seems bizarre to me. We use this to cook, but now we're also using it to run engines. I mean, why were people so stupid about this? We almost completely destroyed the planet pulling fossil fuels out of the ground, and we could easily have been using this for the last however many years. People aren't just assholes. They're stupid assholes," she sneered.

"It's not just that. Dad was telling me they were fining people in the states for converting their cars to run used deep-fryer oil. The worst part about it was that it was the EPA that was doing it. How does that even make sense? The Environmental Protection Agency was fining people for protecting the environment. When he told me that I almost choked. But then that's what happens when government is run by corporate interests."

"Mom complains about the same thing. Even now, when it's past the point of it being an issue, you should hear her go off on her rants about all those corporations that were destroying the environment. Like the company that was illegally harvesting groundwater from California when the really bad drought started, or the two brothers who were lobbying against anything to do with clean energy.

"Actually, I think she said it was more to do with controlling the media to the point where people just didn't believe clean energy was possible. I could never wrap my head around how gullible people were. They just believed everything they saw on TV, or on the internet. Those were the real zombies. At least that's what mom always called them."

"Dad, too, I think. He wasn't into trying to buck the system, though, because he didn't think there was any point to it. People believed the climate change denial messages, because it was easier for them than having to do something about it. They could just relax and sit in front of the TV, and not have to worry."

"Okay, so I amend my earlier statement then. People are lazy, stupid assholes. Or they were. This had to be one hell of a wake-up call for anyone who's still alive. Then again, anyone who's still alive probably has a working understanding of what it means to provide for themselves. Like farmers and preppers."

Once everyone had eaten, including Jake with his usual puréed vegetables, Cam left the room to pace beside the open kitchen counter. They needed to find whatever was causing the sensor issue before darkness fell. If they didn't, it would mean everyone remaining armed and on guard until the sun rose again. There was also a smaller sensor perimeter in place around the occupied portion of the property, which was all well and good, but people needed to be awake and aware if someone got that close to the house. Besides, those were only passive infrared sensors, and with their current low-sensitivity setting she didn't want to rely on them.

Instead of continuing to pace uselessly, Cam started to pull together a plan in her brain. By the time Chuck radioed back to her, she was ready with it.

"Hey, Cam. We got nothin' here. I'm not saying there isn't anything out here, but we're not finding it if there is."

"Okay, could you grab Gilles and come to the back of the main house then? Have Jim stay out by the sensor, and maybe get his son out there with him. I don't want to leave him by himself, just in case. We'll need to talk about what we're going to do here. I'll bring Billy with me."

"Uh, sure. Okay, Cam."

Cam could hear the amusement in his voice, and it very nearly set her off, but she held her temper in check. As soon as they were gathered together, she was going to have to make them understand a few things, or nothing would get done. She went back to the living room for Billy, and as they went through the greenhouse off the kitchen, she spoke to him softly.

"From Chuck's tone of voice, he's not taking me very seriously as a person in charge on this farm, so I'm guessing it'll be the same for you. That's something we have to fix right now, because someone needs to be in charge so everyone is cooperating. So, can you do me a favour and just go along with me for a few minutes while I act like a dictator?"

"Don't I always?" He grinned at her.

"Very funny," she said, but she was smiling.

She wasn't smiling anymore when no one made an appearance at the back door. More than fifteen minutes had already gone by, and she knew from first-hand experience walking the property that there was no way they shouldn't be back by that point. After twenty-five minutes she'd had enough.

"Where the *fuck* are you two? Did you think I was fucking joking about needing to talk?" Even her eyes felt hot as she stared at the radio and waited for a response.

"Oh, sorry Cam. We just got to talking. We'll be there in a second," Chuck responded.

Again Cam found herself staring at the offending radio. This time in disbelief. They just *got to talking*? Either they weren't taking the sensor breach seriously, or they were making plans of their own without consulting her or Billy. She was just going to have to ask when they got there. It didn't take long.

"Exactly what did you think was more important than discussing the safety of everyone on this farm?"

"That's what we were discussing," Gilles said with a shrug, his arrogance implicit in his tone.

"And you didn't think Billy and I were necessary to the conversation. Is that it? You do remember whose farm this is, don't you Gilles? Has it slipped your mind that this is not your property, and that you're living here, surviving, because me, my mother, Billy, and his dad, were prepared and ready to go when disaster struck … while you and Chuck were not?

"Have you forgotten, Gilles, that you called my mother paranoid for thinking she needed a self-sustaining property? Because I haven't. My mother knows you, and trusts you, but I don't even remember you from before. Either of you. So I have no interest in blindly putting my safety, or the safety of everyone we're responsible for, in the hands of someone I barely know. Billy and I are the ones who are responsible if something happens, and until we're certain you two are something more than small-town cops who did nothing but give out speeding tickets, the decisions are going to come from the two of us.

"You don't have to like it. You don't have to agree with everything. And when you disagree feel free to say so, but you don't get to pat us on the head and ignore everything we say. We'll listen to whatever comments or suggestions you have to make, because you were cops at one time, so you could very well know something we don't.

"Now, for tonight I have a plan. Billy, I haven't discussed it with you yet, so if you disagree let me know. We need people on watch. Four-hour shifts of three or four people. No one here is used to long hours keeping watch, so we can't ask them to patrol any longer than that. They could fall asleep, or simply miss something. We don't have enough people to keep watch over a big area, so we'll circle just outside the inner sensor perimeter. Get in touch with one another every hour. When it's daylight again, we'll need to go back to that sensor and take a look for anything that would indicate another person. You've got hunting experience, Gilles, so I already know you can handle that."

She raised her eyebrows and waited. Gilles seemed to be chewing his own tongue. He was pissed, but she was right and he knew very well that he and his family would have been dead if they hadn't taken them in. Finally he spoke.

"That's pretty much what we were already talking about," he said, his tone full of grit. He cocked his head to the side and glared at her.

"Then obviously my ideas aren't for shit, and you should respect the fact that Billy and I are supposed to be handling things. We don't know everything, but we need to cooperate for our own safety, and the safety of our families. We can't have everyone thinking they're in charge, because nobody will be cooperating then, and that's when we're going to end up with gaping holes that could put us all in danger. Billy and I are the ones who are supposed to make sure everyone is okay, which means we need to know everything that's going on. Alright?"

"Understood," Gilles said, his tone only slightly less antagonistic. Chuck, meanwhile, was shuffling his gigantic feet.

"Sorry, Cam. Your mother and Neil did make it clear that you and Billy were in charge when they left. I guess I was thinking you were too young to handle it, but you're a lot like your mother. She would have told us where to stick it, too." He gave her a sheepish smile, and Gilles turned his glare toward him, as though Chuck had betrayed him.

They finalized the details of who would be doing the actual patrolling, and at what times, and by the time all that was settled, Gilles had lost most of his snotty attitude. He wasn't used to having his authority questioned by anyone, from what Cam could tell, but the fact remained he had no authority here.

She also had a sneaking suspicion there was something of the chauvinist in him, but it wasn't consistent if that was the case. He treated her mother with respect usually, and the rare times he slipped up she called him on it, but then most people showed her mother respect. She'd earned it. Cam had yet to prove herself to everyone on the farm, and it hadn't helped that she'd been stuck in her own head for so long. Nobody here knew her, and they didn't know what she was capable of, any more than she knew what Gilles and Chuck were capable of. She needed to acknowledge that.

"Look, Gilles, you don't know me any better than I know you. You've got no more reason to trust me, either. For the time being you're stuck with my decision-making, and I'm sure it's not easy for you to entrust the safety of your family to an unknown. Especially after I've made one mistake. But I learn from my mistakes, and usually right away. So, how about we try to give each other the benefit of the doubt and work together. If we share our ideas, then we can see whether or not those ideas will work, and whether or not we can trust each other. Okay?"

She didn't hold her hand out for a shake, because that just seemed stupid to her. Besides, she'd made all the concessions she was willing to make for the time being.

"Like Chuck said, you sure seem a lot like your mom right now. That's a good thing, so I think we can make this work while they're gone." He nodded and clapped a hand on her shoulder, then left with Chuck to make the arrangements with everyone who would be getting security duty for the first shift. Cam went back inside the greenhouse with Billy, her hands shaking, and immediately bent over at the waist and took a few deep breaths.

"Cam? You okay?" He sounded worried. She just held up a finger to ask him for a minute. After she'd taken a few more breaths, she stood up.

"I'm okay. I just hate confrontations like that. I don't entirely know what I'm doing, but I knew I needed them to take us seriously or we'd lose all control. By the time our parents got back, we'd either have chaos, or Chuck and Gilles would have taken over, and that is not something I'm willing to let happen."

"Well, I think you did great! I know Gilles can be a bit full of himself. I'm not sure if I like him very much, to be honest. I do like Chuck, but he's a pushover with this kind of thing, not a leader. You're better at this kind of thing than I am, so I appreciate you making sure they knew it was both of us they had to listen to. It'll make things easier for me, too."

"Yeah, I'm sorry we didn't get a chance to go over any of that stuff before we got out there, and I didn't want to talk about it outside where someone else could hear us. I took a bit of a risk just talking to them, because if Gilles had decided to be an asshole and ignore what I said, and someone else overheard that, every bit of authority we were trying to lay claim to would be gone. *Nobody* would bother listening to us then. And then I had to get his temper to back off. Probably the French in him," she said with a laugh.

"Isn't your dad part French?"

"Yeah, which is why it's sort of a joke around here. Mom and I tease him about it, and I've heard her do the same with Gilles."

"Oh, okay," Billy said, nodding his head in understanding. "Yeah, my dad and I didn't really know a lot of people around here, other than with the knife store. I mean, they came in, bought a knife, and left, so we'd nod or wave on the street. That kind of thing. We know Jim, of course, because he ran the gas station, but we didn't know his son, or that John was married to Gilles step-daughter. Not until they came here. It's kind of weird how everyone just sort of knew each other."

"Not really. Not if you think about it. This is a small community, with large families. My mother comes from one of those families, though not in this community, so she's told me what it's like. She said when she was growing up that it was damn near impossible to find someone to date that wasn't related to her,"

Cam said with a laugh.

"Ewww."

"Yeah, and the worst of it is, there are actually cousins that are married to one another. First cousins, no less. My mom told me about one little kid that was actually born with teeth. I mean, that's just gross. The idea of having a baby inside you that already has their teeth is pretty fucking freaky. I can't even imagine being pregnant, and that's kind of like some sort of parasitic monster to me. I'm probably being mean, but it gives me the creeps."

"Yuck. I don't think we need to keep talking about that. We need to decide who's going to man the radio for the first shift, and when we're going to sleep and all that."

"I'm not sure I'm going to be able to sleep. For one thing, I slept late like I usually do. I didn't go to bed until after we got the radio call from our parents, to say they were starting on the next leg. They'd get there a lot faster if they took shifts and sailed at night, but they don't want to risk it even with the sonar thingy they have on board."

"I think it's called a depth-sounder," Billy said.

"Yeah, that thing. Mom found the manual for it, and for the boat itself, while they were at anchor last night, so she's probably read everything cover-to-cover, but she's playing it safe. Means we'll have to wait longer for them to get back, but we won't have to worry about them so much.

"As for taking shifts with the radio, if it makes you feel better you can have it for the next four hours, and then I'll take it. I'm going to be up all night, and you probably got up early this morning. In the meantime, we still have a game to play." She grinned at Billy, and they both took off running toward the living room.

Kirk, Leigh, and Lisa, were sitting on the sofa, chatting and awaiting their return. It was the sort of game that couldn't progress without all the players, so they'd been stuck in limbo while Cam and Billy dealt with the sensor issue.

"Just out of curiosity, why the hell did you decide to make a post-apocalyptic survival game, when we're actually living that nightmare right now?" Lisa's question made Leigh laugh.

"To stave off panic attacks," she responded.

"What do you mean?"

"Well, there we were, the world was going to hell, and I was freaking out. I kept thinking we were all going to die, and all these nightmare scenarios kept popping up in my head, so I kept trying to figure out the solution to them ahead of time. In case they actually happened. I talked to Mac a lot about it, too, and she told me what she had in mind. Not only did it relieve me to know that she'd already figured out all that shit, but it gave me the idea that my panic could be used as a sort of learning tool for everyone. My brain already kind of goes in the direction of game development, so it was sort of a natural. I've got other ideas, too, but this one became a sort of therapeutic obsession."

"Oh, okay. You guys are going to have to tell me what all happened with that guy who was here a few weeks ago, though. I know Mac seemed pretty freaked about it for a bit, and then was worried about leaving. Would he be the one making the sensors go off tonight?" At Lisa's question, everyone looked at Cam. The tension in the air was palpable, because it wasn't something that was really talked about openly. Cam knew they were trying to be sensitive, but it was time to just talk about it and get it over with.

"It's possible it's Brian, but I don't think so. He seems okay. The reason my mother was worried, was because I killed his son. And he knows it." Cam held up her hand when Lisa's jaw dropped open in shock.

"He was stalking my mother and was holding a rifle on Neil when I shot him with the arrow. He was already pulling the trigger by the time my arrow went through him. He fell over, trying to reload his rifle for another shot. He'd have killed my mother, too. Probably after raping her," Cam said, her tone defiant.

"I already knew you had killed someone, from the conversation your mom was having with Gilles the day I got here. I just didn't know the whole situation with the intruder," Lisa said.

"Oh. Anyway, I went to see Brian and Geraldine before mom and Neil left. They both say they know what their son was like, and that they've forgiven me. I'm not sure how anyone can forgive someone who kills their kid, but then I've never given birth to a potential rapist and murderer. Apparently he tried to rape his own mother, and they'd spent his whole childhood trying to get him straightened out with various kinds of therapy. It didn't work," she finished bluntly.

"Holy shit! Like there aren't enough problems in the world right now," Lisa replied.

"I know, right?" Cam was smiling. "Still, it was hard after I killed him. I felt guilty for it, and then felt guilty for feeling guilty, knowing if I hadn't done it that both Neil and my mother would likely be dead, so I figured it was shitty for me to feel guilty at all. Believe me, I was really confused for a while. Then my mother told me something that kind of straightened me out a bit." Cam wasn't about to confide in anyone but Kirk and Leigh what her mother had told her, but apparently Lisa already knew.

"Yeah, she told Gilles she'd killed your father when you were a baby." It turned out Billy was the only one in the room who didn't know, because his jaw dropped.

"What the fuck happened? Does my dad know about this?" Cam cringed at his tone.

"Yeah, he knows. It was self-defense. She called the cops right away and everything. Actually, it was even more than self-defense, I guess, because she said it looked like he was going to go after me."

"You guys really attract some weirdoes," Billy said in wonder.

"Hmm," was Cam's only response.

"Oh, shit, Cam. Sorry. I didn't mean that the way it sounded. Especially since my dad was obviously someone who was attracted to your mom," he said, flustered. Cam laughed.

"It's okay, Billy. There were a lot of weirdoes out there, and believe me, every woman on this planet probably had to deal with them at one time or another. We'll see what happens in the future, but without some form of law enforcement or legal system to keep violent people away from the general population, who knows? Mom already ran into a bunch of cannibals in Huntsville, and they apparently prefer eating people to other food sources, so I don't think violence is going to disappear, especially toward women. We're going to have to be ready to look after ourselves if we get into a bad situation."

The second she finished speaking, another sensor went off, putting an indefinite hold on game night.

9 ~ MAST CONFUSION

It had taken them another two days to reach Sarnia, and between the two of them Mac had lost count of the Gravol they'd been forced to take. Neil was now taking a full one every four hours that he was awake, though Mac continued taking only half a tablet. It still made her slightly woozy, but it was the only way she could handle being on the boat.

So far they'd had good weather, but the sky had darkened a few hours before they planned to stop for the night, and between the two of them they figured it might be a good idea to pull the boat closer to the shore, just in case something bad happened. Then at least they could see the shore to swim to it, or take the dinghy. Their complete lack of experience on the water did not make them confident they could handle turbulent weather.

The combination of nausea and pharmaceutically induced exhaustion had them heading for the very nice queen-size mattress tucked in the back of the boat. Mac knew it was called the stern, but she wasn't going to start speaking in nautical terms as though she knew what the hell she was talking about. She just considered herself lucky to be alive at this point, even with the nausea.

They had talked about heading to shore each night, and sleeping on land, but Mac figured that would only delay their adjustment to the motion of the boat. Neil displayed a great deal of skepticism regarding his ability to adjust, and told her he would have preferred the break from the constant sickness, but he also acknowledged that it was risky to go too near the shore if they didn't need to.

They both fell asleep almost instantly, but awoke to the alarming realization that the boat was pitching every which way. They had to brace themselves against the wood cabinets surrounding the bed to keep from crashing into them, and into one another. It took Neil several minutes to stand up, and took just as long for Mac to do the same.

"Well, we're not going to get any sleep that way!" At her smart-ass comment, Neil glared at her, and then headed toward the built-in ladder-like stairs, grabbing a coil of rope as he went.

"We need to make sure everything is still properly tied down. We haven't opened up any of the sails or anything, and I'm sure the owners tied everything off for storage before leaving it at the marina the last time, but with this movement I don't want to leave anything to chance," he said.

"Alright. We'll check everything, but if I get thrown overboard I'm coming back to this boat as a ghost to kick your ass," Mac replied in irritation. As a response, Neil jabbed his finger toward a second coil of rope.

"Yeah, yeah. I'll tie myself off. Doesn't exactly guarantee

anything, really, but it's better than nothing."

She had to wait several more minutes before Neil could even get up the ladder ahead of her. She wanted to make sure he wasn't going to come crashing down on her when she started up.

"Mac," he hollered. "Would you get your ass up here? There's shit to do!" She bared her teeth at him, but started up the steps, holding tightly to the metal handrails. Her shoulders bumped into the framing on both sides of her. She tightened her muscles to keep her upper body still, and let her legs bend and flex with the motion of the boat as much as she could. Just as she reached the top, the door swung back and smacked her in the face.

The instant numbness of her lips and nose told her she was really going to feel that when it wore off. She shoved the door back with a growl deep in her throat, and finished her climb up the short steps.

"You asshole!" Mac yelled it through her numbed lips and teeth. Neil turned toward her to respond to her insult, but instead of fighting with her his mouth gaped open like a fish.

"Oh my God, honey. What happened?"

"You didn't latch the door open, that's what," she replied, beyond irritated. The worried look on his face, however, mollified her to some extent. It wasn't until he grabbed the towel they'd been using to clear moisture off the inside of the cabin's clear plastic windscreen, that she realized there was blood on her face. She still couldn't feel her mouth, so she hadn't noticed it.

"Oh for fuck's sake! Are you kidding me?" She'd looked down

by that point, and saw that the blood was even soaking through her jacket.

"Here. Sit down, pinch your nose, and tilt your head back," Neil said as he led her to the chair in front of the fancy navigation equipment she hadn't figured out how to use yet, and didn't know whether or not it still worked. She hadn't intended to bother with it, but now she stared at it as a way to distract herself from her annoyance.

Neil remember to latch the door open this time, then turned around to go back down the stairs into the living quarters. In a few minutes he'd come back with some ice from the tiny freezer. Mac was constantly amazed by the features on the boat they'd chosen. If she hadn't felt so shitty for the last three days, she might have been able to enjoy the luxury of it. TVs, DVD players, a combined washer-dryer unit, and enough room for at least four adults, with two toilets, a shower, and two big beds. As it was, she couldn't enjoy a damn thing, and it didn't look like she was going to be feeling any better about it in the near future.

"I think you broke my nose," she whined. "And I actually *like* my nose, damn it. In fact, what I liked most about it was that it was still in the centre of my face. Now it feels like it's smeared all over it!"

"Yeah, it kind of is. Man, is it ever swelling. More than anything I'd love to be able to stand here and baby you, but at the moment that's not really an option. The cover on the dinghy is loose, and a couple of sails need to be retied. Or at least that's what it looks like from in here. I won't know for sure until I'm up on the deck."

"I'm coming with you. You're not going up there by yourself," she said, when it looked like he was going to protest. "If something happened to you, I wouldn't be there to help, and I wouldn't have a clue what was going on."

"Alright, but we need to make sure you're not bleeding to death from the nose before we go up then."

"I'm fine. I might *want* to be babied right now, but I'm not gonna die from a smack in the face from a door. It's undignified. You can baby me later, if you're not hanging over the side of the boat, heaving your guts out."

"That's just mean. It's been at least an hour since I did that," he said indignantly.

"Let's go tame this bronco, cowboy."

When they got up on deck, Mac tied herself off on one of the many cleats. She assumed they were there for the sails, and served an important function, but she had no idea what that might be. Nor did she have a clue what sort of knot she should be tying. She'd never been a Boy Scout. So she created something like a noose, tightening it once the loop was around the cleat. If it was good enough for hanging people, she figured it would keep her on the damn boat, or at least she wouldn't float away from it if she fell over.

She helped Neil tie off the sails, and retie the cover on the dinghy so their stuff wouldn't go flying everywhere. There was no rain yet, but she didn't think they'd have long to wait for that. The sky was lighting up, with the thunder rumbling almost ten seconds after. If the lightning and thunder got too close together, they were going to have to try to head closer to shore. She didn't relish the idea of being hit by it, and had no idea if there was any sort of system on the boat for protection from lightning, or if that were even possible on a boat. She hadn't seen anything about grounding or lightning rods in the books she'd read.

They were heading back toward the cabin entry door on opposite sides of the deck, when a large wave hit the side of the boat, knocking them both off their feet and half on top of the area in front of the cabin that only jutted partway out of the deck they had been walking on. Mac felt her forehead crack against the mast, and then she was rolling helplessly toward the cable-like railing. Her hip ground into a support, and she continued to roll until her stomach was pressed against the same support, her head and arms thrust, flailing, over the water between different cables, while the cables dug into her collarbone on both sides.

All the breath had been knocked out of her. She tried to inhale, but couldn't. Her diaphragm had been sent into a spasm, and there was nothing she could do but wait for it to stop. To keep herself from rolling anymore, and accumulating further damage to her various body parts, she brought her hands back to grab the cables. Then she waited. There was nothing she could do until she was able to breathe again.

"Mac! Honey! Please tell me you're okay. I can't see you," Neil called out, and even though she knew he was terrified there was no way for her to allay his fear. Speaking required air. Her vision was starting to darken at the edges, too, and she wondered vaguely just how much damage had been done by the mast when she'd slammed into it. Her grip slackened without her realizing it, and the next roll of the boat had her tumbling toward the back of the boat.

It wasn't until her hair caught on something that her momentum was abruptly halted. It kept her from falling down to the lower level, and possibly off the back of the boat, but the pain as her scalp tore made her wish she'd just gone over. She couldn't even scream from it, because she still couldn't breathe. The hot blood on the back of her neck had her very worried.

Mac reached back to try to free her hair from whatever had caught it, but she wasn't able to release it by the time the boat pitched once again. She nearly blacked out from the agony from the additional tearing of her scalp. Her hand floundered at her hip for a moment before she was able to bring her knife up to slice her hair off at the back of her neck. Still gripping her knife, Mac plunged it into the fibreglass of the deck and held on.

"Honey, please! Will you answer me?" Neil sounded frantic, and despite the pain her breath was starting to come back to her, so she let out a sound that was a cross between a moan and whimper. It wasn't until she felt his hand on her shoulder that she was even sure it had come out loud enough for him to hear.

"Oh, fuck, there's blood everywhere! What happened? Can you

tell me?"

Mac wished she could have shaken her head to let him know she really didn't have it in her to explain anything at the moment, but there was no way she was moving her head if she didn't have to.

"Hit my head. Got scalped." It was all she could get out, since she was still gasping for air. His understanding, or lack thereof, was no longer of any concern to her, however. Reddish-black flooded in from the edges of her vision once again, but this time it continued its trek across her eyes until not even a pinprick of light could be seen.

ഇ ◆ ൽ

"Open your eyes, honey. Come on now. You have to look at me. I need to know you're alright."

The voice was familiar, but it annoyed her. She didn't want to be in this place right now. It hurt too much. She wanted to let go for a while, maybe catch her breath, before she went to the trouble of opening her eyes. Even hearing the voice was painful.

"If you don't come around soon, I'm turning the boat around and heading back to the farm. I don't know how else to help you," the voice said, and it was telling her something she didn't want to hear, but she had no idea why that should be the case. Why wouldn't she want to go to a farm? Still, it felt important enough that she forced herself to speak.

"Can't," she rasped.

"What do you mean? Do you mean you can't open your eyes, or we can't go back to the farm?"

"Both. Don't know why. Just can't." Those few words cost her all her strength, and she began to fade again.

"Oh, Jesus," said the voice, as she let herself slip away again.

ᛒ ◆ ᛞ

"Tell me what the hell to do, Annette! I have no experience with this kind of thing," she heard the voice say. A man, she realized. Someone she knew, but for some reason she couldn't remember his name, or how she knew him. And it hurt so much to try to remember.

"There's not much I can tell you from here, other than make suggestions, because I can't even look at her wounds to see what kind of injuries she might have. Where, exactly, is the bruise, Neil?" A female voice this time, and crackly, which had her picturing someone talking into a microphone. A radio? *Sure hope they don't put on any music*, she thought. She was pretty sure music would hurt her. A lot.

"It's right in the middle of her forehead, and I didn't see any others on her scalp. Hard to tell with all the blood still matted in her hair, though. What's left of it," he muttered.

"Did you have to cut it off when you used the Superglue to close her scalp?"

"No. She'd already cut it off to free herself when I got to her, and by that point she was out of it. Doesn't matter anyway. I just need to know how to take care of her. It's been hours, and she's only said a handful of words. Words that told me she had no idea what the hell was going on. Please, just tell me what I have to do to keep her alive," he begged.

"You're already doing it, Neil. There's nothing else to be done. Her pupils are reactive, so if she has cerebral edema it hasn't reached a critical stage yet. Hopefully it's only the frontal lobe that sustained the injury, and her brain didn't hit the back of the cranium as well. And hopefully there's no internal shearing of the vessels. That's all I can give you at the moment. Hope. It may be a severe concussion, and it may be a subdural hematoma. Without doing an MRI, I have no way of knowing, much less diagnosing an injury I haven't actually seen.

"I would tell you to come straight back, but she shouldn't be moved. And there isn't much I could do for her anyway. Not without resorting to semi-medieval surgical procedures, because I don't have the equipment I'd need to do things right. I don't have any of the drugs that might help. There are a lot of differences between species, and the drugs that work for a goat aren't necessarily compatible with human anatomy."

"Just tell me she's going to be okay, Annette. Give me *something*," he pleaded.

"Mac is a fighter, and that's about all I can really say. If I said anything else you wouldn't believe me anyway. Keep checking for pupillary response with your flashlight. So long as her pupils continue to contract in the light, her odds are good. I'll stay here at the house in case anything changes."

"Okay, thanks. Can you put Cam back on? If anything will bring her back, it'll be her daughter's voice."

"Mom?" At the sound of the new voice, she smiled. She *did* know her. She could picture her face even, though she didn't remember any details.

"That's it, Cam. Keep talking. She just smiled," he said, and she could hear happiness in his voice, but by then she was too tired again. She just needed to rest for a bit.

☜ ◆ ☞

A bright light was shining in her eye. Just one eye, and it was really pissing her off. She raised her hand to bat at it.

"Would you *stop* that? Christ! I'm trying to sleep here," she snarled.

"Mac? Honey? Is that you?"

"Who the fuck do you think it is?"

"I wasn't sure for a while there. Then again, you didn't seem to know either. I couldn't even get you to tell me your name," he said. "You didn't know mine either, but I figured not knowing your own was a little worse, so I tried not to be too insulted."

"Look, cowboy, my head is pounding, and I feel like I'm going to throw up. At the same time I feel like my stomach is gnawing a

156

hole in my backbone. I'm not in the mood for lame jokes." She cracked open her eyelid again to take in the bright light shining through the curtains over the small windows.

"What time is it? It looks like it's afternoon out there. Why the hell isn't the boat moving?" Her demanding, bossy tone had him chuckling.

"Honey, this boat hasn't moved in three days, aside from being thrown around by that storm for a few hours. I figured I should make sure you were going to live before we got back on our way. I'm glad to see you're back to your usual self, though."

"Very funny. If you're not planning on doing anything useful, like getting this boat moving, could you get out of my way so I can get some fucking coffee? I'm in desperate need of caffeine right now."

"I'm not sure if you should be having coffee, honey," he began, but she interrupted him.

"Caffeine works on migraines for scientific reasons I'm not inclined to explain at the moment, so I'm going to have some coffee, even if I have to go through you in the most violent manner possible in order to get it! *Capisce?*"

"Stay there," Neil said with a sigh. "I'll get it. You're definitely not supposed to be walking around a rocking boat, chancing another head injury."

Mac pondered his words. She didn't like the sound of that, and began to wonder how many brain cells she might have killed. After just a few seconds, though, thinking became an exercise in agony, so she allowed herself to drift for a while. It wasn't long before she began to smell the brewing coffee, and a sudden flood of gratitude welled up in her. Along with a helping of shame for being so mean. Granted, he was well aware she hated being woken up, and he didn't seem to be taking offence, so she wasn't going to worry about it too much.

The additional smell of toast had her mouth watering. She smiled wryly. It didn't smell like it was burning, so she assumed there was no seizure coming on. Not that she had ever had one, but she'd known people who were epileptic. Of course, her one friend from years ago, who had grand mal seizures, never remember smelling a damn thing, so apparently it wasn't an exact science.

"Drink this first, honey," he ordered, as he walked through the curtain that gave the bedroom area some privacy.

"Wait a minute. What happened to the toast? I know you made some," she whined.

"I did, yes. That was for me. This is some broth I found in the cupboard. You haven't eaten in a few days, and at the very least you have a severe concussion. You're not getting anything but clear liquids for a little bit. I have to make sure you can keep it down before you try solids."

"I baked that bread myself, damn it. I should at least be allowed to eat it," she grumped at him. Still, she took the broth and drank it. By the time she was finished, she felt full enough that she no longer cared about toast. Coffee was a different story. As she handed back the empty mug from the broth, she opened her mouth to ask for her coffee, but he held up a hand.

"Don't worry, I'm getting it. It'll be finished brewing by now. I'll get us both a cup."

She felt well enough by then that she started to think about what she remembered from the last few days. When she realized Cam knew about her injury, it got her dander back up.

"Did I hear Cam on that radio over the last few days?" Raising her voice so he could hear her turned out to be a pretty stupid move on her part. She groaned at the instant punishment she received for her actions, and pressed both her hands into the sides of her head to try and relieve the pain. It pulled on her scalp at the back of her head, though, and her breath hissed through her teeth. Mac dropped her hands back on the bed.

"Yes, you did," he replied, though he'd waited to answer her until he was handing her a fresh mug. Probably thought she'd be less pissed off at him if she had her coffee, she decided cynically, but then he'd be right.

"Why did you have to worry her like that?"

"Are you *kidding* me? I needed to talk to Annette. I thought you were dying. I couldn't ask for Annette without explaining the situation. You raised her. You tell me what she's like for that."

"Fuck."

"Yeah. Fuck. But I'm going to radio her now so she knows you're okay. Alright? It wouldn't surprise me if this eases her mind about the rest of the trip, though. Once something bad happens, people tend to think the worst is over and they relax a bit. It's not logical, but it's human nature."

"I sure hope so, because she's already going to be pissed at me for this."

"Oh yeah," he said with a smirk.

"Gee, thanks for the reassurance. Before you get Cam on the radio, though, I need to go to the bathroom. I'm not even going to ask what happened with respect to that sort of thing for the last few days. I don't want to know the gory details," she said, with an embarrassed hunch of her shoulders. Neil just laughed.

"You might want to avoid looking in the mirror for a couple of days, honey. I set your nose to the best of my ability while you were out, but there's a lot of bruising and still some swelling just from that. Never mind the giant knot on your forehead, or the tear in your scalp at the back of your head."

"If my looks were the least bit important to me, cowboy, I'd have spent my life in total misery," she replied in a snarky tone. "Guess I'll just have to muddle along without what little I normally have for the time being. Seeing as it's so vital out here in the middle of nowhere with most of the world already dead."

"I'm just trying to prepare you for the stranger you're going to see looking back at you," he said with a roll of his eyes. "Sheesh."

"I guess it's a good thing I lopped off most of my hair," she said with a groan, as she dragged herself out of the bed.

"Why's that?"

"Because my head already feels like it weighs a hundred pounds without it. God. We really should have gone with a motorboat instead. I could have done without an intimate acquaintance with the mast. 'Nobody wins with a head butt,'" she quoted.

"Is that what cracked your hard head? I was wondering. Figured it would take a large chunk of diamond to do that to you."

"Nice to see *your* sense of humour hasn't suffered from my head injury," Mac said grouchily. "Course, it's hard to take away something from nothing." Then she stuck her tongue out at him.

"You've aged a bit, I see," he teased.

"At least a whole year. I might actually act like a twelve-year-old at some point. Miracles do happen," she returned as she stepped through the bathroom door.

Her bladder was speaking rather urgently to her, so she decided to satisfy her curiosity about her wounds after she was done. The shock that dropped her jaw when she finally looked, however, in no way lessened the horror of her face.

"Well, fuck me sideways with a tuna fish!" A muffled chuckle told her Neil had been listening for her reaction. She washed her hands, but didn't even attempt to set her hair and face to rights. She needed a proper shower for the blood in her hair, and she wasn't up for that just yet. A quick sniff at her armpits suggested it was certainly time for one otherwise, but she already exhausted just from the quick trip to the bathroom.

"I heard Annette saying you used Superglue on my head," she said as she sidled past him in the very short hallway.

"Yeah. I wasn't into sports in a big way or anything, though I did a short football stint in high school just for the hell of it. We used Superglue for injuries a fair bit, just to keep ourselves in the game. It was either that or do the stitching myself, and I couldn't bring myself to do it."

"No, that's fine. I was just surprised you'd think of it. Not saying you're dumb. Most people wouldn't. Well, if I had to tear my scalp, at least it's in a place where the scar won't be visible to scare small children. I have better ways of doing that," she said.

"Scaring small children?"

"Yeah. Much more fun ways. Sadly there are so few children left to terrorize anymore, and Chuck won't let me at his," she said, pretending disappointment.

"Well, you can always hope Lisa will be more cooperative," he said with a bit of a laugh.

"Doubt it. For some reason parents are protective of their young. And speaking of parents and their young, I guess I'd better get this conversation over with. Besides, I'd like to know what's been going on at the farm."

"I would, too," Neil replied.

"What do you mean?"

"I mean, I've been a little panicked about other things for the last three days, so as long as Billy and Cam were talking to me, and nobody had died, I wasn't going to worry about it. Now we can find out together."

"Oh, okay. I thought maybe you thought something was wrong, and that they weren't telling you about it."

"Not that I'm aware of, but now we can grill them like a couple of fish and see what they have to say for themselves. Will that make you happy? I mean, they're not actual children anymore, so terrorizing them might not be as fun for you as, say, a four-year-old, but it should still give you a bit of a lift," he said, patting her on the shoulder.

"You know me so well."

10 ~ BLASTING THE PAST

"Mom, is that really you?" Cam knew it was a ridiculous question to be asking, but she'd been terrified over the last couple of days.

"Why is everyone asking me that? Yes, it's really me. There are no pods in the bottom of the boat, and I haven't suddenly developed a super-nice personality or anything. Sheesh!"

"Honey, two people have asked you that question. Two. That's hardly 'everyone,'" Cam heard Neil chastise. Her mother hadn't released the button on the mic.

"Fine, yes, it's me. I'm okay, alright? What all is going on there? And why are you forgetting how to use a damn radio? You're supposed to say, 'Over,' when you're finished talking, remember? Over."

"I'd think there are more important issues to worry about right now," Cam said with a giant eye-roll. When her mother refused to say anything in response, Cam swore and then sighed.

"Fine. Over," she said, exasperated. She couldn't resist asking, "Happy now? Over."

"You're still doing it wrong, and I'm still a cranky bitch, so no.

Anyway, what's going on at the farm? Over."

"We're fine here. We're not the ones getting tossed around on a boat, cracking our heads open, are we? Over." Cam figured her best defense at the moment was a good offense. She had no intention of telling her mother or Neil about the sensors going off every night. They had more than enough to worry about, and there wasn't anything they could do from that distance anyway, other than rush back.

"How are Pickle and Squeaker? They getting lonely? I hope you're spending some time with them. Over."

"I think they miss you, but I've got them in my room with me now. The idea of sleeping in your bed kind of creeped me out. I didn't want to have weird images of the freaky things you get up to with Neil bouncing around in my head while I was trying to sleep. They've been a little bit crazy in my room, though. Really excited with all the new stuff to explore and climb. Over."

"No doubt. Hopefully they're not getting stressed by that. Even happy things will stress them out, so be careful. Bring them back to our room when you're not in your own, so they have some familiarity while we're gone. There have been so many changes for them over the last seven or eight months. Over."

Cam subjected her ocular muscles to another workout, as her eyes rolled around in their respective sockets, but she told her mother that she would do as she asked. It was just easier to agree, and in truth she was almost as protective of the boys as her mother was. In the meantime, she had another topic she wanted to cover with her mother.

"I thought you said you were going to be careful, mom. This whole head injury thing doesn't qualify. Over."

"I was tied to the boat and my hair might have saved my life, so I think I did okay under the circumstances. Besides, Neil's the one who broke my nose. Over." The grouchy note in her mother's voice made her smile. It sounded like she was completely back to normal. But the information about her mother's nose made her frown again.

"Wait a minute. What do mean he broke your nose? Do I have to shoot him or something? Because I will. Over."

"He didn't punch me, for fuck's sake. He just forgot to secure the door at the top of the built-in ladder thingy, so when the boat lurched the door came back and hit me in the face. I still have all my teeth, but I don't think they're going to help much with my looks at this point. My face is a mess, and I'm not sure it'll ever look normal again. Over."

"Serves you right. Over."

"Look, miss bossy-pants, I've had enough of being lectured for one day. I'm going back to bed once I browbeat Neil into getting this boat moving. We should have been in Cleveland by now. Unless there's something specific at the farm you need to talk to me about, I need to get going. Over."

"No, mom. We're doing okay here. Go get some rest. Over."

After they said their goodbyes, Cam released the button on the mic with a sigh of relief. She'd gotten away with it. At least for now. The hardest part had been not snapping at her mother too much. Bitching about her safety was one thing, but if she'd shown just how tired she was, her mother would have known something was going on.

Only slightly less difficult had been convincing Gilles not to say anything, though in some ways she knew he agreed with what she was trying to do. If Neil and her mother came back to the farm to deal with the current situation, assuming it wasn't already dealt with by the time they got there, it would mean them turning around and attempting another trip to Cleveland. It would involve more risk, and it wasn't necessary. There wasn't a damn thing they could do that Cam, Billy, and everyone else on the farm weren't already doing, other than provide two more bodies for security detail.

She hadn't slept much, and Cam knew it showed in her temper, but at least no one was questioning her on the farm. She was careful to discuss things with Billy, because they needed to present a united front if they wanted to keep things under control, but for the most part she was the one looking after everything and making all the plans. Billy seemed content to let her run the show, and Cameron had a feeling Lisa had a lot to do with that.

Cam closed her eyes and took what her mother called cleansing breaths. In through the nose, and out through the mouth. After five of those, she felt more settled, and the possibility of getting some sleep didn't seem like such an unattainable dream now. Her mother appeared to have most of her brain back in gear, so that was one less thing to worry about. Billy was fully capable of keeping an eye on things if she crashed for a while.

Thankfully Billy was carrying a two-way, because she was too exhausted to hunt him down physically. It was bad enough the upper floor on this side of the house didn't connect to her bedroom on the other side. There was a sort of catwalk, but in her present state there was no way she was up to doing any sort of balancing act.

No. Two sets of stairs were in her immediate future. The circular ones that would take her down to the bedroom her mother shared with Neil, and the wide, straight set that led to her own room. She could sleep in the bedroom below, but Pickle and Squeaker were in her room, and she felt guilty about them being left alone so much lately.

Billy readily agreed to take over at the radio, and his relief at her mother's recovery made her smile. He was really a decent guy, she knew, and if he was content to be her friend or something like a little brother, they'd get along fine.

The fact that it was full daylight made it easier for her to relax anyway. The sensors only went off at night, so she didn't really think anything would happen while she was asleep. Eventually she managed both sets of stairs, and after snuggling both ferrets, she crawled into the cool softness of her sheets. Her last thought before dropping off had to do with how glad she was her mother had insisted on buying really good sheets. *Definitely worth it*, she agreed in her head.

℘ ♦ ℭ

"Cam, are you there? Come in Cam!" The crackled, staticky sound jolted her from her sleep. She pushed up on an elbow, and peered blearily around the room. The sound had grown fainter while she'd been struggling to pull herself from her dreams. Suddenly she understood why. Squeaker had grabbed the two-way's antenna in his teeth, and was making off with the radio to hide it in his newly created stash behind her dresser.

She wanted to smack her own forehead for not keeping it out of his reach. The rubber coating on the device had undoubtedly been a siren's song of temptation for the little guy. He was the reason every one of the drain plugs in the house were the mechanical kind that operated with a little plunger-type valve. He'd declared war on all things rubber at the moment of his birth, as far as Cam could tell.

"Squeaker! Now I have to move the damn dresser you little bugger. You can't have the radio." So saying, she angled the dresser away from the wall, and then had to engage in a brief tug-o'-war with the ferret.

"Mine, Squeaker. Not yours. Mine," she stated, and then shook her head at herself. She was trying to bargain with an animal that could not be bargained with, though she was pretty damn sure he understood everything she was saying. Ferrets were far from stupid, and her mother had always told her they were supposed to be smarter than cats or dogs. Considering their behaviour, that

169

wouldn't surprise her in the least.

Finally she managed to extricate the radio from the firm grip of Squeaker's teeth, and pressed the button to radio back to Gilles.

"I'm here. Sorry. Squeaker stole the radio so I had to get it back from him." Silence greeted her response, but then she heard a squelch and a bunch of laughter.

"Is that anything like, "The dog ate my homework,' Cam?"

"That would probably be easier to believe. You'd have to know ferrets to understand why this is true. Anyway, what's the problem?"

"We found someone near the driveway. He showed up on the cameras while Billy was keeping watch on the monitors, though he didn't set off any of the sensors. He says he knows you," Gilles finished.

"You're kidding me. What's his name?"

"He says his name is Mitch, and that he was married to your mom. I never met her second husband, and can't remember what his name was supposed to be, so you'll have to come out here to verify."

"Holy shit! Let me get dressed. I'll be down in a minute. If it's him, my mother is going to be so relieved. Be right down."

If she hadn't been forewarned that it was Mitch, she never would have recognized him. He had wasted away to almost nothing, and he'd been a pretty big guy. Muscular, with a bit of heft, too. Now his clothes were hanging off of him, and he looked near death.

"It's him," she said to Gilles. "It's okay." Then she turned to Mitch.

"First, food and something to drink. Then we can send you off for a shower and fresh clothes," she said to him. The relief on his face was immense.

"Thanks, Cam. I didn't think I was gonna make it here."

She led the way into the kitchen through the greenhouse at the back, and had him sit down at the counter's serving area that separated the kitchen from the area with the partially-assembled pool table.

"From things mom has said, if you've been starving I should probably give you something light to eat at first. Otherwise you might just throw it up. We've got some veggie soup that will do for now. It's got vegetables that are high in protein, so even though there's no meat in it, it should help."

She ladled out a small bowl and heated it up in the microwave. Serving him made her feel a bit funny, since Cam would normally have told him to get it himself, but even she wasn't that heartless. She didn't like him, and he'd been a dick to her mother as far as she was concerned, but now he needed help. Of course, it pissed her off that he was in this state in the first place, because her mother had made a couple of attempts to get him to the farm when things started to hit the fan. It was his own damn fault he'd ended up in this condition.

"How come that guy called you instead of your mom? Isn't she around?" Mitch's question raised her hackles, and she was leery of answering it, but there was no point in not doing so. He would hear the details later anyway.

"Mom will be back soon. They went to get Ian in Cleveland," she said shortly. The microwave beeped, so she pulled out his soup and put it on the counter in front of him.

"Oh, thank God," he said, and started spooning it up. He finally resorted to drinking it directly from the bowl, apparently unable to get it in his mouth fast enough. Not that she blamed him, but she was still a little disgusted. She knew it was because they didn't get along, though, rather than a disgust with his actual manners. Generally Cam just wasn't that picky.

"Too bad I couldn't get in touch with her. I could have used the lift. I didn't think anyone would still have a working vehicle," he finally said, once the bowl was empty.

"They didn't go that way. They took a boat. If they'd gone by truck, they could have been there and back in a day, but it was too risky to go through so many cities, not knowing what was happening in them," she said, and went back to the fridge for a loaf of bread and some butter.

"I can't give you a lot of bread, because grain is something we'll be short on for a while. We just brought in the winter wheat, but we need to make sure the chickens and all that are fed from it first. We've got other stuff we can eat, but you're still hungry and you need something a little bland right now. The butter is from goat's milk, but I don't think you'll taste much of a difference." She pushed the plate with the four slices of homemade bread toward him, along with the container of butter.

"You mean all this stuff is homemade?" His surprise made her laugh.

"Yeah, I know. Mom was never Suzy Homemaker, but if we weren't making the stuff ourselves, we'd have starved to death. We've got chickens for eggs, goats for milk and cheese, and then vegetables, mushrooms, that kind of thing. Our first garden wasn't that big. Just enough for a few of us, but we've got more than twenty people on the farm now, so we're stretched until we start harvesting from the bigger garden.

"And we're breeding chickens like crazy so we have eggs for the ferrets. Mom ended up rescuing fifty of them from three different shelters. You know what she's like with ferrets. Anyway, we've been weaning them from kibble onto the eggs, so we don't run out of food for them.

"I'll show you where the shower is, and find you some clean clothes. Did you bring anything with you? Spare clothes or anything?"

"Yeah, but that guy took my pack and said he had to go through it first," he complained.

"We're pretty strict about security right now. We'll get your clothes back and I'll show you where you can wash them. Chuck or Gilles will probably have something that you can wear in the meantime. If you're short on clothes we'll have to figure something out, because mom and Neil only got kids' stuff when they raided stores in Huntsville. We weren't expecting anyone else." Cam fell silent, part of her wishing she could tell him that her mother had written him off for dead, but she knew it was a shitty thing to say.

"Neil the new guy she hooked up with?"

"You mean married? Yes," she said, her tone turning snotty. She wanted him to be very aware that her mother was no longer available to be used by him.

"That was fast," he said with a derisive snort.

"Yes, it was. They got married five days after they met. And I've never seen her so happy," she gritted out between her teeth. When he was finished his food she led him out back.

"Here's the washer and dryer. We keep it here for a few reasons, but mostly so that everyone has access to it, and so we can wash clothing from the non-tested area of the ferret building. Anyone who comes in contact with those ferrets has to go through something similar to decontamination procedures, just in case one of them has ADV. It was a group that came from a shelter where we didn't get their vet records. We have to protect the other ferrets, including Pickle and Squeaker, so they're basically quarantined."

"I can't believe your mother did all this. Stupid," he jeered. Cam's temper hit the boiling point.

"And yet *we're* not the ones who were starving to death, and begging for a fucking meal. You're here only if Billy and I allow you to be, so you might want to be a little less cocky and judgmental about something you know nothing about."

"Oh, please," he said, and his condescending laugh was so

infuriating Cam wanted to slap him. "So, what? I just bow and call you, 'Your Highness,' or something? Give me a fucking break." He laughed again, and now the urge to sink her fist in his face was almost irresistible.

"You're standing on land I own, with your gut full of food the people on this farm have all helped to grow, myself included. I have no idea what my mother ever saw in you, and I don't think she's going to be anything but disgusted when she gets back. *You* will be very lucky to still be here at that time. You've got one chance. If you stay here you work, just like everyone else. You show me and Billy respect, and you treat everyone with dignity. If I hear that even one bigoted or racist remark has come from your fat mouth, you're gone, too. And believe me, I'm perfectly capable of personally making sure you leave. The last person I forced to leave had to be taken away in a body bag, so don't test me.

"I've hated your ever-fucking guts for as long as I've known you, and even now, when it's up to me whether or not you even get another meal here, you talk down to me and laugh at everything we've accomplished. I won't be bullied by an asshole like you. You'll do what you're told, or you're gone. For tonight you can sleep outside where everyone can keep an eye on you, and bathe in the river instead of getting a hot shower and another meal or two. Maybe you'll be a little nicer after that. I haven't forgotten the time you stole fifty bucks from me for a fix, when my mother and I were just scraping by. I'm not willing to turn you out to die just yet, but watch your step. We've got a couple dozen people here who would be just as happy to not have to share their food with you.

"And just so you don't get any stupid ideas, we're all armed. Believe me, my mother made damn good and sure I knew how to use my gun. Consider yourself lucky she's not here. If she *had* been, she might have shot you herself by now. She'd already gotten used to the notion that you were dead, after all, when you were too stupid to come here before." Cam took a few steps away, and spoke into her radio.

"Gilles, we need to talk about our new guest. Meet me at the house as soon as you can. It's important. And ask Chuck to keep an eye on him in the meantime."

"Yeah, okay. I was wondering about him. I'll take care of it."

"Thanks."

"Wait! Cam! What the hell did I do? I was just joking around." Just the sound of Mitch's voice had her clenching her jaw again, but she spun around and retraced her steps.

"You mean aside from stealing from me? Yeah, you're right. It *was* only fifty bucks, though it was still pretty contemptible. No, it was the fact that you were dealing drugs for some of the worst slime in the city, and then stole from them so they came after my mother. You put *her* fucking life at risk. She was a mother raising a kid, and you thought it was perfectly okay to let scum like that threaten her for forty grand here, another thirty grand there. She went so deep in debt to bail you out, so they didn't *kill* you, that we ended up getting evicted when we couldn't pay our rent anymore.

"Is that enough for you? No, you probably still think you're a stand-up guy, right? You were a spoiled, lazy, piece of shit, who was too good for a regular job, but you weren't too good to hang out with bikers and mob guys. You sucked my mother dry, and nearly destroyed her. She had nothing left to give after you split up, because she was just too fucking tired. Even the *thought* of a relationship made her gag.

"It took her a couple of years before she even considered dating, and by then she was too busy working her ass off so that between the two of us we could afford to buy this place you've just been laughing at so contemptuously, despite the fact that we got it through honest hard work. Everyone laughed at her for the dreams she had for this place. Everyone. Including you. Everyone told her it was paranoid, stupid, ridiculous, impossible.

"I watched every one of you hurt her almost non-stop, even if I only heard the phone conversation at our end. And she *still* took everyone in. The people on this farm, with the exception of Neil and his son, Billy, are alive because my mother was smart enough to plan for this. You knew who it was that warned her, and that he was in a position to know what would happen, yet you still laughed. So, fuck you if you want to laugh now, because you won't be staying here to do it.

"You've come back to use her, yet again, because you're incapable of looking after yourself and making smart choices. You're a heartless fuck who doesn't deserve to be here, so if you want to stay you'd better make damn good and sure you earn it from now on. And if you do one single thing to hurt or betray my mother, there isn't a force on this earth that will keep me from shooting you for it.

"Now wash your clothes and take a bath. You stink and we don't need lice and disease here," she said, disgust oozing through her voice, and when she turned away this time, she started walking and didn't look back. She kicked off her shoes and then slammed the door behind her as she walked into the quiet kitchen. She let the cold from the tile seep into her feet and soothe the heat of her anger.

"Cleansing breaths," she said aloud, reminding herself to chill out and calm down. It wasn't just anger flooding her system with adrenaline at the moment, either. Exhilaration and terror were fighting for second place. She'd been longing to say that stuff to Mitch from the time she'd been twelve years old. She remembered hiding in her bedroom, holding a knife while she listened to him scream like a lunatic at her mother. It seemed almost a miracle to her that he had never actually resorted to physical violence. At least not with her mother.

Instead he had stomped around in a temper tantrum, destroying everything they owned, so that her mother would once again have to work herself half to death to replace everything. She lost count of the number of times the cycle had repeated itself, but eventually her mother had completely lost any feeling for him. One night she had told him she'd had enough and she wanted him gone. He hadn't gone quietly, but at least he'd gone. Cam was only fifteen, and had already been contemplating murdering him in his sleep. Not that she would have been able to go through with it. As she had discovered, it was a lot harder to kill someone than she would have thought, but now that she had … well, if he became a threat she would do what had to be done.

"Okay, let it go. You've already said what needed to be said, so just breathe."

"Cam? You weren't talking to me, were you?"

Cameron laughed at the confusion on Lisa's face, and shook her head.

"No. Just talking to myself. A habit I picked up from my mom, I guess. We'll both hold entire conversations with ourselves, never mind just answering. We gave up on sanity a long time ago, I think."

Lisa snorted.

"You're not the only one. You should've seen me over the last few months. Of course, I could pretend I was talking to Jake, as though my sanity weren't in question, but since I was the one talking back I don't think the argument was a valid one."

"Not surprising. I can't imagine being stuck in town with a kid, hiding from a roving band of cannibals. You seem to have come out of it okay, but I wouldn't blame you if you were a little bit crazy. Sometimes you have to be to survive. Anyway, I need to go talk to Billy and Gilles for a bit, so I'll see you later." Then she paused. She needed to warn Lisa first.

"My mother's ex-husband just showed up here, after months of us thinking he was dead. They became friendly years ago, after my mom got over being pissed at him, but he's not someone that can be trusted. Not with anything. I started out trying to help him, but he got really rude so I lost my shit. He's not allowed in the house, or any other building. At least for tonight. I don't think he's physically dangerous, but he'll steal things, or try to get his hands on the drugs over at the ferret building. That kind of thing. Just thought I'd give you a heads-up."

"Oh, okay. Thanks for letting me know. I think I'll keep Jake inside for the rest of the day anyway. Billy showed me how to access all the movies and stuff, and I think Jake would enjoy watching some Disney," Lisa said tentatively, as though she expected Cam to say she wasn't allowed.

"Alright. I'll see you later probably. Have fun."

Her feet felt heavy as they took her up the circular stairs. Her hand gripped the railing the whole way up, as she pulled her sluggish body upwards. Gilles was waiting in the room when she got there. He must have come in the house through the front while she'd been laying into Mitch.

She was glad the ferrets were in her room for the time being, because she didn't like so many people tromping through her mother's bedroom to get to the monitors upstairs. It was too easy for a ferret to sneak out through a door, even when someone was used to them, let alone people like Gilles who probably wouldn't even notice them. The last thing she needed right now was another crisis, and losing one of the boys would kill her mother. Cam knew she'd never forgive herself either.

"Hey Billy. Gilles," she said, nodding wearily at them. "Like I said to you a few minutes ago, Mitch isn't someone we can trust. My mother might care what happens to him, but she knows what he's like. She wouldn't allow him to put other people on the farm at risk. He's selfish, careless, thoughtless, inconsiderate, dishonest, and lazy. He's a former, and perhaps current, junkie, liar, and thief. He used to hang out with bikers and mob guys, but only because he's a total loser, not because he likes killing people.

"I can't stand a single molecule of him. I gave him a small meal to keep him from getting sick, and took him out back to show him the washer and dryer. Then he got rude, like he was planning to sit around here for a free ride and do whatever the fuck he wanted, and laugh about it. Seems to think he can live off the hard work of others his whole life. I told him he'd either work or he'd leave, and if necessary I would shoot him so he left the hard way. I made sure he knew we were all armed, too."

"Cam, you're too soft. You've got to open up a little and tell us what you really think," Billy said with a smile, making Gilles laugh.

"So, what are we doing with him then?" Gilles asked.

"I told him to sleep outside and to make sure he bathed in the river. I did say I'd see if there were any clean clothes around here for him, though that's more for our benefit than his. He's filthy, and I don't want to see him walking around naked. It would scare the crap out of me, never mind the kids. We'll need to find out if he's the one who's been setting off the sensors, but I'm too mad to go near him right now. And we'll need to watch him."

11 ~ KEEL-HAULED

The loud scraping and crunching noise sent fear searing up her spine. Obviously they'd bottomed out, which couldn't be a good thing. Despite Neil's earlier demand that she remain in bed while he got them the rest of the way to Cleveland, Mac bolted from the bed and struggled up the steps to the cabin.

"What happened? Are we okay?"

"Mac! You're supposed to be resting," he scolded.

"You're kidding me, right? You give every appearance of sinking the boat, and I should just lie around in bed with my smelling salts?"

"Okay, well, maybe not, but I don't think we're sinking. We just scraped a sandbar. Probably sounded worse than it is," he said soothingly.

"I sure hope so, because from where I was sitting I figured there had to be at least an iceberg involved. Then the rich people would all have to leave while the orchestra played on deck to calm the peons," she returned, still shaking a bit, and not entirely convinced everything was okay.

"Well, the world such as it is these days, we'd probably be considered pretty damn wealthy right now, so I think we'll be okay."

"You know, I could still sell off the family jewels. You won't think you're so wealthy then, will you?" Then she had to laugh as he cringed. Worked with every male she'd ever encountered. They all made the same face, even when it wasn't their own balls that were threatened. Mac remembered watching *Commando* in a room full of guys, way back in her early teens. The scene where Arnie used an axe on another guy's nether regions had had every single guy in the room groaning, and nothing had changed since. Apparently not even her husband was immune.

The scraping and grinding hadn't lasted long, but it had her concerned all the same. Neil might not think it was a big deal, but from what she'd been reading about boats, the keel was vital. If it was destroyed, they might as well say goodbye to the boat and set off in the dinghy.

"Neil, I think we need to check and make sure nothing is wrong under there. Switch over to the diesel for a few minutes, and then shut down the engines. I'll get ready for a quick dive." Before she'd even finished speaking, Neil was shaking his head.

"No way. You're still recovering from a head injury," he began.

"And you've never gone diving," she interrupted. "Not to mention the fact that you're perfectly capable of hauling me up out of the water if something goes wrong, whereas the reverse wouldn't likely be possible. Maybe under normal circumstances, and with adrenaline to help me, I could, but my muscles are shaky right now. This is easy stuff for me, okay?"

"You took a damned introductory course. You said so yourself. You don't have enough time or dives logged to be certified. Whichever it is they use for that."

"I did three out of four open water dives, though, so I know what I'm getting into. It was on Lake Ontario, rather than just some small town lake, so Lake Erie won't be a stretch. You don't know how to use the equipment, and me muttering a few instructions to you won't be any help if you find yourself in any sort of emergency situation. It's too likely you won't remember what to do.

"Not that I'll be going more than a few feet under, but you can get hooked by things, or smack a valve on something. Kelp, or whatever else might grow in the water here, can tangle you up. There are just too many variables for three minutes of instruction, okay? We'll hang a guide rope from one side to the other. We can let it go under the hull, and tie it off on both sides. I'll even let you tie a rope to me, and I can use that for a signal if necessary. Now stop arguing with me and let's get this done so we can get to Edgewater Park when we said we would. It's too late to contact Ian now, to tell him there's been a delay."

Neil apparently couldn't summon any additional arguments, but his jaw was rigid. She knew he didn't like it, and felt like he needed to protect her, if for no other reason than the fact that she was already injured. Mac couldn't say anything else to make him feel better, so she headed to the back of the boat and started getting ready. She was duct-taping her knife to her calf, when Neil's voice startled her.

"What the hell do you need a knife for down there?"

"See? This is exactly the kind of thing that would get you in trouble. A knife is vital. And generally speaking you should have everything in redundancies. Spare regulator, spare dive light, et cetera. This isn't considered a dangerous type of diving, like wreck or cave diving, but you still have to have proper equipment. A KA-BAR isn't a dive knife, obviously, which you would know better than I. It's kind of overkill, but I don't have a dive knife. If I get tangled in something, which is the most likely danger for me in shallow waters like this, I have to be able to cut myself free. Kelp and seaweed may not look very strong, but don't let appearances deceive you. There's no way in hell I'm getting killed by a fucking plant."

"Alright, you made your point. You ready to go then?"

"Almost. Just some last-minute checks to do on the equipment," she replied.

"Is there a list or something?"

"Yup. Thankfully I won't need a dive computer or tables, because I won't be diving deep enough or long enough to have to calculate decompression or anything. That makes things a lot easier, but I still feel funny going under without them. Being tied off means I can't get pulled away by an undertow, but I don't like not having everything on me. Say hello to life after the end of the world as we know it," she said with a shrug.

"Great. Thanks. Now you have that song stuck in my head, and I never particularly liked it," Neil said sardonically.

"Well, try to pay more attention to what we're doing than to your earworm, so we can get this done safely. Now, loop this rope once around one of the cleats, so it's loose enough for me to move around, but will take some of my weight if you need to reel me in. Great. I'm a fish. Call me Flounder." Even Mac couldn't resist making wisecracks, though. It was in her nature.

She went down her mental safety list. Once she was done checking both regulators, breathing deeply from each, made sure the dive lights were working and would be bright enough, and was certain nothing on her person was flapping around unnecessarily that might get caught on something, she sat on the low back rail of the boat and put on her fins. Then she tied one end of the rope Neil would be holding to a strap on her buoyancy compensator vest, leaving a long tail that she wrapped around her waist and tied again, making sure her weight belt wasn't caught up in it, just in case she needed to drop it for some reason.

Mac knew she was being overly cautious, but Neil was right about her head injury. If something went wrong, and for some reason she wasn't conscious, the rope needed to be secured to her body and not just equipment that could come off. It wasn't likely it would, but she had the damndest luck with injuries. Being a total klutz didn't help matters, and her general state of impatience put her at risk more often than not, because her body just couldn't keep up with what she usually tried to make it do. Her brain was often twenty steps ahead of her feet.

"Righty-tighty, lefty-loosey," she said once she was ready.

"What?"

"Nothing, sorry. It's kind of my way of saying 'Right-o,' or, 'A-okay,' or something. I'm surprised you've never heard me say it before, but maybe I don't talk to myself around you as much as I do when I'm by myself."

"Probably a good thing. Bad enough to be ignored, but to have you prefer to talk to yourself than to me, I think I might take offense," he said.

"I doubt it. If you haven't been mortally offended by me by now, I doubt there's much I can say to put you off. Alright. Let's get this show on the road." With that she popped in her main regulator, waved at him, and slipped backward off the boat and into the water a couple of feet below. She would have laughed at him instinctively grabbing for her if she'd been able, but the device in her mouth made that difficult, and she was also mentally cursing the pain at the back of her head from her still-healing scalp. Mac popped her head out of the water and pulled the regulator from her mouth.

"What were you trying to do? Save me from drowning? How the hell did you think I was getting into the water?" Then she laughed at his sheepish expression.

"Damned if I know, but yeah, it was kind of stupid. Just reflex, I guess. You see someone falling off a boat, you grab for them," he replied.

"Alright, loop the rope so you don't lose me to the five foot abyss here," she said sarcastically.

"Very funny," he said, but complied all the same. "You know, you look kinda goofy with that mask on. Does weird things to your face."

"Like my face isn't already weird and distorted right now. I'll be back in less than ten minutes, probably. I'm going to take my time and check everything." Mac stuck the regulator back in her mouth, and adjusted the air in her vest. Then she flipped over into the strangely noisy peace of the lake, where she was deaf to the world outside the water, but overly aware of the sound of air passing through her regulator, and the bubbles that escaped when it flowed in the other direction.

As she inhaled, the pressure from the tank gently pushed air into her lungs. Not forcefully, but enough that her lungs expanded in her chest more quickly than usual. Exhaling felt different underwater, too. Slightly more difficult, because she had to breathe against the valve trying to release air. One of the best things about diving, aside from the serenity, was the purity of the air she inhaled. She always felt so good after she got out. If they could scavenge a compressor from a dive shop, she could have some fun messing around in rivers and lakes, she thought, but rolled her eyes behind the mask. She needed to start paying attention.

They were pretty far from the sandbar that had scraped at the keel, so at least there was no silt or sand stirred up to impede visibility. It was dark under the boat, though, which meant Mac had to turn on her light. Then, with a shrug made awkward by her diving equipment, she turned on the second light she'd brought with her. Now she was grateful for the redundancy, because she wanted to be sure she didn't miss anything.

Air hissed and burbled as she used her fins to propel herself down to the bottom of the keel. The manual had said the boat had a maximum draft of just under five feet, which meant they couldn't go into waters shallower than that without running the risk of serious damage. Running aground would likely mean using the dinghy for the rest of their journey, just the same as catastrophic damage to the boat would.

From what she could see, there was nothing worse than scraped paint to mar the keel. Not that she thought the owners would be happy about that, should they be alive to complain. Still, that sort of damage wouldn't cause them any problems on this particular journey. Mac ran the light over the entire keel, front to back, and bottom to top. It wasn't until she got to the front, right where the keel curved down from the hull, that she saw anything to concern her.

Just barely visible, a line, possibly a crack, ran back about six inches from the front, on both sides. She would need to keep an eye on this. To conserve what oxygen she could, for future forays into the water to check the hull, Mac decided to return to the surface. She had already been submerged pretty close to the ten minutes she had planned on taking.

"Well, you broke the damn boat, Neil," she accused as soon as she spit out the regulator.

"Seriously?"

"Actually, I don't know what you've done. There's visible damage, but it might not cause us any problems. I just don't know. We'll have to keep checking it. Here. Take these," she said, and tossed her fins up to him so she could climb back into the boat without them getting in her way. She heard him curse as they slapped him in the chest, probably soaking his shirt. She reached up and waited for Neil's hand, placing her foot on a small rail. Neil mostly hauled her up over the back railing, though.

"Okay, explain what you meant," he said, after giving her damp mouth a relieved kiss. Then he stripped off his sodden t-shirt, giving her an idea. She grinned wickedly.

"Nope. Not until you explain the tattoo," she bargained. She'd been trying, on and off, since he'd been shot, to nag the details out of him, but he wouldn't give them up. He had a compass rose covering part of a shoulder blade. Thankfully it hadn't been damaged by the bullet that had punched through his lung, because she actually really liked it.

"You're kidding me, right? You realize you can't win that argument, I hope. Every time you try we end up in bed together," he reminded her. Her shoulders slumped.

"Damn it. Fine. There's a really fine crack, but I can't tell if it's serious. It's fibreglass, so I don't know what it will do. There's no force on it right now, because it's not travelling forward. Then again, maybe it was already there and it's a normal thing. I doubt it, but it's a possibility I suppose. Whatever it is, I won't feel comfortable unless we're keeping an eye on it, and by that I mean me. I can show it to you next time I go down to look at it, though.

"We should go into the lowest part of the boat and lift up all those panels in the floor. Make sure there's no water inside. I have no idea if that's possible, either, but I'm still going to check all that on a regular basis. If I use the tanks to check the hull, I'm only going to have enough air to check it a few times. So I'm thinking I'll space out the more thorough checks, and then occasionally free-dive to take a look at it with just the mask on. I can hold my breath long enough for that, no problem," she finished.

"It's too bad we don't have an underwater camera. It would make things a lot easier."

"Damn. I knew I was forgetting something. Should have ordered one from Amazon," she said, her sarcasm apparently annoying enough that Neil gave her a dirty look.

"You're hysterical. I was just thinking that maybe the owners might have left one on board somewhere. It wouldn't surprise me. Makes sense if you're on the water enough to own a boat like this. From the little I know about boats, even a used one would probably go for a hundred grand, at least. Even double that. We haven't really gone through their things, so maybe we'll find something."

"I suppose. Just feels weird to do that. I know we stole their boat and everything, but invading their privacy just makes it seem worse. The stuff in the cabin was different. It was all related to the boat itself, and provided some valuable information. Their other stuff is more personal." She held up her hand to stop him from chiding her.

"I know they're probably dead. Maybe some part of me is still in denial that this is all really happening, which is completely ridiculous. Not spending much time off the farm hasn't helped. We haven't seen much emptiness that would provide evidence of most of the world's passing. Even when we went scavenging, we saw people living fairly close to us. That makes me think we might recover. And maybe someone who is still alive is the owner of this boat, and has a right to their privacy."

"Okay, honey. If you want to stay out of their stuff, I understand. We can take turns doing quick checks underwater. It's only for another week, barring further complications."

"It could very well take us longer than that to get back. We're operating under engine power, sure. We made sure we had enough oil to get us here and back, so thankfully we won't have to rely on the current. However, the trip south was the easy route," she said.

"In what way?"

"We've been going with the current. We'll be going against it on the way back, though there are apparently some eddies on the Canadian side of the two big rivers. The current reverses there, but I don't want to risk going too close to shore. Especially now. Shallow waters aren't our friend anymore," she said, eyeing him balefully.

"Yeah, yeah. I broke the ship. I broke the bloody ship," he mimicked in a terrible attempt at a British accent. She recognized the paraphrased line from *Galaxy Quest*, and laughed.

"That you did, cowboy. And we have no replacement beryllium spheres on board. Guess we'll have to find another planet that might have some. Or maybe Ian will be carrying one. But speaking of Ian, I think we'd better get this broken ship moving. He left about five hours ago, which gives us three to get there if we don't want to leave him exposed. God only knows what things are like in Cleveland."

"I'm sure he'll be fine, honey. Worry and fret; that's all you ever seem to do. Well, when you're not rescuing those macho men in distress," he said.

"It's obviously not that he can't protect himself, generally speaking. It's just possible he could be outnumbered if there's someone alive who thinks he has something they could use. He planned to carry at least one handgun, though, so violence isn't likely to be something he can't deal with.

"It's more the health issue. He's got insulin with him, but he may have burned too many calories. He won't know if his sugar has dropped until he starts feeling the symptoms, because he doesn't have any test strips left. So, yes, I'm worried. That's why I brought candy bars, granola bars, some milk that's still frozen, and one of the last remaining cans of frozen orange juice. We might have to get his sugar back up really fast if he's low. I've seen diabetics bottom out, and it's fucking scary. Not to mention potentially fatal. Besides, if I wasn't worried about him, I wouldn't have made this damn trip in the first place, ruining my great good looks just for his benefit," she said with a grin.

      ❧   ◆   ☙

The worrying and fretting were all for naught. They made it to Cleveland with half an hour to spare, so Neil took the boat in toward the yacht club area very slowly, Mac at the front of the boat to make sure the waters weren't too shallow. As they approached Edgewater Park, however, Mac shook her head and called out for Neil to stop. She walked awkwardly on the slanted deck until she was able to lower herself and go into the cabin.

"Too shallow?"

"I think so, yeah. I'm looking at the boats they have docked over there at what I assume is the yacht club, and they don't seem very big. I can't really tell exactly how deep the water is, either. No point taking chances when we've got the dinghy. Probably be safer to row ourselves in, too, rather than make noise with the motor. We'll still be able to see if someone gets a little too curious and tries to board her."

They had to unload everything from the dinghy first, because they had made sure it held all their vital stuff in case the boat sank for some reason. Now they didn't want the extra weight, and wanted more room for three people. Otherwise Ian would have to squeeze in. In addition to a small quantity of insulin, and a syringe,

Mac made sure she had everything she needed to bring his sugar up, too.

Once they had lowered the dinghy into the water, and climbed down into it, it wasn't long before they had managed to row themselves to the shore on the east side of what looked like a long pile of giant, asymmetrical stone cubes jutting into the water from the beach. They pulled the dinghy out of the water, but kept it as close to the cubes as possible. They were hoping no one would notice the new addition to the area. Late afternoon gave the place some pretty deep shadows, which Mac knew would help. Ian was supposed to meet them just east of the beach, but from where they were they couldn't see him.

"That looks like the willow tree he mentioned, where those other big cubes are sitting. Are they supposed to be a retaining wall maybe? I kind of want to call this thing here a breakwater, though I'm not sure if it's the right word for it. It's not a dock, that's for sure, but those cubes can't be a natural phenomenon," she said hesitantly. She didn't like not knowing what she was talking about.

"You're probably right. It seems like it would be the right word for it, anyway. That other long thing sticking out on the other side of the willow looks like a pier. It's too far above the water to be a dock," he said, pointing further east toward the yacht club. "And those concrete things sticking out in the middle of the water would be pretty dangerous for boats."

"Not that it matters much anymore. The whole world has gone to shit, and I'm sitting here worried about what someone called a pile of rocks," she said, laughing at herself. Neil gave a soft chuckle.

"Well, we can have fun debating it some other time. Why don't we go find your friend, so we can get our asses back home some time before summer kicks in."

"Hey! This is my first time in Cleveland. Give me ten minutes to look around, would you?"

"Does *Wet Foot, Dry Foot* apply, do you think?"

"Hardly matters since I have no intention of becoming an American citizen. Assuming there is such a thing anymore. Be kind of interesting to see what the Peace Bridge looks like in Niagara Falls now, though. If there's any sort of government left at all, I doubt patrolling the border is a big priority. Though the GPS was still working on the boat, so that could mean the US Army is still maintaining the ground stations, but that's not a for sure either," she said.

"In what way?"

"Well, from what little I know about how it works, the ground centres have to adjust the clocks on the satellites to match real-time on the planet, and then there's the orbits. I guess they don't stay the same all the time and have to be reset to new location information, and until they're reset they're marked as bad data so the receivers don't use the information for navigation. I didn't quite understand it as I was reading it, but it told me enough that I knew GPS would eventually become unreliable without the ground stations. Still, I figured it was worth having a receiver anyway. It's probably going to be the last thing the US military will allow to fall apart, if there's any kind of organizational structure left."

"That actually sounds hopeful," Neil said.

"How's that?"

"Well, it makes me think that the armed forces would prioritize their needs, such as food, clean water, defense, navigation, and maybe power. I guess I just think they probably made sure right from the start that they had a plan to keep themselves going. They would be thinking of stuff like protecting the ground stations, and how many MREs they had left. It's possible that the vast majority of civilians were fucked, but there may still be a lot of people who used to be military."

"Maybe. Neither of us knows anyone we can talk to on the radio who's still in a major city, so we can't get any hard information. Which, of course, is what makes this little jaunt a lot more dangerous than we've been treating it thus far, so I guess we'd better keep our heads in the game. You were right. Let's get Ian, and get the hell out of here."

By unspoken agreement they had both brought their handguns with them. Not knowing if there were humans left alive in the city, or how desperate they might be, they weren't going anywhere on shore without weapons. Neil's was a Sig Sauer 1911 Stainless Super Target. It wasn't her weapon of choice, but they'd hardly gone shopping for it. It had come from a bunch of wannabe thugs who had taken advantage of the early chaos from the collapse of the power grid. Neil had kept it simply because he didn't already have a handgun. Mac had already owned the Gen 4 Glock 22 she now carried.

Of course, they both carried proper survival knives, too. She had purchased her KA-BAR Becker 22 from Neil, in fact, which was how they had met. It had saved her life a few times since then, so she was even more fond of it than she was of knives in general, and that was saying quite a bit. Neil carried a Cold Steel Leatherneck SF, but she only knew the model because it was stamped on the blade. Not that they had a shortage of knives, since Mac and Billy had emptied Neil's store of its stock shortly after Neil had been shot. Everyone on the farm had taken a knife from that stock, and there were still plenty to go around.

They were quiet as they walked along the sand toward the elevated rocky area, and kept their eyes peeled for any movement. It wasn't until they were a few feet away from the willow tree that they heard a whining sound. Mac was instantly alarmed, and ran to the other side as she pulled out her gun.

Ian was lying on the ground, with his German Shepherd, Bella, lying there with him, alternating between nosing his rib cage and turning her head to lick his face. Mac holstered her gun and dropped to her knees on Ian's other side.

"Ian? Can you hear me?"

His hazel eyes snapped open, but he seemed to have a hard time trying to form words, so Mac shook her head.

"Just tell me. Is it high or low?"

"Low," he whispered.

"Kinda figured. Neil, can you help him sit up a bit? His muscles are going to be useless at the moment if he's this bad. Here, Ian. I've got some orange juice for you. We'll get that into you first," she said, as she tilted the spout of the plastic bottle until the juice started running into his mouth.

"Hang on. This isn't coming out fast enough. You're conscious, so you can swallow it fine. Let me get the lid off."

She managed to get the entire litre of orange juice into him, and after a few minutes he started coming around a bit. As the extreme lethargy dissipated, she noticed that he was shaking. He still had some way to go before he was back to normal, so she handed him a candy bar.

"We've got milk on the boat, but I wasn't sure if it would keep if we had to wait for you, so we're keeping that for later."

"Okay, thanks. Fuck, I hate that feeling," Ian said. She could still see the sweat on his face, and knew it must have been a bad episode.

"Well, you should be feeling better soon. Did you bring food with you or anything?"

"Not much. Fish don't keep well in a backpack, and what I did have I had to share with Bella. She has to eat what I do, now that the kibble is gone. We ate a good meal before we left, and had one on the road, but I burned up a lot of energy coming here."

Ian's blood sugar was finally back up enough that he could eat one of the granola bars to sustain him, though he gave the second one to his dog. It wasn't very good for her, Mac figured, but desperate times called for desperate measures, and Bella needed to eat.

It was another twenty minutes before Ian was okay to head back to the dinghy with them, but as they were standing up to go Neil suddenly went rigid. Mac swung around, her gun back in her hand without her even having to think about it.

12 ~ A JAILBIRD IN HAND

"So how did he get here? And if he wasn't the one setting off the sensors, who the hell is?" Cam's questions had both Chuck and Gilles shrugging. Unsurprisingly, it was Gilles who chose to answer.

"He came on a bicycle and used the directions your mom gave him last August, which included coordinates. He has a GPS, but he followed the road to get to the driveway. I guess your mother described the concealed entry well enough that he knew what he was looking at, but didn't know how to get in. Since he knew she had cameras, he just waited for someone to see him, basically."

"That doesn't solve our other problem, though. Since it's the same group of sensors going off every time, I think maybe we'll have to put at least two people in that area until the person is caught, rather than spreading them out to walk the whole perimeter. I'd really like to know why they aren't showing up on camera, though. We've got stuff missing, and we can't afford to allow that. Whoever this is, they know we're here, and if they were a decent person just trying to survive, I think they would have introduced themselves by now," Chuck said, speaking for the first time since they had gathered to discuss Mitch.

"I agree," put in Billy.

"I've had a thought about the cameras, Cam," said Gilles.

"What's that?"

"I think maybe he saw them and changed the direction they were facing. I mean, does any of us know off by heart exactly what tree configuration every camera was pointing at? Would we notice if it was changed, if we didn't see it while it was being moved? He may not have seen the sensors, which would explain why they're still picking up the intrusion. If we hadn't done a basic inventory and found we were missing stuff, I would have thought maybe it was just a sensor malfunction, but no one here has any reason to take anything and lie about it. We're all well-fed, and nobody is getting anything that the rest of us aren't getting," Gilles finished.

"That makes sense. He could have changed the angle, or even moved a camera or two to completely different trees. There's only one way for us to find out. Mom got maps from the Land Registry Office in Parry Sound, right before all the power grids went down. She made a bunch of copies of our land while she was there. She didn't make copies of Neil's at that time, because she didn't know then that she would need them, but she scanned them in to the server and printed out letter-size copies later. Every single camera is marked on those maps, including the ones that you did right before they left for Cleveland. We'll have to take the maps and visually confirm each camera. At least the ones in that area."

Four sets of shoulders slumped at the thought of all the walking they were going to have to do. Not one of them had had a full night's sleep since the first sensor had gone off. Despite the fact that they knew it was necessary for their own safety, they were all exhausted.

Cam was really worried, but nowhere near as worried as Chuck. He had three kids to think about, and they had no idea whether or not the thief was a physical threat. Cameron was going to assume they were all in danger, until she knew for certain they were safe. The problem was, there was no way they could be effective if none of them were sleeping. Of course, so far Cam was the only female who was involved in dealing with the problem, and that was going to have to change.

"Gilles, we're tired. Every one of us, including Kirk, John, and Jim. It would be nice if my dad was here to help, but I haven't seen him. He keeps disappearing into the bush. We need more people involved in this. Chuck's wife is already busy with the kids, and Kelly and Annette have their hands full with the animals, but there are seven other people who could at least be watching the monitors while we all get some sleep. If I'm capable of walking a perimeter, they're capable of watching a screen. They're not stupid just because they're female," she said.

"I never said they were," Gilles said in surprise.

"Why the hell aren't we asking them to help, then?"

"I have no idea. It's weird. It never occurred to me for some reason."

"Some outdated sense of chivalry or chauvinism would be my guess, but now that you've been made aware of it, we need to get them organized so they can help. You can talk to Melanie and Felicia when you go to your cabin. We'll set up a monitoring schedule that doesn't conflict with anyone's chore day, and this way, even if this problem goes on for weeks, we'll all still be allowed to sleep and take a day off once in a while.

"For that matter, having seven extra people will mean they can each take a night for monitoring. Those of us who have been doing so-called guard duty can switch off every other night. There's seven of us doing that, too, so four one night and three on another would mean we've still got enough bodies actually out there."

With the help of the other three, Cam had a good schedule worked out a short while later, and she could see that the others were relieved to know they would soon be getting a decent amount of rest. Between the sensors and the worry over her mother while she'd been out of it from her head wound, Cam was tapped out. Mitch had shown up at the wrong time to test her, though it appeared he'd been respectful and cautious since she'd gone off on him. For his second night on the farm she had caved and given him the tent and air mattress they no longer had a need for, along with a sleeping bag for warmth. He hadn't made any snide remarks, instead muttering a thank you before going off to set up his new temporary home.

They had already decided that he would be shown how to do chores by Gilles the next morning. He'd had three days to get some rest and sate his hunger, so it was as good a time as any for him to start earning his keep. If he wanted a cabin later, they would help him, but he would have to build it right alongside them. He was a freeloader by nature, and Cam had been sick of it long before he'd ever come to the farm.

They broke up their informal meeting, but Gilles remained behind after Billy and Chuck had traipsed down the stairs. Cam looked up from the map she was marking, when he cleared his throat.

"What's up?"

"I just wanted to say that I'm not the asshole you seem to think I am."

"I never called you one. If I thought you were, I would have. I'm not shy when it comes to that," she said with a self-deprecating grin. Gilles laughed.

"No, you're not. You're pretty good at speaking your mind."

"Mitch I called an asshole. At least I think I did. You just tend to take charge of things, and I'm not the type of person who likes someone trying to take charge of me."

"Don't blame ya. I just wanted to say that I think you're doing a decent job. I didn't expect that you would, but I was wrong. After you went off on your own and ran into Brian, I didn't think you could handle things after your mother left. It gave me a bad impression, so I didn't really give you a chance," he said.

"Well, thanks, but the problem hasn't been solved, so don't congratulate me just yet," she responded, though inside she was glowing with pride at his compliment just the same. Cam still didn't feel like she knew what she was doing, but she couldn't let him see that.

"I think we'll have him soon, whoever it is. This isn't a giant ranch here with thousands of acres. There's only so many places the person can go, and with a couple of us concentrated in that area, like you said, it's unlikely he'll keep getting past us." He tipped his cap at her and left.

Gilles' words proved prophetic. They managed to catch the culprit that same night. When they found a camera that had been moved from its original location, Chuck and Jim climbed a couple of trees and watched the area that the camera's lens could no longer pick up.

The radio woke Cameron once again out of a deep and exhausted sleep. To keep it out of Squeaker's greedy paws, she had put it in the drawer of her nightstand after cranking up the volume so she could still hear it. As much as she groaned about being jarred out of the best sleep she'd had in months, she was extremely relieved when she realized it would mean she would be able to go back to sleep without worrying anymore.

"I'm on my way. Wait. Where am I on my way to? Where do you have him?" She was still a little sleep-muddled, she realized.

"We brought him into the central yard between the two big buildings. We didn't figure there was any point keeping him out, since he's already been in here to steal," Jim said.

"True. Be right down." Two minutes later Cam was in the yard, facing a man she couldn't quite place. She knew him, somehow, but beyond that she couldn't remember.

"I assume you followed him to find out how he was getting through the inner sensors without getting picked up," she said to Jim.

"Yup. I don't think he even knew they were there. It's just how the sensors are positioned. There's a tree on the ground right there that he was climbing over, so he never tripped them. We'll have to move the tree," he concluded. Cameron nodded.

"I'll make sure that's taken care of tomorrow. I think I'll walk both perimeters and check that none of the other sensors are in a position like that. I doubt it, because my mother is pretty careful about stuff like that. I can't believe she would make that kind of mistake in the first place. It's not like her."

"Actually, I don't think she did. The break looked fresh. The tree was probably still standing when she put them in place."

"Okay, that makes sense. Anyway, now that we've found our intruder, all we need to do is keep an eye on him. You can call in the others so everyone can get some sleep. I'm going back to bed. You can decide between you who watches him for how long, so long as he's kept under guard. Give him food and water for now. Once we've all slept enough that we can think, we'll talk about what to do with him."

Their thief hadn't spoken during the entire exchange, but had glanced back and forth between Cam and Jim as they spoke. Now he finally opened his mouth.

"I was here before. You don't remember me kid? I sure remember you," he leered. Cam narrowed her eyes. That leer didn't bode well for his future, she decided. He was not only a thief, he was a creep, too.

"Shut up," she said, and walked away. She would figure out where she knew him from later. Right now she was just too tired.

Minutes later, Cam was lying between Egyptian cotton sheets with both ferrets climbing all over her. And she was perfectly okay with that.

𝕭 ◆ 𝕮

"I think we'd all like to know how you wound up back here, Mike," Cameron said to the thief. She had been in the shower when she had finally placed him. He had been at the farm with his wife, Lianne Langston, in a van full of ferrets from the shelter in Ottawa.

She was pretty sure twenty-eight of the fifty ferrets her mother had taken in, or brought home herself, were from that shelter. And she remembered something else, too. She remembered being relieved that they hadn't planned on staying, because this guy had been drunk and he had leered at her and Leigh even then. No, this guy was *not* going to be staying on the farm, whatever she had to do to make sure of it. For now, though, they would see what he had to say for himself.

"Well, see, it's like this. Lianne and me weren't getting on so

209

good. We were supposed to stay with her parents on their farm, and they never liked me. First time something bad happened, I got the blame for it. Her dad ran me off with a shotgun, saying if I came back he'd use it."

Cameron could easily believe what he said was truth, as far as it went, but it was an awfully short story for about seven months' worth of events.

"What was it they blamed you for?" Gilles asked from beside her.

"Accused me of nasty stuff with my wife's niece, and I never touched her," Mike responded.

"I'm sure they had good reason to think you had," Cam said in disgust. "You don't exactly act like an innocent man. You hit on me the last time you were here, right in front of your wife, and did the same with a friend of mine. You were drunk then, but it doesn't look like you're any better when you're sober.

"You fucked with our security camera so you could get in and out without being seen, and you stole our food. And even now that we've caught you, you're trying to act like you haven't done anything wrong. You could have come to the house and asked for food the honest way, but you chose to steal it instead, which tells me you're not the kind of person we want around here."

"Well, I doubt very much it's up to you, little girl," he sneered.

"And that would be where you're wrong, asshole," Gilles said. "She and Billy run this place, and if one of them says you're gone, then you're gone. One way or another."

Cameron felt a huge wave of relief that Gilles was backing her this way, but then she figured he would. There was no way he would want this lecherous piece of shit anywhere near his family, and of course Chuck had a teenage daughter to worry about, so she knew his silence meant consent. Nobody really knew this Mike guy, or anything about him, beyond the fact that he'd been married to someone who ran a ferret shelter.

The problem she was having had nothing to do with whether or not to get rid of him. She already knew they couldn't let him remain on the farm. The problem was that she didn't know *how* to get rid of him. He hadn't done anything that deserved a death sentence, so killing him, or kicking him off the farm without a way to survive, weren't choices she could justify. Not even in her own mind. Well everyone else had a brain, too, so she decided to take advantage of that.

"Gilles, Chuck, Billy, I think we need to discuss what we're going to do with this guy. He's a bit of a complication, and I'd like to hear your opinions, so why don't we leave him under guard with John for now, and go talk about it," she said. Mike immediately started toward her, though she never found out his intentions. John swung his rifle up before Mike had even gone two steps, the barrel jamming into Mike's forehead.

"I wouldn't, if I were you. You'd be making things so much simpler for us if you gave me a reason to shoot you," he said. Cam gave an evil smile.

"Thanks, John. Yes, that's definitely an option, Mike, so you might want to relax and behave yourself. I don't *think* any of us are going to suggest killing you outright, but you never know. Your first, second, and now third, impressions haven't gone so well." She turned and headed straight back to the house. She wasn't surprised when Gilles was the first to speak.

"That guy is bad news. I think we're all in agreement on that, but we really can't kill him just because we think he's going to be a problem in the future. I sure as fuck don't want him around here, though."

"You won't get any argument from me," Chuck put in. "He's given every female here the once-over, including Katherine. What do you wanna bet he really was trying to fuck with that niece of his?"

"I've seen the same thing with the women here. And Katherine's still a kid, for fuck's sake! It doesn't seem to matter how young or old. He's a pig," said Billy. Chuck nodded along. Cam was pretty sure there was relief on his face, too, after hearing Billy say his daughter was still a kid. With Katherine's crush on Billy, he'd probably been wondering if Billy would think she was fair game.

"Okay, and I agree with all of you," Cam said. "But that doesn't fix the problem. Sending him away from here without some way for him to survive on his own is basically the same thing as a death sentence. And when he gets desperate he'll just come back here. He won't care anymore about hurting any of us, because we didn't care about his survival. Not to mention the fact that I'd feel like a piece of shit for doing it. I don't want us to start becoming judge, jury, and executioner of everyone who shows up here, or getting into that whole lynch mob mentality. We're just trying to survive here, that's all.

"We need to find out how he got here, too. If they needed half a tank of fuel to get where they were going, assuming they were telling the truth about that and they used up all the fuel, how many kilometres are we talking about? A couple hundred?" She looked around at the others.

"What kind of van was it? Minivan or full size monster from back in the seventies? Because that makes a difference," Gilles said. "When you gave them the fuel, did you keep track of how much fuel went into their tank? Was it treated?"

"It was a newer full-size van, that's all I know," Cam answered.

"I was the one who gave them the fuel. I dumped two of the ten-litre jerry cans into their tank, if I remember right," Billy said. "All of Mac's fuel was treated. Ours, too, for that matter. The van was one of those newer Dodge cargo vans. The really tall, squared-off ones. I can't remember the name of them."

"Probably a Sprinter then," Gilles said with a nod.

"Yeah, I think that was it," said Billy.

"I don't think we should count on anything he said being the truth. For all we know, his wife's parents could live a mile from here. I can't remember whether it was him or her asking for the fuel last summer, and even if she was the one asking, he might have had her lie for him. Besides, he could have siphoned the fuel from the van and dumped it into a car or motorcycle. They didn't need much cargo space once they left the ferrets here," Cam said. Gilles' shoulders slumped. Apparently he'd already been busily calculating mileage, and was enjoying the mental exercise.

"Well, damn. Look who's the smart cookie," Gilles mocked, though the tone was friendly and teasing, not jeering.

"Very funny. Anyway, if he's got a vehicle hidden around here, I think it would be a very good thing to get him as far away from it as possible. Now that you've managed to convert one of the trucks over to vegetable oil – and I guess that also makes you a smart cookie, Gilles – there's no reason we can't just use up our remaining gasoline to take this guy as far away as possible, and then give him enough supplies to get him started somewhere else. If he doesn't make it from there, it's his own fault. Does that sound feasible?"

When the other three nodded, they quickly worked out what they would have to give him so that he could survive. The only thing left was to figure out where to take him.

"How much gasoline do we still have? All the car tanks were full, as well as the storage tanks and jerrycans, except for the ones mom and Neil used when they went to Sault Ste. Marie. We haven't really used any since then, have we? Annette and Kelly's cars were both filled after they got here, along with Kirk and Leigh's rental," she said, pausing to try and think.

"Dad's car was full, too," Billy put in.

"I think most of us followed Mac's advice and made sure our

tanks were full before we came here, and we added preservative to all the tanks right away. So, basically we could take this guy across the country if only we had a tank big enough for it, or some way to strap enough storage tanks to a car," Gilles said.

"Okay, I don't think we need to go quite that crazy. Just far enough that we can be sure he won't want to walk back," she said, and waited for the others to say something.

"It takes two or three weeks to starve if you've got no food, and he might be able to carry a week's supply in a pack or something, so any place it would take a month to walk to would probably be good," Chuck suggested.

"How far can a person walk in a day?" Cam asked, frowning.

"Depends. A normal pace for a human is *maybe* five klicks an hour, but that's pretty tough to maintain. And if you're starving you're not going to move very fast, either," Chuck said.

"Yeah, but at that rate a person could do fifty kilometres a day. He could come back from Toronto in a week. Look at Mitch. He made it here from Hamilton, which is even farther. I don't think distance is going to be what we need here. Maybe we should just blindfold him and drop him off in the bushes somewhere, so he has no idea how to get back," Cam finally said.

"Mitch had a bicycle," Billy reminded her. "But you're probably right. If he doesn't know where he is, he won't know where to go, and there are plenty of places with big forests in this province. If we can find a hunting cabin or something, he'd be set up pretty well. He'll have chickens for eggs, and seeds to grow vegetables for later. We have some plastic bottles he can use for carrying water and stuff. It'll be really rugged for him, but it serves him right."

"We can give him a couple of books if he doesn't know what he's doing. We have a couple of duplicates, like the SAS Survival Guide. I don't really like the idea of giving him live animals, but there's no other way he'll survive. Thankfully there weren't any signs of abuse in the ferrets that came from his wife's shelter," Cam said.

She looked around at the three men to be sure they were all in agreement, and after a few more minutes of discussion led the way back out to the yard to give Mike her decision.

"This is how it's going to be," she began, as soon as they reached him. Then she laid it out for him. He wasn't happy.

"You're just going to leave me to rot in some strange place?"

"Pretty much, unless you decide to do something to help yourself with the tools we intend to give you. You're not going empty-handed, so stop whining. You've already stolen from us, and now we're giving you more free stuff that you've never done anything to earn, so count yourself lucky we don't go medieval on your ass and chop off one of your hands," Cam snarled.

She didn't bother to continue reassuring him. Cameron had too many things to do at the moment, including making arrangements for his departure. They needed to box up the three hens and a rooster they no longer planned to use for breeding, since he'd already been bred to a couple of the chickens. The hens were young, and had plenty of laying left in them. He could have a good thing going for himself if he was smart about it. He would need seeds, feed for the hens, and a way to contain them.

She would have to talk to Carol. She still had keys for the hardware store she managed before the shit hit the fan, so maybe they could get some stuff from there, and they wouldn't have to part with their own things. And it would be good to see what they could scavenge from there at the same time. They could do with a lot more building materials. Some of the stuff they'd been planning to use in the main house had ended up being used to put the cabins together, so the house still needed some finishing touches.

Gilles had already suggested a place to take Mike. He'd gone hunting there as a kid. Even when civilization was still in full swing, it only had road access during the summer and fall, so they would use the four-by-four that ran on gas to get him in there, just in case the potholes were too big for one of the cars. Gilles had said he didn't think it would be a problem with the small amount of snow and frost, but that it was possible there was damage from previous years that hadn't been repaired.

Cam was just heading to the ferret building to delve into their seed storage, when her dad fell into step beside her.

"Hey, Cam. How ya doin'?"

"Dad! Where the hell have you been? I haven't seen you since mom left with Neil."

"Just on walkabout," he said vaguely, making Cam roll her eyes. Apparently he'd taken in a little too much Crocodile Dundee

217

for his own good.

"Dad, seriously, what have you been doing? Things are kind of crazy here, and I don't need to be worrying about you at the same time. In fact, we really needed your help." She explained about the intruder, and their plans to take him somewhere else.

"Then what did you need me for? You're doing just fine, kiddo," he said jovially, not taking things seriously, as usual. It frustrated her to no end. If he was given a specific task to do, he did it without argument, but he didn't bother to think ahead or make plans for anything either. Cam could completely understand why her mother had ended her relationship with him. It was like talking to someone who never intended to grow up. It wasn't that her mother had wanted to be with someone particularly ambitious. Just someone who believed in a little bit of personal growth, which was the exact opposite of Cam's dad.

"What was I thinking? I should have known," Cam said, allowing her anger and frustration to show.

"What do you mean?"

"I mean you aren't living like you're a part of this whole thing we've got going here, when everyone else is. We've got a new person here that you may or may not know, we've got an intruder to deal with, we have to go on a scavenging trip to the hardware store, and probably a zillion other things. It would be really nice if you bothered to pay attention to the fact that I'm completely stressed out, and you're supposed to be my dad!

"Mom is doing what she has to do to save the life of a friend, which is more important than what's happening here. She's got enough on her plate without worrying about us. She got hurt part of the way there, too, and you don't even know about that. I could have used a shoulder, or at least someone to talk to who wasn't going to use it as an opportunity to judge me for my ability to keep things going here.

"Everyone else here is joining in to share in the work and concerns. People are coming up with ideas for things, and ways to help. Everything that's happened in the last week has been dealt with by me, Billy, Gilles, and Chuck, with additional help from everyone but you. You do your day of chores, but that's it. Of course, you're barely here to eat the food, so maybe I shouldn't complain," she said, winding down from her rant.

"Your mom was hurt? What happened?" His concern was genuine, so Cam filled him in on that, too.

"You haven't been telling her anything that's been happening here?"

"No, because she can't help, she'll worry, and it would be stupid for her to turn around and come home when they're almost there. Or they should be by now. I'll tell her when she gets back," she said with a sigh, already knowing her mother's reaction.

"She's not gonna be happy you kept it from her," her dad warned.

"Believe me, I know." It didn't escape Cam's notice that her dad still hadn't told her what he'd been up to.

13 ~ HITCHHIKERS

There was a wild and hungry look on the faces of the two young males coming toward them, and Mac was prepared for just about anything. Bella growled beside Ian.

"Stop right there. I can give you a little bit of food and help you get more. Then we're leaving," she said.

"Wha'd'ya mean you'll help us get more? Ain't no food left in this city. They don't drop it no more," the one on the left said, his voice shaky and panicked. He had a bit of an accent, but she couldn't place it.

Instead of arguing while they were starving, Mac reached into her pack to pull out the last two granola bars she had with her. She threw one to the ground in front of each of them, and waited until they had finished inhaling them to explain what she meant.

"My friend here can teach you how to fish, if you want. It might keep you alive until you can figure out how to grow some food. What do you say?" They were already shaking their heads, and the one on the left spoke again.

"We ain't even spose'ta be here. We come to Cleveland 'cuz

they got the Rock and Roll Hall of Fame, but we couldn't get no gas to get back home. We mostly hid when the people went crazy, and they were killing each other all over the place, but then they started dropping the food so people calmed down. Then they just stopped, so people got crazy again. I don't know how you got this food, but we could sure use some more, and we need to get out of here. Without no car, we got no way to get back to my folks." His 'tos' all came out sounding like 'tuh,' but she still couldn't figure out where he was from.

The words had all come out in a panicked rush, and when he finished his breath started hitching. Mac felt bad for them, but had no idea how to help them without knowing more about their situation.

"Where are you from then?"

"My folks got a small farm in Westland, just outside Detroit. If we could find a way back there we'd be okay, but we can't walk there with no food."

"Be a lot faster on bikes," Ian put in. Mac couldn't see his face, since she was keeping an eye on the young men, but she could hear from his tone that he wasn't too keen on the idea of helping them, beyond offering some suggestions. She knew he was naturally suspicious, and she couldn't blame him. Things were a bit different in American cities from what she was used to in Canada. He had every reason to think these two young men would just as soon rob them as look at them, but Mac knew they had the advantage here.

"If you're telling us the truth, there may be a way for us to help you get home. It's better than you starving to death in this city if you're really from where you say you're from. Why don't we get to know each other a little bit better first, and then we can talk about helping you, okay? I'm Mac, the guy who suggested bicycles was Ian, and the tall, dark, and silent one is my husband, Neil."

"I'm Vigo, and this is my cousin, Denny," he said.

"Hey," Denny said, nodding.

"Your mom's a fan of Viggo Mortensen, I'm guessing," Mac said with a smile, but Vigo shook his head, embarrassed.

"Nah, she liked the name from that *Ghostbusters* movie with the painting. She's kin-uh weird, my mom, but I'd really like to see her again anyway."

"I was named after Denzel Washington," Denny piped up, making them all laugh.

"God, how old are you two?" The question came from Neil.

"I'm seventeen, and Denny here is sixteen. I learned to drive last year, and we saved up the gas money to come out to Cleveland last summer. Worst mistake of my life," Vigo muttered.

"Ian, can you check and see if either one of these boys is armed? I'd really like to stop holding a gun on them if possible."

Ian gave them both a thorough pat-down, which caused Denny to yelp when he felt a hand at his crotch.

"Sorry kid, but people store weapons in some of the strangest places," Ian apologized, and patted him on the shoulder. He stepped back over to Mac's side.

"They don't have anything. Damned if I know how they

survived like that in Cleveland," he said quietly.

"Doesn't look like they would have for much longer," Mac replied, holstering her gun. Then she pulled out a couple of chocolate bars and gave one to each of the boys.

"I didn't want to give these to you on an empty stomach, but these should add a few calories now that the granola bars have settled a bit. Why don't you tell me about your parents' farm, Vigo? You don't have to tell me exactly where it is or anything. In fact, you shouldn't give that information to anybody. You don't want to cause your folks any problems. Just tell me what they grow, and the kind of work they get you to do. Young boy like you must be a big help on a farm," she flattered him. She wasn't trying to get him to like her or anything, though he seemed to glow at her words. At the moment she was just trying to find out if he was telling the truth about the farm.

"We got a lot of turkeys there. Organic. I mean, we got vegetables, too, but turkeys is how my folks make money. The rest is just for food. Mostly potatoes, carrots, that kin-uh thing," he said with a shrug.

"You eat a lot of turkey eggs for breakfast?" Mac watched him while she waited for his answer.

"Nah. We eat chicken eggs like everyone else. We keep the turkey eggs to get more turkeys, 'cuz we get more money that way," Vigo replied. Mac relaxed a little bit. She didn't figure a seventeen-year-old kid would know that much about turkeys, if they weren't dealing with them as a way of life.

"If we could get you to Detroit, do you think you'd be able to get the rest of the way?" The question came from Neil. Apparently he'd been thinking the same thing she was.

"You guys are peas in a pod," Ian said, shaking his head. Mac frowned at him.

"What are you complaining about? We got here to help you didn't we?"

"Okay, okay. Don't get all riled up. I'm just saying you guys are pretty damn trusting. Must be a Canadian thing."

"You guys are from Canada? Cool! Do you guys have snow all year?" Denny's question had her laughing. Apparently the American school system hadn't done these kids any favours.

"Our weather isn't much different from yours. In some places it's warmer. I used to live in Hamilton, which is south of most of the Canadian border, and it got way too hot there for me. We barely got any snow in the winter, and the last few years were even worse. We live further north now, and even then we barely got snow this year. A couple of inches for about two months. That heat is the reason everyone lost their power," she finished.

"Everyone? You mean it wasn't jus' Cleveland?" This time Denny's question made her sad.

"As far as we know, the whole planet went dark. The extreme heat overloaded every major system, because everyone had their air conditioning running, which contributed even more to the problem. Sorry to say, you boys may be going back to a place with no more PlayStation or Xbox. Unless Vigo's parents have another power source." She looked questioningly at Vigo, who nodded his head.

"Yeah, we do. We got a big gas generator."

"Well, I don't know how much fuel they'll have left in it, but when they run out they won't be able to get gas for that, any more than you could get it for your car. Anyway, Neil asked if you could get home from Detroit okay. How far is it, do you think?"

"What part of Detroit could you take us to?"

"Anywhere on Detroit River, basically. I don't know where Westland is, or I might have a better idea where on the river," she said.

"Probably a twenty-minute drive on the other side of the city," Vigo replied.

"About twenty miles, then," Ian put in. "Could take up to a day. Long walk for a couple of kids. Do you even know how to get there from the river?"

"I think so, yeah. Just gotta get on Marquette, other side of the city. Ain't far off that. I'm pretty good at navigatin' anyway. Made it to Cleveland without getting lost. Found all the places we wanted to get to, no problem," Vigo boasted.

"Yeah, but you don't have Google Maps anymore. You can't print directions out on your computer, because there's no internet or electricity," Neil reminded him.

"Not having the 'net is really gonna suck, man. What the hell we gonna do for school projects when we get back?"

It was obvious Vigo was having a hard time grasping what was really going on in the world. School wasn't going to be a big problem for him. Mac was really starting to worry about them, because she had no idea if his parents would even be alive after all this.

"What about you Denny? Your parents in the same area?" Neil asked. Denny shook his head, and let Vigo answer for him.

"Denny's folks got killed a coupla years back in a drive-by. He came to live with us then. After that we became like best friends. We didn't hardly know each other before that, 'cuz my parents didn't wanna go to that part of Detroit too much, and his folks didn't have no car to come see us." Denny smiled at his cousin, though there were tears in his eyes. Then he looked away, obviously trying to pretend there was nothing wrong. Mac made her decision.

"Okay, here's the deal. We've got a boat. We can get you to Detroit if you really want to go there."

"For real, lady? *Yeah*, we wanna go. It's all we talked about since the lights went out. Even when they was droppin' those big crates of food, all we wanted was to get back home. My folks gotta be goin' crazy, wondering what happened to us. We were supposed to go back the next day. I went to fill up on gas, and the guy at the station said the pumps wasn't workin', but it didn't matter anyway, 'cuz they didn't deliver the gas like they was spose'ta. Then I didn't know what to do. I promised I'd take care of Denny, here, but I didn't do a very good job of it."

"Vigo, you obviously did a perfectly fine job. The two of you

226

are alive, when a lot of people aren't. When trouble came you kept your heads down, and when there was food you made sure he got something to eat. Your parents will be very proud of you," Neil assured him.

"Okay, we might as well get back to the boat and get started. We'll get some more food into you as soon as we're on board. We don't want to send you back to your parents all skin and bones," Mac said with a smile.

"Uh, Mac, could I talk to you for a second?" Ian walked off to the side a bit, waiting for her to follow. She knew what was coming, but she let him say his piece.

"These kids could be playing you, Mac. Whatever you do, don't let them leave your sight for a second before we get to the boat. They didn't have any guns on them, but they may have some stashed around here, just waiting for the right moment to get the jump on us."

"Did you know that about turkey eggs, Ian?"

"Well, I know I don't eat any for breakfast, if that's what you mean."

"No, I mean about it being more profitable to breed them, rather than eat the eggs. Did you know that was the reason we don't eat turkey eggs?"

"Never thought about it, to be honest, but I see your point. I still think there's a possibility these kids are a lot more dangerous than they might appear, and I don't particularly want to leave my life in their hands," he finished stubbornly.

"We'll make sure they don't have any opportunity to retrieve weapons. The three of us will be the only ones carrying. And you're a jiu-jitsu master, are you not? Trained in hand-to-hand, and foot-to-face? I'm pretty sure you could kick their asses if it became necessary," Mac said with a smirk, laughing a little at his paranoia.

"Not if they manage to grab one of our guns, I wouldn't. They could shove us off the boat in the middle of the lake, and just leave us to drown," he said, refusing to let the matter drop.

"To what end? What good does a boat do anyone right now, except to get them somewhere else. We're already taking them somewhere else, willingly. They don't need to point a gun at us for that. If they were just looking for a boat to hole up on, they could have picked any of the thirty or forty at the yacht club. Yes, this happens to be a working boat, but a lot of those boats will have some form of solar power, too. They could have lights, entertainment, whatever they want. So, obviously they want to go somewhere. Probably somewhere with food," she said.

"Okay, okay. I just wanted to make sure you knew what you were getting into. Kids here in Cleveland probably aren't what you're used to up in that Utopia you call Canada," he teased.

"Yeah, we're just basking in sunlight, drinking wine and dining on ambrosia. The goats and chickens all look after themselves. Weirdo," Mac said, nudging him with her elbow.

"You come all the way to Cleveland just to get little old me, and I'm the weirdo?"

"Well, yeah. What are friends for? By the way, it's good to

finally meet you in person. Where's my hug? I think I at least deserve one of those for all the trouble you've put me through," she demanded. He laughed and wrapped her in a bear hug until she was gasping and begging him to let her breathe.

"Hey, I thought you said you wanted a hug. Jeez, Louise! Wimpy Canadian."

"I think someone needs to teach you the difference between a hug and a vise. I've got no boobs left! And I think you broke at least three ribs. Bloody American," she muttered, making him laugh.

"I think I'll let your husband check out the situation with your boobs. He's already glaring at me."

Mac looked over at Neil, who was in fact glaring, though she didn't think it had anything to do with her breasts. She rolled her eyes and stalked over to him.

"I told him to hug me, cowboy, so get over it."

"What? I didn't say anything."

"Your face did all the talking for you. Relax. Ian's harmless. He wouldn't even check to see if he flattened my chest with that hug," she teased.

"Harmless. Uh, okay," he said sarcastically, which instantly lit up her temper, but it wasn't the time to start a fight. They had things to do.

"Let's just get back to the boat, then," she said tersely. "Hopefully it won't take as long to get back as it did to get here."

"Yeah."

಄   ◆   ಋ

There was no place for a private conversation on the boat. Without the constant, happy chatter from Vigo and Denny, though mainly from Vigo, there might have been a lot of quiet time in the two days it took to get back to Detroit. Before they started out on the second day, Mac managed to convince Ian to take a quick dive with her to check out the hairline crack between the hull and the keel, but it wasn't easy. He seemed to have lost the majority of his suspicions with regard to the two boys, but he eyed Neil warily when Mac made the suggestion.

"Oh, for fuck's sake! We need to know if we're taking on water. Our lives may depend on it. So let's put aside whatever the hell this other issue is and be grown-ups for two little minutes, shall we?"

Her loss of temper eased the tension a little bit, and finally Ian went into one of the bathrooms to change into a pair of shorts he'd brought with him. Then he tied up Bella on the deck so she wouldn't jump in after him. Mac went to change into her own shorts and t-shirt.

"I'll let you wear the equipment. I've been down there and know where I'm going, and I can hold my breath for as long as it takes to show you where it is. That way you can stay there and look at it as long as you need to," she explained to Ian.

"Okay, but you better not drown or anything. I don't look

forward to explaining to that surly bear you married that I'm still alive while you're feeding the fishes."

"Could you take things seriously for a minute? You might be able to kick my ass, but I might just be fast enough to get a shot in and make you regret opening your soon-to-be-swollen mouth," she retorted. With that she just jumped into the water off the railing, and waited for him to fall in. When they got halfway down the side of the boat, Ian turned in the water to look at her.

"You know, you didn't actually have to show me where the keel meets the hull. It's not exactly a difficult place to find."

"Then why did I have to come with you?"

"If I have to freeze my ass off, you should, too," he said, and then disappeared beneath water just in time to miss the splash she sent at his face.

"Aargh!" Then she waited stubbornly for him to finish looking at the crack. A few minutes passed before she felt a hand grab her ankle and yank her under water. She flailed and spluttered to the surface, hearing nothing but laughter from Ian.

"You freakin' jerk," she hollered, making Bella bark at her from the boat, which only made him laugh harder. When they got back on the boat she called him an American idiot, and stomped down the hall toward the bedroom to get changed. Neil was standing there, giving Ian an appraising look through narrowed eyes, and Mac had no idea what to make of it. All she knew was that she was irritated as hell and wanted to spend the next few hours of her life completely by herself. Something that wasn't so easy to do when trapped on a boat with four other people.

Whatever it was that had gone on between Neil and Ian, however, tensions decreased to a tolerable level for the remainder of the trip to Detroit. They were able to discuss the issue of the hull in a reasonable and mature manner, with Ian providing what little expertise he could.

"It could just be crazing in the gelcoat. It's only a single line, rather than a bunch of cracks in a concentric circle. I pushed on it with my finger, and there doesn't appear to be any give, but I'm not an expert by any means. When I had a boat I took it in to other people to get things like that looked after. Probably got taken to the cleaners more than once by not knowing more about it, though."

"So, what does that mean for us then?" Neil asked.

"It means doing what you planned to do in the first place. We keep an eye on it, and check to make sure we're not taking on water. When we go into the water to check it, we can see if the boat is riding lower, and since it'll be heavier if there's water in the hull it may not go as fast, or steer as easily."

"Might be hard for us to tell. We came down here with the current. Now we're going against it, so that's going to affect our speed all the way back. Still, if we notice it getting progressively worse, that should tell us something," Mac said.

"You've got bilge pumps, too, which will start running all the time if the water is coming in," Ian added, rubbing Bella's ear as she sat contentedly beside him.

"Oh. Is that sort of like a sump pump for a basement?"

Mackenzie asked him.

"That depends what a sump pump is," Ian replied.

"Oh, right. I forgot who I was talking to … the hopeless handyman himself. A sump goes in a basement. It's got a float valve on it, or something similar, that turns on the pump if the basement starts getting water in it.," she explained.

"In that case, yeah. The bilge pump is like a sump pump. I would think this boat has more than one, considering the size of it, so if you start hearing a new pump motor coming on all the time, when it wasn't before, then you've got water coming in. Still, I don't think it's something we need to worry about. It's very unlikely it's going to be an issue in the amount of time we'll be on the boat, and the pumps will keep the boat from sinking unless the water volume is too much for them to pump out."

"I was hoping you'd be able to use the boat to get back, though. We can get more vegetable oil easily enough, but having to find another boat that's suitable for conversion, and then getting Gilles to do it, will be a pain in the ass. My ass, in fact. Gilles can be cranky," Mac explained, when Ian gave her a questioning look.

"You don't have one normal friend, do you?"

"Nope. They're all jerks. I must like jerks or something."

"Gee, thanks, honey," Neil said sarcastically.

"Hey, I said I like them. I didn't say I was in love with them, so it doesn't automatically imply you're a jerk, but I'll let you decide whether or not that shoe fits. By the way, what happened to Vigo and Denny? You didn't toss them overboard, did you?"

"Wow, you must really think I'm some kind of asshole. No, I didn't toss them overboard. They finally crashed. I guess it's the excitement of being on a boat for the first time. They spent most of the night lying on the deck, pointing out all the stars. Now they're exhausted."

"What the hell are we going to do when we get to Detroit, Neil? They're kids! Are we really going to let them walk twenty miles by themselves?"

"They survived several months in Cleveland, honey. They'll survive a day-hike."

"Maybe, but have you stopped to consider what will happen to them if they get there and things aren't the same?" She didn't want to say that Vigo's parents might not be alive, just in case one of the kids woke up and heard them talking, but Neil caught on to what she was saying.

"Shit. You're right. We'll have to take them all the way there. Besides, if they have to go through downtown Detroit, God only knows what they'd be facing. So, Ian, it looks like you'll be guarding the boat in the meantime," Neil said, leaving Mac with the impression that he was looking forward to some time alone with his wife. Well, she could certainly do with a few moments of privacy with her husband, too. She wanted an explanation for his behaviour. Not that it would be easy waiting for the return trip to get it, but she could be patient occasionally.

"I've been meaning to ask you why the hell you look like you've had the shit beat out of you, and what the hell is going on with your hair," Ian said, interrupting her thoughts. "I know your husband isn't beating you, or you'd have shot him by now, so what happened to you?"

"Oh, not too much. My face met a door, which *was* Neil's fault, so maybe I should have shot him, and then my head met the mast. After that the boat tried to scalp me. It was doing a good job of it until I lopped off my hair. Neil used Superglue to put my scalp back together, and set my nose for me – thankfully while I was still unconscious from the blow to the head.

"Aside from a couple of dives to check out the hull, I haven't managed a shower just yet, much less a proper haircut to tidy myself up. Sorry I didn't spruce myself up for our meeting, but you know me … I'm not exactly queen of the runway. You're mostly lucky I bothered changing out of my pyjamas."

Ian just laughed at her.

"You have the damndest luck, don't you? When was the last time you walked ten feet without falling down and hurting yourself?"

"Oh, shut up. I better not be that clumsy, or it's going to take a week for us to take those boys home. Meanwhile you and Bella will be lying around on the boat, soaking up the sun, drinking wine, and eating ambrosia. American Utopia. Can't compare to the Canadian version, but we all have our problems. Not your fault you couldn't be born in Canada, though, so I guess I shouldn't rub it in. It's not nice to make fun of those born with disadvantages."

"You know, I can actually kick your ass now. We're no longer in two different countries for you to be getting away with shit like that, Ms. Thane. Or should I call you Ms. Thing? Oh, wait, you're married now. What the hell is your name?"

At that Neil started to laugh. Mackenzie pointed her finger at him.

"Don't you start," she warned. "That did *not* happen."

"You could call her Mac-Mac like I did, though I get the funny feeling she doesn't like it," Neil said, trying to keep a straight face. Once Neil had explained his last name to him, and how everyone called him Mac, too, Ian's laughter carried across the water. Even Bella looked like she was laughing. Mac could feel her face burning, and covered it with her hands.

"I'm going to kill you for that," she muttered through her fingers. "He's never going to let me live that down. I think we've done enough of this sitting around and talking. I'm going to get us moving, so we actually get to Detroit some time before midnight."

As she pulled herself up the steps into the cabin, she made sure they heard her muttering about the jerks she had to put up with, though it was with some relief. It may have cost her some future embarrassment, but at least Ian and Neil were having a laugh together.

Once they made it to Detroit, Mac switched over to diesel for a few minutes to run out the oil, and then shut down the engines. She was going to get a few hours' sleep, and then they would have to head out with Vigo and Denny. Not that she was looking forward to it. Assuming nothing bad happened, they could make it back in twelve hours, but after everything she'd been through she really hated assuming anything. She was better off expecting the worst and being pleasantly surprised if it didn't happen.

When she tried to sleep, however, Mac knew within minutes that it just wasn't going to happen. It was far too early for her, and those boys were raring to go. She could hear the excitement in their voices as they talked about the first thing they were going to do when they got there, so Mac gave up on sleep. She knew she wasn't likely going to be able to sleep outside, either, so there was every likelihood she wasn't going to get any rest until they got back.

"Coffee," she muttered. "I need lots and lots of coffee."

14 ~ SUSPICIOUS MINDS

Billy was left in charge of things at the farm, while Cam took Chuck with her to scavenge at the hardware store. She would have taken Gilles, since she trusted him the most with respect to safety and security, but that was also the reason she left him behind. She needed to make sure someone competent was keeping a sharp eye on Mitch. So far she hadn't had any problems with him, but leaving the farm without proper supervision could be disastrous. Billy could run things easily enough, but he needed good support, too.

At least Chuck had a hell of a reach on him. She'd seen him ducking under door frames, so she figured he was at least four inches over six feet, possibly five. He'd be able to reach anything on high storage shelves, without them having to mess around with forklifts. Carol had said they were battery-operated, which meant they might still work, but they had been sitting there for months. The charge in the batteries may have trickled out in that length of time.

Chuck was driving, because Cam wasn't at all comfortable with a trailer, and the horse trailer was huge. It was meant to haul three horses, so it would give them plenty of space for any building supplies they might be needing, including anything they might take to the hunting cabin so Mike could make it habitable for himself. They sure as hell weren't going to do the work for his thieving ass.

It galled her to have to take care of someone like Mitch, but he was going to need a roof over his head, too. Lisa's cabin was in progress, and there were plenty of trees on the property to finish it, but the less they had to cut down the better. They were trying to keep themselves shielded from view, after all. Of course, it would take a long time for them to cut down that many trees. Between their property and Neil's, there were plenty to go around.

"Okay, pull up to the shipping bay door there so I can unlock it. We can back the truck and trailer right in, if you're okay doing that with a trailer," Cam said.

"No problem. This has more than one axle, so it's not that bad. Doesn't sway back and forth so easily. Your mom's open trailer is a bit more difficult, though this one doesn't have so much visibility," he replied as he drove up alongside the garage-style door. She got out, went in through the side door, and opened the roll-up door. Cameron waited while Chuck pulled around and started to back it in.

He left about four feet of open space behind him so they could still get the trailer doors open. The loading dock was too high for the horse trailer anyway, so Cam figured they could use some strong boards as a makeshift ramp to put everything inside. Since the shipping bay was meant for giant tractor-trailers, there was plenty of room for them, and she ran over to close the garage door. Hopefully no one had seen them come in.

She had just closed the door, and was looking through the row of windows to check for any unwanted company, when she saw some movement about a block away. She was about to call Chuck over to watch with her, just in case there was trouble, when she recognized the strut and stature. It was her dad. He was a short guy, and like a lot of short guys he strutted. Some form of compensation for lack of height, she supposed.

At first she just thought it was a little weird. A coincidence, maybe, running into him this way. She thought about getting him to come over and help them, since it would make the work go faster, but then she saw movement out of the corner of her eye. She looked over, and saw a woman heading toward him. She had a long stride, and was fairly tall for a woman. The moment she saw Cam's dad, she began to hurry her pace. They met in the middle, and were immediately locking lips in a tight embrace.

"Well, isn't that interesting," Cam murmured. "Dad's got a girlfriend." She knew there were other people still alive, so she wasn't too surprised, though she did wonder why her dad hadn't simply brought her to the farm. Obviously this was something that had been going on for some time, seeing as he'd been disappearing for his 'walkabouts' for weeks, if not months. There was no reason she could think of that he couldn't just bring her home with him, and then he wouldn't have to walk so far to meet her all the time.

Unless she was married, of course, and for that she would really have to kick her dad's ass.

But then she recognized the woman. Cameron sucked in her breath so fast from the shock that her saliva caught in her throat and she started to cough. Her first instinct was to run out there and confront them both, but a small voice in the back of her mind advised caution. Whatever was going on here was a bad thing, and she needed to get to the bottom of it. Maybe it was just an affair, but maybe it was something a whole lot more sinister.

She very sincerely wanted to smack her dad upside the head at the moment, because she couldn't think of any good reason why he'd be getting himself involved with the mother of the man she had killed. But then, maybe he didn't know who she was. Still, he at least had to know she was married, because he was keeping their relationship a secret.

"You gonna stand there staring out the window all day, or are we gonna get this trailer loaded?" Chuck's voice carried across the shipping bay, echoing slightly. Cam shook her head to clear it, and tried to ignore the sick feeling in her gut. They had a job to do. She would have to figure out what to do about her dad later.

ဢ ◆ ಚಿ

When they got back to the farm, Cam didn't even bother unloading the truck and trailer. There was no urgency there, and she had something a whole lot more important on her mind. By the time Chuck had pulled away from the hardware store, there had been no sign of her dad, or of Geraldine, but she hadn't expected any. People conducting clandestine affairs generally didn't bang one another in the middle of a street where anyone could see them. In fact, it had been a little stupid of them to meet on the street in the first place, because she herself had seen them.

The problem, of course, was that she had no idea when her dad would get back so that she could talk to him. He must have left the farm the day before, in order to walk so far in that length of time, which meant he'd probably disappeared right after she'd complained that he wasn't there for her. It made her understand once again why her mother hadn't stayed with him.

Thinking about it, she realized this wasn't the first time he had given some woman priority over his own daughter. He'd done it when she was really young, which had resulted in fights between him and her mother. Finally her mother had issued an ultimatum. He either had to do what he said he was going to do, or he wouldn't be allowed to see Cam. It must have been shortly after her parents had split up, because she vaguely remembered the woman her dad had been seeing at the time, and that she hadn't liked her very much.

She considered his situation as she walked over the bridge to get to Kirk and Leigh's cabin. It wouldn't be hard to find at least one of them puttering around the place, and Cam needed someone to talk to. She preferred talking to Kirk, but she was pretty close to Leigh, too. They were the only people she could really trust to

242

keep things to themselves, because they were her own friends, rather than just people who were in her life because of her mother.

Cameron found both of them outside with their archery equipment, which made her sorry she hadn't thought to bring her own. She could have used the practice. For now, though, she would need to interrupt theirs. After a quick greeting, she explained what was going on.

"Oh. Shit. That's bad. That's really bad," Kirk moaned.

"Tell me about it. It gives me a whole new perspective on the kind of person she is, and I let the filthy woman hug me! Hell, I cried on her shoulder. God, I can't stand cheaters," Cam snarled.

"You have no way of knowing what their marriage is like. He might be beating the shit out of her, or maybe they were about to get a divorce when suddenly their kid is dead and the world goes to hell. Now they can't," Leigh said pragmatically.

"If she was being beaten, I'm sure my dad would know, and I guarantee he would have made sure she got away from her husband. It's possible they were splitting up, or that me killing their kid ruined their marriage, but they sure didn't act like that when I was there. I only met her once, and him twice, so I can't be sure, but I just didn't get that vibe from them. Of course, I didn't get the vibe that she was fucking around on her husband, either," she said bitterly. She was really starting to feel like a fool for crying on Geraldine's shoulder.

"I don't know what to tell ya, Cam. All I can say is that I don't think it's a good situation. Even if it's just them having an affair, the last thing we need right now is to have some crazy husband showing up at the farm, pissed at the guy fucking his wife. As shitty as it is, you're going to have to do something about it. Not only is he your dad, but you've also got to deal with all the shit on the farm right now, so you're stuck with the job."

Kirk was right, she knew. There was no one else, and it was her responsibility for the moment. If her mother was here, it would have been her dealing with it, but she wasn't. Cam was really starting to resent Ian for her mother's absence.

"What I'm worried about, is what her intentions are," Cam said, gnawing at her bottom lip.

"Well, yeah. She could be madly in love with your dad, of course, and she hasn't known for very long who it was that killed Gerry, but she could have started something with him just to get inside information on what was going on at the farm. I'm sure by now she knows exactly where we all are, and what our set-up is. It's not a good thing. I hope you took care of the holes in the security where that guy was getting through."

"Of course I did, Kirk. I improved on the original set-up a bit, too, I think. Not only did we get the camera back in place so that everything is in view again, but I made sure there were screenshots printed so we can verify that the cameras are still pointed to the same place. I even kept an extra copy of them in my own file, in case someone fucked around with it and printed new reference images to keep people from being suspicious.

"Instead of moving the sensor by the dead tree, though, we cut up the tree and moved it. Mom will find a use for the wood, I'm sure. We checked all the other sensors, and I'm going to walk both perimeters every once in a while to make sure that doesn't happen again without us knowing about it. Mom is going to freak out when she gets back, and finds out nobody told her about all this shit happening, but we did a damn good job taking care of everything."

"You won't get any argument from me, though I don't envy you when she gets back. She's going to chew up one side of you and down the other," he said.

"I know. I'll have to wait out the storm, and explain my reasoning when she's done having her shit-fit. I know I'd be pissed, too, so I can't blame her but it's not going to be much fun for me."

"Well, what was she going to do, other than worry? Every time you had a problem, you resolved it long before she'd have been able to make it back here to do anything," said Leigh.

"I know, but she's not going to see it that way. At least not at first. She has every right to be kept in the loop, just like when I got pissed at Gilles for trying to take charge. He and Chuck were making plans without consulting me. The plans were the same as mine, so the result would have been the same, but they kept me out of the loop. It pissed me off, and it's going to piss her off, too. Still, it won't be a question of her not trusting me after this or anything. She might not believe I'll tell her everything if she has to leave again, but she'll at least know I can handle whatever comes up," she finished.

"Won't be much comfort while she's chewing you out, but it'll pass," Kirk said. Cam had to laugh. It didn't matter that she was an adult. The thought of getting in shit with her mother still had her stomach knotting. Then again, her mother was pretty intimidating when she was riled.

"So when do you think we can get together again for a real game night? I really want to see what everyone thinks of that game once we've really gotten into it," Leigh said.

"God, I wish I could. We still have to ship off that asshole who was stealing from us, and we've got two cabins to get built. Of course, Mitch is going to be stuck doing a lot of the work himself, because I want him to get a taste of what it takes to do the shit we've been doing. He won't be laughing when he's got splinters, and blisters on top of blisters. Might be the first he's ever earned anything in his life, and I'm looking forward to seeing that," Cam said, grinning evilly.

"You already know that game is great, babe," Kirk said, poking Leigh's shoulder.

"I *don't* know. Lisa was right in a way. I mean, we're already dealing with all that shit, so how is it any fun for anyone?" Leigh looked worried, so Cam put in her two cents.

"Of course it's fun! It's competitive, for one thing, which isn't something we can do in real life. And for another, the consequences aren't real. It's not the same thing at all. In a way it's just like *The Sims*. You can do stuff in the game that you can't do in real life, like drowning your Sims, or starving them to death. And you get to try different ways of doing things, to see what works best. Of course, I'm hoping you're planning to make other kinds of games, too, so we have a little more variety. No rush, though. We've still got a zillion games to play. I made sure of that when mom and I were planning for all this."

"Well, the next one is definitely different, but I'm not telling you anything more about it. Trade secrets," Leigh said with a smirk, which had Cam rolling her eyes.

"Yeah, because the competition is so fierce out there now. Industrial espionage is at an all-time high, right?" Cam's sarcastic comment had them both laughing, and the ridiculous statements only got worse from there. By the time they decided to go inside the cabin to get something to eat, they were almost wheezing with laughter. Cam forgot about her problems with her dad until they had finished eating, but then she brought it up again.

"It sounds mean, but the two of them looked silly together. Not just because she's tall and he's short, but because he's not at all someone who would normally attract a woman like her. She seems so polished, and dad is really rough around the edges. And no, I really don't want to hear comments about his potential skills in certain areas. It's not something I want in my head."

Kirk and Leigh laughed, but decided not to pursue that particular topic.

"Yeah, it doesn't seem likely someone like that would fall in love with your dad. Some immature women might go for bad boys, or whatever, but that's not really your dad's thing either. He's more the cute and cuddly type," Leigh put in.

"Ugh. Okay, forget I brought it up, because there isn't any part of this that I'm really comfortable talking about or imagining," Cam said, wrinkling her nose. "I'd better get back. I told Chuck I'd come back later to deal with the trailer, and it's going to get dark soon."

"Alright. You know where we are if you need backup," Kirk said, making her smile. She didn't know what the hell kind of backup she would need for a confrontation with her dad, but it was nice to have friends who were there for her anyway.

ಬ ♦ ಌ

"I don't wanna be dumped off in the middle of nowhere," Mike whined, as Chuck blindfolded him and they led him to the truck. The trailer had been hooked up to Chuck's four-by-four, which was the only one that used gasoline. There were two other four-by-fours, but they used diesel, and Gilles' truck was just a rear-wheel drive. Eventually, when they ran out of gas, it looked to Cam as though they were going to have a lot of scrap metal they could use. When she made that comment to Gilles, though, he corrected her misconception.

"Nah. Most of the cars have a lot of plastic on them. Not that we can't find a use for that, too, but there isn't as much sheet metal there as you might think. There's some fibreglass, too. Very useful

248

for certain applications, though."

"Like what?" she wondered.

"We can use them as roof tile, for one thing. They're waterproof, don't rust, and don't rot. All the cabins we've been building are going to start leaking eventually, because we haven't been using proper roofing materials," Gilles replied.

"Does my mom know this?"

"Of course. But we all needed places to live right away. We've got some of that thick plastic sheeting over the roofs, top and bottom, but even though that will keep the water out it will also trap moisture so the wood rots faster. For now, we'll fix what needs to be fixed until we can come up with another solution."

"But how the hell did people do roofs before they had roofing tile? I mean, there must be a way where they weren't getting rained on or whatever."

"There are lots of different ways to put on a roof, like those adobe roofs that were used on Spanish houses. It would take us a long time to start making our own bricks and tiles, though. And the fact is, roofs start to rot and leak eventually, and need to be replaced. Even the ones using regular roofing tiles. Roofing companies could give a warranty of a certain length, but it still meant replacing the roof in twenty years or so. Don't worry. We're all doing okay with what we've got for now," he finished, patting her shoulder.

She didn't take offense at the gesture, because it wasn't meant patronizingly. He was just offering reassurance. Granted, she wasn't the touchy-feely kind, but it didn't bother her. At least nobody on the farm tried to hug her.

"You and Chuck going to be alright with this guy?" she asked, making Gilles laugh.

"I think we can handle this putz. We are cops, you know. It's kind of what we do," he reminded her. She grinned sheepishly.

"I think I'm starting to do the same thing my mother does. Jesus. She worries about every damn thing, and now I'm doing the same."

"It's called responsibility. Wait until you have kids. I don't have any of my own, but I watched my friends go through it. I mean, look at Chuck. Not only does he have to worry about his own safety when someone like this Mike comes along, but he's got a wife and three kids he wants to keep safe, and the fact is you can't protect someone twenty-four-seven. It's impossible. We just do the best we can.

"*You're* worrying, because you know everyone's safety and wellbeing has become your responsibility, and if you fuck up then other people suffer for it. It's actually a good thing that you're aware of it. Not everyone is able to understand that, and the fact is you're holding up really well for what you're having to deal with. I gotta say, I'm impressed. Then again, Mac wouldn't have raised an idiot. A weirdo, maybe, but not an idiot," he said with a smile.

"Look who's talking … jerk," she said with a grin, and a quick punch to the shoulder. She was starting to see why her mother was friends with Gilles, who hadn't impressed her initially. The first time she had met him was after killing Gerry, and he'd been really nice to her then, but when he brought his family to the farm, she began to think he was an arrogant know-it-all.

He liked to mock women, too, which pissed Cam off at first. Her mother just gave as good as she got, however, which Gilles took no offense at. Maybe he really was just teasing, even though that hadn't been Cam's experience with men who made chauvinistic jokes. They quite often hid true misogyny behind the mockery. In the long run, Cam had decided she just had to trust her mother's judgment. There was no way her mother would be friends with a guy who hated or disrespected women.

She didn't ask Gilles any questions about where they were taking Mike, because she didn't want Mike to overhear and figure out how to get back to the farm. Instead she just stood there and waved them off when they left, accompanied by the music of Mike swearing at her through the open window in the back seat. He wasn't taking his situation very well at all, she noted with a smile.

A wave of relief went through her. They would continue to keep watch, and make sure the farm was safe, but no longer having a visible threat would be a major morale booster. No one had enjoyed seeing someone under guard, and it wasn't as though they had a jail cell set up for that sort of thing. Chuck and Kayla had made sure their kids were kept from seeing it, and Jake was too small to understand anyway, but it had still been uncomfortable for everyone else.

Her dad wasn't back, so there wasn't a damn thing she could do about that. The only other problem she might encounter now, was Mitch, but he seemed to be doing okay. He couldn't live in a tent for the rest of his life, however, so she went to the house to grab a copy of the building plans they'd used for the one-room cabins, and then tracked him down. When she found him he was leaning against one of the goat pens, watching them and smiling.

"Hey Mitch," she said, causing his smile to disappear.

"Cam," he acknowledged. His tone had been emotionless. He was still being careful, which was for the best. Cameron didn't want to be friends with him. She just wanted him to do his part and not fuck things up for everyone else.

"We got some more supplies from the hardware store, so you can start building your own cabin if you want. Ask a couple people to help you with some of the awkward or heavier stuff. Everyone here is willing to help everyone else, just so you know. They're not afraid of a little bit of work, and nobody wants to see anyone suffer or do without. You're learning the ropes just fine according to Gilles, and there really isn't that much work with so many to do it. Believe it or not, you could have your own cabin in a couple of days, if you ask enough people to help.

"We haven't really been rushing with Lisa's place, because she's already got the room in the house. We also needed to get more wood and stuff. We've got the trees for the outer walls, but they're not so great for the inside part unless they're planed and dried. At least according to my mom. She's always complaining that it would be so much better if we had a wood kiln, but I honestly don't know what it's all for.

"Anyway, here you go," she said, and handed him the papers. "Make adjustments if you need to." She was already walking away when he spoke.

"It'll be nice to not have to sleep in a tent, so thanks." She didn't turn around, but just lifted her hand in a wave to acknowledge what he said. God, was she ever looking forward to having her mother back on the farm. This responsibility shit sucked.

଼ ◆ ଷ

Cam was getting very worried. Gilles and Chuck still weren't back, and a number of hours had passed. Since her mother didn't know anything about the reasons for them leaving, Cam wouldn't have been able to share her concerns with her, even if she had been on the radio to share them with. It was Ian who had answered when she called to check in, which freaked her out more than a little bit.

"What do you mean she's not there? Where the hell would she go? Over."

"I mean she's taking a couple of kids home, and it might be two days before she gets back to the boat. Over."

She signed off shortly after, having little to nothing to say to Ian. She didn't know him at all. Only once had she answered the phone when he'd called, and she'd immediately handed the phone to her mom. She wasn't even sure it was his voice she was hearing, so for all she knew there were pirates on the Great Lakes that were killing people and stealing their boats.

As if she didn't have enough things to worry about, now she was stuck waiting a couple of days to find out whether or not the voice on the radio was really Ian's, and if her mother was okay. Of course, the guy on the radio had known who she was, so most likely it was Ian she had talked to, but she worried all the same. She needed a vacation from all this stress, and the thought made her laugh.

Cam had no idea if anyone would ever take a typical vacation again. The world was full of dangers that hadn't been as blatant before, even though they might have already been there. It was just that now there were no controls in place. No authority figures were there to step in and put their lives on the line to protect the people. It was a problem that was too big for her to solve, so she let that one go. Instead she thought about what it would be like to be on a boat, having no one to bug her, and no responsibilities to deal with.

Boats had never really been her thing, so Cameron did something even better. She went to her room and played with the ferrets for a few hours. She still had the radio on her, in case someone needed to reach her, which sort of dented the illusion she was in her own private world, but it was better than nothing.

Squeaker licked her face as she snuggled him. He was extremely gentle until he got to her eyebrows, where he attempted to gnaw at them. She had to pull him away before his tiny front teeth really started to dig in.

"Those belong on my face, you know," she told him. Not that it helped. So she flipped him on his back on her bed and refused to let him wiggle away for a few seconds. By the time she let him up he was already dooking and squeaking at her. In seconds he was bouncing across the bed, backwards of course, until his butt dropped off the edge and he was scooting onto the floor. Then he skittered backward until he was behind her dresser, expecting her to give chase and chattering away.

"You sound like a monkey sometimes. You know that?" At the sound of her voice he came leaping back out, unintentionally pouncing on Pickle, though it hardly mattered. Except to Pickle, of course, who'd been curled into his usual doughnut shape, sleeping. He grunted at the interruption of his nap, but joined in the fray by yipping at Squeaker and wrestling to regain his spot on their bed.

Cameron sat back and watched them play, which seemed to push everything else from her mind. *Ah, ferrapy*, she thought. She was damn near asleep when her radio finally squawked.

"Cam? You there?"

"What's up, Billy?"

"They're back. Something must have happened, because they're both a mess and mad as hell."

"Okay. Let's find out what happened. I'll be down in a minute."

15 ~ BITTERSWEET RETURNS

They had trudged through the quiet streets of Detroit for half the night. There were bodies everywhere, and despite the fact that Mac didn't think it was something a couple of teenage boys should see, there was no way of avoiding it if they were going to get them home. The map she had taken from a convenience store didn't cover the outlying areas, and there was no way she was adding several days of walking to their trip.

While they had considered the bicycles Ian had suggested multiple times, they never found any within the city that weren't heavily chained or locked up somehow. What few belongings people had owned in the economically decimated city, they had done their best to protect. Since they didn't have any bolt-cutters, and weren't about to go wandering the streets to look for a hardware store, they just shrugged and kept walking.

Before even leaving the dinghy, Mac had cautioned both boys not to talk. If there was something really important, they could whisper it, but she reminded them what it had been like in Cleveland when people were rioting and looting.

"People are going to be even more desperate now, if there are any left alive. They will stop at nothing to take everything we have. We ran into cannibals in our home town, and that's even more likely in a city like Detroit," she had told them.

It didn't look like the warning had been necessary, however. Both Vigo and Denny looked sick and terrified. Despite their natural caramel complexion, both were pale. They took their steps carefully. It shouldn't have surprised her. They had survived Cleveland somehow, while people were killing one another over scraps of food. Most likely they had chosen to stay out of the way, hiding quietly until the threat passed. It was very possible they had resorted to eating things they couldn't bear to think about, and she would never ask them.

They took Ford Road most of the way, but Vigo said he'd recognize things a bit better if they went down to Marquette Street, so they moved south the few blocks to Marquette. Then they continued west, constantly passing mostly-skeletal human remains, though some were more fresh. Some bodies appeared to have shattered, making Mac wonder if they had fallen out of buildings, been thrown, or maybe jumped of their own free will. Others were lying there, bones intact but picked clean. Either rotted away, or eaten by other animals, human or otherwise.

She seriously wished she had a far less graphic imagination at the moment. It had been a useful tool when designing and implementing her plans for the farm, but now she wanted so much to shut off the little movies that played in her head, showing her everything these people had been through. It must have been the same in Cleveland, though Ian hadn't mentioned it, and neither had Vigo and Denny.

Before winter the stench would have been horrible, and there would have been no way she could have walked through it. The smell of anything rotting made her gag, and the images in her head would have added to it. Only a mild hint of decay remained, usually, and Mac still breathed through her mouth, even though she knew whatever particles remained in the air were going right down her throat. She was well aware of the mechanism of smell, and that actual pieces of what people smelled entered the olfactory senses. The knowledge was no longer an interesting piece of trivia she could bring out to disgust her friends, and it made the journey with the two teenagers almost unbearable. She was, in a small way, ingesting dead people.

When Neil tried to touch her she shook her head, and he seemed to understand that she couldn't take it. She didn't want to associate any romantic or comforting gestures with this horrific scene, and the tiniest hint of softness or sympathy would have her shattering like china dipped in liquid nitrogen.

Vigo and Denny were stoic, despite their obvious fear. They trudged on, and Mac knew it was only hope that kept them moving. If they came to the end of their journey, and Vigo's parents were gone, she had no idea what it would do to them. Maybe the only thing that had kept them going all those months was the hope that they still had a home and family to go to. Mac didn't know what she would do if she were in their place. They had each other, at least, and that would have to be enough if there was no one else.

It took them seven hours to reach the small, pale green house with the wood siding just past Wayne Road. They hadn't stopped to eat, because they had no appetite, but none of them were accustomed to walking such long distances either, so they hadn't moved as fast as they might have hoped. Mac, knowing she would have to make the exact same trip back, through the countless dead, all she wanted was to sit down and cry when they arrived. They had a responsibility to protect Vigo and Denny, however, and they needed to be sure of the situation inside the house before they let them go rushing in.

"Vigo? Denny? Are you listening to me?" She waited until they both nodded in answer to her whispered question before continuing. "We're going to make sure nobody bad is in your house, okay? Someone could have just stolen it, or taken it over because your family had food, even though it's back behind these trees. Hopefully no one saw it, but we have to check. We'll be right back. You stay hidden. What are your parents' names Vigo? I want to be able to call out to them if they're there."

"Sharon and Lloyd Morris. My dad's black, but my mom's half-and-half, and she kin-uh looks white. You want to see a picture of them?"

"That's a really good idea, yeah," she said, and waited until he pulled the wallet out of his back pocket. He flipped it open to show her the worn image of a handsome, but tired-looking couple. She didn't doubt that he had taken that picture out a lot over the last few months, just to remind himself what they looked like and take comfort in a loving face. She nearly broke down in tears, and had to push the thought aside.

"Thanks," she said gruffly, and waited until Neil had also taken a good look. He gave her shoulder a quick, almost-stinging squeeze, which was exactly what she needed. Rough comfort worked for her.

They walked quietly through the trees, and across the dark yard. Without the half-moon shining its light on them, they wouldn't have seen anything in the deep night. Even if the streetlights had still worked, their light would not have reach this small home. Mac stepped onto the very right edge of the bottom step, attempting to keep it from creaking, but the effort was in vain. The wood was so old it could barely hold its nails. The second and third steps were only slightly better, though the porch itself was sturdy.

She nodded to the sidelight, which was broken beside the knob. In all likelihood someone had broken into the house, and Mac wasn't very hopeful about what they would find. Still, they had to be sure.

Neil tried the knob, which turned out to be locked. It was the first sign that someone might actually be in the house, though alive or dead they couldn't know. He reached through the hole in the glass, slowly curving his wrist to avoid cutting himself, and unlocked the door. They both stepped through quietly, and pushed the door shut behind them.

"Should we call out for them, you think? If they're still alive, we don't want to end up shooting each other because one of us gets startled," Neil whispered directly into her ear, his breath just barely moving the hair she had yet to trim.

"I'll do it, and you conceal yourself," she whispered back. He nodded, understanding what she had in mind. A female voice would be less threatening, so anyone who might be in the house would be less alarmed and more likely to show themselves, friend or foe. If Neil hung back, he could keep his gun aimed, and reduce their chances of getting killed.

"Sharon? Lloyd?" She called their names softly. She didn't want to alert anyone outside, though it didn't seem as though anyone was alive out there anyway. A sudden gasp echoed through the house.

"Sharon or Lloyd Morris, are you in the house? Please, I'm not here to hurt you. I need to know if you're here. I'm armed, and I don't want to shoot anyone accidentally. I'm here about your son and your nephew," she called, hoping to diffuse any fear.

"That's not possible! They're dead. They're all dead. You get outta my house. Ya got to the counta three, before I come down there to shoot ya," the woman shouted.

"I'm telling you, your son and your nephew are here with me. We found them in Cleveland and brought them back." Dead silence met her statement at first, but then there was a heart-wrenching sob. Apparently mentioning Cleveland had made an impact.

"Vigo? You got my Vigo? And Denny, too?"

"Yes, ma'am. I made them wait outside, because I didn't know who would be in the house. If you give me about ten seconds, I can get them in here. Okay?"

"Oh my God. Please! Yes. Bring them inside!"

Mac slipped out the front door and called softly for Vigo and Denny. They sprinted across the yard toward her.

"Your mother is inside. At least I think it's your mother. She hasn't shown her face, but she knew your names before I said them. She only started to believe me because I said I found you in Cleveland. We still need to be careful, until you at least hear her voice and you're sure it's your mother, okay? Or we see her face. One of the two. I don't want to take any chances."

The moment Vigo called out for his mother, though, the woman came clattering down the stairs.

"Vigo, izzat you baby?" A second later she was nearly smothering him, her arms wrapped tightly around her son. Mac holstered her Glock.

"Denny? Where you at?" Denny shuffled over, as though he'd been worried about his welcome at first, but now that she had called for him he was reassured that she wanted him there. He was pulled into her embrace, despite the fact that she refused to release Vigo, and the three of them were an indistinguishable mass in the shadows. Mac heard the sobs as they poured from the woman, and she had to try to block the sound from her heart. Otherwise she'd be bawling until she dissolved into her own puddle of tears.

It was a good fifteen minutes before Vigo's mother remembered that anyone else was in the house.

"There was a lady here wit'yu. I need to thank her for my babies, but then you can tell me everything. Where you at, miss?"

"I'm right here. My name is Mac, or rather Mackenzie. My husband, Neil, is also here with me. We took a boat down to Cleveland to help a friend of mine, and your boys found us at a park there. Detroit was on our way back, so we were just going to bring them to the city, but it didn't feel right letting them walk all that way by themselves," Mac said, trying to keep the explanation short. She was exhausted, and the emotional scene had worn her out even further. She could have fallen asleep where she was standing.

Neil moved over to stand beside her, and he put his arm around her. Since he had managed to sleep while she'd been at the helm, he was nowhere near as sleepy as she was, though the long walk had likely tired him out, too.

"Hello, Mrs. Morris," he said politely.

"Please, call me Sharon. Hang on a minute. I got a candle here to light, so we can see a bit. I want to see my boys anyway." Mac heard the rasping flick of a butane lighter, and a sudden flame flared in front of her eyes, blinding her. Then the softer flame of a candle stub let them all look at one another.

Sharon had tear tracks down her face, and so did both Vigo and Denny. They were too happy to even try to hide them or wipe them away, until Vigo asked the question Mac had been dreading.

"Mom, where's dad?"

"He's gone, son," she said, and tears of a different sort gathered in her eyes.

"What do you mean gone? Where did he go?" Mac could see that he already knew he hadn't gone anywhere in particular. He was just buying time for himself, wanting to believe there was nothing wrong with his dad.

"He was … he was … well, they hurt him real bad when he tried to stop them from stealing our food, and when they saw what they had done, they ran for it, but it was too late for him. I tried to help him, best I could, but I couldn't stop the bleeding," she said softly, sounding almost beyond the pain. Of course, it had probably been months, and living on her own with no hope that anyone she loved was still alive, she probably *had* gone beyond the pain. It might be a while before she even believed her son and nephew were truly alive and with her again, and she would probably reach out to touch them almost constantly, or hold them, just to reassure herself she wasn't crazy and that they were really there.

"Sharon, we can't stay here much longer. We need to get back to the boat, but I don't want to leave you here if you don't have a way to survive. Do you have food to live on? What about water?" Sharon looked up at her as she spoke.

"Oh, yes. We're fine that way. I still have quite a few toms and hens, and more than enough jakes and jennies to breed once they're older. The neighbours took what vegetables I had left in the garden, but seeing the way the wind blew I had taken out anything that was edible. I walked to the garden centre to get some organic seeds for this year, so I could still get seeds from them when I picked them, and just keep on going, even though a part of me didn't want to. I guess there was a reason I hung on," she said quietly, looking lovingly at the two teenagers.

"What about water then? I don't think city water would be safe, even if it's gravity-fed and still running. The sewage treatment plants wouldn't be working anymore," Neil added.

"Plenty of water around these parts, and we have a rain barrel. A block away there's a bunch of ponds if I need them, though I haven't yet. No electricity, but farmers got on without it for hundreds of years. We'll do the same."

"Okay. Just so you know, though, we do have electricity on our farm. And we have a whole bunch of people with different kinds of food. We're up in Canada. If you want, you can come with us," Mac offered. Neil smiled beside her. He must have known she was going to make the offer, but then it wouldn't have been difficult to guess. If she hadn't, he probably would have.

"Oh, no. We're fine here. We have a couple of neighbours here still, who had no hand in what happened to my Lloyd. Those people ain't around no more. This small area has a couple people who have gardens and such, so we share what we have." Sharon smiled at them sadly, and Vigo and Denny sat quietly beside her on the sofa, both still crying from the loss of Vigo's dad. Sharon had had time to deal with it. For them it was a fresh wound.

"Alright then. So long as you'll be okay after we're gone. I don't want to leave you if you're in any danger here," Mac said, still reluctant to take the woman at her word. Neil rolled his eyes at her.

"See? You like to worry and fret," Neil teased her, making Sharon smile even though she didn't know the story behind the teasing.

"You two are welcome to stay and get some rest, and something to eat if you're hungry. I don't want you going off empty-handed after the gift you've given me," Sharon offered.

"I'm sorry to say we really have to go, though it's not easy to say goodbye to those two boys. We haven't known them long, but we're going to miss them," Mac said, making Vigo and Denny look up at her, both with small smiles despite their grief.

"Yes, I'm afraid our kids are going to be anxious that they haven't been able to talk to us on the radio. They probably tried to reach us on the boat last night. Mac's friend, Ian, will have told them what's happening, but we weren't planning to walk through a major city on this trip, so they're bound to be concerned about our safety," Neil said, making Mac cringe at the thought of her daughter's reaction when they finally spoke again.

Neither of them mentioned that the walk through the city had probably ruined their appetites for a while anyway.

They said goodbye to Vigo, Denny, and Sharon a few minutes later. There was no way for them to ever communicate with them again to see how things were going, so it truly was goodbye. Mac felt her eyes burning when they closed the door behind them, but the need to pay attention to their surroundings kept her from focusing too much on her sadness. The fact that the boys were back where they belonged made a huge difference in how she felt about it, too.

It began to rain about half an hour into their trip back, and it wasn't a soft rain either. Mac was actually relieved to see it, though.

"You know, this is the first time I've actually seen rain this spring," she said.

"Not me. It rained for a couple of days after you conked yourself on the head. You just didn't see it."

The rain soon stopped, and they were dry by the time they made it back to the river. Once they were settled in the dinghy, however, Mac remembered her irritation with her husband.

"Now, cowboy, would you mind telling me why the hell you decided to be such a jerk about Ian all of a sudden? I'd like to get this straightened out while we have some privacy and don't have to worry about being overheard by the city of Detroit," she said with a snippy tone.

"He had a look on his face when he hugged you. I didn't like it," he responded with a sigh.

"What? Are you fucking kidding me?"

"Nope."

"What the *fuck* kind of look could he have possibly had on his face, that would have you of all people acting like an asshole all of a sudden? You aren't the jealous type," she added.

"Who says? You're my wife. He's a good looking guy, and there was a time you had a thing for him. The look he had on his face made me think he had a thing for you, too, so I wasn't too pleased about it. You went to some pretty extraordinary lengths to make sure he was okay, and for a while there I wondered if he was going to take that as a sign there was another reason you had come to get him," he said with a huff.

"A good looking guy, huh? Maybe I'm the one who should be jealous," she retorted. His mouth dropped open, and then he rolled his eyes at her.

"Oh, absolutely! I'm just going to forget all about my forty-five years of heterosexuality and jump on some guy."

"It could happen. How do I know you don't have any latent bisexual tendencies? Maybe you've been hiding them from me," she said, laughing at his expression.

"Well, if I had, I'd hardly be willing to admit it to you now. You'd just make fun of me," he said, making her smile.

"You would deserve it. In fact, I still have to get you back for telling him about the whole Mac-Mac thing. I will never live that down. He's going to be calling me that until one of us keels over dead."

"He's older than you, so you might have a few years' peace and quiet before you die," Neil offered.

"You say that, but you don't know his family. Not that I ever met them, obviously, but they all lived well into their nineties.

He's probably got another forty years left in him. I'll be lucky if I get anywhere near that. Anyway, all kidding aside, are we okay now? Are you going to stop acting like you're hopped up on testosterone, and behave like a rational human being, or am I gonna have to start smacking you around?"

"I suppose. I'd fight him for you, but then he'd beat the crap out of me. He'd get to demonstrate how truly manly he is, and I'd be left to limp off into the sunset. Alone."

"Idiot," she muttered. "Row the damn boat. I want to get some freakin' sleep before I start hallucinating."

"Yes, ma'am." He grinned cheekily at her and rowed the damn boat.

⅚   ◆   ⅘

Ian took the first day at the helm to give them both some rest. They were at anchor when Mac dragged herself out of bed, and she could hear the two men talking out in the galley area. She smelled something amazing, and for the first time since she had set foot in Detroit, her stomach gave a happy leap. Bella was already inhaling her own plateful.

Gathering up some clean clothes, Mac headed for the tiny bathroom. She wanted a shower. Her scalp hadn't opened up at all, so she felt safe giving her hair a light shampoo. She couldn't scrub too hard, but it was better than nothing. When she stepped out and toweled off she felt almost human again. She had to struggle into her clothes, what with the humidity in the bathroom making them stick to her skin, but eventually she managed to make herself decent. Everything felt crooked on her still, but it would all straighten out once her skin was properly dry.

Neil put a plate on the table, and shoved it in front of her when she sat down in the cramped dining area.

"Eat, honey. You've been losing weight," he criticized.

"What the hell? Jerk! You don't get to tell me I'm too skinny. Or too fat. You're supposed to think I'm perfect. It's your job," she instructed.

"It's my job to worry about my wife, who hasn't been eating," he said through gritted teeth. "I had to watch you at death's door just a few days ago, so shut up and eat. Get your strength back."

"Oh, fine. Jerk," she muttered again for good measure. Ian just laughed at her. She hunched her shoulders, and dug into her eggs. They were from their farm, and were a couple of weeks old, though they were probably still a lot fresher than what people used to buy at the grocery store. She dipped her toast into the runny yolk and groaned at the first taste.

"Okay, you're forgiven," she finally said, when she pushed away her plate.

"I don't recall asking for it, oh cantankerous one," Neil intoned solemnly, so she stuck her tongue out at him.

"So, how far did we get today, Ian? Do you know?"

"You keep forgetting I can kick your ass now. Of course I know. We were passing Sarnia just when it started getting dark, since we only had about eight hours' of daylight by the time you two got back today."

"Oh, good. It'll be nice to be able to tell Cam and Billy we should be home in three days, if we can get twelve or thirteen good hours' travel in each day," she said.

"Shouldn't be a problem, so long as the weather cooperates, though I did forget to tell you that Cam radioed last night," Ian said.

"Yeah, Neil said something to Sharon when we were about to leave, which made me realize one of them would probably try to get in touch. I felt like an idiot for not thinking of it. She's going to be pissed that we went through Detroit like that. We weren't supposed to go into any of the cities. She was already worried about us going to Cleveland. We had plenty of oil from the restaurants back home, so there was no need to risk it, or so we thought. Best laid plans, though," she said, waving her hand airily.

"I'm sure she'll forgive you," Ian said with a shrug. "How did all that go anyway? You mentioned a woman's name. Was that Vigo's mother?"

Mac filled him in on everything while Neil put the plates into the tiny dishwasher. If there hadn't been one on board, they probably would have left the dirty dishes until they got home to throw in the dishwasher there, and then brought them back to the boat. Neither of them could stand washing dishes.

"It was the same walking through Cleveland," he said, when she finished describing the remains on the streets.

"I'm guessing there are plenty more inside the buildings, too, since the number on the street wouldn't coincide with the original population."

"Probably," Ian agreed.

"It's just such a hard concept to wrap my head around, and maybe part of me didn't think it was real. It's not until you see that there are really that many dead people, that it sinks in," she said.

"Well, things were pretty quiet in Huntsville, too, honey. And don't forget the cannibals," Neil reminded her.

"You know, I don't think, even if I live as long as Methuselah, that I will ever forget the cannibals, but thanks so much for the reminder," she said sarcastically.

Ian was tired, and heading off to bed with Bella trailing behind him, so Mac and Neil went into the cabin to radio the farm. Nobody answered at first, but then they were calling a little earlier than usual. They waited another half hour before trying again. This time Cam picked up.

"I'll have to talk to you later, mom. Something has come up that I have to deal with. I'll explain when you get home. Over."

"Well, put Billy on so he can tell us what's going on. Over."

"He's busy. We're all busy. I have to go. Over and out." Mac stared at the silent radio for a full minute.

"Huh," was all she could come up with.

"Couldn't have said it better myself. Looks like those kids have got some explaining to do," he said.

"Sadly, they're not the only ones. Great. I was just starting to relax a bit, and was looking forward to getting home soon. Now I'm probably gonna worry until we get there. Damn it."

"Could be she's just pissed at you," Neil suggested.

"I'm pretty sure she would have started giving me shit if that was the case. Though maybe it's part of why she didn't feel the least bit inclined to explain what was going on there. Makes me wonder what else might have been happening there."

"It doesn't look like we're going to find out tonight, so why don't we go up on deck and look at the stars for a while. Maybe if we get tired enough we can get a bit of sleep so Ian doesn't have to take the wheel for the whole day tomorrow."

"I *hate* not knowing what's happening at home, though," she whined.

"Yes, I know. Worry and fret all you like. I know I will be. I'll just be doing it up on deck. You coming?"

"Fine. Might as well do it there as anywhere else," she muttered.

16 ~ A Developing Courtship

Cam couldn't even derive any satisfaction from cutting off her mother and not filling her in. She had too much to do. She wasn't particularly worried or anything, but she couldn't sit up here chatting when they had a fugitive to find.

Gilles and Chuck had only been gone about twenty minutes when Mike decided to jump out of the moving truck. Neither of them knew how he had managed to free his hands, let alone remove his blindfold and see well enough to do it, but until they caught him it didn't do any good to speculate. They would figure that part out later.

As it was, she had enough trouble dealing with two men whose egos had been stomped. Both of them were ashamed, but still trying to justify the escape.

"Stop it, would you? I'm trying to deal with the larger issue here. We need to find him first, and then you can debate the matter all you want. We don't know if he's going to try to come back here, but it's a good possibility, and I do not want him getting through our security again. We've taken steps to keep that from happening, but no security is perfect, so let's catch him before it's a problem."

She organized the same sorts of patrols to cover the perimeter, but realized they would have to cover the whole thing now, instead of that one area. If he was coming back, he would pick a different spot. This time, however, the women would be involved no matter who liked it and who didn't. One person would be on the radio, and six people on patrol. They would switch off at three in the morning. They could cover a lot more area with more people, so she was involving everyone she could.

The exceptions would be Lisa and Kayla, who had young kids to look after, and Kelly and Annette, along with Mitch who would be given chore duty until their security issues had been dealt with. She might not trust him with security, but he could damn well milk a few goats. She'd still be checking to make sure the work was done, but that would only take a few minutes a couple of times a day.

Everyone except Mitch would be armed, but they usually were anyway. Chuck and Kayla's youngest was only seven, so they really hated having guns around her, but Cam solved the problem by loaning them the small biometric safe she used to store her own gun in. She'd had to add Kayla's fingerprints to it temporarily, but it was better than having little Amelia get her hands on a loaded gun. Their son, Chris, was ten, so he could be made to understand the danger, but nobody wanted a ten-year-old boy around a loaded gun either.

Katherine was becoming sort of the opposite problem. She'd been pouting and whining about how they had been so mean to the nice man who told her she was pretty, and Cam wanted to slap her. Chuck was not happy with her behaviour, and had already threatened to make some kind of a latch to lock her in her room if she didn't shut up.

They were probably going to have to start giving that girl birth control pills with her breakfast if any single males showed up. Fourteen sucked at any time, but in a world with no potential boyfriends, it was probably a teenager's worst nightmare. What Cam really wanted to know, though, was how the hell Katherine had gotten close enough to Mike to hear him call her pretty. He'd been under armed guard the whole time he'd been in the yard, and every one of those men would have told Chuck if his daughter had gotten that close.

"Chuck," she said suddenly, coming to a decision.

"Yeah?"

"I think we need to talk to Katherine about Mike," she said.

"Huh?"

"I think she knows something. Has anyone mentioned to you that Katherine was near enough to Mike to hear him call her pretty?"

"No," he said slowly, working it out in his head. "Hmm. I'll go get her." He was back in ten minutes, Katherine's arm firmly in his grip. Then he turned to Cam.

"You were right. She knows something alright. And she has no fucking clue the kind of damage she's done, either," he said, disgusted. "Feel free to explain it to her, because I'm too angry with her right now."

"You've been talking to Mike for a while now, haven't you?" Cam directed her question at the sulking teenager.

"So what?"

"So, you could have gotten yourself raped and killed. Not to mention any of the rest of the people on this farm. This isn't playtime, or find-Katherine-a-boyfriend time. This is end-of-the-world time where the grown-ups have to make decisions, and the children have to listen. Otherwise people get killed. Most of the world is already dead, and there is nothing out there to protect us from harm, so we have to rely on ourselves.

"And here's this other little thing you might have forgotten while you were flirting with a man at least twice your age. You're here because I allow you to be. You have food to eat because of me, Billy, Neil, and my mother. And if you want to continue eating that food, you will obey the rules we put in place. There aren't many of them, but they're not negotiable.

"This is no longer a world with juvenile detention halls. This is a world where people who break the rules go without a place to live and food to eat. Your dad could have been killed when that guy escaped. And if that had happened you would have had to live with that for the rest of your life. It's entirely possible someone might still get hurt because this guy got away. He was run off at gunpoint from the last place he was staying, because he couldn't keep his hands off his own niece.

"Now, what did you hide in the truck?" Both Katherine and Chuck looked at her in surprise. Chuck had been listening, but apparently he hadn't quite understood where she was going with it until she asked that question.

"I don't know what you're talking about," Katherine said, and her petulance was the final straw for Chuck.

"Cam asked you a question. You're going to answer it, and you're going to tell her the truth, or so help me God I'm going to spank your naked ass in front of every single person on this farm!"

Katherine looked at her usually mild-mannered father in shock and horror. Cam wouldn't be at all surprised to learn that no one had ever threatened to spank her before. Chuck was a very gentle person, normally, and Katherine acted like a spoiled, ungrateful little snot.

"I just put my little penknife on the back seat." She answered so quietly they could barely hear her.

"What else?" Cam glared at her until she squirmed.

"Just a note! That's all. I swear."

"What was in this note? Did you ask him to meet you somewhere?" Chuck looked at her in shock this time. Apparently it hadn't occurred to him that his daughter would step that far out of bounds, but Cam knew better. Chuck could blind himself to his daughter's behaviour all he liked, but Cameron couldn't afford to stick her head in the sand.

"Yes," Katherine whispered.

"Did you promise to bring him anything? Things like food or blankets?"

"Yes," she responded again.

"Where are you supposed to meet him, and when?"

"Same place we always meet. I just use one of the canoes to get there, so it only takes me about five minutes. He's got a van parked near the river bank on the other side of the bridge. I said I'd be there every day at three, just in case it took him a while to get back here."

"The same place you *always* meet him? Well, that's great. How many times has he raped you, Katherine?" Father and daughter both gasped, but for completely different reasons.

"Never! It's not rape when it's love. He makes *love* to me."

"You're fourteen. He raped you. You're not old enough to give consent." Cam felt terrible for Chuck, who had collapsed into a chair at his daughter's answer.

"I'm sorry Chuck. If it turns out she's *not* pregnant, you might want to get her on the pill. We have a whole bunch in storage. She'll be a grown-up long before we run out or they expire. You might as well take her home for now, though. I don't think there's anything else she can tell us that will help us catch him."

Chuck looked like he'd aged twenty years in the last ten minutes. He ran a shaky hand over his face and hair, stood up, and finally led his daughter down the stairs. Nobody said a word until they heard the door downstairs open and close again.

"Holy shit!" Gilles' comment pretty much summed it up for all of them.

"I know. I wasn't sure at first, but because her comment about him calling her pretty pissed me off so much, it sort of stuck in my head. After a while I realized there was no way he could have been that close to her without someone knowing about it. So, the only person to blame for Mike's escape, aside from Mike himself, is the little girl who fancies herself in love with him. Ugh."

"Chuck is going to want to cut his balls off when we catch him again. And if I'm honest I'd have to say I wouldn't mind holding the sick fuck down to make it easier for him," Gilles said. Billy nodded in agreement.

"I'm only nineteen, and it really freaked me out just to have her flirting with me. I can't imagine doing anything with her, and not just because of Chuck. She's basically still a little kid, and she acts like one, too."

"That's because she's spoiled," Cam put in. "Doesn't matter, though. I don't care what she did, or how she acted. What Mike did was rape, which is a whole different crime from stealing food. We all knew he was bad news, but now that he's acted on it we're going to have to do something about it. We can't allow anyone to rape a fourteen-year-old."

At least catching him should prove to be pretty easy, now that they had all the information about his van's location. Cameron thought there was a very good chance Mike would show up where Katherine offered to meet him. After all, in his eyes Katherine was more than willing to be alone with him and let him do whatever he wanted. And even if he wasn't a first-rate pervert, the food alone would probably be enough to convince him to show.

The real difficulty was now going to be finding a way to deal with a rapist. One that would satisfy Katherine's dad. Of course, there were lots of things they would all *like* to do to him for it, but everything she could think of was on the extreme edge of violence and cruelty. What would they become if they went to those lengths to punish someone?

Cameron tried to compare their current situation with the laws that used to be in place for rapists, but couldn't find a way to connect them. Rapists were supposed to go to jail, but there was really no such thing as a jail anymore. They couldn't take him up to Parry Sound, or over to Huntsville. Either Chuck or Gilles could get access to the holding cells there, but someone would have to drive there every single day to make sure the prisoner was fed. The only other option for keeping him imprisoned was to build their own jail on the farm.

They had no court-like system set up to hear charges, or allow anyone to present evidence of a crime. The closest they had come to that was listening to Mike tell them what he'd been doing. They had no impartial judges, and no one to defend or try a case against an accused person. When they had been planning the farm, not once had she or her mother considered the possibility that they would have to punish anyone for a crime. The closest thing to that had been the agreement that they would run people off the property with their guns.

Cam dropped into the chair that Katherine had so recently vacated, propped her elbows on the desk, and put her head in her hands. She was in way over her head here, and she knew it. Now was the time to rely on people like Chuck and Gilles. They were the ones who had been trained in law and order, and right now they were the last people who could help her. Suddenly her head snapped up.

"Kelly!" Her sudden shout startled both Gilles and Billy. She was a little startled herself, since she had completely forgotten until then that Kelly was a Justice of the Peace. Cam had no idea what sort of training that involved, or how much she knew about the law, but it was something anyway. If she couldn't let Chuck or Gilles handle this, she should at least talk to someone who had worked in the legal system.

"Okay, here's where I'm going with this so far. We'll do the patrols as planned, but there's a good chance we'll catch him if we surround his van. In the meantime we have to figure out what we're going to do with him. I'm going to talk to Kelly about it because she was a JP. She's the one who married Neil and my mother. She's got some legal training, and was given the legal right to do certain things, though I don't really understand what those were.

"I'm just going to get some advice from her, or maybe some suggestions, and we'll see what we can come up with. The thing is, we're all going to have to agree on how we're going to deal with this sort of thing in the future. If we start going crazy, cutting off men's balls, there's no telling where we'll end up with that kind of thing. Next thing you know someone is going to accuse someone of rape just because they hate them, and by the time we find out it's a lie we have a eunuch on our hands.

"And saying that, it occurs to me that we have no idea whether or not Katherine is lying. Maybe he hasn't touched her, but she knows he'll get in trouble if she says he did. Maybe he hurt her feelings. Any number of things could have happened. Or the kid could be crazy, and she's created a whole fantasy in her head that he's proposed marriage to her. She's fourteen after all.

"We can't go around punishing people just because someone says they did something. It's probably true that he took advantage of Katherine, and he most likely deserves whatever fate we want to dish out, but what if it's not?"

"Shit," Gilles said succinctly.

"This is so fucked up," Billy chimed in. "What the hell are we going to do?"

"Well, whatever it is, we can't leave it up to Chuck to decide what to do with this guy. He's not blindfolded justice right now. He'll just be in a blind rage," Cam said. "For now, let's figure out how we're going to catch him tomorrow, and make sure that little security weakness with the river is dealt with. People can't pass through because of the bridge there, but if Katherine can get a canoe across the property line in the other direction, without triggering a sensor, we need to move those sensors."

When Chuck came back through her mother's bedroom, and

climbed the stairs to the security room, Cam realized she was going to have another problem.

"Chuck, as hard as this is going to be for you to hear, your daughter is a teenager who is angry and sulking, and there's a possibility she's lying about Mike. He might have hurt her feelings, and so she's saying things that will get him in trouble. She has to know every one of us, and especially you, will be itching to punish Mike for touching her. She might have already been aware of the whole thing with his niece. She might think that saying she was with him because she loves him will keep her from getting into trouble, while still putting him in a world of hurt.

"I'm not saying she is lying. I'm saying there's a possibility of it. We have no way of knowing the truth right now, so we can't just go cutting his balls off. There was a reason we had court systems in place. People can lie, and we have to do our best to find out the truth. Right now we don't have anything like that."

"I don't know, Cam. Do you think maybe she was asking for it?" Chuck's question made her angrier than she could ever remember being.

"I don't care if she was sitting in his lap and grinding against his cock. She's fourteen fucking years old. She can't ask for it at that age. It's rape. It's our job as adults to protect teenagers from whatever self-destructive behaviour they exhibit, not take advantage of it. Any man who can't keep his dick out of a fourteen-year-old girl has no business walking the fucking streets. Would you fuck a girl your daughter's age?" Her question had him hanging his head.

"Never in a million years."

"So how can you even ask a dumbass question like that?"

"Isn't that what everyone else is going to be saying? That she asked for it?"

"Some, maybe, and they can bloody well get their asses the fuck off this farm if they're going to talk like that. She made some bad choices, and sadly she's probably going to pay a price for that. If nothing else she's going to realize the kind of slime that Mike is.

"Anyway, the point is, you can't be there to bring this guy in. We need to do this without you. It would be like having a doctor operate on their own family. That means no patrol, and no being there at the van for whatever day he might show up. He's got a bit of a walk to get back here, so it might not be until the day after.

"We need to do this right. This is really serious, and I don't want to start off on the wrong foot. Maybe we'll never have to deal with something like this again, but we probably will. If not rape, then theft. Maybe murder, maybe child abuse, or maybe someone beating up their spouse. The more people we get together in a group, the more likely those things will start happening, and even if it's not one of us, outsiders cause problems, too. Like Mike."

Chuck was still hanging his head, but he didn't argue with her. He wasn't a violent man, and Cam had a feeling he was relieved that the decision wouldn't be his. That didn't help her, since she was still stuck with it, except for the fact that she wouldn't have to fight with Chuck over it. Hopefully that would make things a little bit easier.

They brought everyone together who would be surrounding the van to try to catch Mike, and talked about strategy until everyone agreed that they had planned it as well as possible. There was always the chance something could go wrong, but with input from Chuck and Gilles for the more complicated parts, they managed to settle on a plan that would probably work. As soon as they were finished deciding how best to confine him after he had been caught, Cam went to find Kelly. It wasn't hard. She was standing outside, staring up at the stars just in front of the ferret building, which also happened to be the building she lived in with her girlfriend.

"Hey Cam. How's it going? I heard there was some excitement tonight," she said, obviously wanting to hear some of the details. Cam didn't blame her. They all had a right to know what was happening.

"Yeah, the guy who was stealing from us managed to jump out of the truck about twenty minutes from here. He had help," Cam told her, still disgusted with Katherine for that. She filled her in on the rest of the details.

"I actually came over here to ask for your help. Or maybe just your advice. You were a JP when we still had a legal system, and you have some familiarity with our courts. We have two former cops, but they never really had to go to court. Maybe if someone fought a speeding ticket, but that's about it. Now we've got a guy who might have raped a fourteen-year-old girl, so we have to figure out what to do with him once we catch him. Of course, I have no idea what a Justice of the Peace does, or did, so I don't even know if you can help me."

"Believe it or not, JPs aren't that different from judges in Ontario. We just didn't hear big criminal cases. I used to issue warrants and hear minor cases like by-law and *Highway Traffic Act* violations, as well as deal with bail hearings. True criminal cases were heard by judges, who had to be lawyers. I just needed lots of volunteer experience and a college diploma. So, I can definitely explain to you how the system used to work, and maybe give you some advice on your current problem. Not that I have any real say on things anymore, since I don't have a provincial government to back me up now, but I'll help if I can," Kelly offered.

"How would you feel about being a judge then?" Cam's question wasn't a joke. They needed someone to handle this kind of thing, and Kelly was the only one who had a clue what she was doing.

"Well, why don't we see what sort of system we can come up with? We're such a small group of people that we're going to need to take everyone's opinion into account, but I think you're doing the right thing by not engaging in some form of vigilante, wild-west justice. I'm sort of surprised, actually. It's very easy to fall into that trap when you're talking about the possible sexual assault of a teenage girl. It's very hard not to want to string the guy up by his testicles.

"I'll have to set aside my own bias, for that matter, but I had to

287

before, too. As a JP I wasn't allowed to be politically active once I was appointed. When I started the whole application process, I had no idea how involved it all was. I just wanted to be able to marry two of my friends, but it turned out to be a great thing for me. I enjoyed what I was doing, and there wasn't as much stress as there would have been as a judge. Not that I could have been one anyway."

"What about now? Will you have a hard time with hearing these kinds of cases? I don't think we're going to have to deal with a lot of this kind of thing, but we also need you to look after the ferrets," Cam said.

"Cam, I did the JP thing in addition to running my own shelter, with very little volunteer help. The small amount of cases I would need to deal with here on the farm won't be a problem. We can get more people involved with the ferrets if necessary. Plenty of people here love them, so I don't think it would be hard to find help. I can also train someone to take over as a JP or judge, for that matter. It's not like we have to worry about real legal requirements anymore. We're just trying to set up a fair system so people don't get hurt."

With Kelly agreeing to hear cases, Cam felt like they were heading in a good direction. They would need to get a confinement area set up for Mike. One that a fourteen-year-old couldn't break him out of, of course. And they would have to organize some sort of trial or hearing. That meant everyone on the farm should know about it, and be allowed to attend.

She decided it might be a good idea to have some sort of notice board to announce things like that. It could be used for all kinds of things. Cam's head was nearly spinning with all the possibilities. She didn't think she was much of a community-type person, but whether she liked it or not the farm had become exactly that. Eventually people would start having get-togethers, playing sports, having dances. When she realized the sorts of things her mother was going to be coming home to, she started to grin. Her poor mother was going to end up mayor of this crazy town, and Cam knew she would sit back and laugh her ass off when she figured that out.

She was walking around the yard, looking for the best location to confine Mike, as well as for putting up a notice board, when she saw her dad heading toward his cabin. Thankfully he'd come back faster than usual this time, because she had a lot of things to say to him right now, and she'd been hoping to get it out of the way before her mother got home.

"Dad!" Her voice carried across the yard enough for him to hear, though she tried not to be so loud she woke anyone up. Most of the people on the farm still preferred sleeping at night, even though they no longer had to keep a regular schedule other than on their chore days. And now Mitch would be getting up early to deal with the animals.

"Hey, kiddo! How ya doin'?" His casual greeting irritated the crap out of her, considering what she had to discuss with him.

"I saw you with Geraldine, dad. Do you have any idea who she is?"

"What do you mean?" He was trying to be nonchalant, but his face turned ruddy.

"I mean, aside from the fact that you're obviously fucking a married woman, do you know who her son was?"

"I knew she had a kid, yeah. Of course. She doesn't like to talk about it, so I haven't really asked."

"Jesus, dad. You're sleeping with the mother of the guy I killed! How can you be so blind that you haven't figured that out? There are so few people left alive, and his parents are two of those people. It's not that big a stretch to think that anyone you meet right now could very well be connected to that family. Hell, damn near *everyone* is connected to one another here!"

"She makes me happy, Cam. We're consenting adults, and it's not like she can get a divorce, so what else can we do?"

Cam's jaw just dropped. His complete lack of understanding of the true problem made her wonder if there wasn't something seriously damaged in his brain.

"You mean you're getting laid, so what the fuck do you care if she might be a danger to me and everyone else on this farm, don't you? I was already suspicious because she seemed to be just a little too nice about the whole thing. And now I find out she cheats on her husband. When I saw them together there was absolutely nothing to indicate that they weren't happily married. I don't know what she's been telling you, but it's probably flat-out bullshit, and you're probably quite happy to believe it, because you're getting something out of it.

"I do not need this right now. You've been away, *yet again*, and aren't aware of the fact that we have an escaped rapist on our hands. Now we have to catch him and hold some sort of a trial, because we can't even be sure what he's guilty of unless there's actual proof of his guilt. Now you're off banging some woman who could very well be another serious problem, but you just don't give a shit because you're getting laid."

Cam could see he was getting angry, but there was also shock on his face when she brought up the rapist.

"Who?"

"Are you asking who got raped, or who did it?"

"Both, I guess," he said weakly.

"Chuck's daughter Katherine. A fourteen-year-old girl who thinks she's in love with a thief and a pervert. The rapist being Mike, of course. That's assuming you've been around here enough to even know who Mike is," she said angrily.

"Isn't he the guy you had in the yard yesterday? I thought he was under guard. How the hell did he get his hands on Katherine?"

"She was meeting with him before we caught him, apparently. Or maybe I should say, 'allegedly,' since we're trying to do this whole court thing right. It's statutory rape, I guess, but no adult male has any business touching Katherine."

"Disgusting fucker," her dad said in agreement, which was a huge relief. She really didn't want to have to kick him off the farm for saying Katherine deserved it.

"Dad, if you don't stop seeing that woman, we're going to have a very big problem on our hands," she said finally, hoping like hell he listened.

17 ~ INFORMATION BLACKOUT

They managed a full fourteen hours' travel toward home on the first day, each of them taking the helm for close to five hours. Ian took the first shift, since he had gone to bed relatively early. Mac woke up after about six hours' sleep, feeling awake and refreshed, and took the second shift. Neil was awake an hour later, so he kept Ian company, while Mac kept her mind on what she was doing.

As soon as she was done her stint at the helm, however, she went through the steps to shut down the engine and dropped the anchor. She changed into her board shorts and a bikini top, and grabbed some goggles. She wasn't diving at pressure, so she didn't need a mask. She just needed to be able to see underwater. Neil followed her to the back of the boat and watched her jump off. When she was done checking the hull, he helped her climb back aboard. By then Ian was standing beside him, holding Bella's leash while she did her business.

"So? We gonna sink?" Ian asked. He leaned over with a baggie to clean up after Bella.

"Doesn't look like it so far. It doesn't look any bigger than it did the first time I went down, and we're travelling at our top speed, which is supposed to be up to seven or eight knots. I would think the additional stress on the hull would have shown if the crack went beyond the … what did you call it?" Mackenzie asked, looking at Ian for the answer.

"Gelcoat. Of course, the hull is painted, too. It's not just fibreglass and gelcoat I don't think, so maybe it's just the paint that's cracked. Like I said before, I always took my boat in to the people who actually knew what the hell they were doing, so I can't really tell you much," Ian replied. He handed Mac the leash so he could wipe up the rest of Bella's mess.

"Well, whatever it is, it doesn't look like we're riding any lower in the water, and I'm not hearing any pumps going crazy, so it looks like we'll be fine. Still, it's always better to be sure. We have zero experience with boats like this, and it scares the crap out of me that something could go wrong. We wouldn't know what the hell to do," she said.

"Did you say seven or eight knots? I thought this thing seemed slow. Jesus. You could have taken a regular motorboat and been there and back in a damn day or two. Instead it'll be more like two or three weeks."

"Well, Neil and I figured we didn't want to end up in the middle of one of the Great Lakes with a blown motor or something, and no way to keep going. If we got halfway there, and suddenly blew the motor because of an unknown mechanical issue, we'd have been fucked. We can't call in the Coast Guard or any sort of rescue. A dinghy isn't really adequate for a trip of around four or five hundred nautical miles, and swimming or walking weren't options either. We could have converted a diesel car or truck, and easily done the trip in a day, but we didn't know what was happening in the cities. We figured a boat would keep us away from any remaining population. What the hell do you want from me? I'm not perfect, ya know."

"Why the hell not? I certainly am!" Ian's comment had her laughing. He quite often said stuff like that about himself, but she knew he wasn't being serious. He was a lot more of a softie than he let on, and his ego often appeared rather dented. Sometimes she felt sorry for men. Particularly those of his generation. He'd grown up in a confusing time where women were supposed to be equal, but men still had to act macho or be told they were women, as though womanhood was synonymous with weakness.

"Okay, cowboy. It's your turn to fly the bird. I probably didn't need to purge the oil from the line since it was such a short stop, but I did, so you'll have to switch it back," she said, directing her comment at Neil.

"Aye-aye, Captain!" He saluted smartly and headed for the cabin.

"Jackass," she called after him.

"You two have the strangest relationship," Ian noted.

"Probably, but it works for us," Mac said with a shrug. "For the most part anyway. We're pretty blunt about everything, and yet we almost never argue or fight, so it's probably best that we don't rock the boat there."

"I still can't get over the fact that you married him after only five days," Ian said in amazement.

"I know. Totally out of character for me. I mean, when I married Cam's father I was really young, but we had still been going out for quite a while before we got married. I wasn't surprised my parents gave permission either. I was only sixteen, but they couldn't wait to get rid of me I don't think. Probably thought we should be back in the old days, where girls married at fourteen and started popping out kids at fifteen. Well, my father thought that way anyway. My mother just went along. I was with Mitch for a few years before we got married. Guess it just goes to show," she said.

"Goes to show what?"

"That it's not about waiting. It's about knowing who's right and going with your gut. Most people ignore the red flags that say someone isn't right for them for one reason or another. I know I used to. This time everything felt exactly right, even if it felt crazy. Of course, I thought Cam was gonna kill me at first. It was so reckless, and it was the worst possible timing. If I had been wrong about him, it would have been a complete disaster."

Ian gave her a considering look, but didn't say anything. They decided to take a look in the galley cabinets to see if there was anything interesting that they could nibble on. Food was kind of Ian's thing, and they wouldn't be having a real dinner until Neil stopped the boat for the night. Of course, Ian had to eat pretty frequently to keep his blood sugar as level as possible anyway, and to stretch out his insulin supply, he had to eat very small meals, at least five or six times a day.

There wasn't a lot, which wasn't surprising for a boat that might have been docked for a while. It was more surprising that nobody thought of checking out the boats to see if they had any food. There were some dry goods, like rice, pasta, and barley, which would have been a pretty great find, as well as some canned stuff to go with it, like tomato sauce. It was mostly healthy, and would have been very filling. They also found a tall jar of mixed nuts, which was perfect for Ian to snack on between meals. Hopefully it would keep him pretty steady.

"How are you with your insulin now?" she asked him.

"Well, I'm not dead. Without being able to check my sugar with a monitor, it's not easy to know how much I need to inject myself with. The meal-time insulin is just about to expire, so I'll be finding out how good your old-fashioned insulin is soon enough. I've got a few more months left on the long-acting stuff, which will keep me relatively stable, but once that goes I don't know what it'll be like."

"Yeah, I'm sorry there wasn't anything I could do about that. In order to make synthetic insulin, I would have needed some sort of reactor thingy, and the long-acting insulin wasn't even made in North America, so none of the facilities are here, even if we found a way to power them and a person who knew how to operate them. The only way to do it would be to go overseas, and I'm pretty sure that's beyond my very limited boating skills. Flying a plane is completely out of the question, unless we find someone who's a pilot. I don't know anyone who is. Or was."

"Well, it's really too bad you can't solve every damn problem in the world, Mac. We were all really relying on you for that," Ian teased.

"I have a damn brain. I do my best to use it. Sorry," she said with a roll of her eyes.

"I'm just teasing you. You know that. You've done a hell of a lot as it is, and not just for me either. It seems as if you've helped a lot of people. You make a difference. You always have, but especially now."

"Maybe, but it never feels like it's enough. I had to watch as the whole world imploded from its own idiocy, knowing what was happening and what it would take to change it. But you can't force people to do anything to help themselves. They all just wanted to sit in their comfortable homes and watch TV, and what I wanted was to smack the shit out of them for it.

"They paid too high a price for their complacency, but then a lot of other people paid the price who were trying to change things. How many Mozarts did we lose? How many Einsteins? So many people who could have been a huge help rebuilding this world are gone, too. Our very best minds are either dead, or we have no way of finding them and talking to them."

"It makes no difference now. It can't be undone," Ian said flatly. "All you can do is make a difference for the ones who are left. And then there's me. Who says all the great minds are gone? I'm still here."

Without thinking about it, they started munching on peanuts and cashews, continuing to talk until the sky began to darken. Only a day and a half, maybe, until they were home again, Mac realized, and she couldn't wait. She was still going to demand to know what was going on when she got on the radio later on, but there were probably a lot of little details she wouldn't find out about until she got there.

When it got to where they were turning on the lights, Mac decided it was time to start something for dinner. Spaghetti would be good, she figured. They didn't eat a lot of pasta at home, since they only had what was in storage. She hadn't learned to make it yet, so she'd been using what they had pretty sparingly. They had some goat cheese with them that she decided to use for protein. When the pasta was cooked and she'd poured on the sauce that she'd heated up, she crumbled the cheese over their plates. Aside from the goat cheese, it certainly couldn't be considered anything fancy, but both men ate with flattering enthusiasm.

They had a couple of hours before it would be time to get on the radio, and played a few hands of poker to pass the time. When she saw that it was close to midnight, Mac squeezed out from behind the table.

"Is it that time?" Neil asked.

"Yup. And I'm really looking forward to hearing about what the hell was so important last night, that Cam couldn't talk to us."

"You're not the only one. It's been a few days since I talked to Billy, too. Hopefully he's there this time."

"Think we'd get more answers from him than we would from Cam?"

"I'm not sure, but there's no sense trying to second-guess the situation. All we can do is talk to them and find out," Neil said pragmatically.

It took ten minutes before anyone picked up at the radio, and by then Mac was starting to freak out a little bit.

"Hey Mac! How's it going? John here."

"John? Where is everyone that's supposed to be operating this radio? Not that I don't want to talk to you or anything, but it doesn't sound like you had your licence to broadcast. Cam and Billy are supposed to be operating this thing, or even Chuck or Gilles. Over."

"Over? Am I supposed to be saying that? Sorry. Yeah, I really don't know what I'm doing with this thing. Cam just wanted me to keep an eye on the security monitors, so I'm the only one up here right now. Uh, over."

Mac and Neil looked at one another, wondering what the hell was going on at the farm if not one of the people who were supposed to be using the radio was actually there to use it.

"John, what the hell is going on there? Over."

"Not much right now. We've got some people out on patrol, keeping an eye out for Mike, but we don't really expect him to show up until tomorrow. Oh yeah. Over."

"Who the hell is Mike? Over."

"Just some guy who showed up and started stealing things. We caught him, which is how we found out who he was, but he got away again. Over."

"Maybe you'd better explain. From the beginning. Over."

"I can't. I don't really know the whole story. I just know he was tripping the sensors and my dad finally found him. Gilles and Chuck were taking him somewhere to get him away from the farm, but he jumped out of the truck. The only people who know what happened really are Cam, Billy, Chuck, and Gilles, but they're not here right now. Over."

"Where are they then? Over."

"Well, they're still somewhere on the farm, but I'm not sure where. I'm not seeing them on the monitors. Over."

"Aren't they carrying the two-ways we picked up when Neil and I went into town? Over."

"Yeah, but I'm not allowed to contact them unless it's an emergency. They're looking for Mike, and they said the radio might give away their position. You want me to try anyway? I mean, do you really need to talk to them? Over."

"No. I don't know what's going on there, so I won't put anyone at risk when there isn't an absolute need for it. When you talk to Cam, you let her know I want her to radio back as soon as she gets in, though. Okay? Over."

"Yes, ma'am. Over."

"And John, when you finish a conversation, you say, 'Over and out,' alright? Before we sign off, though, is everyone alright? How are the animals doing? Over."

"Everyone is fine, I think. Nobody's been hurt, and I don't think anyone even has a cold. Mitch is doing alright with the animals, but we're still keeping an eye on him like Cam told us to. Over."

"Mitch? Who's Mitch? Over." Mac had to ask, because she could not quite bring herself to believe it was who she thought it was.

"I thought Cam said you knew him. That he was your ex or whatever. Over."

"I do have an ex named Mitch. I just didn't think it could be him. He was still in Hamilton last I heard, so I figured he was dead. Over." She was mouthing the words, 'Holy crap,' at Neil.

"Mighta been close to it from the looks of him when he got here, but he's doing okay now. Over."

"How long has he been there? Over."

"A week maybe? Dunno. Been a while anyway. Slept outside the first night, but he's got the tent now. Looks like he's going to start work on his own cabin soon, because he was asking my dad for help. Doesn't seem to know a whole lot about using tools, but Cam wants him to do most of the work himself. I guess he was kinda rude when he first got here. Dad heard Cam go off on him the first day, but from the sounds of it he's been okay since then. Over."

"Doesn't surprise me in the least. Cam's probably been waiting to have a go at him for years now, and it wouldn't have taken much to set her off. I wonder what he said, though. Over."

"Dunno. Not sure if my dad heard that part. If he did, he didn't fill me in on the details. He just said something about him laughing right before Cam tore him a new one. Over."

"Well, hell. Sounds like it's been pretty interesting on the farm since we left. Anything else been going on? Over."

"Cam and Chuck got some more building supplies, so we can finish the new girl's cabin. Lisa, I think her name is. The one with the baby. And there should be plenty left over for the inside of your ex's place if we use logs for the main structure. He's got the plans for the one-room cabin. I guess Cam gave him a copy. Over."

"Cam and Chuck went to get supplies? Over." Mac had said it very slowly, just to be sure John heard the question right, and she got a full answer.

"Yeah. Carol gave her the keys to the hardware store, so they filled up the horse trailer and truck box with all kinds of stuff. As soon as they got back, though, Cam went over to see her friends. We didn't unload until later. She looked pissed, but I don't think she was mad at Chuck. He didn't look like there was anything wrong with him. Of course, he's no longer on patrol, either. I just realized that. Cam's got him doing other things, like helping Mitch with the animals, and building a jail cell. He doesn't seem like he's upset about it, though. In fact, I think he's got it in for that Mike guy, because he's seems pretty happy to be building the jail. Over."

"Jesus Christ! A jail cell? What the hell do we need a jail cell for? Over."

"Something to do with Mike. I think there's more to it than just him stealing and escaping, but I haven't been told what it is yet. There's been a rumour going around that they're going to have some sort of trial. Sam was talking to Kelly, who said something about resuming her old JP duties, but she wouldn't say anything more than that. Over."

"Alright John. I'll let you get back to what you were doing. There's no point in talking about rumour and conjecture. I'll just get the story straight from Cam when she gets in touch. Over."

"Sure, okay. I don't think she's gonna be back at the house tonight, though. She left about an hour ago, and wasn't planning to be back until morning. She asked Billy to check on the ferrets while she was gone, but I'll let her know you want to talk to her as soon as I see her. Over and out."

Before Mac had a chance to say anything further, he was gone.

"So," Neil began.

"Yeah," Mac responded, shaking her head. She got up slowly from the tiny navigation desk, and the two of them were silent as they headed back into the galley and dining area.

"So, how's it going at the old homestead?" Ian's question had Mac shaking her head again, as though trying to activate some sort of coherent thought.

"Uh, they're building a jail cell," she finally said, still having difficulty taking it all in.

"For some guy named Mike," Neil put in. "Oh, and Mac's ex is still alive, because he's there now. And Cam went off on a scavenging mission. And everyone who really knows anything is out on patrol. Looking for Mike. There's more, but my head is spinning and I can't remember it all right now."

"I take it this is all news to you?" Ian asked, looking back and forth between them.

"I'll say," Mac replied in a wondering tone. She still could not wrap her brain around the concept of the jail cell, much less the fact that Cam had gone on a scavenging trip, or that her ex was still alive and had somehow managed to make it to the farm. Though she did feel a streak of pride that Cam had told him off.

"Well, it sounds like they've got everything under control then," Ian said with a hint of laughter in his voice.

"Very funny. There was something about holding a trial for this Mike person, who is apparently a thief, but John thinks there's something more to it. It was all very confusing, but they had apparently decided to drive him somewhere and drop him off, just to get him away from the farm. The guy escaped, which is saying something in itself, because he escaped from two former cops. They haven't caught him again yet, but I guess they're pretty sure he's coming back to the farm, and they're no longer talking about just taking him somewhere, so it makes sense that there's another issue. I just don't know what it is.

"The scary part is, our kids are out there on patrol for this person. They've got some sort of formal security detail happening, and John was told not to contact them on the radio because it might give away their position. Now tell me, does that sound like something we should be laughing about?" She raised her eyebrows at Ian, who sobered immediately.

"No, it doesn't. Sorry. It was just the stunned look on your faces when you came back in here. It takes a lot to shock you like that. Your kids are armed, right? I mean, they're not going out there to look for someone who may or may not be dangerous without weapons of some sort, are they?"

"Cam's got her Glock. Billy will have a rifle or shotgun most likely. Not everyone has a handgun, but there are plenty of weapons on the farm. Both Chuck and Gilles have their service pieces still. And then there's the knives, too," she added.

"Knives?"

"Yeah, from my store," Neil answered. "My whole stock is there. I ran a knife store which is how Mac and I met."

"Oh, right. Sorry. Mac told me that at the time, but I forgot. Anyway, they're armed at least. Doesn't Cam have a bow, too?"

"Yup. That's how she killed that Gerry guy last summer," Mac reminded him. "I'm not sure how much she'll be using it, but she had just started carrying it around with her again before we left, which was when she ran into Brian. That's the situation I was really worried about when we came to get you, even though we talked to both Brian and Geraldine and everything seemed okay there. Hard to say for sure, but John didn't mention anything about them."

"Who's John?"

"My friend Gilles is married to Felicia, whose daughter, Melanie, is married to John. John's parents are also on the farm. I knew Jim from the gas station in town, but I didn't meet his wife, Donna, until they got there."

"How many people are on this farm of yours, Mac?"

"You know, I don't think I know anymore. I would have been able to tell you a couple of weeks ago, but there seem to have been a couple of additions since then, invited or otherwise."

"Trying to start your own town or something?"

"I really wasn't. I don't know what the hell happened," she said helplessly. Ian laughed at her again.

"I do," Ian said.

"Yeah, yeah. Shut up. You're one of the people I'm trying to help, so you've got no business complaining."

"Hey, I'm not complaining. If you want to go rounding up all the survivors in the world, that's up to you. You should put up signs, though. *'Need help? Call 1-800-4-Mac-Mac.'*"

"Oh, go to hell," she told him, having to raise her voice to be heard over the sound of Ian's laughter. Then she pointed her finger at Neil. "*See?* The rest of my life he'll be doing that. I guarantee it!"

ॐ ◆ ♋

She didn't hear back from Cam by three, so Mac finally decided

307

to go to bed. Neil was already in bed, waiting for her, and she could hear the sounds of Ian's snores coming from the other end of the boat.

"Still no word?"

"No, but then John said she was probably going to be gone all night. I'm better off just getting some sleep so maybe we can get there a little faster. It's the only way we're going to know for sure what's happening there. That's assuming I can sleep, of course."

"I think I might be able to help you with that," Neil said, and she could hear the warm promise in his voice.

"I'll just bet you can, cowboy. Wanna take a stab at it?"

"A stab? If that's what you want to call it," he teased, as he rolled over to cover her with the warmth of his body. Her quiet laugh turned to a gasp as he slid inside of her. It wasn't long before she was sinking her teeth into his shoulder to keep from crying out at the intensity of her release, which instantly had him following her.

Despite the warm contentment she felt in her physical being, her mind was unwilling to let go of the thoughts that spun around inside it. She put on Neil's t-shirt, which covered her to mid-thigh, grabbed shorts and underwear, and went to the tiny bathroom that didn't have the shower to use the toilet and clean herself up. She pulled on the panties and shorts, but didn't worry about a bra. The t-shirt was dark, though she couldn't remember if it was black or navy, and even if Ian woke up she didn't have to worry about giving him a show. Not that it sounded like he was getting up any time soon, since his snores continued unabated.

Mac went out onto the slightly tilted fibreglass of the deck to lie on her back and look up at the stars once again. It made her wonder why the hell she had never made it a priority to buy herself a boat. Then again, the boat they were using probably cost just as much as their whole entire farm and everything on it, but she would have been happy with something much smaller. In fact, it might have made for an interesting choice if she'd gone with a houseboat instead of a farm, though it might have made gardening something of a challenge.

They had done vertical container gardening at the apartment in Hamilton, so she knew how to grow a lot of food in a small space. It wasn't impossible to be self-sustaining on a boat. Just a lot more difficult. Instead of chicken eggs and goat's milk, fish would have provided their protein, but she didn't like the idea of killing fish either. She'd done it as a kid without a second thought, though she'd at least knocked them out before gutting them.

It was just so peaceful on the boat. Day or night. She loved diving because of the serenity, but even lying up on deck by herself was eerily quiet. Or at least it was until she heard the footsteps shuffling across the deck toward her. She was surprised to see Ian standing there.

"I thought you were sleeping," she said.

"I was until a few minutes ago. Got a little shaky, so I grabbed a glass of orange juice. Hope that's okay."

"Of course! Take anything you want. Bella still asleep?"

"Yeah. I saw you through the window, so I thought I'd come out. Or maybe I should call it a porthole, since we're on a boat?"

"Don't ask me. You're the only one with any boating experience. I feel stupid even using the correct terms, like I'm some kind of poseur. Makes me think of Joe Pesci in *Lethal Weapon 4*, where he was ranting about them getting 'all nautical' when they were around boats."

"Haven't seen it," Ian said, even though he laughed at her discomfiture.

"Yeah, you're not much for movies. You don't know what you're missing. You've got plenty of time to catch up now, though. We've got a zillion of them on the server." Just then she heard Cam's voice on the radio through the window. She jumped up and instantly tripped over her own feet trying to rush to the cabin. Ian caught her by the arm just as she was about to fall.

"Thanks!"

"I think you need training wheels," he called after her, but by then she was pushing the button on the mic to talk to Cam.

"What the hell is going on there, Cam? Over." She was going to get answers this time, whether Cam wanted to give them to her or not.

18 ~ ANSWERS

Cam looked at the radio in misery. She had really been hoping no one would be there to pick up. She thought maybe she would be able to avoid talking to her mother until at least the next night, when hopefully Mike would be caught. Apparently not.

"What do you mean? Over." Cam wanted to find out what her mother knew, before she started spilling her guts.

"According to John you're building a jail, going on scavenging trips, setting up security patrols, you've got an escaped convict, Mitch is there, and you're going to be holding a trial. There might be more that I'm forgetting at the moment, but that's quite enough to be getting on with for now, don't you think? Let's start with all that. Over."

"Well, if you know that much, why are you asking me what's going on? It sounds like John's told you everything. Over."

"Right. Why don't you start by telling me who this Mike person is? He was apparently stealing and setting off the sensors. You caught him, but then he got away when you were trying to send him somewhere else. Now there's something else, because you're suddenly building a jail to put him in, and Kelly is apparently going to preside over a trial. Have I got everything right so far? Over."

"It's kind of a long story that involves Chuck's daughter, and I'd rather sit down and tell you the whole thing when you get back here. I'll just say that it's a possibility Katherine is pregnant, but we don't know the whole story. I didn't think it would be a good idea to just let Chuck cut off his balls, if we didn't even know for sure if she was telling the truth. We do know that she made it possible for him to escape, though. Over."

"Oh, God! She's fourteen! Is this a grown man we're talking about here? Over."

"Yeah. Do you remember those people from the Ottawa shelter? Mike was the husband. He brought the van back here, so I'm guessing he lied about how much gas they needed to get to her parents' place. He's got to be around thirty years old, so even though Katherine is calling it lovemaking, we're treating it as rape. It's statutory rape if nothing else. Over."

"Jesus. I don't know what to say. You seem to be handling it the right way, though. I can't imagine how bad things would get if we just started chopping off balls without some sort of due process. Over."

"Yeah, that's kind of what I figured, and Kelly agreed with me. She's the nearest thing we have to a judge, and I guess JPs used to hear actual cases as long as they weren't criminal cases, so she's not that far off. At least she understands how the legal system is supposed to work, and can keep things respectable. Over."

"Yeah. Wow. I still don't know what to say. How long has this situation been going on, though. This can't have just been in the last couple of days. Over."

"Well, no. We were getting sensor alerts for a while, but nothing was showing on the cameras. It turned out that he found one of the cameras and moved it. He was getting through the inner sensors because a tree fell over in front of it, which meant the sensor was blocked and wasn't picking up his body heat. It was just luck that the tree fell the way it did. We've moved it now, and the camera is back where it's supposed to be. We took screenshots so we know exactly how each camera is supposed to be positioned. Before it was hard to tell, because they all just looked at trees. Nobody was going to remember exactly what the trees looked like for each camera. Over."

"I guess it's a damn good thing he wasn't there to kill anyone. Over."

"Yes. And now you know the big news. Anything else? Because I'm really tired right now, and I still have a lot to do before we try to recapture this guy tomorrow. Over."

"What do you mean? How are you going to do that? Wouldn't he be far away from there by now? Over."

"Katherine left him a note, telling him to meet her at his van, and we think there's a good chance he'll show up. She offered to bring him food and stuff, and obviously he thinks he can continue molesting her, too. Over."

"So you're going to surround the van at the appointed time and then put him in jail once you have him? And you didn't think I should know about all this, Cam? It never occurred to you that I might have something to say, or that I should know you were putting yourself at risk? How the hell did you convince Gilles and Chuck not to tell me about this? Over."

Cam let out a long sigh. She had known this was coming, but it would have been so much easier to do this in person. It was a pain in the ass communicating over the radio.

"Look, I'm doing the best I can here, and making the choices I think are the right ones. You aren't here, and there's nothing you can do to help. You'll hear all about it when you get home, but for now I really have to get going. Talking to you is taking up time that I could be using to sleep later. How long before you're back? Over."

"If we're not back before nightfall, it'll be the following day. And you and I are going to have words when I get there. I don't like being kept in the dark. Over."

"Yeah, well, neither do I really, but you still went traipsing off through the streets of Detroit without discussing it with me first. So, yeah, we can have words when you get back. Until then, I've got work to do. You brought most of these people here, and then left them for me to deal with, so that's what I'm going to do. I'll talk to you when you get back. Over and out." She release the mic button and turned off the radio.

She knew she was going to pay for that, but Cam was just too tired and irritated to give a shit. She was sick of being given the responsibility of an entire group of people, only to have her mother treat her like a child and second-guess everything she was doing. Besides, she really did have more important things to be doing.

Mike hadn't shown up at his van the first day, so Cameron figured he was going to get there in the afternoon. She'd been up all night as part of the patrols, and she still had to go out and figure out how to fix the sensors on the far side of the bridge. Once she was done that, she might actually be able to get some sleep. Assuming Pickle and Squeaker didn't decide to dig at the base of her door for an hour, like they had the last time she'd been trying to fall asleep. They wanted out, and they most likely missed her mother. Usually she missed her mother, too, though that wasn't the case at the moment.

Nobody knew about the situation with her dad, except Kirk and Leigh, and until her mother was home there was no way she was telling her about it. If she was freaking out over the situation with Mike, she was going to be a lot more upset about Geraldine sleeping with Cam's dad. Her mother wasn't stupid, any more than she was, and Cameron really didn't believe Geraldine was the kind of woman that would find her dad irresistible.

Now Cam was at odds with both her parents, which was not helping her state of mind in the slightest. Her dad had damn near blown a gasket when Cam had told him he needed to stop seeing Geraldine, and he hadn't spoken to her since. Her mother's reaction was going to be even worse, but at least it would be directed at her dad, rather than at Cam.

Her dad would be lucky if he still had a place to live after this, and Cam was more than happy to let her mother make that decision at this point. The fact that her dad considered getting laid more important than whatever risks he was exposing his daughter to, had hurt Cam a lot more than she was willing to show. He was acting like a selfish prick, and he wasn't even trying to be there for her when she was shouldering so much responsibility she wanted to scream.

Making a noise of disgust, Cam shoved away from the desk and stomped down the stairs to let John know he could go back to watching the camera feeds. She wasn't too happy with him at the moment either. He should have kept his mouth shut. But then, in Cam's experience men were worse for gossiping than women. They just didn't call it that.

It was an hour before she got back to the house, and just to give herself some peace and quiet later she decided to take the ferrets to her mother's room for a while. They could play themselves out from the excitement of it all, and then she might be able to get some decent sleep before they went back to surround and watch the van. They had temporarily mounted a camera to keep an eye on it anyway, but they wanted to be close by so they could move in when he showed up.

"You guys really miss her, huh?" Cam asked the ferrets as they wandered the room, sniffing and searching. Every once in a while they would tilt their heads way back to look up at her, as if to ask her where she was hiding their mama.

"Poor babies. She'll be back in a day or two, though, and then you can get all excited about her for an hour or two before falling asleep again."

Pickle looked up at her just before nipping at her sock-covered toe. As soon as she yelped, he made a huffy, laughing sound and bounced backward, wagging his head from side to side.

"You're such a little shit, Pickle," she said, but she was laughing. He was so ridiculous. He did the exact same thing to her mother all the time, if she happened to be wearing socks. Something about socks just got ferrets going. Squeaker wasn't as bad for nipping, though he did tend to grab the socks and try to pull them off with his teeth.

Cameron pulled off one of her socks and dropped it on Pickle's head, who went absolutely nuts attacking the offending item. All four paws were gripping it as he rolled around on the floor, 'wrestling' with it. Every once in a while he would bounce onto his feet only to start rolling around with the sock again after pouncing on it. Squeaker decided to get in on the fun, and pounced instead on Pickle, who yipped at him and forgot all about the sock. Until it touched his fur, of course, and then he forgot about Squeaker to attack the sock again.

She sat on the bed and watched them play until her head started rolling on her neck. Then she yanked her sock away from Squeaker, who had apparently commandeered it, and put it back on her foot. She got a whiff of her own foot, which wasn't pleasant, but Cam had no interest in a shower right then. All she wanted was her bed. Scooping the ferrets into her arms, she trudged off to her own room, trying to keep the wriggling bundles from falling to the floor as they struggled to get down.

"Nope. You guys have had all the fun-time you're getting right now. And if you start digging at the door again, I'm locking you up." It was an empty threat. They didn't even own a cage for them. Her mother had gotten rid of it years ago.

The instant she closed her bedroom door behind her, however, and set the boys on the floor, they ran straight to their bed. They curled up like a couple of quotation marks and went right off to sleep. *Probably depressed now*, she thought. They weren't used to spending this much time alone, and her mother had never been away from them for more than a few hours at a time, so Cam felt sorry for them. It wasn't like she got mad at them anyway. Still, it was a relief to be able to strip off her clothes, slip into shorts and a t-shirt, and let her body ooze between the sheets. She really was falling in love with her bed lately, she realized, which was her last thought before she passed out.

℘   ◆   ℀

"You've been keeping a close eye on Katherine, I take it?" Cam asked Chuck.

"You'd better believe it. That girl isn't allowed to leave the house right now. Hasn't been out since I took her back the other night. She can get fresh air when the front door wafts it in," he said bitterly. Cam wasn't surprised. It had been a very rude wake-up call for him to find out what his daughter was really like.

The price of spoiling your kids, she thought. It was one of the reasons she didn't really like kids. Or at least other people's kids. And why she had thanked her mother more than once for not letting her turn out like that. They might have their disagreements, but being raised to be responsible and independent, instead of expecting everyone to give her whatever she wanted, was something she was grateful for.

If she had ever shown any signs of behaving the way Katherine had done, she'd have been stomped on for it. In fact, the closest she had come to that had been going out on her own the day she met Brian, and adult or not, her mother hadn't let her get away with it. Most of the arguments she had with her mother came about because they were too much alike, though. Lately the tendency for them both to rely solely on themselves was getting to be problematic. They each had a hard time operating within a team, which was what they had to do now.

Not that Cam wanted to run the show on the farm. Far from it. It was just that she had been given the responsibility for a short period of time, and she was damn well going to do it. Once her mother was back, and knew everything that was going on, Cam would feel nothing but relief. She kept wondering when someone was going to ask her who the hell she thought she was, giving them all orders. She could easily see someone like Katherine saying,

'You're not the boss of me!' The thought nearly made her smile, but she contained it. She didn't want Chuck to think she was laughing at him.

"Cam?" Chuck's query startled her.

"Sorry. Did you ask me something?"

"I just said we need to find a way to lock our new containment cell so that asshole can't get out again."

"For now we can just bar the door. We can angle a beam from the ground to the door. Dig a pit, and maybe line it with fast-drying cement, to brace the beam. Sort of like those metal door bars you see in movies of people living in apartments in shitty neighbourhoods. For now anyway. We can think of something else later. Just make sure your daughter doesn't go anywhere near the building once we have him."

"I will. Like I said, she's not getting out of the house right now."

"Alright. You'd better get your door bar set up then, and we'll make sure we have someone to put in your fancy new jail. Okay? We can improve on it with a trip to the hardware store later," she said. Chuck nodded and clomped down the stairs. When he was gone she turned to the other people in the room.

"I know we went over this yesterday, but we're going to refresh our memories so we don't forget any of the details. Felicia, you'll be watching the monitors for any signs of him. Radio the person who's furthest away from him once you see him. That person will let the others know his location, and we can surround the van with that in mind. We want to box him in without him seeing us, if possible. We stay on the property on this side of the sensors until he shows. It's unlikely he'll go on the property now that he knows about the sensors, but if we're circling his van he could run right into one of us while we're waiting.

"We'll move in and surround the van in two circles. If he runs through one group, he'll be caught by the second. Please, for the love of Christ, if you have to fire at him watch where you're shooting. I don't want us shooting each other. Gilles, I'll let you give the instructions there. I went through the firearm training for civilians, but I don't have police training."

Gilles took over and gave them a rundown which wasn't far off what he'd started teaching her about hunting. The same safety precautions applied. The exception was that they weren't shooting to kill. He made that clear a few times, and double-checked to make sure everyone understood. The rumours had finally circulated that something had been done to Katherine, so it was entirely possible someone would get a little too trigger-happy. When Gilles finished, Cam only had one thing left to say.

"Some of you have some idea why we're so determined to catch him, and some may think we know all the facts. We don't. There's a distinct possibility we've been fed a steaming pile of bullshit from a rebellious teenager. *If* he's done what he's been accused of, and we have to be absolutely certain of that, we need to make sure he can't hurt any of us again. If he *hasn't* done it, and we turn into a bunch of animals and do something we can't take back, not one of us will be able to look at ourselves in the mirror again. I do not want to be responsible for that. Okay? We're going out there just to catch him and confine him. If we do this right, there is no reason we can't bring him back here alive and unharmed." She glared around at the ten people who would be going out with her, and every one of them looked sober-minded rather than wrathful, which was what she wanted.

"Okay, please be careful with your own skins, too, and do not approach him while still carrying a weapon than he can take from you. Let's get our asses over there and be ready."

Cameron felt something like a parrot, because she had said pretty much the same thing the day before, but it didn't hurt for everyone to have a reminder, or the extra bit of training Gilles provided. People learned through instruction, practice, and repetition, and so they would be better prepared on the second day than they had been on the first. So long as it didn't get to the point where they were rolling their eyes at her, but if it stretched on much longer she would be rolling her own eyes and telling herself to shut up.

Cam knew he was going to show up that day. She didn't know if it was instinct, or what, but something was going to happen. Because she felt that way, the afternoon air felt like a surreal swirl around her. Some sort of calm stole over her, until she was so in the moment that it felt like time stopped.

It didn't, of course, and it wasn't long before she saw Leigh walking toward her. Apparently she'd gotten the notification over the two-way, which meant Mike was at the other end of the group. Leigh had let everyone know as she passed them on her way to tell Cam, so they had followed her. They gathered up the rest of the group. Then the second radio call came in to let them know Mike was at the van.

Now they could safely surround his van in the two circles. Four people inside, though still shielded by trees, each coming toward a corner of the vehicle so they were watching two sides of it. The other seven people formed a wider circle, showing little from the van side, other than the business end of a rifle, and an eye with which to aim. No one carried a shotgun, because the risk of collateral injury was too great. Until everyone was exactly where they were supposed to be, and all had nodded to the person closest to them to indicate they were ready, they remained silent. Once they were ready, however, Gilles called out.

"Michael Langston, we're armed and have you surrounded. Come out of the van, slowly, and put your hands in the air where we can see them. Do not bring a weapon out with you, or we will fire on you."

Cam distinctly heard the word 'fuck' from inside the van. The cargo door latches clicked open, and the doors began to swing wide very slowly.

"I'm coming out. Jesus. You didn't need to go to all this trouble just for me. I haven't done anything other than take some food, for cryin' out loud!" He held his hands way up in the air, using only his legs to climb out of the back. From where Cam was standing, she could see blankets and cushions piled up. At the very least he slept back there, and had potentially done much worse.

He had to know Katherine had told them about their meetings. Otherwise how would they have known where and when to go looking for him? However, he continued to play the innocent.

"What did you expect me to do, man? Starve to death? And it's not like you had the right to take me somewhere I didn't want to go," Mike continued, blithely unaware that every word he spoke had Gilles clenching his jaw.

Cam had to admire Gilles' restraint, because he didn't even mention Katherine. Gilles handed his handgun to Cam for safekeeping, and took out the handcuffs he'd dug out of storage. Mike was searched and cuffed without incident, then told to walk ahead of the group. Against his better judgment, Gilles had agreed to cuff his hands in front, because they would be walking over uneven terrain, but they were all warned not to walk in front of him. Maybe they were being paranoid, and it was just as likely Cam had seen too many movies, but they wouldn't risk the possibility of Mike getting his hands on someone's gun.

The trip back to the yard seemed to take a long time, though it couldn't have been more than ten or fifteen minutes. The van hadn't been far outside the property line. The tension during their journey made the time stretch, however, and it wasn't until Mike was safely behind the barred door that Cam was able to take an easy breath. The only opening in the structure was a horizontal gap in the wall opposite the door, which was just big enough to pass food through, and provided fresh air.

She didn't know enough about plumbing to outfit him with a proper toilet, so they would have to bring him to one for the time being. It was either that or have to deal with a bucket, and nobody wanted that responsibility. If they had been dealing with a criminal mastermind she would have been a lot more concerned. A thieving pervert they could handle, so long as he had a gun held on him at all times. He was a coward at heart. Jumping out of the truck when Gilles and Chuck had both holstered their weapons was the extent of his bravery.

Still, it nagged at her enough that Cam knew her mother would be bothered by it, too. In all likelihood a brand new structure would be built once her mom had had a chance to think about it. Until then, Cameron wouldn't feel comfortable without a constant watch. She would be taking the camera off the van anyway, so they could use that.

As for the rest of it, Cam was in over her head. Kelly could deal with it. Or her mother. She was just going to ask Kelly whether or not it was considered humane to hold him without trial for a couple of days, because she seemed to remember something about that being in the Canadian *Charter of Rights and Freedoms*, though she didn't actually have a copy of it on hand.

Kelly would be in the midst of carting out the day's ferret poop, and since it had been a while since Cam had been able to help her with all that, she decided they could talk while they worked. She grabbed some spare clothing to change into after she was done.

Even if they had already been looked after, she wanted to spend some time with the ten that were quarantined. She always felt so bad for them, even though they had each other to play with, and both Kelly and Annette spent time with them. It was like they were being discriminated against or something.

"What it boils down to is this, Cam," Kelly said in response to her question. "Are you going to follow the laws that were in place, or are you going to create new ones? If you're going to create new ones, the fair thing to do would be to involve everyone in the crafting of them, and give everyone an opportunity to learn what they are. Until that's been done, it's probably best to stick with the original laws, because it doesn't seem right to suddenly throw someone in jail and subject them to laws that never existed until you made them up. Conversely that applies to rights they may have had before.

"The laws in place before everything went to hell meant that a person had to be given a bail hearing or released within twenty-four hours. Whether or not someone is granted bail depends on many factors, but what applies here is that he's already shown he's a flight risk. By running from two police officers during transport, I think it's fair for me to deny bail on those grounds. If you want to do things right, though, so that we maintain peace and order, we should really set up a bail hearing for first thing in the morning. Has he been informed of the charges?"

"Not yet," Cam said, and hunched her shoulders at the look Kelly gave her.

"He has to be told. Gilles should know that, since he's a trained police officer. Why didn't he do so?"

"We weren't sure what the hell we were doing, and I asked him not to say anything. In fact, nobody even told him he was under arrest, because it just sounded so stupid under the circumstances," Cam added.

"Well, it's not like there's anyone he can complain to. He won't have a defense lawyer or anything, who can get him off on a technicality. For that matter, there are no prosecuting attorneys, and we won't have DNA evidence or even hair analysis from a sexual assault evidence kit. Chuck and Gilles are the only people on the farm, aside from myself, with any legal training that I'm aware of, and I can't see either of them defending him. Be a bit much to ask of Katherine's father, I'd think, and if Gilles went along with you on not telling the guy why he was being detained, he's probably not inclined to help him either."

"This whole thing feels ridiculous. I'm beginning to feel stupid for not just letting Chuck have a go at him."

"Cam, you're doing exactly the right thing. It's complicated when you only have a few pieces of a very big puzzle. The Canadian Department of Justice was no small thing, and you're doing your best to be fair to another human being. That's not a bad thing."

"She's right, you know," Annette piped up from across the room. Cam hadn't realized she was even there.

"Thanks, but now I have to explain to everyone else why I've turned it into some kind of circus, when it could have been such a simple thing. Every one of us knows he's a pig with females, and none of us wanted him to stay here for that reason."

"But it's not at all simple," Kelly admonished. "Frontier justice is a terrifying thing. If you allow it to happen now, it will only get worse. Besides, you've already got everyone going along with it. They brought him in without hurting him. You had all those people out there with guns pointed at him, and not one of them pulled the trigger. They're already on your side with this, in case you haven't realized it. If they weren't, someone would have had an 'accident,'" she finished, using her fingers to form quotes in the air.

Cam thought about Kelly's words later as she headed to Gilles' family's cabin. She was actually feeling sort of proud of herself, even if they had made a couple of mistakes. Now it was time to correct them, though, and for that she needed a police officer.

"Get your badge," Cam told Gilles when he answered the door. He frowned at her, but went to get it.

"What's up?" Gilles asked when he came back with the badge in his hand.

"We're going to inform him of the reason for his arrest, and then you need to read him his rights. I don't know how they're worded in Canada, but I know we've got something similar to the Miranda warning they use in the movies."

"What for?"

"So we can do this right. I should have let you do it the way you wanted to in the first place. We're going to have a bail hearing tomorrow morning, so we should let everyone know. Kelly says he's a flight risk, so we don't have to worry about her letting him out or anything," she said, trailing off when she saw a shadow moving near the jail. Gilles turned to look at the same time.

"What the hell is he doing there?" Gilles asked, and put his hand on his gun.

19 ~ HARRIED HOMECOMING

They decided to push it in order to arrive that night, instead of waiting until the following morning. Mac was far too agitated to go to bed, after Cam had said goodbye so abruptly on the radio, so by four-fifteen she was warming up the engines, and at four-thirty she was pulling up the anchor. She could just barely see the shoreline, and that was enough for her. Neil wasn't quite as anxious as she was, though he'd woken up at the sound of the engines, and then listened while she told him what Cam had said.

"It sounds like she was just tired, honey," he had tried to soothe her.

"They're going to stake out this guy's van, Neil! I can guarantee your son is going to be in on that. Can you honestly tell me you're not the least bit concerned by that?"

"I'd be lying if I said I wasn't, but I'm trying to be rational about it. First of all, there's no way in hell we can get there by then. Whatever is going to happen will be over long before we get there, or it won't happen until tomorrow afternoon, in which case we'll be there to deal with it. Either way there's nothing we can do until we're home. So do us all a favour and make sure you don't drive the boat into a rock trying to do the impossible."

Pragmatism hadn't worked for her, though. She'd had the boat at top speed the whole way, not bothering to check on potential leaks or anything. Neil had shoved a sandwich in her mouth at some point, nagging her to chew and swallow until she finished it, though it might as well have been cardboard for all she noticed of its taste. She let Neil take the helm just once so she could pee, and then glared at him until he surrendered the wheel to her again.

"We should be there soon. Get on the radio and let them know we need a pick-up at the docks," she ordered rigidly. Neil stood there, stubbornly waiting for an apology. At first she just got angrier, but then she realized it was terror making her behave that way.

"Look, I'm really scared right now. I'm sorry I'm being an asshole, but I can't help it. And I need to concentrate right now. It's getting really dark, so I can't think of a bunch of pretty words to convince you. Help me, here!" Pretty or not, her words were enough to get him moving. She had to remind herself that having a husband with a backbone was usually a good thing.

Neil sat down at the navigation desk behind her, and started calling on the radio. Eventually a female voice answered.

"Hey, Neil. Donna here. How's it going? Over."

"Donna? Uh, okay. We're almost home, and we need someone to come pick us up right away. Is anyone available to do that right now, or has Cam arrested the lot of you and stuck you in her new jail? Over."

"Ha! That's a good one. I'm sure I can find someone to come and get ya. Cam only stuck that one guy in jail, and he ain't from around here anyway. Over."

"So you caught him then? Over."

"Yup. We were all there. Went off without a hitch. She was smart about it, and we were careful. No worries. You should hear Jim rave about her. What time you need your ride? Over."

Mackenzie frowned at what she could still see of the shoreline, though relief poured through her at Donna's words. According to the GPS they were only about forty-five minutes away. She sure hoped the lights on the boat would be able to pick out the features around the docks when they got there, but she'd use the dinghy if necessary.

"Tell her we'll be there in forty-five minutes or so, though I can take it a bit more slowly now that I know everyone is okay," Mac told Neil. Neil finished up the conversation, and Ian poked his head into the cabin.

"Did I hear that right? They caught the guy?" Ian asked.

"Yeah. Thank Christ!" Neil responded. Apparently he'd been a lot more worried than he'd let on. Probably trying not to make her worry about the situation even more than she already had been, she realized. Suddenly the view before her got really blurry, and a sob broke free before she could contain it. She just barely had a chance to cut the throttle before Neil had pulled her into his arms. He didn't say anything. Just held her.

"I thought everyone was okay!" Ian was confused, which made her tears turn into a short bark of laughter. She flapped her hand at him to get him to shut up.

"They're all fine," Neil assured him. "She's just venting."

"Oh. Okay," he replied, still sounding unsure. Mac started giggling, though she still had tears in her eyes.

"It's hard to explain," she finally said. "That's the thing about having kids. They can scare the living shit out of you. It doesn't matter if you trust them and you know they're smart. I don't know what I would have done if she'd become a cop or gone into the army. Doubt that's a concern anymore, but what she's been doing has been bad enough."

"You're a nut," Ian said.

"Tell me something I don't already know. I probably wouldn't be crazy if I'd never had Cam. Then again, you don't have any kids, so what's *your* excuse?"

"Watch it, or I'll have Bella bite you on the butt!"

"You can say 'ass,' you know. We're all grown-ups here. Besides, I think Bella likes me. She's not gonna bite me," Mac said, then wiped her eyes and got the boat moving again. Even if everyone was safe, she was still anxious to get home, and get back to what had become her daily life. That thought made her wonder if her daily life would still exist when she got home. It sounded as though everything had changed.

Chuck was waiting with one of the crew cabs when Mac let the boat drift slowly toward the dock. It was hard not to be disappointed that Cam wasn't there to meet them. Neil had already packed everything they had brought with them, so they were able to disembark as soon as Ian had jumped down and tied off the mooring lines. Neil picked up Bella, and lowered her down to Ian, and climbed down the ladder. Mac kissed her fingers and patted the boat with them, murmuring her thanks for it getting them back again safely, despite Neil scraping the sandbar. Then she climbed down to the dock and gave Chuck a giant hug.

"Hey Mac," he said, grinning down at her.

"Hey Chuckles. Hear you've had some rough weather around here. You doing okay?"

"Not too bad. Cam caught the guy," he said, which let her know he was willing to acknowledge the situation.

"So I heard, though I think there's a lot more I probably haven't heard. Hopefully I'll get the whole story when I get home. Where's Cam then? I mean, she caught the guy, so why isn't she here?"

"She's trying to decide whether or not to shoot your ex, I think," he said with a laugh.

"Jesus. Which one?"

"Mitch again, though I don't think she's too happy with Allan right now, either." Chuck explained the latest situation while they got their gear loaded, and finally got themselves buckled into their respective seatbelts.

"I think I might shoot him myself! What the fuck was he thinking? Anyway, Chuck, this is Ian. And Bella, of course. Ian and Bella, this is my friend Chuck." Ian reached over the seat to shake hands with Chuck, and then Mac continued the conversation.

"You know, I think Cam has been more patient with Mitch than I would have been, and she hates him. Mitch has this nasty habit of not taking things seriously. Particularly women. And Cam is young, so he probably didn't think there was a serious reason for the guy being locked up. I don't think he's going to be with us much longer. I'll talk to him first, but in all the years I've known him that's one aspect of his personality that's never changed."

"Well, I think the real reason Mike is locked up has been kept pretty quiet, so Mitch probably only knows about him stealing food. Not that, uh, well, the stuff with Katherine," Chuck said. Mac could see the sheen in his eyes from the dash lights, even though they were dim. She wanted to comfort him, but knew from experience that sympathy could make a person even more emotional.

"Wasn't anyone guarding him?" Neil wanted to know.

"John was out there, but had to take a quick bathroom break. There's no way for Mike to get out, so he didn't think it would be a problem. Besides, you know what he's like. Nice guy. Good kid and everything. Just doesn't think anything through yet. He's still pretty immature, and it's not like he's got any training for this kind of thing. Jim chewed him out for it, so I don't think he'll make that mistake again, but he's been taken off guard duty. Cam's not letting me anywhere near the guy, either, which is probably for the best," Chuck said. Mac patted him on the arm.

"It's better that you won't have the chance to do something

you'd have to live with. Trust me on that. Cam knows what she's doing there. So do I. Gilles probably already told you what happened after Cam was born, I'm guessing?"

"Yeah. I think he was still in shock. Not at what you did, but that none of us knew the whole story. You could have told us, Mac. We would've understood."

"Uh, Mac? Who the hell did you kill?" Ian's question had her hanging her head.

"My first husband. I'll tell you the whole story another time, but it was self-defense, and yes, Neil knows all about it. I'm pretty sure everyone at the farm knows now. You boys gossip worse than a bunch of hens. I didn't tell anyone because I was trying to make sure Cam didn't have to deal with any of that while she was still a kid, and then later I just didn't want to talk about it," she said, uncomfortable with the direction of the conversation.

"But you told Cam anyway," Chuck said.

"Because she was trying to deal with killing Gerry. You saw what she was like for those first six months. Completely disassociated from everyone and everything. And that's what she's trying to spare you from, Chuck. If you do something you can't take back, believe me when I tell you you'll regret it. Not because of what happens to the other person, but because of what it does to you. It changes you, whether or not you think it should."

Neil hopped out when they got to the concealed gate and went behind the tree to press his thumb to the pad. Ian watched in amazement as the gate swung open.

"You said you were paranoid, Mac, but I don't think I really believed you until now," he said as Neil hopped back in the truck and closed the door.

"Well, now you've got proof. Neil was my one shot at total reckless abandonment. Pity he's been so irritating lately, because now I can't get rid of him," she needled her husband. He needled her back in a more direct way by poking her in the ribs, making her yelp. Chuck glanced into the rearview mirror at Ian.

"Ignore them. They're always like this," he said. Ian laughed.

"I know. I had to share a boat with them. Bella shows more dignity," Ian replied. Mac just rolled her eyes.

"By the way, Ian. I'd advise you not to touch Cam," Mac warned as they were getting out of the truck in front of the main house. Chuck waved and headed back toward his cabin.

"You calling me some kind of pervert? Jesus. I'm only, what, thirty years older than her?" He looked mortally offended in the light shining over the front entrance. Neil laughed, shook his head, and went into the house to look for Billy and Cam.

"That is not what I meant. Get your brain out of the gutter. I meant when you meet her, don't try to hug her or anything. It freaks her out, and you're one of those touchy-feely people. She'll start running away every time you're around otherwise. Just shake her hand and she'll be okay with it."

"I thought you wanted me to teach her jiu-jitsu? How the hell am I supposed to do that without touching her?"

"That's different. It's physical affection she can't stand from people. Even me. It's not anything that happened to her. She just doesn't like it. Fighting with someone won't bother her in the slightest.," Mac explained.

"Didn't you say she's had boyfriends and all that?" Ian wondered.

"Yup. She's okay with sex, apparently, but she kicks them out of her bed afterwards. Every boyfriend she ever had has complained about it. She won't cuddle, and won't spend the night. I always thought maybe she'd meet someone one day where she'd feel comfortable that way, but considering the state of the world now, it's not bloody likely."

"Wow. You're all crazy, I think. Every one of you. Besides, don't most guys think that's the ideal woman?"

"They start out that way, until they get serious about her, and then they're all upset that she isn't the clingy type. Weird, I know. Mostly it's that she likes her space, and she hasn't found anyone she's fallen in love with yet. But she's happy this way, too. She never really cared about having a boyfriend, so it doesn't matter.

"Anyway, this is it! What do you think? Well, what do you think of what you can see of it at least?" Mac asked him. Ian looked around, peering into the darkness. Mac decided to look around, too, wanting to see the changes.

"How many buildings are there? I'm seeing at least five or six, though just barely."

"I'm not sure now. Kelly and Annette live together in that big building there, which is where all the ferrets are housed. Chuck and his family are in that cabin. Carol and Samantha have the small one over there. Allan's little cabin is behind theirs, so you can't see it from here. Gilles and his wife are there, while her daughter and son-in-law, which is the John we mentioned earlier, are in that one. John's parents, Jim and Donna, have their own cabin as well, and the one that's partially finished is for Lisa and her little boy, Jake.

"Kirk and Leigh have Neil's old place, but it's about a ten- or fifteen-minute walk from here, across that bridge. I'm guessing the tent is where Mitch is still sleeping. Hmm. That little building in the middle must be the new jail cell where Mike will be living for a while. Good location for it, but I'll have to take a look at it from a construction standpoint when it's light out. Wonder what they're doing for plumbing," she muttered to herself.

"Holy fuck!" Ian exclaimed. Mac's head jerked up.

"What?"

"What do you mean, 'What?'" Ian was gaping at her. "You've got, what, twenty-some-odd people here. You said 'Chuck's family,' so I don't know how many that is."

"Wife and three kids. From the sounds of it, he could very well end up being a grandfather, too. We'll have to wait and see. It's not like the kid will have a choice if it turns out she's pregnant. Abortion is no longer an option, though it would be far safer in her case," she said sadly.

"Where did all these people come from?" Ian asked.

"Me, mostly. I can't help myself. I even offered to bring

Sharon, Vigo, and Denny back here. I guess they're okay, though. They have neighbours that are still alive, so at least they're not alone. Well, let's head inside and see where the hell my wayward daughter is."

At the sound of shouting, Mac turned to Ian.

"Never mind. I found her," she said with a laugh. "Come on. I'll introduce you to Miss Crankypants."

Mac didn't want to interrupt whatever was going on, because it could be something serious, so she walked up to her daughter without calling out. When she heard what was being said, however, she almost started laughing.

"You're so lucky my mother isn't here," Cam was winding down. "But I can tell you this much. If she decides to kill you, I'm not throwing her in jail for it!"

"Well, thanks! Will you help me hide the body, too?" Mac couldn't help it.

"Mom! Oh my God! When did you get here? And why didn't anyone tell me you were coming?" Cam ran over and flung her arms around her, shocking the hell out of her.

"Sure, make a liar out of me," she muttered, but hugged her back. "Wow. You must have missed me." Cam pulled back.

"No. I'm just happy I'm no longer going to have to deal with this kind of bullshit," she snapped, flapping her hand toward Mitch who looked seriously pissed. Mac figured it was probably something to do with the earlier incident, so she wasn't about to smile at him.

"Yeah, I heard something about that. Have you told him why the guy was in jail, or is he still under the impression it's for stealing food?"

"Oh, he knows, but apparently raping a fourteen-year-old girl isn't a big deal in his books, and he thinks we're all overreacting. He knew exactly what Mike had done when he tried to let him out," Cam snarled.

"How the fuck is it rape when she said she wanted it?"

"Mitch," Mac growled, her mood instantly changing at his words. "Are you telling me that you've been out raping fourteen-year-old girls?"

"No! You know me better than that."

"I don't think I do, if you can stand there and tell me it was okay for another man to do it. You know it's wrong for you to do it, but not for someone else? That doesn't make any sense to me. In fact, the only thing that makes sense is that you're lying, and that you have no problem with the idea of raping a child. Do you understand what it means to give consent? Are you at all aware of the definition of sexual assault? Did you know that sixteen is the age of consent in this country, and that there's a good fucking reason for it?" Mac was beyond livid, and she could see Ian's disgust on his face. She knew how he felt about pedophiles, but then all decent people felt that way.

"I thought it was fourteen!"

"No, it's not, unless you're less than five years older. Any older than that and it's sexual assault. The very thought that you could

341

stand there and try to justify a grown man raping a child sickens me. You can't stay here. You'll have to find somewhere else to go, and you won't be welcome back," Mac said, rigid in her anger.

"We can do the same thing for him that we were going to do with the pedophile before we found out about Katherine," Cam suggested.

"What's that?"

"Gilles was taking him to a hunting camp beyond walking distance, and leaving him with the supplies he needed to start a small farm. He wouldn't die, but he'd be away from decent people," Cam sneered. Mac nodded.

"Let Gilles know. Mitch, have your things ready tomorrow if you prefer that to simply getting kicked off the farm and starving. You've been learning how to deal with animals and gardening shit, I hear, so you probably won't die."

"Mac, listen. You can't do this to me. I walked all this way so I wouldn't be alone."

"I don't actually care, Mitch. You're a piece of shit. I don't ever want to see you again," Mac said, and walked away. He must have started to go after her, because she heard Ian's voice.

"If you take one more step, I'll break every fucking bone in your body. And if you get past me, she'll kill you. You're already scum. Don't be stupid scum."

Mac smiled and continued walking without bothering to turn back. She walked with Cam back toward the house.

"So, when *did* you get here?" Cam asked.

"About two minutes before you saw me. Donna was on the radio. I guess everyone thought you needed to finish dealing with Mitch before they told you. We must have got back before you were done."

"Between getting Mike back into the jail cell, and reaming out Mitch, that doesn't surprise me. Plus Gilles had to tell him why he was being detained, and read him his rights and all that. We're trying to do things according to the original laws as much as possible," she explained.

"God, I'm proud of you! I can't even begin to tell you how proud I am. It's just barely possible I would have killed the guy, instead of trying to do the right thing. You'll have to tell me all about it. Granted, I spent the last seventeen hours having a panic attack after you cut me off on the radio, and I really want to kick your ass for that, but right now I'm just so damn glad to be home and finding you safe and sound. I think I need to go cry. Where are my boys?"

"They're still in my room, but I did let them play in your room a couple of times. People have been walking through there a lot to get to the monitors upstairs, though, so I couldn't leave them in there. I was afraid they'd get out and then get lost or hurt."

"Okay, can you go get them? I really need to see them right now, but Ian needs to be let in the house. I'll have to set him up on the locks later."

"Okay, I'll be right back. They're going to be really happy to see you. They've started moping," Cam called back as she ran through the greenhouse and into the kitchen door. Ian walked up to her maybe thirty seconds later.

"How the hell did you end up married to that loser? I seriously felt like snapping his neck just then," he said.

"You're not the only one. I was really young when I met him. He seemed cool at the time. I hadn't exactly come into my own at that age, and was still desperately looking for love. When we split up, though, I didn't think I'd ever be interested in another relationship again. It was years before I had feelings for anyone again, and even that didn't work out. Neil was a complete shock for me."

Mac wasn't about to remind Ian who it was she'd had feelings for. Those feelings had disappeared long ago, and she knew he didn't remember. She assumed that was the reason Neil had been so pissed off at Ian in Cleveland and on the boat, even though he hadn't really done anything.

"Let's go in the house so you can see that it's not as ugly as it looks from the outside. Cam's bringing the boys down to me. God I've missed them. Wait until I take them into my room before you bring in Bella, okay?"

"Sure. She's tied up outside for the time being."

"Should be interesting when she meets Gowan, though he's usually with Billy so he's not in the house much, or he's in Billy's room. Jake seems okay with dogs, but he's still only a year old, so we'll have to watch," Mac said.

"Me being here is a big pain in the ass, isn't it?"

"You're always a big pain in the ass. Here or in Cleveland," she teased. Cam came down the stairs then, and Mac nearly wept with joy. Two bundles of fur wriggled in her arms and licked every inch of her face. Pickle was pretty much exfoliating her skin with his abrasive tongue, while Squeaker merely licked delicately, though still quite thoroughly.

"I told you they were starting to miss you," Cam said with a laugh.

"I'll say. I thought they were bad when I left the house for a few hours," Mac exclaimed, but then had to close her mouth to keep from getting a really weird French kiss from Pickle. She buried her face in their fur, her eyes burning.

"Cam, can you do me a favour? Can you get some of the guys to move all that security stuff out of the room over our bedroom? It sounds like we still need to keep an eye on things with Mitch, and I really want to be able to sleep without people going through our room. I'll walk Ian around, show him the house and where he'll be sleeping until Lisa's cabin is finished. I'm guessing the security issues have been delaying the construction?" At her question, Cam nodded.

"They've been screwing up everything. Mitch was given the animals to deal with, though he was supervised, so everyone else was free to do patrols and watch the monitors. I have to say, I didn't expect all this crap when you left."

"Neither did we! You'll have to tell me all about it once we have a moment. Oh, and by the way, Ian, this is Cameron.

Cameron, this is Ian. Though you both have brains, so I assume you already know that."

Ian sort of smirked at Mac when he politely reached out to shake Cameron's hand.

"I was warned not to hug you," he said drily. Cam laughed.

"Mom's worried I'll punch someone for it one of these days. Though I don't think I'd try that with a jiu-jitsu Master. Especially since you're supposed to be my sensei very soon."

"Not if you don't want to wind up crying on the floor, no," Ian said with a chuckle. "Though I do try to be a little nicer to the children of my friends."

"Alright, Cam, go get John to deal with the security monitors. I'm assuming you took him off guard duty after his little bathroom break."

"Yeah. Jim took over, after reaming him out." Cam got on the two-way and got things in motion, while Mac dragged Ian around the place. Neil was in the security room with Billy when she took Ian up there, still holding Pickle and Squeaker. Neil grabbed them both from her, so he could spend some time cuddling them. She grinned at him. Apparently he'd missed the boys, too.

"John is coming up here to move all the security stuff. He can move it to the wall end of the kitchen counter for now. Nobody ever sits there anyway. We always sit at the open end. There's a wired LAN plug there, too, so it won't be on Wi-Fi. People have been treating our bedroom like Grand Central Station, from what I hear. Be nice when everything settles down again," Mac said with a tired sigh. Cam came running up the stairs then.

"Mom, before John gets here, I wanted you guys to know about something. I haven't told anyone yet, and wanted to wait until you got home. My dad's been having an affair with Geraldine. I saw him with her when Chuck and I were at the hardware store. I told him who she was. That she was Gerry's mother, I mean. And when I told him he would have to give her up if he wanted to stay on the farm, he just stopped speaking to me," Cam said miserably. Everyone in the room, except possibly Ian, was shell-shocked.

Mac turned and looked at her daughter, suddenly more terrified than she could ever remember feeling.

20 ~ STRANGE ANIMAL

Cam had slept neither well, nor long. The first thing she thought of was the jiu-jitsu training she was supposed to be getting from Ian. She needed that right now, so she went straight downstairs to find him, once she was showered and dressed. Thankfully she no longer had to worry about things like bail hearings and arranging for Mitch to be moved off the property. Her mother would deal with all that later.

Cam wouldn't have stopped in the kitchen for food, since she could never eat when she first woke up without feeling sick, but she found him there anyway when she was on her way through.

"Hi," she said, feeling awkward. "Do you think it would be possible for you to start teaching me today?"

"Sure. Just let me finish my breakfast and we can find a place to work. I don't suppose you have any mats, do you?"

"We do, actually. They're in the room Lisa's using. That's where the workout equipment was before she got here, but we took most of it out so Jake wouldn't get hurt."

"Cool. Maybe we can pull those outside, then, so we have some room. In the meantime, you can tell me what it is you're looking to get out of your lessons. When I teach martial arts, I teach them so they work in real situations. I don't teach them so my students win trophies or get belts. I teach so you can survive when it really matters. I hope you're ready for that," Ian said seriously.

"Oh yeah. I was already looking forward to learning. I've wanted to go into martial arts since I was little, but it just never happened. That was for the coolness factor back then, and I wanted to kick some ass. Now I just want to be able to protect myself, because I might have to. I'm good with a bow, as well as a gun, but I don't want to rely on them as my only defense," she explained.

"Good. Give me ten minutes, and we'll get started," he said.

Cam was relieved. For one thing, she needed to burn off the nervous energy she was feeling over the issue with her dad, and she didn't think walking the perimeter like she used to do was such a good idea right now. Not when there was a very real threat, and it was directed specifically toward her. She really wished she could convince herself that Geraldine's affair with her dad was innocent, but it would be stupid to try.

It was a good thing it wasn't high summer yet, because it was already uncomfortably hot under the mid-morning sun, and dragging out the mats was enough for Cam to work up a sweat. Once they were set up to Ian's satisfaction, he looked at her with a very serious expression on his face.

"What you really need to know, and remember at all times, is that one strike is never enough. Once you start going after someone, you have to keep going after them until they're no longer a threat. Never forget that. Do you understand what I'm saying?"

"I'm not really sure," she replied.

"Alright, let me explain then. If someone comes after you, and you hit them, that isn't going to be enough to stop them for very long. Especially if they're very determined. What you do is you keep hitting them, over and over, until you're absolutely certain they're not going to be able to continue coming after you. Your first strike doesn't even have to be all that powerful. It's a surprise more than anything, but then you have to follow up on it.

"Your follow-up strikes have to be stronger. But speed is important, too. You don't want them to have time to think in between. You also want them to hurt, and hurt badly enough that they're causing damage. I'm going to teach you three simple moves for now. We're not going to do anything fancy to start out with, because you need to learn to defend yourself as quickly as possible against a real threat. You're not worrying about your next belt test or scoring points in a competition. Point strikes don't cause any damage. They're not supposed to. I don't teach that.

"The first thing you're going to learn is the hand-heel strike. It's also called a palm strike, depending on who's teaching you. It's very effective, especially when used against someone's nose. If you hit someone in the nose their eyes automatically close and tear up. It hurts. A lot. And it gives you an opportunity to come at them with something a lot more powerful and debilitating after. Later we'll do an elbow, or forearm, strike, as well as a front kick. Those three things, if you use them one after the other, multiple times, will be a huge help to you.

"Later on we can get into some of the fancier stuff, maybe, but this is what I've taught my students for many years. And I can tell ya, it works. Not only can it work for women, but it can work for little kids, too. Sometimes all you need is a chance to get away, so even if these moves seem simple, they can save your life. Alright, let's get started," he said, finally.

Stretching took up the first ten minutes. Then it was slow-motion repetition of the hand-heel strike, progressing to full speed, which had Ian complimenting her on the rate at which she was picking it up. They moved to the front kick, which he pushed her a little harder on, after seeing that she caught onto that just as fast as she had the hand-heel strike. The elbow strike went even faster, with him saying it was because she needed to be challenged.

"It would be better if we had a heavy bag so we could go through some scenarios. We'll just have to find a volunteer to stand in as *uke*."

"*Uke*? What's that?" Cameron asked.

"Someone you pretend to beat up," Ian said with a grin.

"Oh, okay. I can handle that," Cameron said, laughing.

They grabbed a startled Billy, who had been talking to Jim nearby, and spent the last half hour with Ian encouraging Billy to pretend he was trying to rob or attack Cameron, while getting Cameron to start out looking intimidated, but suddenly launching her offensive. Of course, she couldn't really hit Billy, so she had to stop short on her strikes, but it made things very interesting for Billy for a while. Cam laughed at the way he cringed when she came within a quarter-inch of his face. Still, she had to admit it took courage for him to just stand there and trust her not to hit him.

Lisa came up and watched the spectacle for a little while, which made Billy blush. Cam could see the interest on her face, too, so it looked like that would be a done deal pretty soon. She was happy about it now. She liked Billy, and wanted him to be happy. Lisa seemed like a good match for him. Slightly older than he was, but not enough that there was a weird gap between them. Cam didn't let him off the hook, though, just because Lisa was there. She continued to enjoy scaring the crap out of him with her various strikes, grinning every time he flinched.

After two hours, Ian said he was going to take Bella for a walk, and Cam staggered off to the kitchen for a drink of water. She had hated drinking water in the city, but their water on the farm was amazing. No foul taste of chlorine or fluoride. She filled a tall glass and drank the whole thing in one go. Then she refilled it, sipping until she had finished the second glass. Partially revived, she headed upstairs.

A cool shower revived her further, though a hot bath probably would have been better for her muscles. She'd have one of those tomorrow, if they were as sore as she thought they might be. Once she was dressed, she decided it was time to hunt down her dad. She didn't really expect him to come back on his own for a few days, because he'd been mad when he left. His lack of maturity was one of his more irritating qualities, and that was on a good day. This wasn't a good day.

Cameron was pissed that she was left to worry about the safety of a person who obviously wasn't worried about hers. So much for his protectiveness. Looking back she started to feel as though it had been more of a show that he put on, whenever she had mentioned a guy she was going out with, or that liked her. He'd acted like he was so concerned. Now, when it really counted, his worry had disappeared. Still, whether he truly cared about her or not, she still cared what happened to him, whether the threat came from her mother going after him, or from Geraldine. She had no choice but to try and find him, and she thought she might know where to start looking.

Their meeting place near the hardware store indicated to Cam that they were likely using a nearby house for more privacy. Her dad was a creature of habit, and had probably picked one and continued to use it. He wasn't exactly a mastermind of strategy, and his lack of forward thinking meant he would continue business as usual without worrying over consequences.

If he had told Geraldine that Cam knew about their relationship, however, that would change things. Geraldine seemed like a sharp woman. Still, Cam hoped that her dad wouldn't betray her quite so readily by telling Geraldine about their conversations. It was one thing to continue an affair. It was another thing entirely to knowingly expose someone to further danger. Knowing who Geraldine was might make him more cautious in his speech. Or, if nothing else, he might be too interested in getting laid to bother talking about anything important.

Cameron passed through the kitchen on her way out, and considered eating. She was starving, especially after two hours of kicks and strikes. With her stomach tied in knots at the thought of her upcoming confrontation, however, she decided she would wait until it was over before she stuffed her face.

She took her mother's old BMW, since they still had treated fuel in the tank and planned to use it up before it went bad. Cam didn't tell anyone where she was going, and knew she was going to catch hell for that when she got back, but it was the only way she could get to her dad without her mother dragging his possible location out of her first. She was starting to think it might actually be a good idea just to move all his stuff out of his cabin and take it to him, so he wouldn't have to come back and face her mother's wrath.

Sadness welled up in her as the car rolled over the pressure plate and the gate opened. This could easily be the last time she saw her dad. He was already angry with her, and this confrontation wasn't going to make him any happier. He might decide he didn't have to be her dad after all, since it wasn't as though they were related by blood. In a way, Cam already felt like that was what was happening. Like he'd been pretending to love her all those years or something.

Tears filled her eyes and rolled down her face, making it difficult for her to see the road. The complete lack of traffic was a blessing at that moment, because she was pretty sure she was too upset to be driving had there been other cars on the road. As it was, she rounded a corner and nearly ran someone over. She just barely veered enough to avoid hitting the person who was wandering on the side of the road. She hadn't used her brakes while swerving, because she didn't want to lose control of the car on the dirt and gravel road, and end up hitting the person she was trying to avoid. Now she slammed her foot down on the pedal to stop the car.

She touched her hand to her back as she got out of the car, making sure both her knife and her Glock were where they were supposed to be, and tucked the tail of her shirt behind them so it wouldn't get in the way. Then she knuckled the tears from her eyes so she could see clearly.

He had stopped moving once he'd seen the car, but there was a fair bit of distance between them so she couldn't really see his features. She just knew he was male, and looked pretty tall with dark hair. She walked very slowly toward him. Like her mother, Cam hated the thought of anyone suffering or going hungry, but she wasn't stupid. *People are assholes*, she reminded herself silently.

As she got closer she realized he had no pack, which meant he had no food or supplies of any kind. He could turn out to be extremely dangerous, or very grateful for any help she could provide. They had emergency packs in every vehicle; it was something her mother had done for as far back as Cam could remember. Every pack had non-perishable food in it. If he was hungry, she could help him, but she had to be sure he wasn't going to kill her out of desperation.

"Hello," Cam said tentatively. He eyed her warily, his face gaunt and haggard, but he didn't reply to her greeting. She couldn't help thinking that maybe he hadn't seen another human being in a long time. If that was the case, he was probably wondering if she was real.

"My name is Cameron. Are you hungry? Hurt? I have a few supplies with me that you can have if you want. I'll let you take them all. That's why we have them in the car. Would you like something to eat?"

His expression was one of disbelief. She was still a fair distance away from him, but if he wanted food he would have to come back to the car with her. Not wanting to turn her back on him when she didn't know what he would do, Cam gestured to him to indicate that he should follow her, then started walking backward. He began to shuffle along toward her, and his gait suggested that he was barely able to keep to his feet at the moment. He was definitely in need of some help. Whether or not he was a danger to her was a different story.

It took some time, but they reached the car. She kept her eye on him as she opened the trunk and pulled out the duffle bag with the food, water, and first-aid kit in it. There were other things in the trunk for emergencies, like Mylar blankets, candles, jumper cables, and all that, but those were more for breakdowns than anything else. She unzipped the bag and pulled out an energy bar. She hoped it wouldn't be too much for him, since he obviously hadn't eaten for a while, but it was the only type of food in there.

"Try to eat this slowly, okay? It's got a lot of calories in it, and it might make you sick if you eat it too fast. Maybe have half now, and wait a few minutes to eat the other half," she suggested, though she wasn't surprised when he just sank down onto his knees in the middle of the road and ate the whole thing.

"I can give you more, but you gotta wait. Seriously. It'll make you sick otherwise, and you don't want to be wasting your food right now." He looked up at her then, and she noticed that he couldn't be much older than she was, despite the lines his face had accumulated. His silvery eyes caught hers, locking on and pulling her in. She could feel his misery beyond any empathetic reaction she'd experienced previously. Her lizard brain was fighting with her more evolved intellect, telling her that he was safe. She wasn't dumb enough to trust that, however, having learned a few lessons from her mother's mistakes. Cam needed time to trust someone, and this guy would be no different. She broke off eye contact and pulled a bottle of water from the bag.

"Here," she said as she handed him the bottle. "I know there are a lot of lakes and rivers to drink from around here, but this water is safer. It's been treated already, so you won't get sick from it. Drink a little bit and I'll give you another power bar, okay?" When he began to drink, she kneeled on the road facing him, just out of reach. She didn't want to sit down, because that would make it more awkward for her to reach her gun if she needed it.

"What's your name? Do you remember?" she asked. He sat there silently for a while, and she could tell he was thinking rather than ignoring her. Cam could also see that he was getting upset. Apparently he was having a hard time remembering who he was at the moment, so her question had agitated him. She decided to change the subject instead.

"I can probably help you, so that you don't have to go hungry anymore," she said. He looked at her in disbelief, despite the fact that she'd already given him food.

"We have a farm not too far from here. We grow our own food. There are lots of people there now, too, so you wouldn't have to be alone anymore. You look like you've been alone for a long time. It must have been hard out here by yourself. Do you know what's been happening?" She knew that would probably upset him, too, since it was a pretty unsettling topic, but she was hoping to get him to talk. He just kind of shrugged in response to her question, though, as if he wasn't quite sure.

"Maybe this isn't such a good time to talk about it. Have you seen any other people lately?" He shook his head, his expression sad and scared.

"Well, you have now," she said as brightly as she could, though perkiness and optimism weren't really her thing.

"Would you like to see more people? You could meet my mother and her husband. He's got a son a bit younger than me, so I guess you could say he's like a step-brother to me. A couple of my friends came to live on the farm. Kirk and Leigh are a lot of fun.

We like to play video games when we have some time. We actually have electricity on the farm, because we put up a bunch of solar panels, so we can still do pretty much everything we did before the power grid went down," she continued, trying to put him at ease with a constant stream of chatter. She knew somehow that he was a lot more scared than she was. Whether that made him safer or more dangerous, though, she didn't know yet.

"Look, I was on my way to do something pretty important. I can leave this food here with you and then come back for you, if you want. Or maybe you can come with me. I don't know you, so I don't know if I can trust you, but I don't want to leave you all alone either. What do you say? Are you willing to go in the car with me?"

He pointed at the bag with a questioning look on his face.

"Yeah, we'll take that with us. You should be okay to have another power bar now if you want. Just dig through the bag and see what you like. You can have it all if you want. Just go slowly. Like I said, we've got food at the farm, so you don't need to share any of that. This is just an emergency pack in case one of us runs into someone who needs some food. Like you, basically."

He got into the passenger side of the BMW, his expression still wary. She had to wonder what kind of life he'd been forced to live over the last several months. Maybe she didn't really want to know, either. Survival sometimes meant doing some pretty nasty things, and Cam didn't want to imagine a lot of those things, but she knew she would do whatever it took for her own survival.

Logically she couldn't blame someone else for doing the same, but that didn't mean she wanted to picture it in her head.

She didn't put her seatbelt on this time, keeping herself unfettered just in case he turned out to be violent. As she drove, she kept glancing over at him, relieved every time she saw that he was either digging through the bag for more food, or using his hands to eat what he found.

Cam parked the car in a driveway around the corner from the houses she planned to search, on the side opposite the direction Geraldine had come from when Cam had seen her meeting up with her dad. It wasn't especially well-concealed, but she didn't think it would stand out, sheltered under a maple tree as it was.

Being a '98, Cam knew the central locking system wouldn't automatically engage like some of the newer cars did. The stranger in the car would be free to leave if he wanted. She rolled all the windows down, anyway. Otherwise the black car would start to feel stifling in the afternoon heat, even in the shade. She wasn't leaving it running with the air conditioning going, just in case he had a mind to take off in the car. Instead she pocketed the keys, and told him she would be back as soon as she had seen whether or not her dad was in one of the houses.

"I'm trying to find him right now to give him an important message, but I'm not really sure where he goes, so this could take me a little while. Half an hour maybe. Try to remember to take it slowly with that food. When I come back we can go to the farm I told you about, and then you can have some real food, like eggs and potatoes, that kind of thing, instead of that stuff with all the preservatives in it. See you soon," she said, as cheerfully as she could, though it was strictly for his benefit. She wasn't feeling the least bit cheerful.

As Cameron walked toward the first house, she wondered how the hell she was going to know if anyone was using a place. Then she started to think about the possibility that she might end up finding a bunch of bodies if she just started going into the houses. The only thing she could think to do for the moment was watch and listen.

Cam walked around to all the windows of the first place, carefully peeking in. When she didn't see anything, she would press her ear against the glass. Eventually she went up and tried the door, but it was locked. Since there was no reason to continue locking a door, she thought maybe the house that her dad was using to meet with Geraldine might already be unlocked. They would want to be able to get in and out without dealing with keys, or going in through windows, so Cam moved on to the next house.

She was really starting to get tired by the time she circled the third house. She didn't have much energy left after her lesson with Ian, and she was starting to feel foolish. She had no idea if her dad was in the area, and, even if he was, she knew he wasn't going to listen to her. He never did. Still, it wasn't in her to give up so easily, so she continued on to the fourth house, and then the fifth. This was the one that was closest to the place she'd seen them meeting, so it was the likeliest location.

Cameron went through a small gate at the front of the yard, and gradually circled to the back yard, checking each window as she went. She didn't see or hear anything, and continued around the other side toward the front again. A loud rustling sound came from the bushes behind her. She spun around, her hand already going to the holster at her back, but the tail of her shirt had fallen over it again. She couldn't get underneath it in time to pull out the gun. By then Geraldine had her own gun pointed directly at her face.

Cam lashed out with her hand, using what Ian had taught her earlier that day. The hit to Geraldine's face obviously threw her a bit, but not enough to make her drop the gun. Instead of pulling her hand straight back, instinct had Cameron swinging her forearm over and down to connect with the hand holding the gun. It was enough to push her hand away and keep her from aiming directly at Cam, but it didn't jar her arm enough to make her drop it.

Geraldine's determination made her fierce, and Cam was weakened by her own fear. Hatred poured from Geraldine's gaze. Hatred that gave a light of insanity to what had seemed such a nice face. Cam knew she couldn't give up. There was no way this woman was going to let her walk away alive. She lunged into her, trying to use her body weight as a weapon. Turning sideways to free her right arm, while still pressing forward with her body, Cam attempted once more to free her Glock, but Geraldine shoved back at her, making her stumble and throw her arms out for balance.

She tried another hand-heel strike to buy herself some time. Geraldine lifted her chin up and away, so it merely glanced off her jaw. She only staggered back a little, still trying to bring up her hand to aim at Cam with the gun. Cameron kicked out at the weapon, and Geraldine jerked her arm back to avoid losing her grip on it. Cam was too far away to use her hand or elbow now, so she tried another kick, which had Geraldine skittering backward a couple of feet. Cam ran forward, knowing she needed to keep the woman within reach, or the last thing she would see would be Geraldine pulling the trigger.

Both women were panting and gasping with their efforts. Despite being younger, Cameron had started out the struggle already tired, and with no food to give her any energy. Geraldine might have been psychotic, but she was older than Cam. She was closer to Cam's mother's age, which meant she didn't have the automatic benefit of youth and agility. She didn't look like she was out of shape, but age still had an effect.

Cameron kicked out once more, missing, despite the speed and ferocity brought on by panic and desperation. Her next kick connected, hitting Geraldine in the knee, but it didn't stop the motion of her arm as she finally managed to move the gun into position. Cam instinctively brought her arm up to shield her face and head. She turned a little, ducking her head slightly just as she heard the gun go off.

She felt nothing at first, which made her think she hadn't been hit. Then a cold burning sensation turned to fire and her whole forearm exploded with pain. Cam dropped to her knees in shock, which jarred her arm and sent white-hot shards of agony through her bicep, into her shoulder, and even across her chest. She wanted to cradle it protectively, but even the idea of touching it was unbearable, so it dangled at her side. Looking at it was out of the question. Cam felt sick just imagining what she would see.

Her hand was completely useless. Even if she were able to move it, she figured the pain would make her pass out if she tried to do so. Her brain insisted on showing her mental pictures of a hand and wrist dangling from a small scrap of flesh, and she wondered vaguely if she was going to lose her hand. Physical shock, in addition to the emotional, began to creep through her, chilling every part of her body except for her right arm. When her body started shaking, it reverberated through her injured flesh. She wanted to gnash her teeth against the pain, but was incapable of anything beyond incoherent whimpers. When Geraldine spoke to her, Cam could only stare up at her in bemused misery.

"There, that's better. I'm glad I didn't have to kill you outright. After all, you've caused me more pain than you can possibly imagine, and I've had to live with that pain for months now. You stole the only thing that ever mattered to me, and for that you're going to pay dearly. First with pain, and then with your life. I knew there was more to the story than what that cop told us, and it turned out I was right, though I doubt any of you told us the full truth. After all, that cop was a friend of your mother's. He would have told us anything she wanted him to.

"Of course, I needed to make you suffer like I did, and the only way to do that was to take away someone that *you* love. Someone like your dad." She paused, apparently waiting for her words to sink in.

"You have no idea how unbearable it was to let him touch me, though it was a necessary step in my plan to draw you away from that farm. I figured once you knew about us you would eventually go looking for him, and then I would have my chance at you. He was stubborn, though. Refused to tell you about me, even though I pretended I wanted to meet his daughter, and that I was hurt he wouldn't introduce me to his family.

"Such a disgusting little man, only interested in having something to stick his dick in. He had to pay for the privilege, and so he did. If you had only looked in that one last window, you would have seen how he paid," Geraldine said, her tone sickeningly sweet. Cameron's stomach lurched as she tried to concentrate, to understand the meaning behind her words.

"Of course, I kept a record of it. I keep records of all the important memories of my life, and I had a few pictures left in my old Polaroid camera. See for yourself," she invited, and tossed a picture on the ground. Cameron gazed at it with horror, incapable of comprehending what she was seeing. Whatever that was in the image, it couldn't possibly be her dad. She should be able to recognize him, shouldn't she? All she could see was what looked like a mass of bloody meat. She shook her head at it.

"Trying to deny it, aren't you? I'm sure you don't want to believe that he's dead because of you. I'm sure this close-up will convince you, though," Geraldine sneered, and tossed down another image. This time Cam could see human features. Hazel eyes, though one looked as though it had been sliced through, matted brown hair that looked nearly black with all the blood soaked into it, and a brown goatee streaked through with silver and smeared with more blood. Beyond that he was unrecognizable as her dad, but she knew deep down that it was him. Her body went numb, and her heart froze.

"If only you hadn't killed my son, your dad would still be alive. He was a waste of life anyway. Not like my son. No. He was nothing like my beautiful Gerry, the product of my loins, my namesake, and the true keeper of my heart. His father was never anything more than a means to an end, though his end was maybe meaner," she said with a little chuckle. Another picture dropped in front of Cam, and since she was still looking in that direction, at the picture of her dad, she saw what had been done to Brian Newman. His entire lower half was soaked in blood.

"What … " Cam started, but was unable to finish the question.

"What did I do? Oh, I just paid him back for his refusal to have more children with me. Served him right for taking the decision from me by having that vasectomy. But now everyone has paid except you, my dear, and I think your time has come."

21 ~ BLOOD OF MY BLOOD

Kelly had done just what she had said with regard to the bail hearing, so the formalities were out of the way with Mike now. The second escape attempt, aided and abetted by Mitch, had prompted Kelly to simply come down to the little cell and inform him that bail was denied. Not that he had anything to offer as surety even if he had been granted bail, but the process had been run through just the same. Mike would be held until Kelly got around to providing him with a trial.

Then there was Mitch. He saw Mac as she was walking across the yard to witness Mike's informal hearing, and tried to waylay her.

"This is just a misunderstanding, Mac. Seriously. You know me better than this. I'd never do anything to a kid," he pleaded.

"Fuck off, Mitch. Pack your shit. Chuck will be taking you to your new home, and if you show up here in the future you'll be run off in a hail of bullets. You got that, or do I need to write it down for you?"

"Cunt," he snarled at her.

"What was that?" Mac asked icily.

"You heard me," Mitch said, his tone filled with hatred.

"Ah, so the truth finally comes out. I'm no longer any use to you, so I'm nothing but a cunt. You know what? You just lost your supply privileges. You'll still get the chickens and the seeds for growing your vegetables, because I'm not going to give you a death sentence just for calling me names, but I sure don't feel obliged to make life easier for you anymore. You can do things the hard way now. If you don't survive, it'll be your own damn fault. But, call me a cunt just one more time, and see how far my patience stretches.

"You have to be the dumbest motherfucker I have ever encountered in my life. You were given the chance for a decent life here. If you'd been smart you would have had to work one day out of every ten. Instead you insulted the one person who had total say over what happened to you. Cam went easy on you, because she knew I cared what happened to you, but even in your precarious position you decided to help out a fucking child-molester. Nice work. So you were exiled, but were still being given everything you could possibly need to survive in a relatively easy fashion. What do you do? You insult the person who's trying to keep you alive.

"Maybe one day you'll stop and ask yourself what the fuck is wrong with your brain, because you have completely screwed yourself over. Now, get the fuck out of my way, because I'm done with you. If you force me to continue speaking to you, it won't be words you'll be hearing." If he muttered anything else as she left, she didn't hear it.

Once Mac had finished with Kelly and Mike, she'd stood and watched Cam for a while. It was a relief they were starting right away, because Mac did not have a good feeling about what was going on with Allan. An hour later, she had watched Mitch being carted off in the truck. Just to be on the safe side, she'd sent both Jim and Gilles with Chuck. They had gone through Mitch's things to destroy the scrap of paper on which he had written the farm's location, and had removed the batteries from his GPS after deleting its history.

She hadn't expected the need to maintain law and order in whatever fashion they saw fit. She had only planned for the possibility that she and Cam would need to defend themselves, and their property, but now they had so many people sharing that property that it had become necessary to formalize a sort of criminal justice. Mac had no idea whether or not she would have done what Cam had managed to do. She might well have fallen into the trap of simply dispensing her own brand of justice, or allowed Chuck to do the same.

It was a lot more work to do what Cam was attempting. If they had prisoners, and they weren't going to simply execute pond scum like Mike, it meant they had to take responsibility for their prisoners' welfare. It made her feel sick in a way, but also made her grateful that they weren't sinking to that level.

Thoughts of her daughter had her mind moving on to Allan, and the sticky situation he'd gotten them into. Cam was right about one thing. If he was involved with Geraldine, he would have to leave. It was too great a risk to allow Allan continued access to the property. He was the kind of person who was easily manipulated, and Geraldine would eventually get whatever she wanted out of him. He might not mean any harm, but he would cause plenty nonetheless. He would have to make a choice, and she would have to give him until at least the next day to make it. They already had three people off the farm to take Mitch to his destination, and couldn't afford more to remove Allan should he remain stubborn.

Mac went looking for Neil to see if he'd managed to find Allan, but it turned out that Allan hadn't been seen for a while. No one was sure when he'd been there last. Cameron might know, and it was possible she knew where he was, too, so she went looking for her daughter to find out. When she went into the house she saw Donna sitting on one of the kitchen stools, keeping an eye on the security monitors.

"You haven't seen Cam, have you?" Mac asked her.

"She left," Donna said.

"Left? You mean she left the property?"

"Yup. Probably half an hour ago, I'd say. Driving that fancy black car of yours," she added, making Mac roll her eyes. She'd worn herself out explaining that she had only paid a thousand dollars for that 'fancy' car, but no one seemed to believe her. In their eyes it was a BMW, and therefore must have been expensive. She'd bought it because it was fast, reliable, rarely required maintenance, and the motor left about the same carbon footprint as a hybrid. It was just too bad it wasn't a diesel, because Gilles could have converted it for her then. Now it was going to end up as nothing more than scrap metal at some point.

"Did you see which way she turned when she left?"

"Went to the right, toward Rosseau," Donna supplied. Mac frowned. She must have gone to see her dad. It was the only thing that made sense. She wasn't scavenging for supplies, or she would have taken a truck, and since she was apparently aware of her own potential danger, only something she considered important would convince her to leave the property. Even when she'd been dealing with her guilt, and had made one bad decision, she hadn't left the farm. That was before Mac and Neil had gone away, though. Since then Cam had gone to the hardware store, for reasons Mac didn't think all that important. Maybe she was getting used to making her own decisions, risky or not.

She hadn't been gone long enough for there to be any reason to think something was wrong, but Mac wasn't letting it go. They needed to find her. Fast. Mac was sure she had gone to convince her dad to give up his illicit girlfriend, which in a way was for her own protection, but she had put herself in potential jeopardy by doing so.

Mackenzie grabbed a couple of two-way radios and ran out of the house to find Neil. They would take separate vehicles and search the streets near the hardware store. She ran into Ian while she was looking for her husband, though, and decided to bring him along with her. When she found Neil, he was with Billy, so the four of them got into two of the trucks and headed to the hardware place close to Neil's former knife store.

They crossed paths in front of the hardware store, Billy and Ian communicating with one another that nobody had seen anything yet. They travelled around what might be considered a block in a larger town, in opposite directions, but couldn't find anything at first. It was twenty minutes before Neil noticed the BMW parked in a strange driveway, with all the windows down, but Cam was nowhere to be found. At that point they all agreed to search on foot, calling her name. It was risky, since it was entirely possible Geraldine was out there and would mark their locations, but Mac needed to find her daughter.

There was no answer. They combed one yard after another, on the street where the car was parked, breaking into each house to search from top to bottom. Mac just kept moving, frantic, ignoring the bodies they seemed to find in every house. Her heart was pounding, and her mouth arid as the desert. Nobody tried to convince her that Cam would be fine. They all knew the danger she was in if their suspicions about Geraldine were right.

They had searched the entire street. All the yards and houses surrounding the car on both sides of the road had been gone through thoroughly. The only other possibility was that she had purposely parked the car out of sight, which meant they needed to search the other streets. Mac kept moving. There was no question of anyone giving up. Directly across the street from the hardware store, however, Mac's heart stopped. She could just barely see a foot, toes pointed upward, and a walkway shielded by trees. Her hand reached out and gripped Ian's t-shirt. He pushed the button on the radio as they moved forward together.

"We've found something. House number twelve right across from the hardware store. Left side of the house on a walkway. We're not sure what yet. Meet us here," he said, his voice cold and rigid, but no colder than Mac's heart. She almost couldn't bear to step forward. She had to know, but couldn't stand it. If that was Cam lying there, Mackenzie's world would end. Nothing else would ever matter again.

Ian stalked forward as her body argued with her mind, and he was back in moments.

"It's not her, Mac," he said hoarsely. She looked up at him, not understanding.

"Who?" she finally managed.

"I don't know. Some woman. I think her neck's been broken. But there's a lot of blood there, too, and it can't possibly be hers. There were pictures beside the blood, too, but we can look at those later. Right now I think we need to find your daughter. If she was with that woman, and that's her blood, she's been hurt pretty badly. Possibly shot, because there's a gun lying beside the dead woman." If anything, Mac's panic increased. Ian was probably right, and that meant her daughter could bleed to death if they didn't find her soon.

There was no answer to their calls. Mac looked at the body on the walkway and recognized Geraldine. She was no forensics expert, but the way her head was twisted seemed to confirm what Ian had said about her neck. They decided to check out the house, to see if Cam had gone inside to look for emergency supplies. There were some in the trunk of the car, but maybe she didn't think she could make it that far. Instead they found Allan.

"Oh my God. It's Cam's dad," Mac explained to Ian. Neil and Billy finally arrived at the house, but Mac rushed out to keep them from going in. Billy didn't need to see that. They would deal with that later, though. For now Cam was their priority.

They criss-crossed through more yards, and then headed back to the other street to see if she'd gone back to the car. Nothing was there. Not even the car, though there was plenty of blood on the ground.

"Wasn't that the passenger side?" Ian asked. Mac thought about it.

"I think you're right. There must be someone with her. I hope to Christ it's someone friendly who can take her back to the farm. Neil, I'm heading back there. Please stay here and keep looking for her, just in case she's still here and needs help. Billy, you come with me so you can come back and let your dad know what's going on if we find her. Ian doesn't know his way around."

Mac wasn't really in any condition to drive, but then neither was anyone else. Empty streets kept them from getting into an accident, though. They went around a bend in the road near the farm, however, and nearly plowed into the back of the BMW. Mac jumped out of the truck while it was still rolling past the car, yelling at Billy to stop the truck.

She leaned into the driver's side window of the car to find a stranger trying to shake her daughter awake.

"I'm her mother. Let me drive," she shouted in his ear. He jumped out of the car to let her in, and she peeled away, leaving him standing on the dirt road. For the first time since she'd installed the biometric fingerprint scanner beside the gate, she cursed its existence. As she pressed her thumb to the pad, she saw Billy pulling up in the truck with the stranger in the passenger seat.

Mac ran back to the car, shoved it into gear, and spun thick clouds of dirt into the air before the tires grabbed hold and propelled the car through the open gate. She slammed on the brakes in front of the ferret building, but not in time to avoid hitting it with the car. The loud scraping crunch had every head in the yard turning in their direction. Annette and Kelly both came running out of the building to see what was going on.

"*Help me with her,*" Mac screamed, unlatching Cam's seatbelt, and half a dozen people came running. She threw open her own door so hard it bounced back against her knee, but she didn't notice as she launched herself out of the car and around to Cam's door. It took a few seconds of clawing at the handle to realize the door had been locked, so she reached in through the window to pull on the inside handle. There was blood everywhere, covering Cam from shoulder to knee, and she knew there was no time to waste looking for the injury. She would have to leave that to

Annette, and let her start repairing the damage right away.

Kelly had run back in to grab a blanket, so they laid Cam out on it and all six people grabbed part of it to take her inside the small shed Annette used for performing exams and whatnot on the animals. She kept it sterile, so it was by far the safest place to take Cam. Mac had built the exam table for her. It was made out of wood, but performed its function well.

"We're both O-positive," she told Annette, who nodded at her.

"I'll still try to double-check for compatibility, unless time turns against us. Otherwise we'll just have to take the chance. It's unlikely she would have a reaction to your blood, but it's still possible."

It was only now that Mac took the time to look closely at her daughter. She saw the mess of her arm and gasped. The middle of her forearm looked like bloody pulp. She could see red-smeared bone fragments sticking out. At least one of the bones had been shattered, but beyond that she had no way of knowing the damage. All she could do was stand there, hoping she wasn't going to lose her arm. There was no point asking Annette for any information, because she wouldn't know anything until she started working on it. Kelly brought in a chair and positioned it by Cam's head.

"Sit down, Mac, so I can draw some blood from you. I'll have Kelly start the typing and cross-matching while I take a better look at Cam's injury. Do you know what happened?"

"I think she was shot. Beyond that, no," Mac answered quickly. She didn't bother to share her opinion about the bone. Annette could see all that for herself, and understand more of what she was seeing. Despite being a vet, she had more medical training than the rest of them put together, and she was their only option when they were hurt.

The only other person she knew who could be considered medical personnel was Sarjit, but he was a pharmacist and didn't actually live on the farm with them. They traded with him, but he stayed in his own home with his wife and children. Annette was trained to handle multiple species, and Mac had a lot of faith in her abilities. She'd been there to help when Neil had been shot, and now she would be there for Cam. She would owe her everything, if she could keep her daughter alive.

"I'm going to keep a sedative on standby, but I don't want to give it to her unless I have to. With the amount of blood she's lost, it's risky to give her anything," Annette explained.

"Alright. I don't want her in pain, but I'd rather that than have her die. Pain is temporary," Mac said, tormented herself at the thought of the torture Cam would go through if she woke up while Annette was working on her.

"What kind of gun was it? Do you know?"

"Handgun. I don't know what calibre it was, but it's still likely low-velocity rather than high-velocity like Neil's wound," Mac said, hoping the lower velocity would mean less damage to Cam's arm.

"Whichever it was, I'll have to deal with whatever I find. I don't have the benefit of x-rays, which means I'm going to have to look at the actual bones to be sure of the damage. To me it looks like the radius, but the ulna may have been damaged as well. I'll see how far the bullet went in once I'm at that point. If the cross-matching checks out, we'll get that set up and ready to go. I need to get some things together, though. Thankfully I have some plates and screws. They were in with all the other stuff I brought from the clinic, and I'm likely going to have to use them to keep the bone together long enough for it to mend. I can take them out later if they bother her, though that might re-fracture it.

"It looks like she brought her arm up to protect her face," Annette mused, and Mac tried desperately not to think of what would have happened if Cam hadn't gotten her arm up in time.

℘   ◆   ℃

Annette had to work on Cam's arm for several hours. With so few medical amenities, there was only so much she could do for her, and it took a lot longer than it would have with a full team in a proper surgery. She had Kelly helping her, since she knew which instruments to hand her, and she usually helped when Annette worked on the animals.

Mac was shoved back into the chair when it came time for the transfusion. The cross-matching had been fine, so at least the blood loss could be replaced. She could hear Neil outside, which meant Billy had gone to get him, but she was too focused on watching Cam's face while she was being worked on to even call out to him.

She knew he had to be frantic, but Cam's need was greater.

Finally Annette closed up the wound, bandaged it, and splinted it to keep it stable. She had the materials to put a cast on the arm, but said she wanted to keep an eye on the wound for a little while before she did that. She stepped back from the exam table when she was done, placed both hands in the small of her back and stretched.

"I'll need to give her an antibiotic. Thankfully we're all up to date on our vaccinations and boosters, but she could easily get an infection. She's allergic to penicillin, right?"

"Yeah. I've got Bird Sulfa if you need it, but I imagine you're covered there," Mac said.

"I'll give her an injection, yes. She can start taking the pills when she wakes up again. She should be fine for pain relievers then, too. And she's really going to want them at that point."

Annette gave Cam the injection, and left to go sit down. Mac couldn't blame her. She'd been standing over Cam for the whole surgery, her back bent. Mac stayed where she was, stroking Cam's undamaged arm, and just let the tears flow. There was a very good chance of nerve damage according to Annette, which might resolve itself within a year or so, but there was no way to know for sure until the injury began to heal. Still, Mackenzie could only think about how grateful she was that her daughter was still alive. Maybe not entirely out of the woods yet, but alive and strong enough to fight if there was an infection to deal with.

She started sobbing, and that's when Neil came in. He was

shaking when he knelt down to hold her, even though he knew Cam was probably going to be okay. Or maybe that was her. It wasn't long before Cam was stirring restlessly on the table beside them. Mac figured it was probably because of all the noise she was making, but she couldn't help herself. She'd never been so scared in her life, and at the moment she was a little bit dizzy, too.

"Mom? Is that you?" Cameron's voice was weak, but it sounded like a miracle to her mother. Mac hiccupped and grabbed for Cam's uninjured arm again.

"Yeah, it's me. Now that you're awake we'll get you some drugs, okay? Annette didn't want to give you any while you were unconscious, because you lost a lot of blood."

"Okay, good. Drugs are good. Hurts," Cam slurred.

"Hang on, sweetie," Mac said. She looked at Neil and he went to get Annette. A few moments later Cam was swallowing a couple of the Percocets they had managed to get from the pharmacist when they started trading with him. As soon as possible Cam would have to be switched over to Tylenol, though. Major narcotics were in dangerously short supply, but they had enough acetaminophen to last them until the pills expired. At least they had plenty of Tylenol Ones which contained a small amount of codeine, since they were available without a prescription at the time she'd started stocking up on various things.

Major drugs were kept locked up in one of the gun safes, however, to which very few people had access. Mac had also stocked up on the chemicals necessary to make ether, but it was so dangerous to make, and hard to administer, that they weren't touching the stuff until they ran out of all other options. That was something else she'd be leaving up to the pharmacist to do for them, since he had a degree in chemistry and understood how all that stuff worked. Mac didn't even understand the periodic table of elements. Just looking at it gave her a headache.

"What happened to that guy who was with me?" Cam finally asked.

"I have no idea. Last I saw he was standing in the yard," Mac said, and looked at Neil for clarification.

"He's still out there, though I had Billy bring him something to eat. I think he's waiting to see how you're doing, though I'm not really sure. He hasn't spoken that I'm aware of."

"He didn't say anything to me, either," Cam said. "I don't think he can remember his name or anything. I nearly ran him down on the road, and then stopped to give him some food. I brought him with me when I went to find my dad … oh, God," she trailed off, her eyes filling with tears.

In all her terror over Cam's condition, Mac had pushed aside thoughts of Allan, but now she felt her own eyes well up.

"I'm so sorry, Cam," Mac said.

"You saw the pictures?" Cam asked.

"Not the pictures, no. We went into the house where Geraldine was found. He was in there," she explained.

"So, she wasn't lying then? The pictures were real?"

"I don't know what the pictures looked like, but your dad was killed, yes." There was nothing else Mackenzie could say. Cam had lost the only father she'd ever known, and there was little comfort Mac could give her. All she could do was grieve with her. She knew Cam would be tormented by the fact that they had been arguing at the time of his death, too.

It didn't matter that it was Allan's short-sightedness that had caused the argument, either. That might even make it worse. Cam would feel anger for that, and guilt for the anger. Mackenzie stroked her daughter's sweat-soaked, and dirt-matted hair, hoping that Cam could feel all the love her mother felt for her in that simple gesture. It was all the comfort she could give her, and it didn't feel like it would ever be enough.

After a while, Mac asked Cameron if she was willing to see the young man who had most likely saved her life. She nodded silently, so Neil went out to get him.

He shuffled in slowly, as though unsure of his welcome, even though he'd been invited in. Mac looked up at him.

"Thank you. I'm not sure what all happened, but I get the feeling it's because of you that my daughter's still alive, so thank you. One day I'll hear the whole story from one of you, maybe, but for now it's enough that she's alive." She would never be able to thank him enough, she knew, even if she said it a thousand times. Neil cleared his throat beside her.

"Cam's not my daughter, but her life is very important to me, so I feel the need to thank you as well. For whatever it is you did to keep her with us. We'll leave you alone for a couple of minutes,"

Neil said, and holding Mac by the hand he pulled her outside with him. She was a bit startled, but didn't question it. She trusted his judgment, and knew Cam would be safe, even though the guy was a stranger to them. All the same, they remained outside where they could hear what was going on. Trust was one thing, but curiosity was something else entirely.

"Maybe one day you'll be able to tell me your name, so that I can thank you properly. You really did save me. She was just about to finish me off when you came looking for me. I hope you'll choose to stay with us. You don't have to be sociable or anything. Nobody expects much from anyone around here. We all just pitch in a bit of work here and there to keep things going, and that way there's plenty of food to go around. Still, when you want company there's lots of it," Cam finished.

"Blake," a voice rasped. Mac smiled at Neil.

"Is that your name?" Cam asked him.

"Yes," he said in the same raspy voice. It sounded as though he hadn't used it in a really long time, or maybe it had been damaged somehow.

"I'm glad you were able to remember it. Thank you, Blake. For everything. You don't have to answer now. About staying I mean. You can just hang out and see if you like it here. Does that sound alright?"

"Okay."

"Cool. Anyway, I'm really glad I'm alive, and I'm really grateful for your help, but they gave me some drugs a little while ago because my arm hurts, so I feel kind of weird and floaty. Not useta drugs. Dunno if I can talk much longer, but you're really nice. Thank you. Glad you're staying. Cute too, I think. Kinda hard to tell, but prolly. Pretty eyes," Cam said, severely slurring her words and trailing off.

Blake walked out of the makeshift surgery with a very odd look on his face.

"Come on, Blake. Let's get you settled in," said Mac. "I have a feeling you're going to be here for a while.

22 ~ RITES

Her father's body had been brought back to the farm, along with Brian Newman's, which had been found in the house he'd shared with his wife. Annette performed a somewhat cursory exam of all of the bodies in order to log their injuries so a record could be kept, though her exam of Geraldine had been done where her body had fallen after Blake had broken her neck. Nobody had wanted her on the farm.

She felt sad for Brian. As far as Cam could tell, he had done nothing but love his wife and son, and had paid for that decency with his life. There was a lot of debate about what to do with Brian's remains, and in the end they had said a few words and taken him to be buried beside his wife and son. Cameron remained behind, not wanting to see the final resting place of any of them. Her dad was a different story.

Allan had been washed in the process of examining him, so the only thing left had been to figure out some sort of ritual to perform. Cam needed a final goodbye. A way to honour the man she had loved as her father for as long as she could remember. It didn't matter right then that they had argued before his death.

Everyone else on the farm would need to say goodbye, too. Her dad had been friends with Chuck and Gilles for as long as her mother had. At one time they had been a tight group, so Cam would not be the only one feeling the pain from his death. It just cut her more deeply. There was a connection between everyone that lived there, though. They had all come through the end of the world together, and this was the first time one of their number had been lost.

Her mother, when not trying to comfort Cam, had spent all her time in the large garden shed she used as a workshop. Cameron didn't look, but she had a feeling she knew what she was doing. Her feeling was later confirmed. Chuck and Gilles brought out a heavy stand, placing it in the middle of the yard, close to the place where Ian had given her that first jiu-jitsu lesson.

A few minutes went by, and then they were carrying out a wooden box. Her mother followed them out of the large garden shed, one arm wrapped around her middle, and her other hand pressed over her mouth as if to hold in her sobs. Tears flowed unchecked down her face. Cam turned away from her mother's grief to fight against her own. She wasn't ready yet.

As she watched, they took the box into the makeshift animal surgery, where her dad's body was waiting. She knew she shouldn't go in there. That it would hurt her to see it. She went anyway. He'd already been dressed when she'd gone to say a private goodbye to him that morning, so now she watched Chuck,

Gilles, and her mother, as they lifted him off the table and lowered him into the simple box. Cam stepped forward, using her left arm to help them carry it out to the waiting stand, though she refused to look in at him as they walked. She didn't want to see him being jostled, moving as though there was still life in him.

Cameron had gone into the bushes with her mother that very morning, still weak from her surgery the day before, and floating on a couple more Percocets she'd taken to keep the pain in check. Together they had chosen the spot for her dad to be buried. Neil and Billy had taken over the digging. It wasn't something Cam could do while her arm was pretty much destroyed, though she would have liked to. She couldn't help thinking she needed the exertion. A way to work off some of the pain building inside her. Instead she had watched for a little while, but it wasn't long before she turned on her heel to disappear a short way into the bush.

Part of her wanted the tears to come, while another part felt a need to hold them in, as if that would keep him close somehow. When she went back to the house, she saw the partially-assembled pool table, and an unreasonable anger at her mother swelled inside her. He had been looking forward to playing pool again, but never got the chance because other things had come before setting up the table.

When she'd gone back outside, however, that was when she'd seen what her mother had been doing in her workshop. It wasn't until that moment that she'd realize the extent of her mother's grief. Cam knew she had loved her dad at one time, but she hadn't considered that she might still care a great deal about him. Cameron had always figured he was more of an annoyance to her than anything else. Someone she tolerated for her daughter's benefit. She could see now that it was a lot more complicated than that.

Maybe love never really died. Maybe it just changed, even if it ended in hate. Cam hadn't truly understood her mother's ability to remain friends with her exes. Kirk was different. They had tried dating, but had never really been anything but friends. So they had gone back to their friendship with no hard feelings. Not for the first time, Cam wondered if she was even capable of loving someone like that. She had never experienced it, and wasn't sure she would recognize love if it ever came her way.

Her eyes fell on Blake, standing by himself near the house, and she quickly looked away. *No*, she thought. *I can't deal with anything even remotely like that right now*. There might be a flicker there inside her, but it was dampened by the heavy grief burning in her chest. If it hadn't been for that, she might have been willing to spare a few moments to wonder. Now her mind spun in a loop that made her shy away from emotional connections of any kind. She could hardly stand to be around her mother right now, because she was assailed by fear. Death could happen to any one of them, would eventually happen to them all, and she could not bear even the thought of losing her mother, yet she was reminded forcibly of the possibility whenever she saw her.

Cameron stared down at her dad's ruined face now, not noticing at first that people were coming toward her. When she did finally see them all gathered around, she wanted to scream at them that it wasn't time yet. She wasn't ready. That they couldn't take him away from her. But she knew he had already been taken. This was nothing more than a formality. All she could really do was hope he had gone somewhere else, and that, in time, she would be allowed to see him again. She wasn't religious, and so her hope was small, but her mother believed there was something beyond them despite the fact that she wasn't religious either.

Finally her mother walked over and guided her a small distance away from her dad's body, so that Gilles could say what needed to be said. He was the only one who knew her dad well enough to speak, who could do so without breaking down. Even Chuck was something of a mess, and Cam knew her mother couldn't even go to the funerals of strangers without crying from the grief of everyone around her. Cameron just didn't feel ready to say goodbye, and she knew that when she was, she would never be able to speak for the grief that would overtake her.

"I've known Allan since just after high school," Gilles began. "We were all a bit wild then, spending far too much time in the local pubs and bars, but having a lot of fun. We kind of made our own family, and when Mac and Allan were together we just sort of congregated at their place.

"Time went on and we drifted into different lives, but we never lost that basic friendship. We always knew that if one of us needed help, the rest would all be there. When things went bad for the rest of the world, we pulled together once again, becoming a family. Allan, though he was always a bit different from the rest of us and never truly settled down, was just as much family then, as he was when we were friends all those years ago.

"He was a good man. One of the few that would never willingly harm another human being, because he just didn't have that in him. There was no hate, and even though he had a temper it wasn't the sort of anger he kept inside himself for long. He forgave everyone for everything, no matter what it was, and was happy to sit down and drink a beer with them again, right then and there.

"Mostly Allan wanted to laugh and have fun. He teased everyone, including himself. There wasn't an ounce of malice in him when he did it, either. He just liked to joke around. His inability to take things seriously could be difficult for most of us to deal with, because we were all so busy moving ahead with our plans and dreams. Allan just wanted to stay where he was. He was content with his lot in life, and I've never seen that quality in anyone else. It's something we can all learn a lesson from, I think. That quiet acceptance of what was handed to him allowed him to live more freely than anyone I've ever known.

"Not everyone here knew him as long, but it wasn't hard to get to know him well. He was exactly as he appeared to be. There were no secrets with Allan. His life was completely open, and he simply didn't care about pretense. He lived the way he wanted to, and let everything else go. I'm not only going to miss Allan's friendship, but the continuous reminder that life is to be enjoyed as much as possible while you've still got a life to live.

"If there's one comfort we can take, it's that Allan didn't waste a moment of his life on being unhappy. He really lived, and by doing so he probably lived more in his time than most of us will do in eighty or ninety years, should we be so lucky as to have that much time. Allan didn't talk much about religion, or life after death, either. He was more concerned with enjoying that moment, than worrying about what may or may not happen to him.

"He loved us all, but most of all he loved his daughter. He joked around a lot, but he talked about Cameron all the time. He always carried her pictures around with him, and bragged to anyone who would listen about how well she was doing, how smart she was, and what a great person she had turned out to be."

Cameron choked on a sob then, unable to continue holding her grief inside because she wondered if it was true, and she desperately wanted it to be. Her argument with her dad, and then her doubts about his concern for her, rose to the surface, strangling her with guilt and pain. She didn't notice when her mother's arms came around her shoulders, but she turned automatically into the comfort she offered, her heart breaking as Gilles continued to speak.

"Allan, I don't think most of us truly appreciated how decent you were. It was easier to think we were all doing things the right way, while you were left behind, but when disaster struck we started to see that maybe you were doing something right. You had your family. You were happy. And until recently the rest of us were behaving like hamsters on a wheel, spending far too much time trying to get ahead for no reason at all.

"We're going to miss you, Allan. I can only hope I remember to follow some of your example. That all of us remember to do that. Because we'll all be much happier for it."

Cameron watched through her tears as Gilles, Chuck, Neil, Billy, Jim, and John, all took hold of the handles on the box her dad would be buried in, and lifted it from its pedestal. She followed numbly, as they carried him through the trees to the place she had picked out with her mother only a few short hours before. They set the box temporarily on the ground, and a lid was put in place. Using ropes they lowered it into the deep hole.

Someone handed her something, which she took with her left hand, not looking down to see what it was. Then her mother led her to the side of the hole and pointed at what she was carrying. Cam stared at the wildflowers as though she had never seen any before in her life. They were somewhat scrawny and unkempt, but yet they were beautiful in a way that reminded her of her dad. No pretense, no overt prettiness. Just that sinewy strength that kept them going when more delicate blooms would die. Except that her dad was dead, and these flowers were dying, too, now that they had been taken from the roots that nourished them.

Cameron tossed the flowers down to scatter across the box that held what used to be her dad, and was now nothing more than an empty vessel that would never again call her, 'Kiddo,' or poke her in the ribs and laugh at her.

She watched as they began to shovel the dirt back into the hole. She watched as the box was covered. And she watched as the last bit of dirt was moved and packed down. Then her mother spoke beside her.

"I thought you might like to decide on the marker yourself, whenever you're ready. None of us will forget where he is in the meantime, but you should be allowed to choose what you want to leave there to honour him." Cam could only nod her head.

ॐ ◆ ೞ

In part as a way to deal with her grief, Cameron decided to continue her lessons with Ian, even though she could only use her left arm. She knew the immediate threat was gone, but having something physical to do made the emotional pain easier to get around for the moment. Their situation was still precarious anyway. Another danger could be lurking around the corner, ready to spring out at one of them at any moment, so she felt better knowing she was doing what was within her power to do.

Eventually the grief would catch up with her, she knew, no matter how fast she ran from it. It was an ever-present shadow, lurking in her thoughts as she went about keeping herself as busy as possible. When she allowed herself to think about her dad at all, she pondered what sort of marker she wanted to leave for him. He'd loved being in the forest, which was why she had chosen that particular spot, but there was no sun for the kinds of flowers they had seeds for. She didn't want to plant flowers and then have them die.

Finally Cam decided she would use a stone. She spent several days probing the earth with a shovel, holding it with her left hand, and using her foot to shove the blade into the dirt. She scoured the surface of the ground with her eyes, going for long walks over the property to see if she could find a stone she liked. Blake watched her for a while, but finally he asked what she was looking for. When she told him, he started going with her. He took the shovel from her, and would dig holes so she could look deeper.

It was about two weeks after her dad's burial that they finally found a suitable stone. Blake went to get the wheelbarrow, and pushed it back to the yard for her. He helped her wash the dirt off, but then disappeared into the workshop for a few minutes. He came back with one of the pencils and a sketch pad her mother used to plan things she wanted to build. Still showing was the last thing her mother had built. Her dad's casket and the pedestal it had been placed on. Cam could see the marks from her mother's tears on the page, as Blake handed it to her.

"Write what you want to say," he said to her, and it took her a moment to understand what he meant.

"I have to think about it. I don't know yet," Cam said, and finally she started to cry. She sat on the ground, her legs folded beneath her, and just cried. Blake sat next to her and put his arm around her, not speaking until her tears had stopped.

"I'm sorry," he said. She knew he was worried that he had upset her, so she shook her head.

"You have nothing to be sorry for. It wasn't anything you did. I haven't been letting myself think about him, because it hurts too much, but I know I have to. I can't keep distracting myself and avoiding it. I did that before when I killed that woman's son. I felt bad for killing him, and I didn't deal with it right away. It changed me." Blake nodded beside her.

"Yes," he agreed, and she knew he meant killing in general, not her specifically. It made her realize what he had done for her that day.

"I'm sorry you had to kill her, but I'm not sorry she's dead," Cameron said to him.

"It wasn't the first time I had to hurt someone. I didn't want to, but sometimes there is no choice," he replied. It was the most she had ever heard him say at once.

"You can talk to me about it if you ever want to, but you don't have to either. I never really did. People around here knew what I did, so I never had to explain, and I don't like talking about how I feel anyway."

"Okay," he said quietly. She looked up at him, really noticing him for the first time since she'd locked eyes with him the day they had met. He was filling out a bit now, some of the gauntness leaving his face, though the lines were still there. He was cleaner, of course, and dressed in decent clothes, so he looked almost like anyone else on the farm now. Healthy and whole. But she could see something different in him. Not just that she looked at him differently than she looked at anyone else, but that he *was* different. His experiences had been different.

It was only now that Cam remembered the look on his face when he had come up behind Geraldine. It had happened so fast, and Cameron had been in so much pain that she barely understood what was happening at the time. She'd also been on the verge of passing out, though she hadn't been aware of it then.

Blake's face had been curiously blank, though his eyes had flashed with some unidentified emotion. It wasn't pleasure. That much she was sure of. He hadn't enjoyed killing, which would have scared her. It might have been determination. As if a job had needed doing, however unpleasant it might be, and he would do it.

ॐ ♦ ☙

In the days that followed, Cam spent a lot of time with Blake. Usually they didn't speak, but the silence was comfortable for her. There was no need to fill it with words that would be meaningless for her right then anyway. Eventually she decided on something simple to put on her dad's marker, and when she wrote it down for Blake he took the paper into the workshop where the stone was now sitting.

She could hear a hammer striking a chisel, so she knew what he was doing, but she didn't look over his shoulder. He would show it to her when it was ready. He took his time with it, and when he took her by the hand and pulled her into the workshop to show her, she could see the care he had put into his work. Every letter was precise. Every number exact.

Allan Bouchard

August 18, 1978 – April 18, 2020

Father and Friend, who lived, loved, and laughed.

"It's perfect," she whispered. "Thank you. I think I should get my mom. She should see this. Maybe everyone else, too. We're all together in this now."

In the end everyone showed up to watch Blake help Cameron as she awkwardly tried to maneuver the stone into place. People were smiling through their tears, which somehow seemed appropriate. Not just because of the finalization of the ritual, but because of who her dad had been. Cameron could feel him beside her, almost, and hear his laugh as he made fun of himself lying in the ground. She began to smile herself, as she kissed her fingers and touched them to the stone.

"I hear you dad," she whispered. And somehow she knew then that he had never left her. She just hadn't known that he was there.

EPILOGUE ~ FLOCK TOGETHER

"Chuck, we need to talk," Mac said quietly, hating what she had to tell him. Four weeks they had held Mike in their brand new jail cell, and in that length of time they had come no closer to proving or disproving his innocence. Katherine was not pregnant, and without forcing a pelvic exam on her, they couldn't even determine whether or not her hymen was intact, which meant nothing anyway.

"I'm not gonna like this, am I?"

"I don't think so, no. We're going to have to let him go, though we have no intention of letting him stick around here. Basically I think we'll have to have the trial, state that there's a shadow of a doubt or whatever, and then he'll be free. It boils down to doing what Cam intended to do with him in the first place, except that you won't be on the expedition to take him to his new home.

"He can hole up with his good buddy, Mitch, since they seem to be birds of a feather. They'll have each other for company, and to help one another with whatever work they need to do, but they won't be around any women or young girls that I'm aware of. I know it's not much, but it's what we've got, and without proper forensics it's actually slightly better than what would have happened in our former criminal justice system. Back then he would have walked away without any sort of punishment at all."

Chuck sighed and spent some time thinking before he said anything.

"I won't go after him, if that's what you're worried about. I had already decided I wasn't going to take any kind of revenge on him, no matter what happened with our little trial. You were right. It's not the kind of thing I want to live with. I became a cop to do the right thing. I was never the kind of guy who was in it so he could wave a gun around and frighten people."

"I already know that, Chuck. You're a decent human being, and you care about people. It doesn't make you weak. In my view it actually makes you stronger. It's easy to let fly with your anger and your fists. It's easy to ignore consequences. It's never easy to take the better road."

Without a surprise confession, the trial would be nothing more than an exercise. So when no confession was uttered during the short trial, it was unanimously decided that Cam's original idea be implemented as soon as possible. Nobody wanted the chore of looking after a prisoner, and they wanted even less to have someone they mistrusted around the farm. Everyone was tired of having to be constantly on guard. It had been one thing after another, and they all looked forward to taking it a bit easier. They couldn't relax their guard completely, but things would still be much improved with one less creep about the place.

Mike was given the same treatment as Mitch. Blindfolded to prevent his return he was sent away under guard, with Gilles' handcuffs being utilized once again. No pocket knife would be there to assist in his escape either. Katherine was kept under careful watch, and the truck was searched prior to transport. Not that Katherine was interested in helping him anymore, after hearing him call her a lying little tramp during his trial.

Neither Mac nor Cam bothered to go on the journey, though they knew the location of the old hunting camp from the maps Gilles had shown them. They just had no desire to visit the place, or see how Mitch was making out. His survival was now his own business.

Still, when Gilles, Jim, and Neil came back, they had some news to report. Mitch had been alive, and upon seeing the truck had automatically assumed Mac had changed her mind and come to save him from his exile. Mac just rolled her eyes at the sense of entitlement he still seemed to have. No matter how badly he behaved, he just assumed he would be forgiven and then he could continue doing whatever he wanted to do. He hadn't been happy to learn that all he'd gained was a new companion, though Mac figured he would eventually feel a little better about his situation once he really understood he was no longer alone. Solitude had never been something he enjoyed.

Cam's difficulties while she and Neil had been gone for those two or three weeks had outlined a problem for Mac, though. Cam no longer had those responsibilities now that they were home, but the responsibilities themselves hadn't changed. They were still going to run into those kinds of situations in the future. People who wanted to take what they had, or even those who just wanted to destroy it because they could. Without the legal and authoritative support system they had enjoyed while civilization still existed, they were all easy prey for those who had no moral code. They were back in the dark ages, unless they could find a way to band together and strike fear into the hearts of those that would harm them.

Mac was only one person, and in order to protect everyone they all had to work together. For someone who had an intense need for solitude, she was really getting the short end of the stick on this deal. Cam had started calling her the mayor of crazy town for some reason, but it wasn't far off the mark. And she had no idea how she had allowed it to happen. Suddenly she was leading people, instead of being left alone to spend her time in happy solitude. Cam was only too happy to point that out, and Mac couldn't bring herself to put a stop to the teasing.

She would do the best she could, of course, but she was really feeling inadequate to the task. Suddenly she heard Neil strumming his guitar out in the middle of the yard. Billy joined in on his, and then they were singing, *With a Little Help from My Friends*. She thought about it for a moment. And so she *would* get by, but in the meantime she had to see a man about a tattoo.

COMING SOON!

SALVAGE RIGHTS
Tipping Point Book Three
Author

For someone who wants to live a quiet and solitary life, Mackenzie is doing a terrible job of it. Somehow she and her daughter have managed to start rebuilding civilization on a small scale. But not everyone wants a return to law and order. There are those who look on the end of society as an opportunity, and they will stop at nothing to ensure Mac and Cameron do not succeed.

IMPERFECTIONS
Anthology
Editor and Contributing Author

A bit of horror, some fantasy, and a dash of science fiction, all with a dystopian twist, *Imperfections* brings together some of the best up-and-coming authors. Don't miss it!

Sign up for Rain's mailing list so you get all the good stuff:

mailinglist@rainstickland.com

(If you have a problem, make sure you didn't put an 'R' in Stickland.)

In case you missed it …

TIPPING POINT

Book One of the Tipping Point Trilogy

Mackenzie knew the power grid was going down. She was warned.
So she spent years coming up with a way to survive and protect her
daughter at the same time. When major cities start going dark, and
supply lines to millions of people are cut, Mackenzie is suddenly
faced with an entire litany of situations she wasn't expecting, and
isn't prepared for.

Paperback ISBN-13: 978-0-9949500-0-0
Paperback ISBN-10: 0994950004
Kindle ISBN-13: 978-0-9949500-1-7

Now available ...

IMPƎRꟻECTIONƧ
Anthology
Editor and Contributing Author

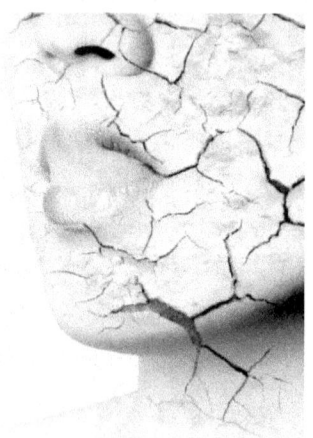

IMPƎRꟻECTIONƧ

Edited by
RAIN STICKLAND

Humanity goes to great lengths to do away with their perceived imperfections, but where does the journey take them, and are they any better for it?

Imperfections brings together some of the best up-and-coming authors, for a veritable smorgasbord of fiction...and no genre is safe. There's a taste of horror, a sampling of fantasy, a soupçon of drama, and a dash of science fiction, all with a distinct dystopian flavour.

Paperback ISBN-13: 978-0994950055
Paperback ISBN-10: 0994950055
Kindle ISBN-13: 978-0-9949500-6-2

ABOUT THE AUTHOR

Rain Stickland has been writing since the age of twelve, when the fever took hold and never truly dissipated. Despite two decades of interest in off-grid living, she was only recently introduced to the vast world of preppers. Her interest kicked up a few notches, however, during the Northeast Blackout in 2003, when the world went dark for millions of people, some for weeks.

Called the Canadian Tornado by friends, she's written and published nearly 400 articles on a wide variety of topics, including everything from stem cell transplants to the care and feeding of cats, dogs, and ferrets. She lives with her daughter in Ontario, Canada. You can find out more at www.rainstickland.com

www.ingramcontent.com/pod-product-compliance
Lightning Source LLC
Chambersburg PA
CBHW060341260626
47160CB00006B/2162